Smoke and Ashes

A Dream Walker Novel

MICHELLE MILES

First Edition May 31, 2022

ISBN: 9798201213152 (ebook)
ISBN: 9781734306873 (paperback)

The search for the Cup of Christ is the search for the divine in all of us.
Dr. Marcus Brody, Indiana Jones and the Last Crusade

And then he took the cup, and gave thanks, and gave it to them, saying, Drink ye all of it.
Matthew 26:27

From the ashes a fire shall be woken, A light from the shadows shall spring.
J.R.R. Tolkien, The Fellowship of the Ring

CHAPTER 1

I HAVE A CRUSH on Kincade.

I stared at the words like they might crawl off the page.

My heart beat a wild, chaotic rhythm. Thinking it was one thing. Putting it down on paper was another entirely. Like writing it made it real.

I didn't want to have a crush on Kincade any more than I wanted to admit it. But there it was. Written in my own hand.

Being in the same house with him is a challenge. Avoiding him has become more and more difficult. Ophelia seems determined to push us together—almost as much as my uncle once did. It's not like we have a future. He's a Watcher and I'm—

I stopped writing.

He was a Watcher. Divine. Immortal.

I was a dream walker. Divine. With the Godlight.

Immortal?

My uncle once said dream walkers lived longer than most. Didn't age the same way. I never asked him what that really meant. I wasn't sure I wanted the answer.

I closed the leather-bound journal with unnecessary force, fighting the urge to tear the page out. Defacing the journal Grace gave me for Christmas felt wrong. Sacrilegious, somehow. I shoved it aside and flopped onto my back, staring at the ceiling.

There was nothing to do about Kincade. Thinking about him didn't help. Not his steady presence. Not the way he always knew when I lied. Not the impossible mix of restraint and intensity that made my chest ache for reasons I refused to examine too closely.

With a frustrated groan, I rolled off the bed and padded toward the balcony. The floor was cold beneath my bare feet. I tugged my sleeves down over my hands and pulled the door open.

Morning gray greeted me. Cold air rushed in, sharp and bracing. Maybe freezing myself half to death would help clear my head.

It didn't.

I shut the door and turned—

—and found a winged man standing in my room.

I yelped, my heart slamming against my ribs. I pressed a hand to my chest, drawing a shaky breath.

"I wish you angels would learn to knock."

"Sorry, dearie."

I froze. My eyes flew open as I stared at the angel in my room. His silvery wings were threaded with gold and spread behind him in a brilliant display. He was simply dressed in dark pants and a matching button-down shirt. He peered at me with familiar dark blue eyes. My knees buckled as sudden tears clotted in my throat. I fell to the floor, my cold fingers pressing against my lips.

"Is it you?"

He reached for me, placing his hand on top of my head. "They call me Cashiel now. My Seraphim name."

A Seraphim. My uncle, Edward, died and became a Seraphim.

I suppose I wasn't surprised because Edward, after all, was connected to everything and everyone, angelic or otherwise.

"Rise and let me gaze upon your face."

I got to my feet and, without thinking, I hugged him hard, fighting back hot tears of joy. He barely hesitated before he reciprocated the embrace. After a long moment, he pulled back and held me at arm's length, looking me over with those familiar blue eyes, contemplation creasing his face. I shifted from one foot to the other, self-conscious.

"Well? Do I pass inspection?" I asked.

A smile tipped the corner of his mouth. "You look tired. Have you been sleeping?"

The truth was, I hadn't. Since the whole ordeal in Acre and Jerusalem, I had sleepless nights. For the last few weeks, I'd dreamed of my mother. My biological mother. I had no explanation for that other than Edward's final words in his letter still haunted me. I memorized them and thought of them often.

You were right about Natasha. I believe there is a good chance she is your mother. My dearest sister. Find her. Help her.

I spent most of my days avoiding Kincade like he carried a communicable disease. Aside from that, I had constant worry about the next relic and how I was going to find it. The last postcard I received was for Valencia, Spain and the Holy Grail.

The relics I'd already recovered—the Horn of Gabriel, the Spear of Destiny, the Staff of Moses—currently resided in the library vault. Hidden away from prying Fallen eyes. Kept safe from the outside world for when I needed them. Whenever that was.

"I'm great," I lied.

He pressed his lips together in that all too familiar expression. That one that said I was lying, and he didn't like it. It gave me an odd sense of comfort. At least that part of my uncle wasn't gone forever.

"I'm glad you're here," I said before he chastised me. "And that you're..." I paused, trying to choose my words.

"I'm Seraphim?" he asked.

I grinned. "Yes, actually."

I was getting used to angels showing up in my life—showing up to *watch over me*, apparently. Joachim had been the first. The one who set me on this whole impossible path to begin with. Others had followed since then, appearing when things went sideways, offering help I hadn't known how to ask for.

Some stayed longer than others.

Some complicated things.

"And you're...okay with that?" he asked, still sounding faintly stunned.

"I don't have much of a choice," I said lightly. "Angels seem to find me whether I invite them or not. Uncle—"

"I'm not. Not really. I'm something else entirely."

I pondered that a minute. "I suppose you're right, but you'll always be my uncle."

"Fair enough." He gave a nod of his head as though in agreement to my stubbornness.

"There's something I need to know. Something that happened to me when you..." My words drifted off. I bit my lower lip. Having him here was almost as though he hadn't died. Almost as though I got him back in my life, even though my rational mind understood I hadn't.

"Died?"

I blew out a breath. "Yes."

"It's still hard for you to accept."

It was not a question, but I nodded as though it were. Hot tears pricked my eyes. I blinked them back at a furious rate to keep them from falling. I pressed cold fingertips against my lips.

"I miss you."

It was an admission I never thought I'd have. His face softened as a small smile creased his lips. "I'm still a part of you."

Sariel said something similar to me the day Edward died. That he lived on in me. It brought me back to my question.

"When I...when you..." I had trouble saying it out loud. Almost as though putting words to it again would bring back that horrible day. That day I pierced his heart with my dagger.

"When I died," he said.

"Yes. There was...a light. I don't remember much after that because it knocked me unconscious."

He nodded. "My power transferred to you."

I blinked, staring at him as though he'd grown a second set of wings. "Huh?"

"When you pierced my heart with the dagger, it eradicated the demon poison. The power residing inside me was released. That was the punch of light you felt when you were knocked unconscious."

I continued to stare at him. I wasn't sure how to take that. Was that why I was able to understand and speak Hebrew? Because he could speak the language? All his knowledge and power came into me? And if I possessed his knowledge and power, then...what did that make me? I sank to the edge of the bed, clutching my elbows, shivering.

"This is a lot for you to take in," he said. "But please understand, Anna, there was no time to tell you. I didn't know myself until afterward."

Afterward...? When he went to the afterlife? When he was resurrected as the angel, Cashiel? How did that work? On second thought, maybe I didn't want to know. Less information was better.

"Why?"

I wasn't even sure what I was asking. Why what? Why did I get his power? Did he have to die for me to receive his power? Why me?

"Because you are extraordinary, Anna. I would have thought by now you understood that."

I scoffed. "There is nothing special about me."

"I think you understand, deep down, you *are* special," he insisted. "You've been denying it far too long. Accept you are the one to lead mankind out of darkness."

"Yeah, no pressure or anything." I pressed my lips together in a thin line. Despite everyone cheering me on from the sidelines, I still felt like a fraud.

"You can do this."

"That's what everyone keeps saying."

"And everyone is right. Kincade, too."

To my chagrin, I blushed to the roots of my hair upon hearing his name. "Still trying to push us together, uncle?"

He lifted an eyebrow at calling him uncle.

I sighed. "It will take some getting used to calling you Cashiel."

"I understand, of course." He nodded as though punctuating the thought. "Your next quest is the Holy Grail."

A tingling of fear skittered up my spine. "Yes."

"You have doubts."

"Yes," I said again and nodded.

"Only those who are worthy will find the Grail. Only the divine will retrieve it." His piercing gaze bored into me. As if to say I was both worthy and divine.

When I retrieved the Staff of Moses in the Holy of Holies, only the divine were allowed to enter the chamber. Even Kincade wasn't allowed in.

"Should I remind you of the Godlight inside you?"

"No, you should not."

His last words echoed back to me yet again. *Be the light of the world, Anna.*

I frowned. And he wondered why I wasn't sleeping.

"You are afraid, but you have no reason to be. Remember that, dearie. Now, I must take my leave of you." He extended a hand to me. I took it. His fingers wrapped around mine and squeezed. "Be strong, Anna. You can defeat this evil spreading through the land. And you will."

I wish I had his confidence.

Before I formed a response, he was gone, leaving my empty hand hanging alone in the air.

CHAPTER 2

After my uncle—Cashiel—left, I sat on the edge of the bed, rubbing my arms as a chill crept over my skin. I glanced toward the balcony door. Closed. Still, the cold lingered, sinking deeper than it should have.

I had his power.

The thought landed heavy and unwelcome. Whatever that meant.

I didn't dwell on it. Dwelling never helped.

Instead, my fingers drifted to the pendant at my throat. The small weight of it was grounding, familiar. Kincade's gift. Thoughtful. Uncomfortably so. I pressed my thumb over the etched angel, then let my hand fall away before I could follow that thought too far.

My stomach chose that moment to growl.

Good. A problem I could actually solve.

I pushed to my feet and headed for the bathroom, already planning coffee strong enough to burn and food I could eat one-handed if the universe decided to interrupt me again.

⁂

I DRESSED QUICKLY—BLACK CARGO pants, tank, Henley. I tucked the pendant Kincade gave me beneath my shirt and checked that the dagger at my waist was secure. Some habits were hard to break.

Yawning, I headed downstairs.

Laughter drifted from the parlor.

I stopped in the doorway.

Ophelia and Darius were playing Twister.

I blinked once. Then again.

Nope. Still happening.

Darius's wings—now brilliant white—were spread awkwardly behind him as he balanced across the mat, limbs tangled in impossible directions. Ophelia was wedged beneath him, laughing, her cheeks flushed and her eyes far too bright.

I took a careful step backward, cleared my throat loudly, and turned to retreat.

"Anna!"

Too late.

Ophelia popped free and grabbed my hand, dragging me into the room. "Join us."

"I'll pass," I said quickly. "Games aren't really my thing."

Darius retreated to a chair, perching carefully to accommodate his wings. I gave him a look.

"She talked you into this, didn't she?"

He flushed, then straightened. "She thought it might help me... recover."

"Mm-hmm."

"It's cold outside," Ophelia said. "And we were bored."

"You could always start taking down the Christmas decorations," I said. "You might finish by next year."

She punched my arm. "You love them."

Maybe. I wasn't admitting that.

My stomach growled, loud and traitorous. "You kids behave."

"Anna, wait." Ophelia caught my arm. "What's the next quest?"

I studied her. "Why do you ask?"

She shifted. "We're restless."

That, I understood.

"Yes, Keeper," Darius said. "We are ready."

"Are you?" I eyed him pointedly.

"I am."

I nodded. "Good. But it'll have to wait. I made a promise to Killian."

The words settled heavier than I expected.

I hadn't thought much about Astrid lately—not with Kincade occupying every spare inch of my mind—but that didn't change what I owed. Killian was waiting. And promises, once made, had a way of demanding to be kept.

Ophelia frowned. "That promise? The one to get Astrid back from Hell?"

"Yes."

"There's no talking her out of it," Kincade said from behind me.

I sucked in a sharp breath despite myself and straightened as awareness skittered up my spine. I hadn't heard him approach. Of course I hadn't.

He leaned against the doorjamb, arms crossed, gaze fixed on me like I was the only person in the room.

"Are you certain that's wise, Keeper?" Darius asked.

Kincade's attention flicked to him, then back to me.

"I made a promise," I said. "I don't break them."

"But Azriel took her to Hell," Ophelia said.

"I know where he took her." I lifted my chin. "And I'll find her."

"Told you," Kincade muttered.

"Oh, hush." I shot him a look.

He smiled like he enjoyed that far too much.

Darius stepped closer and rested a hand on my shoulder. "You must be careful."

Before I could answer, Kincade was suddenly there—too close, his voice low at my back.

"She won't be alone."

I glanced over my shoulder. "You're coming?"

"I am."

Darius's hand dropped away.

Men.

"Well," I said briskly, "then I should figure out a plan and get moving."

I slipped past Kincade, inhaling the familiar sandalwood scent before I could stop myself.

Focus.

My stomach growled. Loudly.

Kincade fell into step beside me as I headed for the kitchen.

"You expected this," he said.

"Yes."

"No argument?"

"What's the point? You'd come anyway."

He huffed a laugh. "You disappoint me, Miss Walker."

"Tragic." I grinned. "I'm hungry."

He grinned back.

Our verbal volleys had become a new pastime.

I veered into the dining room while he continued on, boots fading toward the gym. I made quick work of breakfast—bacon, toast, coffee strong enough to qualify as a weapon—and finally sat, the noise in my head settling into something I could manage.

At least for now.

As I bit into my first piece of heavenly crispy bacon, Piers arrived. He extended a handwritten note to me in the palm of his hand.

"What's this?" I asked around a mouthful of bacon.

"A missive, my lady."

I finished chewing and swallowed. "I can see that. Who is it from?"

"I'm certain I don't know, my lady."

"Please stop calling me that." I took the note out of his hand.

The handwriting was a fancy script. The thick textured envelope paper was sealed with red wax, a sigil of a roaring lion pressed into it. I slid my thumb under the wax seal to break it, opened the envelope and pulled out the letter folded neatly in half.

Dear Miss Walker –

I shall call upon you at three o'clock this afternoon. I look forward to meeting you at last.

Regards,

Alexander Harred

I stared at the perfect script a long time wondering where I'd heard the name Alexander Harred.

And then it hit me.

My mother, Annabelle Walker, was betrothed to him. She never married him and instead took off for the States with her mystery lover. AKA my father.

Why the hell did Alexander Harred want to call on me and why did he use such archaic language?

I checked my watch. It was half past nine. I had some time to prepare.

"Piers, we're going to have a visitor. We'd better prepare tea, scones, lemon cakes and whatever else you have up your sleeve."

"Of course, my lady."

I hated when he called me that but for once I didn't complain as he walked away. He didn't ask who the visitor was, just headed off to do my bidding. I folded the letter, wondering where to find more information on this Alexander Harred and wishing, once again, my uncle was around to ask.

I tapped my forefinger against my chin, wondering how to kill time until the man showed up. Kincade was in the workout room, but I didn't feel like getting my ass kicked by him today. I hadn't seen Grace that morning, either.

After I finished my pile of bacon, I pushed back from the table and wandered upstairs to the library, which also doubled as my uncle's office. My rational mind understood it was my office now, but denial was a powerful thing and my denial allowed me to continue to think of it as his.

I paused in the doorway and peered at the oversized desk with the oversized chair behind it. A small ring of keys rested on the top. Not a speck of dust or scrap of paper.

On the other side of the room was a seating area with chairs, a table, a sofa, and—most important—a liquor cart with half-full decanters. One of them my favorite whiskey. The fireplace was cold. No embers glowed. I shivered, wishing a fire was in its place.

I didn't know how to build a fire but now was as good a time as any to learn. A pile of logs was in the log rack. I set about stacking them in the grate and then sat back on my heels.

In Texas, there wasn't much use for a wood burning fireplace except a few times a year and that was when the temperature dropped below thirty. Here in England, when it was chilly most of the year, I found myself wanting to hover around the fireplace more and more.

I glanced around for the long matches but found none. I sighed, sitting on my knees with my hands on my thighs thinking I should find Piers to help me light it.

I clutched my hand into a fist, imagining a lovely little fire ball in the palm of my hand to fling out and light the logs. Wouldn't that be fun?

I snickered, chiding myself for my ridiculous thoughts as my eyes flickered open. On a whim, I flung out my hand, opening my fingers.

And to my surprise, a ball of flame landed on the wood pile and ignited it.

"What the actual fuck?"

The startled words shuddered out of me as I stared at the beginnings of a fire. The light flickered over my face, warming my chilled skin as I peered into the flickering red-orange flames wondering if I'd actually lost my mind. Could this be some of my uncle's power now residing in me?

No, of course not. I'd never seen him fling a fireball at anyone.

Although he did have a flaming sword.

I hopped to my feet, my heart rapidly beating as I called down his sword. When my uncle did it in the past, the sword would be flaming. He used it to kill demons and the like. But I'd never seen him light it. It was always already lit.

How did he do it?

I held the sword upward, the point toward the ceiling as I chewed my lower lip. I'd lit the fire with my right hand. Maybe

I could light the sword blade, too. I switched hands, holding the sword with my left, closing my right into a fist. I closed my eyes again and thought of the ball of fire in my palm.

My hand warmed. As it did, I opened my eyes, put my hands together and opened my right fist. Flames shot out from my palm and lit up the sword in a brilliant blue-white flame that quickly flicked to yellow and orange.

I sucked in a sharp breath.

I had the power. *Edward's* power.

And now I understood how to use it.

CHAPTER 3

I WAS SO ENAMORED with my newfound power, it took several agonizing, horrible moments to figure out how to snuff the flaming sword. When I gave up trying to figure it out, I put the sword back in the cloud, counted to ten, and then drew it down again.

Tada. No flame.

I relit it.

Put it back in the cloud.

Drew it down.

Relit.

I did this several times until I convinced myself I was (a) not insane, and (b) I really had this awesome power in the palm of my hand.

Hell was in for it now. I grinned as I put the sword away for the last time.

I'd never seen Edward light the sword. Perhaps he used sleight of hand. It was second nature to him, and he did it without thinking. The fire was part of him as much as my dagger was part of me.

The flame in my hand distracted me from my true purpose of coming into the library in the first place—to find information on Alexander Harred. I wondered if there was anything in the family history book.

Where was the family history book? I hadn't seen it in ages. My uncle typically kept the thing locked up somewhere, I suspected, in this room. I went to the desk and snatched up the keys. They were small enough to indicate they belonged to the desk drawers.

The one time I'd riffled through the desk, all the drawers had been locked but the center one. I used the key to unlock one of the drawers and pulled it open.

There, lying there in the top drawer, was the leather-bound family history book.

My heart skipped a beat.

I placed the keys aside and reached for the book, my hands shaking as I picked it up out of the drawer. I ran my hand over the aged dark green cover. Taking a deep breath, I opened the cover which crackled from age.

The Book of Dream Walkers

As written by Edward Clifton Walker I

Edward Clifton Walker I was my great-grandfather.

I flipped past the first few pages with the family tree and the prophecy that had decided my destiny. Past the ripped-out page we found in Antarctica in the lair of the Knights of the Holy Lance, which I replaced by tucking it into the crease of the book. Past the pages full of drawings of the Holy Relics.

As I flipped past the drawings, I halted. There was a letter still in its envelope between the pages. The same seal was on the envelope—the one with the roaring lion—as on the missive, as Piers called it, I received that morning.

No return address. No stamp. Just the name *Edward Walker II*.

It dawned on me my uncle was *Edward Walker III*. I flipped the envelope open and pulled out the letter. The paper had turned yellow from age.

Dear Edward—

Thank you for your letter. It was with great pleasure I received your acceptance of my marriage proposal. However, it has come to my attention Annabelle has refused the betrothal and, hence, snubbed my family. No doubt you are aware of that which I reference. Annabelle has refused to see Alexander when he calls on her. She has rebuffed and ignored him at every gathering. I cannot tolerate such behavior.

A shame, really, as they would have made a handsome pair and a strong dream walker lineage for both our lines to continue well into the future.

You assured me she would abide by the betrothal and accept Alexander's hand in marriage. And yet I find she is not interested in marriage to my son as you have so fervently promised. I request an explanation as to why she is not interested in my son.

I await your response.

Best,

Bascom E. Harred

My heart pounded hard as I read the letter. I sensed the discontent between the lines, the disappointment with my mother who refused to marry Alexander, Bascom's precious son. I, of course, was aware of the timeline of events but I wondered what she'd been up to then and what exactly had happened between her and Alexander.

My grandfather was not amused by the situation. My uncle told me he'd sent him to deal with my mother. Obviously, she refused to listen because here I was. The product of her illicit love affair.

And now Alexander, the boy she snubbed, was coming to see me.

I folded the letter and slipped the paper back into the envelope, back between the pages, and closed the book. I sat back in the oversized desk chair. That was enough learning for today.

Or was it? I wondered if Alexander had a bone to pick with me and that's why he was coming to meet me. I rubbed my forehead with my thumb and forefinger, trying to figure out why he wanted to come here. What did he hope to accomplish?

Sighing, I slid the book back in the drawer, locked it, stood, and pocketed the keys.

I glanced down at my normal attire and suspected it wasn't going to be good enough for Mr. Harred. The last time I wore a dress was at my uncle's funeral. I wasn't even sure what other clothes I had in my wardrobe other than cargo pants and Henleys.

Perhaps it was time to find out.

LATER THAT DAY, I stood in the middle of my bedroom, my stomach rumbling from hunger as I'd skipped lunch while I fretted over the state of my wardrobe. It was a drag at best. I didn't want to wear the funeral dress. And the heels I wore that day were still caked in mud from walking across the soggy lawn.

I didn't own any makeup anymore.

And the saddest thing of all was I didn't care.

I was missing a gene that made me feminine. I was more into killing demons than watching chick flicks and reading romance novels. What did that say about my state of mind?

Oh, fuck it. Who cared what this Alexander dude thought?

I decided my attire was just fine and he could deal.

A knock on my door interrupted my self-deprecating behavior. "Come in."

Grace poked her head in and paused as she eyed me standing before my full-length mirror, frowning.

"Hi, Grace. Come in." I waved her inside the room.

She stepped in and shut the door. "I haven't seen you all day."

"I've been...preoccupied."

"Piers said you're expecting a visitor later." She raised her eyebrows with an expectant question on her face hoping I'd elaborate.

"Someone from my biological mother's past," I said. "From what I gathered, he's kind of a snob." I looked myself up and down in the mirror, convinced I wouldn't be presentable.

"And that bothers you?" she asked.

"A little."

"Because...?"

I huffed. "Because look at me, Grace." I waved at my reflection in the mirror. "I wear nothing but these...these..."

"You wear what makes you comfortable," she put in. "Don't you?"

"I guess."

"And why should you change for some snob?"

I laughed. Why, indeed? "I guess because I don't want to insult him more than my family already has."

She tipped her head to one side. "Who is this person, Anna?"

"The man my mother was supposed to marry and didn't," I said.

"I see." She pressed her lips together as she regarded me. "Maybe I can help you."

"How?"

"With your wardrobe." She held out her hand. "Come with me."

Without thinking, I took her hand. I followed her out of my room and down the hall to hers. She flung open the bedroom door and headed right for the wardrobe on the other side of the room. She opened the doors, revealing a colorful and diverse closet full of clothing. I stared at the vast array of clothes, my mind trying to reason through how in the world she'd managed to accumulate so many in so short a time.

She riffled through the clothes, pushing things to one side and back again. She pulled one thing out—a blue and white blouse—and shook her head, put it back. She did that numerous times until she settled on a red blouse and black pants. She held them up for inspection, hopeful.

I looked over the clothes, wishing I had that excited feeling when she presented them. I bit my thumbnail, trying to decide how to let her down easy.

"You hate it." Her shoulders slumped.

"Not at all," I said, far too quickly. "It's just that I...well...it's not me."

She pressed her lips together and put the clothes back in the wardrobe with a sigh. "You're right, of course."

"Grace, I truly appreciate what you're trying to do, but I'm..."

"You're not that girl." She gave me a small smile as she walked over and took me by the shoulders. "You be you, honey. Don't be intimidated by some snob."

She was right. Why was I letting this Alexander Harred get to me? I didn't know him. I didn't care what he thought about me and my family. I had a job to finish—find the remaining Holy Relics and secure them. I didn't need him getting in my way.

I hugged her, hard. "Thank you."

"You're welcome. Now, go. And be who you are." She kissed my cheek.

It was the confidence boost I needed.

As I exited her room, Piers headed up the hallway in a clipped gait. Relief passed over his face at my appearance.

"My lady, Mr. Harred has arrived. He and his son are in the parlor."

"His son?" I stammered. "He brought his son?"

"Yes, my lady."

I sighed. "I thought he was coming alone."

"He didn't." Piers shook his head to punctuate the thought.

"Fine. Let's go."

He tilted his head back and gave me a once over. "Are you certain, my lady?"

"Is my appearance unacceptable, Piers?"

"Ah..."

"I'm not going to pretend to be someone I'm not," I snapped. "He can deal with who I am or get the fuck out."

"Perhaps, my lady, your language should be in check? Merely a suggestion."

I sighed again. "If I must."

I headed down the stairs. At the bottom, Kincade waited for me looking fierce. His sweat-dampened arms were folded across his massive chest. The neckline of his t-shirt was also damp. Sweat still beaded his forehead and the side of his face. He was fresh off a workout.

And so stupidly attractive it was honestly offensive.

Ugh. I *had* to get my emotions in check.

"Who's in the parlor?" His voice came out clipped, his gaze fixed past me like he was already taking stock of who—and what—he'd find.

"Someone from my mother's past," I said. "Alexander Harred. The man she was supposed to marry."

His eyebrows rose in surprise as he glanced toward the parlor. "He seems like a pompous ass."

"He probably is," I agreed with a nod.

"And you're going to meet with him?"

"Do I have a choice?" I countered.

"I'm coming with you."

My initial reaction was to tell him no, wave him off, keep him out. But then, Kincade was an intimidating force. A force who had my back. I gave a nod. "All right. Let's go see what the pompous ass wants."

Together, we turned and entered the parlor.

I entered first. As I did, Alexander and who I assumed was his son stood to greet me.

Alexander was tall, thin, with an aquiline nose under beady gunmetal gray eyes, a high forehead and hair the color of alabaster. He was dressed in the finest three-piece suit I'd seen—much like what my uncle used to wear—and designer shoes polished to a high shine. He smelled and looked like money. Old money. He had a pinched expression on his reedy face as he examined me with disdain, unimpressed. Then he glanced over at Kincade.

Those beady eyes widened a bit as he took in the massive hulking man standing next to me. Pride swarmed through me. *That's right. He's with me, Sir Pompous.* I choked off the words as I approached him, extending my hand in greeting.

"Good afternoon, Mr. Harred."

He glanced down at my hand with a snort of derision. "Hm. So, this is the niece of Edward Walker. The savior of the world. The one who was chosen to protect us all." He pressed his lips into a thin line to punctuate his scorn. "Tell me, Miss Walker, how do you plan to save the world from Lucifer and his dark army?"

I dropped my hand back to my side. I had no snappy retort. Instead, I shifted from one foot to the other with my discomfort. Alexander Harred made me feel like that lost orphan girl who was made fun of in elementary school because she didn't have any real parents.

"For starters, she has me." Kincade stepped up next to me. His powerful presence sent a warm shiver over me as I glanced up at him. *Pompous ass*, he said in my head.

Alexander tilted his head back and peered down his nose at Kincade, which was a feat because the man was taller than both of us. "And who are you?"

"Kincade belongs to the Brotherhood of Watchers," I said before he could respond. "Surely you've heard of them?"

"The Brotherhood...?" His voice trailed off.

"Perhaps I should ring for tea?" I suggested. I cut a glance to the man who appeared to be about my age standing next to Alexander. "You must be Mr. Harred's son. I'm Anna." Again, I extended my hand in greeting.

Unlike his father, he took my hand and we shook. "Ronan. Pleasure to meet you, Miss Walker."

"Please call me Anna."

I didn't have to ring for tea. Piers seemed to have a sense about these things. A brisk knock sounded on the door before it opened and he wheeled in the tea cart with a teapot, cups, sugar and creamer, and a stack of tiny finger sandwiches and lemon cakes. Bless him.

"Tea?" I waved to the cart as Piers made his exit. Swift as the wind.

"I did not come here for tea," Alexander said.

"Then why did you come?" I asked, growing tired of this little game.

"I came to have a look at you for myself. All this talk of the Keeper of the Holy Relics. You appear to be nothing more than death warmed up." He sniffed derision.

"Normally I would take offense to that, but since I have three of the Holy Relics and no one else does…" I paused to let that sink in.

Next to me, Kincade snickered.

It did my soul good to hear him snicker. I so loved he was on my side.

"You have three of the Holy Relics? I demand you show them to me at once." He crossed his arms over his chest with said demand.

"Sorry, no. They're in a safe place. I'm the only one who knows where and I'm the only one who has access to them."

"How do I know you have them?"

"You're gonna have to trust me, dude."

He took offense to my slang and huffed out a breath. "And what happens to these Holy Relics should something happen to you?"

"You're all in deep shit, aren't you?" Kincade replied.

It made me crush on him even harder, if that was possible.

Ronan tried hard not to smile at Kincade's snap. Alexander didn't bother to hide his offense.

"If she dies, all is lost," Kincade said. "If she dies, there is no way to defeat evil as it spreads. As a member of the Order, you should know that."

The Order? What the bloody hell was the Order? I slid Kincade a questioning glance, but his eyes were fixed on the pompous ass across from us.

Alexander sucked in a sharp breath. "Are you telling me the prophecy has come true?"

"I am. She's living proof." He motioned to me.

"Enough of this. Where is Edward?" Alexander demanded.

I took a deep breath and met those beady eyes. "Edward is dead."

Saying the words aloud to someone else made my gut clench. I hadn't voiced it to anyone until now. It hurt me more than I wanted to admit.

He blinked. Next to him, Ronan exhibited shock but made no sound.

"Dead?" The man's face paled as he stumbled back a step. He collapsed in a nearby chair, his hand on his forehead. "That cannot be."

"It is," I said. "He died in Acre trying to help me recover the Staff of Moses."

He looked up at me. "How did he die?"

"The Prince of Greed killed him," Kincade said, before I was able to form a response.

And I was relieved he had. I didn't want to tell Alexander the truth. He already had a low opinion of me. Why give him more ammo? He wouldn't understand why I had to kill Edward. I still grappled with that decision every single day.

"This just won't do. Not at all." He shook his head.

"I'm sorry if that news ruined your day," I snapped. "But it is the truth. We buried him before Christmas."

Ronan stepped forward then and cleared his throat. "What my father is trying to say in a most undignified and unsympathetic manner is that your uncle arranged your marriage."

The blood swooshed from my head so fast, tiny pinpricks of light danced in my vision. "And just who am I supposed to marry?"

He pressed his lips together again and flushed, his cheeks turning a pale shade of red. "Me."

CHAPTER 4

OH, HELL, NO.

I swayed on my feet. Kincade grasped my elbow and led me to a chair. He pushed me down into the forgiving cushions. He pressed a glass of whiskey into my hand.

"You didn't know, did you?" Ronan asked.

"No, I didn't know!" The words exploded out of me before I was able to stop them. "My uncle never shared any pertinent information with me until he was ready. Why should this be any different? I suppose he was going to tell me on my wedding day."

None of this made sense. Why had he never told me? While he was alive, he tried everything in his power to push me and Kincade together. Why would he do that if I was supposed to marry someone else? Yet another Edward mystery.

"Drink the whiskey, Anna," Kincade said, his voice smooth and low.

I downed the whiskey, remembering the pact we made in Acre. We drank whiskey when I had a tragedy. As far as I—and Kincade, too, I guess—was concerned, *this* was a tragedy. I clutched the empty highball glass until my fingers ached.

"The marriage contract was very clear. Since his sister rebuffed me, he was still going to honor that betrothal by pledging her daughter—you—to my son." Alexander lifted his head to give me a heated stare. Like this was all my fault.

My gut twisted into an even tighter knot. If my uncle arranged the betrothal, then he must have after I was born and quite possibly after he moved me to England. He knew all along and never shared that piece of information with me which sent tendrils of anger spiraling through me. How dare he. How dare he arrange my life for me.

The realization of how much my life paralleled my mother's was not lost on me. And not on Edward either. Likely why we had a lot of strife in our relationship. He was doing everything in his power to keep me under his carefully constructed control. Just like my mother. And just like my mother I left for the States.

"My uncle told me nothing about a marriage contract," I said at last, trying to keep the emotion out of my voice. "And as far as I'm concerned, you can stuff it up your pompous ass."

Kincade's head snapped in my direction, his eyes wide and his brows lifted to his hairline. A ghost of a smile slipped over his lips before he regained complete control. I glanced at him a split second before turning my glare back on Alexander.

That infuriated him even more. His face flushed with anger. "Come, Ronan. We will not stand here and be insulted."

"Yeah, well, I won't be insulted in my own home," I spat with as much hatred as I could muster.

He shot to his feet and stormed out of the parlor, slamming the door behind him. Ronan paused a moment, a sheepish expression on his face.

"I'm sorry for your loss, Anna." And then he followed his father out the door.

I collapsed into the chair, my hands shaking and my gut churning whiskey-laced acid. Without a word, Kincade refilled my glass.

"What the fuck am I going to do about this?" I asked.

I wasn't actually asking.

I didn't expect him to answer my rhetorical question, but he did. "Where would Edward put this marriage contract?"

Fuck all. "For what?"

"To see what it says."

I snorted. "I thought you were on my side?"

"I *am* on your side. But we have to see the contract to know what he promised."

I blinked as I gazed up at him, but he had his back to me. A little voice niggled at the back of my mind. Did he not want me to marry Ronan? Was he jealous of this sham of a betrothal? He refused to turn around as he sipped his whiskey. I'd never seen Kincade sip whiskey. He always downed it in one gulp like me.

As much as I hated the thought, Kincade was right. I had to find that marriage contract. "Maybe in the library," I finally said.

"Then you should search for it."

I swallowed the drink in one gulp. The amber liquid burned all the way down my gut. "Come help me."

"No. This is something you should do alone." Still, he wouldn't turn to face me.

"I don't want to go alone. I'll ask Grace." I set aside the highball and got to my feet.

"So, ask Grace."

By the time I reached the door of the parlor, hot tears were in my eyes.

I didn't understand the tears. I blinked them away as emotion clotted my throat. I also didn't understand Kincade's reaction. But he was hard to figure out on a good day. As I got my emotions under control, I moved from the parlor back up the stairs to the library. Once inside, I closed the door and leaned against it.

I was still infuriated Edward had agreed to a betrothal with someone I had never met. Ronan seemed like a nice enough guy, but I wasn't interested in marrying him. Hell, I wasn't interested in marrying anyone.

I pushed off the door and walked to the desk, pulling the keys from my pocket. I unlocked the drawer with the family history book and took it out again.

Something Kincade said sparked in my mind. He'd mentioned the Order, but I'd been so blindsided by the betrothal thing I hadn't thought to ask him. Perhaps something was written about the Order in the book.

I flipped endless pages skimming the handwriting looking for any mention. Towards the back of the book, I halted and stared down at a page titled *The Order of the Holy Relics.*

My breath hitched in my throat.

The Order of the Holy Relics was formed to support the Keeper in her search for these aforementioned relics in whatever capacity she deems necessary. The Order consists of four clans who have banded together to help bring down evil. These clans are Walker, Harred, MacKeller, and FitzGerald.

The leader of each clan is as follows:
Edward Walker III
Alexander Harred
Malcolm MacKeller
Colum FitzGerald

Upon obtaining the Holy Relics, the Keeper shall call upon the Order to come to arms for the battle of all mankind.

The Order shall call upon the Brotherhood of Watchers to come to arms for the Keeper of the Holy Relics and the battle of all mankind.

The Brotherhood of Watchers shall call upon the Seraphim to come to arms for the Keeper, the Order and the battle of all mankind.

And so it goes.

And with these groups assembled, Dark Evil will be defeated.

So, it is written. So, it shall be.

Holy shit.

I had a ready-made army. I had no idea who Malcolm MacKeller and Colum FitzGerald were, but I planned to find out.

I flipped back to the front of the book and compared the handwriting. It was similar but different enough to indicate two different people. My great-grandfather penned the prophecy but the information about the Order of the Holy Relics was written by someone else.

My uncle?

I wasn't sure but if I had to guess, he would be my first one.

I remembered something I'd read before in the family history book. I flipped back several pages until I found the passage I wanted.

...one of our kind will come. But it will not be the son of a Walker. It will be a daughter. A strong, powerful woman. She will have a pure heart and will be the one to save Man from the evil that walks the Earth.

I know not of whom he speaks. Only that she is a direct descendant. The only one who will become the Keeper of the Holy Relics. The one to save mankind from Hell.

Icy tendrils went up my spine. The person referred to in this passage was me. When I first read the prophecy last summer, I had my doubts. Now, those doubts were shattered. I was the "she" referred to in this passage.

Why? Why had my uncle never told me of the Order of the Holy Relics? Or the marriage contract for that matter.

My hunch was Edward wanted to wait until I had all five relics in hand. The passage *did* state *upon obtaining the Holy Relics.*

I blew out a breath and sat back in the chair, my head throbbing. Edward was never free with information. He kept everything closely guarded. Maybe he was afraid he'd lose me again if he told me everything that first day I arrived in England. He might have been right. He would have scared me shitless and I would have run back to the States.

I reached over and flipped the book closed with a thud.

Once again, the family history book distracted me. I pulled open the next drawer and rummaged through the files but found no marriage contract.

Figures.

Edward likely hidden it in a place I couldn't access.

Like his bedroom.

I had never stepped foot in his room. Not even when I was a child. It seemed like the ideal place he'd hide something like that.

I didn't exactly want to go in now, but a niggling sensation at the back my mind told me that was where the contract likely was. One thing I've learned was always listen to your gut.

I replaced the family history book, closed and locked the drawer. I stuck the keys in my pocket and headed out of the library. Edward's room was on the far end of the hallway in the corner, away from the noise. I likened it to his private sanctuary.

I paused at the thick oak door with the iron hinges. It struck me how much it reminded me of a medieval door. I cocked my head to one side and examined it, wondering why the hell the door to Edward's bedroom was something out of the Middle Ages.

I tried the bronze lever handle, but it was locked.

Huh.

Edward locked his bedroom door?

I stuck my hand in my pocket and fished out the ring of keys. Most of them were small like keys to the desk. One appeared to be a door key. I tried it in the lock, turned the key, and heard a click.

With my heart in my throat, I pushed the lever and shoved open the door.

The iron hinges belched an ominous groan.

This seriously freaked me out.

What did Edward have he needed to keep behind a locked door? Dead bodies?

I stepped into the threshold and paused. The slash of light from the hallway illuminated the plush garnet rug. I ran my hand along the wall by the door until my fingers bumped against a light switch. I flipped it on.

Soft yellow light flooded the room. I stood there, frozen, staring at the huge interior as my heart beat a rapid tattoo.

One on side of the room, heavy garnet curtains trimmed in gold pompoms. They were held back by matching tiebacks. Layered behind the heavy curtains, sheers that filtered the sunlight, giving it a lovely evening glow. By the window, a small antique executive desk cluttered with papers and scrolls. Behind it, a tall leather executive chair—quite modern against the antique wood desk. That side of the room was the work area.

On the other side was a huge four-poster bed with a damask coverlet in dark red and gold. Pillows piled high at the headboard. Nightstands were on either side hosting tall brass lamps. A wardrobe stood in a corner. And beyond was a doorway I assumed led to the bathroom.

Standing there, looking at Edward's room, I realized I didn't really understand him at all.

There was no sign of his personal things. No alarm clock. No television. Nothing electronic. I walked over to the wardrobe and pulled open the door. It was empty.

Piers must have cleaned out his personal belongings after he died. When I returned home after recovering the Staff of Moses, he'd offered me the master suite. I refused.

Piers hadn't removed the mountains of papers scattered across the top of the desk. I headed there next and stood behind it, looking down at the mess trying to make sense of it.

In some ways, I was afraid to disturb the controlled chaos there.

But curiosity got the better of me.

I shuffled papers aside that appeared uninteresting or unimportant. One on side of the desk, a stack of opened letters. Handwritten letters. Letters he likely read and responded to. On the other side, a stack of stationary and a fancy pen.

I didn't have time or patience to read through everything there, so I began to stack the loose pages in neat piles. When I got to the last one, I halted. My hand shook as it hovered over the pages stapled in the top left corner.

Typed in the center of the first page:

Marriage Contract Between

Ronan Harred and Annabelle Walker

Son of a bitch.

I wasn't sure whether to laugh or cry. I was very certain I didn't want to read it because I was afraid, I'd want to light the thing on fire.

But Kincade was right. I had to know if I could negotiate my way out of this sham of a betrothal. I flipped the first page and began to read.

CHAPTER 5

AN HOUR LATER, I peeled myself out of the executive chair. I'd read the marriage contract from start to finish. My uncle agreed to my hand in marriage to Ronan which included my dowry to be paid out when certain events occurred. Four thousand pounds for every year we were married. Five hundred thousand pounds for every son I produced. One hundred thousand pounds for girls.

Insulting. A hundred thousand pounds for girls? That really got to me.

I was a kick ass girl. I didn't back down from a fight. Ever. I was worth just as much as any smelly boy.

Aside from the money, Edward agreed to transfer the estate and title to me upon his death. That title would then be passed down to the eldest of my children, regardless of sex.

I scoffed. Who said I was having kids? I didn't care for children and I wasn't sure I was cut out to be a mom. I was a total walking disaster. I made bad choices.

There was nothing in the contract about terminating it. Pity.

I was just going to have to find another way.

I folded the contract in half lengthwise and headed out of the bedroom. Having seen it reaffirmed my thoughts I preferred my own room. I closed and locked the door behind me.

I had bigger things to worry about than the marriage contract. Like finding Astrid and the Holy Grail. I didn't have time to dwell on it.

As I headed back to my room, Piers ascended the stairs and paused at the top.

"You have a visitor, Miss Walker."

I frowned. My head pounded from the whiskey. I was tired. All I wanted to do now was go to bed. "I don't want to see anyone. Make my excuses and shoo them away."

"I'm afraid he's rather insistent."

That gave me pause. "Who is it?"

"Mr. Ronan Harred."

For fuck's sake. What the hell did he want? "Is his father with him?"

"No, my lady."

Interesting. "Is he in the parlor?"

"Yes, my lady."

I folded the marriage contract in half again and stuck it in my pocket. I shoved aside the fatigue, curiosity winning over to find out what Ronan wanted. I thanked Piers and headed back down the stairs to the parlor. Ronan stood at the fireplace, hands behind his back, as he gazed at the artwork on the mantle. When I entered, he turned. I paused in the doorway.

When he was here earlier, I didn't really get a close look at him. I was too busy being blinded by rage. He was handsome, with perfectly chiseled features. A strong jaw and perfect nose, aristocratic cheekbones. Deep brown eyes were fringed in dark lashes. Perfect dark blond hair. Dressed in a designer suit. I recognized money. Edward preferred designer suits and wore them frequently. Ronan was the kind of guy who was way out of my league. The kind the old me might pine for. The new me didn't give a rat's ass if his suit was Hugo Boss or from the local Goodwill.

"I hope you don't mind me calling on you again this evening, but I wanted to speak to you. Alone," he said.

I closed the door and folded my arms across my chest. "You have my undivided attention."

"First, my father's abhorrent behavior was unacceptable. For that you have my deepest apologies."

I probably should apologize for telling him to stick the marriage contract up his ass, but I didn't. "Okay."

Surprise flickered over his face by my response. Like he expected me to accept his heartfelt apology and we'd have a jolly pint together at the pub. He cleared his throat.

"Second, I wanted to talk to you about the marriage contract."

I stiffened, unsure where he was going with this and remained silent. He shifted from one foot to the other, uncomfortable.

"My father came here expecting Edward to hold up his end of the contract. Needless to say, he was quite shocked when he discovered Edward was dead."

"Sorry to disappoint." Try as I might, I was unable to hide the sour note in my voice.

"Miss Walker, I—"

"Allow me to be blunt," I said. "I'm not interested in marrying you and I'm certainly not going to hold to this ridiculous marriage contract that offers money for children."

His eyes widened. "I'm sorry?"

I pulled the quarter-folded paper out of my pocket and shook it at him. "It says my uncle will pay five hundred thousand pounds for every boy I produce. I am not a broodmare."

His face paled.

It occurred to me he had no idea what was in the contract. "You didn't know."

He shook his head. "My father and your uncle negotiated the contract. I've never actually seen a copy."

I moved toward him and held it out to him. "Then, here. Read it for yourself."

He took the paper from me, unfolded it and read over. When he was finished, a sickly expression on his face, he handed it back.

"You'll notice there is no way out of this thing," I pointed out.

"I noticed." He motioned to a nearby chair. "May I?"

I nodded.

We sat in the wingback chairs facing each other. A proper English lady would have rung for tea, but, well, who was I kidding? I was far from a proper English lady.

"Miss Walker—"

"Please call me Anna."

He nodded. "Anna, I want to honor my father's wishes..." He paused.

I cringed and opened my mouth to object.

He held up his hand to stop me. "But it will be difficult for me to do that."

Well, that was a relief. "Because?"

He gave me a point-blank look. "Do you want marry someone you've never met until today?"

I clenched my jaw as I peered at him. "I don't."

He nodded. "Nor do I. There is someone else. Though we haven't spoken of marriage. My intentions were to ask for her hand."

"Even though you were already aware of our marriage contract," I pointed out.

He gave a little laugh. "Honestly, we thought you were a lost cause. Or, rather, I did. My father, however, was desperate to meet you as soon as we heard you were back in England. I held him off for as long as possible. When I learned he sent the note to call on you today, I insisted on accompanying him. I never expected him to enforce the marriage."

My reputation preceded me, apparently. "How did you know I was back in England?"

"It's a small world, Anna. And we are all dream walkers. Some of us know things before they happen."

I lifted a brow. "Some of us meaning you?"

"I have premonitions. I foresaw our meeting before my father made up his mind to come. I should have come sooner, before he had a chance to blindside you. I would have had I known Edward was dead."

Words failed me. Instead, I asked, "Who's the girl?"

"The daughter of Colum FitzGerald. Her name is Kiara." He sounded wistful when he said her name on a faint sigh.

The name FitzGerald triggered a reminder. I pressed my lips together, trying to decide what to ask him next.

"She has fiery red hair and an equally fiery temper." He gave me a broad grin, clearly proud of his Irish beauty. "My father, though, will see us married if he has his way."

"I don't doubt that. This Colum FitzGerald is one of the clans in the Order of the Holy Relics?" I had the answer, but I wanted Ronan to tell me.

"He is."

"As are you," I added, giving him a pointed look.

"What do you know of the Order?" He cocked his head to one side.

Before I could answer, the door to the parlor opened. Piers wheeled in a cart with a teapot, cups and tiny lemon cakes. Without a word, he poured two cups. The scent of Early Grey wafted to me, reminding me of my uncle and giving me a sense of comfort. Then he dispensed, closing the door behind him.

Ronan reached for the cup nearest him and added a healthy amount of creamer. I was thinking about adding whiskey to mine but refrained.

"I don't know anything," I finally said.

"The Order was formed generations ago between the four clans. Walker, Harred, MacKeller, and FitzGerald. Years after the first dream walker failed and the archangels reclaimed the Holy Relics, the clans were constantly at war with each other. Each one was on a quest to find the relics first. Their war was a long, bloody one. And no one found the Holy Relics. Until..." He paused, gave a small smile. "Your great-grandfather had the gift of foresight."

I thought of the family history book and the prophecy. I filled in the blanks. "That's how he knew, isn't it? That the next Keeper of the Holy Relics would be a girl. That's why he wrote the prophecy."

"It was not merely a prophecy. It was his vision. It was the truth. He envisaged what others did not."

My stomach twisted into a tight knot. My life was determined before I was born. I reached for a lemon cake and popped it in my mouth. I was starting to wish for that whiskey.

"He wrote it down," I said around a mouthful.

"Did he?"

"We have a...family history book." I reached for another lemon cake. This was all too much. "I thought it was prophecy."

"It was *truth*," he corrected. "Your great-grandfather told the others of the vision. On that day, those four men, leaders of their clans, made a pact. They would stop warring with each other. If there was to be a new Keeper, one that would reclaim the Holy Relics, then they would back her. *You*, Anna."

My heart tripped in my chest. I didn't want to hear this any more than I wanted to read it in the family history book.

"They would call upon the forces of the Light to fight this darkness alongside you. You are the savior, Anna. The one who will stop this holy war with the darkness."

"So, I've been told." I didn't bother to hide my sour tone of voice. "I didn't ask for this."

"No," he agreed. "You were born for it."

I resisted the urge to scowl at that. Instead, I asked, "How do I stop the coming war?"

He shrugged. "Only you have the answer to that."

"Great. Then we're all fucked," I said without thinking.

He ignored my pessimism. "There was something else your great-grandfather saw in his vision."

I shoved the second lemon cake into my mouth and gave him a questioning glance. He sipped his tea. The perfect English gentleman.

"What's that?" I asked, my mouth still full.

"The End of All Days."

◆——————◆

I DIDN'T WANT TO believe Ronan, but my gut told me he was right. I wondered if that was something else my great-grandfather wrote in the family history book. The End of All Days. The end of mankind? Did that mean Armageddon? Ronan didn't explain and I wasn't keen to ask.

He finished his tea and took a lemon cake for the road. I walked him to the door. We didn't talk about the marriage contract anymore, but I had some relief with the knowledge he was interested in someone else. That worked for me. After he was gone, I returned to my room, a weight pressing down on me from all the information.

I stuck the marriage contract in the top drawer of my nightstand. Right now, it was out of sight, out of mind. It was hard to push aside everything Ronan told me, but I just didn't have the mind power or the energy to think about it right now.

Fatigue punched through me. Kincade was right. I needed rest. I kicked off my shoes, changed into my favorite sleeping attire, and slid under the covers, peering up at the ceiling. I thought about Astrid, how I was going to find her and rescue her from Azriel. I thought about other things, too, like how I was going to get to Spain and start searching for the Holy Grail and how I was even going to find the Grail.

Before long, my eyes grew heavy and eventually drifted closed. Almost immediately, the dream started. I was in the dream world that was the in-between state. A dangerous precipice where I could easily lose control.

Astrid was there. In a dark place—both mentally and physically. I sensed her erratic thoughts in the shadows, the way her mind seemed to be scattered into a thousand pieces. I caught a glimpse of Killian, her Fae lover and the remaining king of the Otherworld. I teetered on the edge of losing control. I gripped those dream threads and called out to her.

"Astrid?"

"Who's there?" There was no mistaking the fear in her disembodied voice in the darkness.

It was odd. Normally, when I dream walked someone—either on purpose on not—I saw them as though we stood in the same room together. Not Astrid. She was hidden from me, like Lucifer had hidden himself from me when he invaded my dreams. I didn't understand why or how.

"Anna. I've come to help."

"Anna." She exhaled my name on a breath of relief. "You shouldn't be here."

"Where are you?" I asked.

"Where are *you*?" Confusion laced her tone.

"I dream walked you. Tell me where you are. I'm coming to get you."

"No." Her firm response startled me.

"No?"

"Anna, it's not safe in Azriel's lair."

I sensed something then. Another lingering presence. My time with her was limited. Knew someone was invading and trying to control.

"He doesn't scare me." I was no longer afraid of him now that Kincade eradicated the tracking tattoo on my shoulder. Plus, Kincade had my back. "I made a promise to Killian."

"Killian…" She said his name on a hitched sob. "He should let me go."

Killian would never forgive me if I left her there in Hell. I had to bring her back to him.

"He's not going to do that." I kept my tone firm but full of concern. "And neither am I."

She sniffed. "Oh, Anna."

"Fine. Don't tell me. But I'm coming anyway. Even if that means I have to wander through the depths and circles of Hell to find you."

"Anna—"

"You will never find her."

Azriel's voice broke into my dream as he sauntered into view. Too late I realized my mistake—I'd forgotten to put up those mental walls that kept him out. His giant black wings expanded behind him giving him an ominous appearance. He was dressed in his typical fashion—jeans, white shirt, black boots. His dark hair had grown. A tendril curled over his forehead. Even though he was my archenemy, he was still devastatingly handsome.

I instantly tensed, my hands clenched into fists. In my dream state, I was unarmed.

"She has to pay for what she's done," he continued. "I am no longer willing to tolerate your interference."

"You won't win this fight," I said, my voice strong and sure.

"This isn't your business, Keeper."

In the darkness, I heard Astrid whimper. I scanned the shadows for any sign of her but found nothing.

"She betrayed me. She will pay."

"I *will* find her—"

"No, you won't. And if you come for her, I will kill you."

I scoffed. "You can't."

"You destroyed Mammon and Abaddon. You will pay for that, too."

He advanced on me. Gone was the flirtatious Azriel who wanted to get in my pants. This Azriel was all business. Despite the shadowy alcove of my dream, the evil glint in his eye was apparent. It took me aback for a moment as I realized he intended to attack. I stepped back, trying to decide how to defend myself.

Out of nowhere, Kincade burst through the shadows and crashed into Azriel. The fallen angel was totally surprised and unprepared for his attack. They disappeared into darkness.

I stood frozen, wondering what to do and what the hell just happened.

Deep silence stretched for long minutes and then Kincade reappeared out of the shadows. His cheekbone was red and bruised.

"Time to go, Anna."

And then I woke up.

CHAPTER 6

I SAT UPRIGHT ON my bed, my heart throbbing as I stared into the lingering darkness of night. My chest heaved in and out while I tried to catch my breath. Sweat trickled down the side of my face even though the room was cold.

Shoving off the blankets, my bare feet hit the cold floor. Gooseflesh erupted on my naked arms and legs as I padded to the bathroom. I flipped on the light and peered at my haggard face in the mirror.

Dark circles pierced the skin under my tired eyes. I was so desperate to find Astrid I was careless and didn't put my mental walls up to keep Azriel out of my dream.

I swept a hand through my unruly hair and paused as I pulled it away from my face. The white streaks at each temple had not gone away. I noticed them after my first foray into Hell. Briefly, I thought about covering them with hair dye, but decided against it. The white streaks were *earned,* and no one could take them away from me.

Leaning one hip against the counter, I sighed wondering how I was ever going to sleep again. A knock sounded on my door. I stiffened.

"You all right?"

Kincade was on the other side of the door. No doubt coming to check on me after our shared dream and his active participation. I didn't want to discuss it. At least not until he got the nerve up to tell me he was also a dream walker. Frustration edged through me. When was he going to tell me the truth about his dream walking abilities? Was I supposed to accept them and move on with life?

I glanced down at my flannel shorts and long-sleeved shirt. I didn't want him to see me like this, shivering in the cold night air. I walked to the bedroom door and placed my hand on the knob to keep it from turning.

"Fine," I said through the thick wood.

"You sure?" His muffled voice was just over my head.

I pressed a hand against the wood. Knowing his presence was on the other side, knowing he was there for me when I needed him gave me comfort.

"I'm sure."

A long pause, then he said, "Night."

I exhaled a heated breath as I shivered in the chilly shadows of the night clutching my elbows. He'd come to check on me. I didn't want to think about what that meant. So instead, I padded back to the bed, climbed in, and made a valiant effort to sleep.

⊷——————⊶

MORNING CAME. SUNLIGHT FILTERED through the curtains at the windows and balcony door. I laid in the bed starting up at the ceiling, my leaden limbs heavy from a bone-deep fatigue. God, I was tired. My sleep had been fitful after the dream with Astrid, Azriel, and Kincade. I dreamed, but I had difficulty remembering it. As tried to recall the dream, I had the distinct sensation my mother—my biological mother—was in that dream. Dreams with her had been ongoing for a few weeks now. I was starting to wonder why.

The last time I interacted with her was in a dream when she saved me from certain doom. She'd asked me if I comprehended the danger I faced. She warned me to step carefully.

The last time I saw her in the flesh was in Istanbul when she escaped from the Knights of the Holy Lance and disappeared. She called herself Natasha. No longer was she Annabelle Walker. The German doctor did horrible experiments on her brain to turn her into a super dream walker. She'd nearly killed me with her mind. My uncle and I disagreed over whether she was really my mother. I believed she was, but he didn't. Only with his death and the final letter he wrote me did he change his mind.

You were right about Natasha. I believe there is a good chance she is your mother. My dearest sister. Find her. Help her.

Those were the words burned into my memory, haunting me.

I wasn't sure why I had the lingering sense I'd dreamed about her again. Perhaps my subconscious was still thinking about her and my uncle's admission Natasha was actually my biological mother.

I expelled a breath. I could cower under the blankets all day to try to puzzle all that out. Still, though, I couldn't shake the feeling. I truly did want to find her and help her. I wasn't sure where or how or where to begin.

A knock on my door followed by Grace's voice. "Anna, you have a visitor."

Good grief. Who was visiting at this hour?

I rolled over to check the clock. It was a few minutes after eight. I sighed.

"Are you up?" Grace called through the door.

"No," I grumbled.

"I think you should come down to the parlor," Grace persisted.

"Who is it?" I called not bothering to hide my annoyance.

"The woman…" She paused as her voice hitched. "You better see for yourself."

Huffing out a breath, I flung off the covers and muttered *fine*. I didn't bother to shower. Instead, I pulled on my clothes from yesterday I'd left in a pile in the middle of the floor. I swept my long, tangled hair into a ponytail. I didn't bother with shoes.

I flung open the door.

Grace stood on the other side, fingering the tiny gold cross at her throat and looking as though she'd seen a ghost. She didn't say a word as she turned and headed for the stairs.

Odd.

I followed, keeping my thoughts firmly planted in my head. I definitely sensed something was off. My bare feet pounded down the stairs. I wished I had at least pulled on socks because they were cold.

Grace paused outside the doorway of the parlor. Piers was nowhere to be found, which I also thought was odd. He usually hung about if we had visitors.

I yawned, halted and waited for Grace to say something. She merely motioned toward the room. Worry lines creased her face and forehead. This was freaking me out.

I stepped into the parlor and halted as my gaze landed on the woman facing the fireplace. As she turned to face me, I understood why Grace had a stricken look on her face.

Standing in the parlor was my biological mother, Annabelle Walker.

My gut immediately clenched into a tight knot. That sense of dreaming about her crashed through me. Knowing she was a super dream walker meant she understood how to dream walk me, too. She had the ability to get into my mind and find me. She must have. And figured out a way to make me forget.

Her appearance was exactly as I remembered. Long, dark hair hanging over her shoulders. Her purple eyes, the same color as mine, bored into me. She stood stiffly as she stared right back at me. Her clothes had seen better days. She was no longer dressed in an all black catsuit. She wore an oversized red sweater that appeared to be moth-eaten over a long-sleeved gray turtleneck shirt. Her baggy jeans were mud-stained and grass-stained. Her shoes were filthy. She was haggard, as though she'd been traveling for ages. She was thinner than I remembered.

"I dreamed about you last night," she said at last, her mellifluous voice whispering through the cold, dense air.

My senses were not off. I *had* dreamed about her. I couldn't remember. As I peered at her, the dream was nothing but a vague memory of faint emotions.

Natasha glanced around the room, eyeing the furniture. She turned back to the fireplace and ran her hand down the length of the mantle, pausing on a picture of Uncle Edward. I'd put it there after his death to remember him. He looked stoic and handsome. She drew a finger down the gold frame.

"He is familiar," she said.

"You met him in Istanbul with me," I reminded her.

I wasn't sure how she'd take the news he was her brother, now dead. I wasn't sure if she understood where she was. Something drew her here, though. She had found her way home. I didn't understand why or how. I didn't think she did either.

"No." She kept her gaze on the picture.

"We did," I said. "When you took me underneath the Hagia Sophia."

She pressed her lips together. "I understand, yes. But I meant no in that there is something more. Something I cannot recall. I know his face. I know this man." She turned to me. "Tell me his name."

A lump formed in my throat. I clenched my hands into fists. "Edward Walker."

I was proud my voice didn't warble when I said his name.

"Edward." She whispered it, letting it roll off her tongue. "He lives here?"

I swallowed hard. "He did."

"Did?"

"He's dead." I clenched my hands so hard, my nails dug into my palms.

"When?"

"About a month ago."

"How?"

I had no clue how to answer. I took a deep breath, searching for some white lie that sounded plausible. "He was stabbed."

Her gaze met mine. "There is more but you are afraid to tell me." She cocked her head to the side. "I could probe your mind, but I understand it's improper."

I lifted an eyebrow, wondering who told her it was improper. Where had she been?

"Why don't I ring for tea?" I said.

"Not necessary."

She put the photo frame back on the mantle and wandered to the Christmas tree still up and lit. She paused in front of it, looking it up and down. She fingered the ribbon serving as tinsel. Then she turned to look at me once more.

"You live here."

It wasn't a question, but I nodded.

"But not always."

Her mind was working, as though she was trying to resurrect some long dead memory.

"Not always," I agreed.

"Where were you before?" she asked.

Not wanting to answer, I took evasive action. "You have a lot of questions and you need rest. Maybe you'd like some clean clothes, a hot bath and a hot meal. Then we can talk more."

Her gaze flickered back to the photo of my uncle on the mantle. She shifted from one foot to the other, her hands flexing.

"Is it safe here?" she asked.

"Yes. No harm will come to you here."

The silence stretched. At last, she said, "All right."

As I turned toward the parlor door, my heart skipped. Kincade stood outside of it next to Grace, who still fingered the tiny cross at her neck. I never ever heard him walk up. His intense gaze was fixed on me. Question flickered in his eyes. I said nothing as I headed for the stairs. Natasha followed, her footsteps heavy behind mine.

Walker Manor was large and not short of bedrooms. Ophelia and Darius shared one, but Decker, Kincade's brother, hadn't made an appearance, so we had a few of spares.

Not thinking, I led her down the long hallway with the gallery of portraits lining the walls. Her footsteps halted. I turned to face her, and my stomach dropped to my shoes.

She stood in front of her own portrait. The very one I'd stared at many hours. She was sixteen in the oil painting, perched on the edge of an oversized garnet wing-backed chair wearing a champagne-colored gown. Black strappy heels peeked out from the hem of her dress. Her black hair hung long and straight over one shoulder. She had a faint smile on her rosy lips. There was no mistaking her purple eyes in the portrait, either.

Natasha stood rigid as she stared at it. I watched her face crease with question then confusion. Her gaze flickered from the one of herself to the one of her brother, mother, and sisters. People she hadn't seen in decades. My heart ached for her. Likely she had no memory of them and struggled to recall who they were and why her own portrait was hanging on the wall.

I waited, my breath pooled in my throat, wondering if she was going to ask more questions.

"Is that me?" The words came out a whisper of ice.

Indecision flashed through my mind. Should I tell her the truth? Or conceal it from her? I settled on the truth. "It is."

She bit her bottom lip. "I have no memory of this."

"I know." I stepped toward her and put an arm around her shoulders. "Come away. We'll talk more later."

Her gaze was still glued to the portrait until she turned away, walking with me down the hallway. She smelled like she hadn't bathed in days.

I pushed open the last door on the left and flipped on the light. The modest bedroom was small and tidy. She stumbled toward the bed and practically collapsed on it, not even bothering to remove her shoes. She curled up on top of the coverlet, her knees to her chest and promptly closed her eyes. I stood a moment to watch her, turning away when I heard her heavy breathing.

I closed the door and let her sleep.

CHAPTER 7

I LEANED AGAINST THE door, closing my eyes trying to get my erratic heartbeat under control. My emotions ranged from disbelief to confusion to joy to a deep sorrow. Something had happened to her from the time I saw her in Istanbul to now. What happened to her after she left behind the Knights of the Holy Lance? Had she come across some nefarious group who wanted to find out who and what she was?

I pushed off the door and headed back to my room, acutely aware of my cold feet. I pulled on socks and boots. Even though I wanted to ignore the rumble of my stomach, I couldn't. Plus, I needed coffee in a bad way.

I trotted back down the stairs and headed for the kitchen. No one was about. They'd all scattered but I wasn't in the clear. Kincade would be around soon enough to find out who she was and what she was doing here. Grace, though, had a fairly good idea. She wouldn't prod me with questions because she wanted to give me space.

A thick miasma of swirling emotion spun through me. Having Natasha show up here was odd at best. Something of the real Annabelle Walker was still in there, undamaged by the probing of the Knights of the Holy Lance, giving way to memories she likely didn't understand. Something had brought her here.

And now I was going to make sure she was cared for and safe.

In the dining room, Kincade sat at the table with an empty plate scraped clean and a steaming cup of coffee in front of him. I paused. We eyed each other but said nothing. I sat and poured myself a cup of the dark brew. Piers bustled in then.

"Piers, the room at the end of the hall needs fresh linens after our unexpected guest awakens."

"Already handled, my lady. I had fresh linens on the bed moments after her arrival."

Was the man clairvoyant? Or just that good?

"Oh." I clutched the handle of the steaming mug. "She also needs decent clothes."

"I will see she has whatever she needs," he said. "I apologize for not telling you myself she was here, but Grace thought it would be better coming from her."

But she hadn't told me *who* was downstairs. Maybe it was for the best. "It's fine, Piers. Thank you."

He gave a nod, glanced at Kincade and backed out of the room. I sipped my coffee, pretending everything was situation normal. Kincade surveyed me with those keen eyes of his. I finally put down the cup.

"What?" I asked.

"Do you think you can trust her?" he asked.

I stared at him for a long moment. "Why shouldn't I?"

"Just because you think you know who she is doesn't mean she's trustworthy."

I sipped my coffee, letting the caffeine work its magic before I responded. "Am I supposed to turn her away, back out into the cold?"

"I didn't say that."

"You implied it."

He sighed. "I meant you should be careful until you figure out why she's here."

"She's here because she remembered her home." My fingers tightened on the mug as I pulled it closer to my face, letting the steam rise over my cold nose.

"Or someone planted the memory."

My jaw locked before I could stop it. Heat crept up my neck.

"Why would someone do that?" Frustration and annoyance edged my voice.

"Because they want to hurt you, Anna." A hard glint was in his gaze. "They want to destroy you because of who you are."

The room felt suddenly too quiet. Even the faint hum of the house seemed to pull back, waiting.

"Who is *they*?" I asked.

"Whoever she's working for."

I carefully replaced the cup on the table and clenched my jaw, trying not to lose my cool. "Did I tell you what my uncle's last letter said?"

"No."

"He believed Natasha, that woman upstairs, was his sister. My biological mother. He wanted me to help her. That's what I'm going to do."

"I'm not telling you *not* to do that. I'm telling you to be cautious. That's all."

"Why are you so suspicious?"

His expression shifted. He looked at me as though I were the dumbest person alive. "Let's think about this for a moment, shall we? Natasha, a woman you met in Antarctica, tried to murder you with her mind and again in Rio de Janeiro. You said yourself she was working for the Knights of the Holy Lance. That Schneider performed experiments on her brain to make her a super dream walker to give her those powers."

"But she didn't try to kill me in Istanbul," I pointed out.

"No, she took you to Schneider on his orders so you would turn over the Spear of Destiny to him. My point is she was working for the enemy. She could be again."

Kincade was starting to piss me off. "Listen, I appreciate what you're saying. I really do. But I'm not an idiot. She is my *mother*, Kincade. Do you comprehend what this means for me?"

He was silent as he pressed his lips together.

Hell, I didn't comprehend what it meant for me. I had a lot of unanswered questions, too. Like how she managed to make it back here. What brought her here? Why? Was there some deep-seated memory that triggered her memory of Walker Manor?

All my life I dreamed of having a family. My real family.

I stared at the coffee in my cup, watching the steam curl and vanish.

For years I'd wondered who my biological mother was. Now she was here—upstairs, asleep in one of the guest rooms.

My uncle's last wish pressed against my ribs. I had a chance to help her. To do *something* right before he was gone for good.

"I have no reason not to trust her. At least not yet," I added.

He sat back in his chair and ran a hand through his short-cropped hair. "Where has she been all these months?"

He wasn't going to be derailed from his suspicions.

"I don't know!"

"You think she's going to willingly share that information with you? That she's going to sip tea and eat lemon cakes and tell you her life story?" He shook his head. "Don't be so gullible, Anna."

The chair screeched across the floor before I realized I'd moved.

Anger slammed through me, hot and blinding.

"I'm not hungry anymore."

I rose and stalked away without waiting for his reply.

Blinded by my rage, I stormed through the kitchen, ignoring everyone and everything going on, and charged out the back door. A damp bite was in the morning air promising a chilly rain later. Cold pressed into my cheeks and nose as my feet pounded the damp grass.

I ended up at the workout room, the door slamming closed behind me. I stood a long moment, trying to catch my breath and tamp down the anger flooding me. My hands flexed into fists and then released. I glanced around the workout room looking for something—anything—on which to expend my pent-up fury.

My gaze landed on the boxing punching bag hanging from the metal bracket. With my rage surging through me, I headed for it and started hitting the damn thing until I got a rhythm. I started counting punches until I lost track at a hundred and twenty. I beat it until my knuckles were red, raw, and bleeding. Until my hands were numb with pain. Until sweat beaded my forehead and the back of my neck.

Behind me, the door banged closed. I didn't have to turn around to know Kincade was there. Damn him. Why did he have to follow me?

Sweat dripped down the side of my face as I dropped my hands, the bag swaying still from my onslaught. I contemplated punching the bag some more. I turned on my heel and peered at him over my shoulder.

He stood on the other side of the gray workout mat looking ready to spar.

So, I charged him.

He didn't flinch when I crashed into him and shoved him backward. His arms came up around me, holding me in place. I kicked him in the shin. He grunted and released me. I stumbled backward.

"Why are you so pissed off?" he asked.

I huffed. "As if you don't know."

I backed up toward the exercise mat in the center of the room. He matched me step for step and took a ready stance. There were moments when I wanted to kiss him. There were moments when I wanted to punch his face. Now was one of the latter moments.

"I was *abandoned*, Kincade." I spat the heated words. "Where the hell was she my entire life?"

He didn't answer my rhetorical question as he cracked his knuckles and flexed his fingers. "Are you sure you want to do this?"

I hated that calm, measured tone. Furious, my fist crashed against his chest, leaving bloody knuckle marks on his shirt.

"Why didn't she try to find me?" I demanded. "When my uncle came for me, why didn't she come here *then*?" I punctuated the last word with another punch to his gut.

He was rock solid. It was like hitting a brick wall. And he didn't flinch.

"I don't have an answer, Anna."

"She doesn't really know who I am!"

Again, I threw a punch. This time, he caught my wrist, his fingers like a vice grip as he stopped me from hitting him again. I realized hot tears spilled from my eyes. Embarrassment flooded me, heating my cheeks. I jerked my wrist out of his grip and turned away from him.

I hated to cry. I hated to cry in front of Kincade more.

"Why are you here?" I asked.

"You know why." His voice was quiet in the cavernous room.

Did I? There had always been this silent communication between us since the day we met. We were both too proud and too stubborn to talk about our feelings with one another. Not that I *wanted* to talk about my feelings with Kincade, anyway.

I suspected he was here because he was offering his moral support in his own controlled way. He had seen me at my absolute worst. He'd followed me from England to Hong Kong when I was on my quest for the Horn of Gabriel.

When he was captured by Azriel and nearly lost his soul forever, I was willing to move mountains to get him back. We had both made sacrifices for each other. And yet, we couldn't and wouldn't talk about them.

"You should let me tend those knuckles."

I'd made a bloody mess of my hands. The skin was ripped to shreds and now that I'd managed to rein in some of my anger, they were starting to throb with a terrible pain.

"Fine."

I spun on the toe of my boot and breezed by him, shoving open the door to the workout room. Saying nothing, he followed me out of the building, across the lawn, and to the back door in the kitchen. He continued to follow me through the house and up the stairs. I headed for my room.

"I have a first aid kit," he said and passed me on the way to his own room.

I halted, standing in the middle of the hallway watching him enter his room. My heart suddenly did a wild pounding as I stared after him, trying to make my feet move. Did he expect me to follow him in there?

He poked his head out of the open door. "Come on." Then, as if he couldn't help himself, he added, "Princess."

I frowned. That was a new nickname. I hated it—almost as much as I hated when he went all calm and careful on me.

I stomped into his room. He pointed to the edge of the bed before disappearing into his own bathroom. A few minutes later, he came out with the promised first aid kit and a couple of small towels.

He pulled up a chair and sat across from me, opening his kit. His methodical hands sifted through the contents of the kit to find what he wanted. Antibiotic ointment, bandages, hydrogen peroxide.

This was so not going to be fun.

He held out a hand and wiggled his fingers. I placed my right hand in his.

And tried hard to ignore the little thrill that went through me as we connected. I was aware of my rapid beating pulse and hoped he was unable to feel it while holding my hand.

His large fingers wrapped around my wrist to hold me in place while he sprayed the hydrogen peroxide on the bloody mess of my knuckles. I sucked in a sharp breath and tried to jerk away, but he held fast, ready for that reaction. His hand tightened on my wrist, his palm pressing into the beat of my pulse. There was no hiding it.

His gaze drifted from my knuckles to my face. I thought for a moment a smug expression flickered across his face, but if it was, it was fleeting, and I missed it.

"This is going to sting," he said.

"*Now* you tell me," I said through clenched teeth.

"Don't be a baby, Anna."

He gently wiped away the bubbles and inspected the wounds. "Why did you hit the bag without your gloves?"

"Why do you even have to ask?"

I practically growled the words and fervently wished he would release my damn wrist. My pulse was beating at least at two-hundred beats per minute.

He spritzed my hand again with the bubbly evil stuff. I clenched my jaw to keep from crying out. He cleaned off the peroxide and went about adding antibiotic ointment and bandages, which wasn't easy since I'd managed to mangle all four of my knuckles.

"Now the left."

"Super."

I frowned as I gave him my left hand and we repeated the fun and games all over again. He, again, wrapped his hand around my wrist and held me in place. I started to think he was enjoying himself a little too much.

Once my left hand was bandaged, he put everything back in his kit, picked up the bloody towels and trash, and headed off to the bathroom.

"Maybe you give your hands a break for a while," he said from the bathroom.

He turned on the faucet. I assumed to wash his hands.

I sat on the edge of the bed and immediately regretted it.

Him—fresh from the shower, towel slung low on his hips—flashed through my mind without permission.

I stood abruptly, breath tight in my chest. *No. Not now.*

Why was my brain being so traitorous and conjuring up all these sordid memories of the man? I so did not need that right now.

He came out of the bathroom drying his hands on a fresh towel and paused. We stared at each other across the room. Heat rose from my boots to the roots of my hair.

"Well, thanks." I waved my bandaged hands at him and stepped toward the door.

"Anna."

I paused in the doorway, peering at him over my shoulder.

"If you want, I can see if someone in the Brotherhood can help your mother."

My brows knit. "What do you mean?"

"You said Schneider did experiments on her brain. Maybe one of our healers can help her."

The offer landed anyway—quiet and unexpected, coming after everything we'd just said to each other. The Watchers had healers. Angelic ones. If anyone could do something a human doctor couldn't... it would be them.

But I'd seen what Schneider had done. Not damage. Change.

I shook my head once. "I don't think it can be reversed. He didn't just hurt her—he rewired her. Took pieces out and put different ones back." My throat tightened. I hated that it did. "But... thank you. For offering."

"If you change your mind," he said, "let me know."

I nodded and left his room.

It wasn't lunchtime yet and I'd already had several shocks for the day. I wasn't sure how much more my heart could take. Fatigue gripped me hard as I headed back to my room, wanting nothing more than to be alone and sleep for a few hours.

This big manor house was starting to get awfully crowded these days. When once it was just me, my uncle and Piers, now there was a whole motley crew of us.

I closed my door, kicked off my shoes and fell into my unmade bed still fully clothed. It didn't take long for me to drift off to sleep for my mid-morning nap.

And dream.

I was somewhere in a tunnel in the deepest shadowed alcoves of Hell. Voices echoed back to me. I headed for them, my heart in my throat and my hand trailing the wall as I moved through the dark murky depths approaching the end of the tunnel where light spilled inside the entrance. I paused, keeping my body out of the light as I peered around the corner.

Azriel knelt before his Lord Master. Lucifer's thin, reedy body perched on his black-boned throne petting the red-eyed beast at his side. When I saw the dark lord before, he was in human form. Now, not so much. He was a disgusting creature with leathery wings spread out behind him.

"You have failed me," Lucifer said.

Azriel kept his head down, eyes pinned on the ground. "Yes, master."

"Not only did the Keeper escape, but she also managed to kill my Prince of Greed and my destroyer angel."

"She has many allies. She—"

"I care not about the Watcher who has decided to guard her. He is expendable. At least the uncle is dead."

My anger rose again hearing him reference Edward.

"If the Watcher could be turned against her—"

"You tried to use him against her once before. It didn't work. She managed to recover the spear from you. Sometimes I wonder if you're helping her."

I almost snickered. Azriel didn't want to help me unless it was an advantage for him. Like when he released me from the prison after Abaddon captured me.

I kept my gaze on the fallen angel. Sweat rolled down the side of his face. Smug satisfaction skipped through me with glee at his discomfort.

"You were supposed to bring her to me. Instead, what do you bring me? A time shifter."

"She has value," Azriel said.

"Yes, I suppose she does." He sounded thoughtful as he spoke. "Therefore, you will use her to our advantage." He paused, his long slender fingers petting the beast between its ears. Still Azriel did not look up at him. "Yes, we will use her. She will do everything we ask to bring the Keeper to heel and deliver those relics."

He paused again, sighing as though exasperated. Azriel remained motionless as he waited for his master to finish his thought.

Lucifer intended to use Astrid to his advantage. Which made it all the more important for me to find her and get her away from Azriel. How, was the real question. Azriel threatened me. Astrid told me not to come after her. And the dream walk I had earlier still haunted me.

"You will use the time warper to get me those relics and bring me the girl. Won't you?"

"I will do your bidding," Azriel replied.

"Good. You have your orders. Now go."

And with that, Azriel was dismissed from his master. He rose, head still bowed, and backed away several steps before turning to leave. Lucifer watched him go while scratching the beast behind the ears. The thing tipped its head up and looked at him with an almost reverent expression.

"And if he fails me again, my furry friend, I will kill him and go after the girl myself."

CHAPTER 8

I STEPPED BACK INTO the shadows and pressed my back against the cold tunnel wall.

I woke up, my heart in my throat and my stomach in knots. I was so exhausted I hadn't thought to put my mental walls up before falling asleep. I took several deep breaths trying to calm my shredded nerves.

I was almost there when a high-pitched scream ripped through the manor house. I bolted off the bed, out the door and into the hallway.

I heard laughter coming from the room next door and realized it was Ophelia. I took a deep breath, pressed a hand against my still thrumming heart, and blew out. I really did not want to know what was going on in that room next door with the two of them.

"Hey, Anna."

Grace's voice made me nearly jump out of my skin. I spun around to see her coming out of her own room down the hall. She was dressed for her morning jaunt around the grounds.

"You scared me." My voice came out in a breath.

"I'm sorry." She gave me a once over. Concern flickered through her eyes. She reached for me and patted my arm. "Are you all right?"

"I'm fine. Just tired, I guess."

"You look exhausted."

"She looks like shit," Kincade added.

I gave him a sour glance. Why did he always pop up when I never wanted him? "Gee, thanks."

Grace let out a little gasp as she reached for one of my bandaged hands. "What happened to your hands?"

I pulled away to hide the bandages at my sides. "Nothing."

"She got pissed at the punching bag," Kincade said.

I shot him a glare. "You're not helping."

"Anna..." Grace used her motherly chastising voice I was all too familiar with.

"I'm *fine*. I promise. They'll heal in time."

She gave me one more thin-lipped response but said nothing more about the hands. "I'm going for a run."

"Be careful." The words popped out of my mouth.

She grinned. "Why wouldn't I be? You said yourself Walker estate is the safest place for me."

I nodded. "I did."

She gave Kincade a nod of farewell before she headed down the stairs. I watched her go, an unexplainable tightness in my chest.

Bubbly laughter came from Ophelia's room. I rolled my eyes and started to return to my room, but Kincade's voice stopped me.

"She's right."

"About what?" I demanded.

"You *do* look exhausted. You're not sleeping, are you?"

I shrugged. "Doesn't matter."

"It does."

I ignored him and started to leave, but he grasped my upper arm and turned me to face him. "It's not good for you to go without sleep."

I pulled away, took a step out of reach. "I realize that."

"Are we going to talk about that dream walk you did to find Astrid?"

"Are you going to admit you were following me in that dream walk?" I fired back.

He looked taken aback for a brief moment before he recovered. He clenched his jaw, the muscles ticking along the side.

"*Touché*, Miss Walker."

I tilted my head back, looking down my nose at him. "Why?"

"I thought that obvious."

Nothing with Kincade was ever obvious. I sighed. "I'm really not in the mood for mind games."

I turned my back on him and took a step toward my door. He growled low and deep in his throat, as though frustration was eating him alive.

"*Fine*. I'll tell you."

I halted in the doorway, my hand on the jamb. I held my breath and waited.

"I left the Brotherhood of Watchers because..." He paused.

I bit my lip, waiting.

"Because you're the Keeper, Anna. And you can't do this alone. Especially now with Edward gone."

My throat constricted. My eyes heated with sudden tears.

"So..." I said, my voice a raspy whisper. "Are you my guardian then?"

"I'm here to protect you."

Victory. Or was it? He didn't answer the question directly. Even so, I didn't deny the triumph pumping through me at getting that much out of him. I wanted to shout victory to the rooftops. But I didn't. I took a deep breath, got my emotions in check and gave him one glance over my shoulder.

"You're right, too. I'm not sleeping and I'm weary. So weary." My voice warbled a little on the last sentence.

He took a step toward me. "I can't ease the burden of what you have to do. But I can help by making sure you succeed. By protecting you."

Damn him. Why was he saying this to me now? My throat clogged with more emotion I didn't want to shed. Not again. Not in front of him. It was too much to think about. Too much to feel.

"I appreciate that," I said finally. "Now, if you don't mind, I'm going to sleep."

"And I'll stand right here until you come out."

Guarding my door. Something about his presence there gave me comfort.

As my boot crossed the threshold of my room, something dark and evil punched through me. Like an oily black substance taking root deep inside me, taking my breath away as I sucked in a sharp breath. My back bowed. My knees buckled. I was going down.

But Kincade was there. He caught me before I hit the floor. A paralysis not unlike the one Abaddon inflicted upon me surged through me. The difference was I still had some movement in my extremities.

Kincade clutched me in his strong arms, holding me against his chest. Concern, fear, worry all flickered through his eyes.

"What is it? What's wrong?"

I shook my head slowly from side to side, trying to catch my breath. "Something... dark... evil..."

"I don't sense anything."

But I did. The evilness pierced through my entire being, exploding through my head. I shut my eyes as a brilliant light flashed there, an intense pain pounding against my skull.

I'm coming for you. But since I can't have you...I'll take her.

The disembodied voice shattered my mind. And suddenly I understood.

Lucifer's voice was inside my head. How, I didn't know. I shoved away from Kincade, falling to the floor in a heap. I clambered to my feet, trying my best to force my legs to work. Stumbling, I made it to the top of the stairs.

"Anna—"

"Grace is in danger."

He didn't question me. He brushed by me and pounded down the stairs, his boots reverberating off the wood. Meanwhile, I was still trying to get my footing. I finally made my way down to the front door but realized as I stepped out into the late morning, I had no shoes.

I didn't care.

I ran like a newborn colt with new, untested legs. In the distance, Kincade was already halfway across the lawn looking for Grace. She took the same path every day, so she shouldn't be too hard to find.

The black cloud descended from the sky in an oily fog. Even from this distance, I smelled the sulfur, the death, the decay, the rot. My gut clenched into a tight knot as I stumbled after Kincade in the wet grass. My socks were soaked through. I paused long enough to discard them and continue barefoot.

Ahead, Grace took her normal turn and headed back toward the manor. She was so far away she was nothing but a speck. My ragged breath see-sawed in and out of my chest as I made a desperate attempt to catch up to Kincade who was ahead of me. I waved my arms like a maniac trying to gain her attention.

She had her earbuds in listening to music and not paying us any attention. Meanwhile, the black oily cloud formed into a shape of something almost humanoid lowering to the ground and floating towards her at a brisk pace.

I shouted her name. She didn't hear me.

"Hurry, Kincade!"

He ran faster than I'd ever seen. He was almost to her when the black cloud lunged and enveloped her. I saw her halt. Her body bowed, as though she were pulled tight. Every muscle went rigid and unmoving.

Kincade halted giving me enough time to finally catch up to him. "Wh-what is it?"

My teeth clacked together, and I shivered as the damp earth pressed into the soles of my feet.

"A vampire wraith."

"It has her!"

I started to bolt toward her, but he snatched me by the arm, pulled me to him. His arms wrapped around my upper body and held me in place.

"Don't."

"But—"

"It will kill her if we intervene."

A black and purple cloud formed behind the wraith that had Grace. When the smoke cleared, a man I recognized stood there. He held his hands in front of him as though he were enjoying afternoon tea in the parlor with a sickly smile on his brutally handsome face. He wore a fancy three-piece suit. His long wavy black hair brushed his shoulders. And his piercing blue eyes pinpointed me with a frightful glee.

Lucifer.

"Hello, Anna."

"Let her go!" I shouted.

He *tsked* as though I were an errant child. "You should understand by now things are not that easy."

I wiggled in Kincade's grasp, trying to get free. I'd seen too many of my loved ones suffer at the hands of evil. I wasn't about to watch it happen to Grace, too.

"She has nothing to do with this fight," I said.

His gaze flickered briefly to Kincade then back to me. "But she does. You have a fondness for the woman and, therefore, I must use her to get what I want from you."

I stiffened. "Never."

"Do you know what this is, Keeper?" He motioned to the wraith.

"Please let her go." I hated the begging sound of my voice.

He ignored me. "The vampire wraith serves me well, obeying my every command. If I tell it to release her, it will. If I tell it to kill her, it will. If I tell it to remove her soul and hand it to me, it will."

I swallowed the bile rising to my throat. "Please..."

"Give me the relics and she will be as she was," Lucifer said.

It's a trap, Kincade said in my mind.

Of course, it is. This ain't my first rodeo, I shot back.

"And if I don't?"

He sighed, annoyed with me. "Oh, Anna, you do make things so very difficult. I will give you time to decide. If you do not comply..." A rotten smile crossed his rotten face. "There will be consequences unlike you have ever seen."

"Is that a threat?"

"Why, yes, it is. My minions and demons run far and deep into this world. They obey my every command. Do you want the weight of that and her death on your shoulders, my dear?"

I said nothing as I processed his words. He flicked his wrist. The wraith wrapped around Grace in a swirl of black smoke and disappeared. Grace fell to the ground in a heap, unconscious.

"How much time depends upon you, Keeper. Only one thing can save her. The Holy Grail and the remaining relics. Bring them to me and she lives. Fail and she dies."

With the snap of his fingers, he was gone.

CHAPTER 9

As soon as he was gone, Kincade released me. I ran to Grace, falling to my knees at her side. I pressed two fingers against her neck to check for a pulse. It fluttered, proving she was still very much alive.

"Grace, can you hear me?"

"She can't." Kincade moved to stand on the other side of her.

I looked up at him. "What did the vampire wraith do to her?"

"What you would expect. It sucked a little bit of her life force from her. It takes life to sustain its own. That's how it survives."

"And how it kills?" I asked.

He nodded. "When it takes all her life force, the wraith becomes whole again."

My brows knit in question, but I didn't have to ask it.

"A demon," he clarified. "Right now, it's trapped between worlds. Clearly, Lucifer controls this wraith."

Kincade knelt and scooped Grace up off the wet ground. He cradled her against his chest and started for the manor. I followed, hot on his heels. Panting, I tried to keep up with his long strides.

"How do I save her without giving up the relics?" I tried to ignore the panic welling deep inside.

He didn't answer as he pushed open the back door with his foot. It banged against the wall, startling Piers who jumped at our sudden appearance. When he noticed Grace unconscious in Kincade's arms, his face went pale. He cared for her and he deserved to know what happened to her. He'd have questions and I would answer them later. Right now, I needed to understand how to save her.

"Kincade?" I prodded.

He headed through the dining room and up the stairs to her room without answering. My legs burned from the exertion as I followed at his brisk pace, trying to keep up. He laid her gently on the bed, smoothing a damp lock of hair away from her face. As he stepped back from the bed, I perched on the edge. I pulled out her earbuds still nestled in her ears and placed it along with the tiny MP3 player she kept in her shirt pocket on the nightstand. I took her hand in mine. Her cold, clammy hand. My heart ached.

In the lamplight of her room, her tiny gold cross winked in the hollow of her throat.

"I don't know," he said at last. "No one has survived a vampire wraith."

I had no words. I sat there, dumbfounded, not sure what to do next as I held her hand and prayed to the powers larger than me to save her. Kincade left the room. I was vaguely aware of his booted footsteps on the hardwood as he stepped out.

"You can't leave me, Grace," I muttered.

She was the only family I had left. Well, the only family that was within her right mind and understood me.

"There is but one way to save her."

The male voice behind me startled me. I glanced over my shoulder to see Sariel. He moved into the room, pausing next to me as he gazed down at Grace's unconscious form.

I stiffened, my back going rigid. The stubbornness inside me reared its ugly head. "I'm not giving up the relics."

He shook his head. "There is another way."

"You can help her?" I asked, hopeful.

"I cannot. But you can by finding the Holy Grail."

I glanced back at Grace, watching the steady beat of her pulse in the long column of her throat. "How will the Holy Grail save her?"

"The cup of Christ has the power to heal."

"With holy water." I looked back up at him. "I'm fresh out."

"No." He shook his head again as he reached into his pocket. He handed me a small corked bottle. Inside, the liquid was a faint blue. "When you find it, pour this holy water inside the cup and have her drink it."

"And that will heal her?"

"Yes. But Anna..." He sat on the edge of the bed next to me. "This quest for the cup will be the hardest one yet."

"I understand. Many seek the Holy Grail."

"Yes, and not all of them are human."

I recognized a warning when I heard one. He reached for me and placed a hand on my arm.

"For you to find it, you must give up your promise to find Astrid."

Disappointment pierced through me in a flash of heat. "But I told Killian—"

"You cannot help her now," Sariel interrupted. "And you must be cautious."

I thought back to the dream with Azriel and Lucifer. "He wants to use her to get to me."

"Yes. And he will. Both of them will. They will use her to destroy you."

The answer was clear. I had to give up Astrid to save Grace. And I hated that. I hated having to choose between the two of them. But Grace had practically raised me. She meant more to me than anyone. Especially now that Edward was gone.

"I understand."

Even though I said the words aloud, deep down I told myself I would find a way to keep my promise to Killian. I had to find a way to save Astrid from the darkest shadows of Hell and bring her back to the Fae king.

Sariel rose suddenly, glancing toward the door. "I must go."

And he was gone in a blink before I was able to respond. A second later, Natasha appeared in the doorway, looking haggard and frazzled. She ran a hand through her long, dark locks as she glanced around the room. I slowly got to my feet.

"Are you okay?" I asked.

"I thought I sensed..." She looked around again, clearly trying to understand where she was. She shook her head and pressed her lips together.

"Sensed what?"

She took a deep breath, blew it out. "There was a presence. Someone familiar and yet, not. Does that make sense?"

I shook my head. "Not really."

She spotted Grace and moved deeper into the room. She halted at the edge of the bed.

"What happened to her?"

"She was attacked by a vampire wraith," I said.

She stared down at her, not comprehending. "What is a vampire wraith?"

"Evil," I whispered. "Absolute evil."

"Will she survive?" Natasha asked.

"I'm not sure. I have a chance to save her, but I have to leave."

She tipped her head to the side, her brows knitting together. "Where are you going?"

"I'm going to Spain. I have to find something. Something that will save her."

Natasha glanced back at Grace. "Who is she to you?"

I swallowed hard, trying to decide how to answer. Rather than confuse her more, I said, "She raised me."

"Your mother?"

"For a time," I said with a nod. "Until my uncle found me."

"Edward," she said filling in the blanks. Her mind worked as she remembered our conversation in the parlor.

I nodded. "Yes, Edward."

"Then you must go, if it will save her."

"And you are welcome to remain here," I said.

But she was shaking her head before I finished. "I shouldn't. It wouldn't be right."

"I insist," I said. "Piers and the others will take good care of you."

Which reminded me. I needed to talk to Darius and Ophelia about my trip to Spain. And probably Kincade. I had no doubt he would be coming with me.

As though I conjured him by thinking of him, he appeared in the doorway. Concern etched his features.

"Anna, you need to see something."

"Now?" I asked.

"Yes, now. Outside." He thumbed over his shoulder.

I glanced at Natasha who gave a small nod. "Go. I will watch over her."

Can you trust her? Kincade's voice floated in my head.

"You don't mind?" I ignored him as I spoke to Natasha.

"No." She gave me a faint smile as she sat on the edge of the bed next to Grace.

I followed Kincade out of the room, back down the stairs and to the front door. He opened it and stepped out. I was still barefoot and not looking forward to going out without proper foot attire. He didn't seem like he was in the mood to wait around for me to put on my boots.

"What is it?" I followed him outside to the front of the manor.

He walked around the side of the building, heading for the first window which was the parlor. The manor had been attacked by demons not long ago and this window had to be replaced. He waited for me to catch up. When I paused beside him, he pointed to the window.

"There."

I looked at it, but there appeared to be nothing out of the ordinary. "What?" I looked harder but shrugged. "I don't see anything."

"For hell's sake, Anna." He grabbed my hand and pulled me closer, kneeling down in front of the window. He pointed to something etched in the stone under the windowsill. "There."

I squinted, as if that would make the image come into focus more easily. I scooted closer to get a better look in the early afternoon light. Under the window was an etching of an odd-looking hand with an eye in the center. A black substance was smudged over the eye.

"What the hell is it?"

"A hamsa," he said.

"A what-a?"

He huffed. "The hamsa hand is a popular amulet in the Middle East to guard against the 'evil eye,'" he said. He put air quotes around the *evil eye*. "A sign of protection. Also known as the Hand of Miriam. Christians believed it would bring the bearer good fortune. In this case, I believe your uncle used it to ward off evil."

Something inside my brain clicked. I had never actually seen the wards, but I was aware they were there. "Those were the wards my uncle mentioned?"

"Likely."

I reached for it and dragged my finger through the black substance and sniffed it. It was oily and smelled terrible. "What the *hell* is that, Kincade?"

"My best guess is something to eradicate the protection from the hamsa."

I sat back on my heels. "Is this the only one?"

"No. They're under every window on the first floor. I'm not sure about the second floor or the exterior doors."

As I sat contemplating what this meant, I wondered if this was why I had the dream walk with Lucifer and Azriel and why Lucifer was able to attack Grace with the vampire wraith.

"Grace was outside the building when she was attacked," Kincade said, as though hearing my thoughts.

I really hated when he did that but let it slide. "So, she wasn't protected anyway."

"No," he agreed. "And there's something else."

He got to his feet and started around the side of the building. I followed him, curious as to where he was headed. He paused on the side of the manor where there were no windows or doors. Then pointed at the wall. The wall had a cross stamped into the stone. That oily substance was also smeared across it.

"Whoever built the manor made sure to embed these crosses into the stone. Likely to ward off evil."

"My ancestors," I said, thinking of Ezra and his own form of evil.

He was the one who had gone rogue and tried to destroy the dream walkers with the misuse of the Holy Relics. Walker Manor was built long after he was dead, though. I wasn't sure who the builder was, not that it mattered, but whoever it was clearly wanted to keep all manner of evil and dark things out.

"These crosses are on every exterior wall of the manor with the same black substance across them. Someone or something was here and wants to make sure all the protection is eradicated," Kincade said.

Gooseflesh erupted on my exposed skin. A bone-chilling shiver went down my spine.

"Who or what?" I was afraid of the answer.

He shook his head. "I wish I had the answer."

He gave me a pointed look. I suspected whoever it was wanted me dead and/or out of the way. I realized this as much as he did. I didn't want to think it was my mother masquerading as Natasha on the second floor.

"What do I do now?" I asked.

"I'll take care of this." He waved at the smudged cross. "And the others."

I suspected he had a full grasp of what he needed to do to get rid of whatever was on the hamsa and the crosses. I gave him a slow nod, then met his level gaze.

"And when you're finished and we're sure the manor is safe again, it's time to leave for Spain and find the Grail."

I ENTERED THE MANOR, my head spinning with everything I had to do before we left. I had to make travel plans and figure out where in Valencia we were going. I needed to find the last postcard I received to look at it again and commit it to memory. All I recalled was it was a picture of a cathedral.

"Pardon me, my lady, but may I have a word?" Piers stood at the bottom of the stairs.

He glanced at my bare feet then behind me where I'd left wet footprints on the wood floor.

"You're concerned about Grace," I said. "She's unconscious. That's all I know."

"Might I inquire as to what happened to her?"

I shifted my weight from one foot to the other trying to decide how to answer. I wasn't sure if Piers was aware of the motley crew living under Walker Manor's roof. If he knew I was a dream walker, that Darius was a warrior angel, and Kincade was a former member of the Watchers.

"If I may speak freely?" he said.

"Of course."

"I am aware your uncle and the entire Walker family have special abilities. Even you. I have been a part of the Walkers for generations."

This was a piece of information I didn't have. I cocked my head to the side. "I don't remember you when I was a kid."

"You wouldn't because I wasn't the butler then. But I knew your uncle. Even your mother." He glanced upward as if to indicate he understood Natasha's real identity.

A part of me experienced a deeply gratifying relief knowing he understood. I blew out a breath I hadn't realized I was holding. But I also had other questions about Piers and who he truly was. That would come later.

"Then you understand what I have to do and why," I said. "You understand the dire situation Grace is in."

"Please, tell me."

"She was attacked by a vampire wraith sent by Lucifer."

His face drained of color as he glanced away to keep his emotions in check. It was the first real indication I had Piers and Grace cared for each other. It was also the first real indication of emotion I had ever seen from the old butler.

"He's using her to get me to do what he wants," I continued.

His stoic gaze met mine. "Alas, you cannot. For the fate of the world rests on your shoulders."

"I can't. But I *will* save her. I swear it. Lucifer isn't going to win this fight."

It was a vow I made not only to Piers, but also to myself and everyone else.

He gave me a faint smile. It was unusual to see him smile. "Very good, Miss Walker. Then your quest for the Holy Grail begins."

He walked away, leaving me standing in the hall gaping after him. I hadn't told him my next quest was for the Holy Grail. How did he know? Perhaps he overheard me mention it. Piers tended to lurk in the shadows.

I shook it off and headed up the stairs to my room.

It didn't take me long to pack. I tended to travel light and wore the same clothes everywhere. I was in for comfort. I usually ended up with demon guts on me at some point, too, due to Kincade's handiwork.

One of the best things about being my uncle's heir was that he had a private jet and a bottomless bank account. I called the pilot for him to be on standby and ready to leave, called the driver to pick us up, and made hotel reservations in Valencia at a five-star hotel. My job as Keeper of the Holy Relics didn't have a lot of perks, but those luxuries were definitely at the top of the list.

As I finished making arrangements, a knock sounded on my door. I opened it to Piers on the other side.

"You have a visitor in the parlor." He paused a brief moment before adding, "Mr. Harred."

I stiffened. "Which one?"

I sure as hell didn't want to talk to that blowhard, Alexander.

"Ronan."

Confused, I chewed the inside of my lip. What was he doing here again? "I'll be right down."

Piers nodded and headed back down the stairs. I stood a moment longer, biting the edge of my thumbnail and trying to decide if his arrival was timely or not. I took one more glance at my packed bags and my disheveled bedroom before heading down to the parlor.

Ronan sat on the edge of one of the chairs. He was dressed in hiking boots, khaki pants and a black button-down shirt that indicated he might be ready for a safari. A backpack and a duffel were at his feet. I had a bad feeling about this.

"Mr. Harred, to what do I owe the pleasure of your visit?" I tried to sound as cheerful and normal as possible.

But in reality, my insides were jangling.

He rose to his full height. He glanced at first my bare feet and then my bandages hands. Question flickered through his eyes for a brief moment.

"I've come to offer my services."

I cocked my head to the side, eyed the bags at his feet. "What services?"

"You plan to leave soon. Isn't that, right?"

My eyes narrowed with suspicion. "Where did you get that information? I've told no one outside this house."

"I told you before. A few of dream walkers have the sight."

A hot prickling sensation trickled up the back of my neck. Yep. A really bad feeling about this.

"You mentioned it." I said it slowly, cautiously.

"I had a vision of a gala at a royal palace. Something terrible happens. Something that puts your life in grave danger," he said.

I had no plans to visit a royal palace, much less attend a gala. While I believed he had the gift of foresight—and that what he saw might actually happen—I wasn't sure how I felt about him tagging along. "I'm sure Kincade and I can handle—"

"No." He cut me off with the slice of his hand in the air. "You don't understand."

He squeezed his eyes shut, as if recalling the memory. He jerked his head to one side, then another.

"It's the future I saw. I must accompany you."

Oh, shit. Kincade wasn't going to like having the man I was supposed to marry tag along. "Ronan, I appreciate your concern, but—"

"Listen, Keeper." He opened his eyes and moved toward me, taking me by the arms. His fingers pressed into the flesh of my biceps. "I have certain abilities. I can help you on your quest. I can help you defeat this evil."

How was I going to tell him off? "Kincade and I have been through a lot together. I'm sure we'll be fine."

But he was shaking his head before I finished speaking. He gave me a little jerk. Just enough to get my full attention.

"You don't understand, Keeper." He dropped his voice to a whisper. "I have seen your death."

I stared at him, my heart suddenly in my throat. "At this gala in the royal palace?"

He nodded.

"And...so...you're saying if you come with us, you can stop it?"

He dropped his hands to his side. "I believe you'll have a better chance of survival, yes."

I chewed my bottom lip. "What did you see exactly?"

"Images, mostly. Dark feelings of death. Large black wings and a woman who can alter time. Both of them come to do you harm."

I sucked in a sharp breath. *Astrid*. He saw Astrid and Azriel in his vision. This posed a serious dilemma. If I made him stay behind, my death was likely. If I allowed him to come with us, Kincade would hate it. But I wasn't sure I could very well take a chance and leave Ronan behind. Even so, I had questions.

"And your father is okay with this?"

"He doesn't know, and I don't plan to tell him."

"Well, I'm sure he won't be upset at all if he finds out." I prayed he didn't. The last thing I needed was an angrier Alexander Herrad on my tail. "What are these abilities you have?"

He pressed his lips together looking as though he didn't want to answer.

"If you're joining the party I need to know," I said. "You have the gift of foresight. What else?"

He swallowed hard, his throat working. "Only those closest to me know."

"And now me. Go."

"I have divine power."

I blinked, staring at him hard trying to reason what that actually meant. When I said nothing, he shifted from one foot to the other.

"I can harness the power of the divine."

That still told me nothing and I wondered if that meant he had the Godlight, too. Did that make him like me? Perhaps, when the time was right, he would expound upon that information. I had more questions but nodded anyway.

"Okay, then. You're in."

Nope. Kincade wasn't going to like this at all.

CHAPTER 10

THE FIRST THING I had to do was find Kincade and tell him. But as I turned to leave the parlor, he stood in the doorway leaning against the jamb, his powerful arms crossed over his chest looking meaner than a junkyard dog on a short leash. I was in deep shit.

"Oh," I said on a breath. "Kincade, Ronan is—"

"I heard." His voice was terse as his gaze flickered to the man behind me.

"Then you understand why he's coming with us." I tried to pretend everything was situation normal but the glower on Kincade's face made that difficult.

"Do I?" He met my gaze, making me want to shrink into oblivion.

Ronan moved to stand next to me which was probably the worst idea ever. Kincade turned his fierce stare back to him. "She's in danger."

"She's always in danger," Kincade fired back. "That's what I'm here for."

I was torn between laughing out loud, which I managed to contain, and acknowledging the flutter of my heart, which I made a valiant effort to ignore. I combated both with sarcasm.

"I like to live life on the edge."

"I don't think you understand—" Ronan began.

"He understands. He's just being difficult," I interrupted.

"I understand," Kincade said, talking over me. "You think you can protect her better than I can."

"If you were eavesdropping, which you were," Ronan said, "you know I have the gift of foresight. I've seen her death." He tried hard to keep the irritation out of his voice, but I didn't miss the clenching of his fist.

"And?" Kincade looked utterly unimpressed.

"He has divine power," I offered up.

Kincade gave me the flattest look I'd ever seen. His mouth straightened into a thin line.

"Listen, we don't have time for this." The last thing I needed was a pissing match between these two. To Kincade, I said, "He's coming."

"Who says?" he snapped.

"I do. And I'm in charge of this party." I thumbed at my chest.

His face tightened as he managed to control his rage. "Fine."

Kincade stalked away from the parlor and up the stairs, his booted feet angry on every single step as he stomped up them.

"We leave within the hour," I called.

He replied by slamming his bedroom door. I sighed.

"He doesn't want me to go," Ronan said.

"No, but he'll get over it. You're going. Now, if you'll excuse me, I have some last-minute details to finalize. Can I get you anything?"

He shook his head as he entered the parlor. He took a seat next to his bags.

"You don't mind waiting here?" I asked.

"Not at all."

Leaving him seemed awkward but I had to call the pilot and tell him we'd have another passenger as well as add another hotel room to our stay. But first, I needed to talk to Darius. I darted up the stairs and paused at the door to the room he shared with Ophelia. When I was certain there were no shenanigans going on, I knocked.

This was the norm for them. They stayed holed up most of the day and night. I couldn't blame Ophelia, really. Daris was a hot warrior angel.

She opened it a second later and greeted me with a smile. "Hey, Anna."

"I need to talk to Darius."

She pushed open the door wider and stepped aside. He moved from the depths of the room to join her at the door.

"Keeper." He gave me a nod of hello.

"I need a favor," I said. "I need you to watch over Grace."

"Of course, but from what I've seen, Grace can take care of herself."

I shook my head. "Not this time."

I recounted the story of the vampire wraith, Lucifer's threat, the black smudges on the crosses and the hamsa on the walls, and my subsequent trip to Spain.

"Grace will be well guarded. You have my word," Darius said.

"Thank you." It gave me peace of mind knowing he would be here standing guard. And that if anything or anyone invaded the manor, he'd fight back to protect her and keep her safe.

"When did all this happen?" Ophelia was clearly shaken as she and Grace had become fast friends.

"This morning. My hope is to find the Grail. I believe it can heal her."

I thought of the holy water Sariel had given me. I considered packing it but decided against it since it wouldn't do me any good. I needed it here when I returned with the cup.

"I'm coming with you," Ophelia said. "You need me."

I took a deep breath and turned her. "As much as it pains me to say this, I need you to stay here. I have another job for you. I need you to keep an eye on Natasha." I gave a nod to the room at the other end of the hall.

"Your mother? But she poses no threat. And besides, I can—"

"Yes, I realize having you with us would help us fight and kill demons, but I already have my hands full with Ronan and Kincade," I added.

She frowned, her brows drawing together. "Who's Ronan?"

I hadn't talked to her since the appearance of my betrothed. Too many things had happened here at the manor.

"Long story. I'll catch you up later. Will you do it?"

She shifted from one foot to the other, then gave a glance at Darius. As if she decided staying behind to babysit might not be a bad thing after all.

"What do you want me to do if she leaves?" she asked.

That was a great question and one to which I didn't have an answer. "Don't let her leave. I need her to stay here where it's safe."

"Gee, that's helpful." She gave me a sour expression. "But yeah, I'll keep an eye on her."

At that moment, Kincade exited his room with a duffle in his hand. He slammed his bedroom door again, rattling the rafters.

"Let's go," he barked as he stomped by.

Surprise flickered over Ophelia's face as she watched him disappear down the stairs. "Who pissed in his Cheerios?"

"Again, long story. I'll catch you up later. Thanks for being here. Both of you."

"Good luck, Keeper," Daris said.

I nodded and bid them farewell. I hurried to my room, grabbed my own bag. I really wasn't looking forward to being trapped inside the car or an airplane with the two of them. This was going to be a very long trip.

◆———◆

THE CAR RIDE TO the airport was silent. The plane ride from England to Valencia, Spain was even more silent with a whole lot of uncomfortable thrown in for good measure. I ignored Kincade's brooding and Ronan's indifference and took the time to examine the postcard I received of the cathedral in Spain.

I took my cell phone out of my pocket and did a quick search for cathedrals in Valencia and included the words Holy Grail. The first result was Valencia Cathedral. I tapped on one of the photos of the exterior of the cathedral and compared it to the card I held in my hand.

Bingo.

That was it.

But this was too easy. I doubted the Holy Grail would be in that cathedral waiting for me. If it was, how was I going to recover it? Likely it was guarded with security and cameras. There was no way I would be able to waltz in, pick up the Grail, and waltz out. There had to be a catch.

Because there always was when it came to these relics.

After more research, I discovered it *was* in that cathedral on display. How the bloody hell was I supposed to retrieve it without getting caught? I was already likely in some trouble for my theft of the Staff of Moses. It was from a holy site in Jerusalem. Pretty sure

Interpol or whoever was looking for me, but Tamar Mizrahi, my contact there, had done her best to wipe out my existence.

I was grateful the flight to Spain was a short one. We landed at a private airport in the city and deboarded. I had a car waiting for us to take us to the five-star hotel in the heart of the city. My uncle had spoiled me to luxury hotels, private jets, chauffeurs. I wasn't going to give that up.

I put the phone in my lap. I flexed my hands, the skin under the bandages itching. I unwound the gauze and examined my knuckles. They were still raw but were healing from my boxing debacle.

When we stepped off the plane, the cold wind swept through me. I shivered in the depths of my heavy coat. I zipped it up to my neck and shoved one hands, still painful and sensitive, deep in my pockets. I carried my duffle with the other, wincing with the throb as the cold wind bit into the exposed flesh. The driver greeted us with a half nod. We exchanged pleasant greetings.

"Welcome, Miss Anna."

"You have the address of the hotel?" I asked.

He nodded as he opened the trunk for us to store our luggage. "The drive is a short one."

He opened the back-passenger door for me. I slid inside. Ronan started to follow, but Kincade stopped him with a hand on his chest. He gave him a push.

"You. Up front."

Tension rolled off both of them as Ronan stiffened. He said nothing as he reached for the front passenger door and got in. Kincade waited until the door was shut before getting in next to me and slamming the door.

I shot him a glare, biting back the acid words. I resisted asking him why he was being such an asshole because I already had the answer. He didn't seem to notice or care.

We took off for the hotel, silence piercing the air between all of us. I pulled my cell phone out of my pocket and took great interest in the screen. I scrolled through my email and read the hotel confirmation though it was already memorized. Kincade shifted in his seat, the leather material squeaking with his movement.

"Why?" Kincade kept his lethal gaze on the back of Ronan's head.

"If you overheard our conversation in the parlor you know why."

I refused to give him any slack. Nor did I want to look at him. I held the phone in my lap and kept my gaze firmly planted on the window, watching the world flash by. Despite the chill in the air, the sky was clear, and the sun was bright as it beamed down into the car.

"You think he can save your life?" He sounded so disgusted and almost as though he had his feelings hurt.

"I think he can help us." I gave him a glance over my shoulder before turning back to the window. He looked as unhappy as I sensed. I tried to decide what to think about that. Was he jealous of Ronan? We were betrothed, sure, but his heart belonged to another. He had zero interest in me.

"You should know by now, Anna, I'm your best chance."

He said nothing more. My gut twisted at his words. I did believe that. Truly. But something in Ronan's words convinced me I needed him with me. Something told me if I didn't bring him along, I would regret it.

I was a girl who always listened to her gut.

Especially when it came to other dream walkers who had divine abilities.

We arrived at Las Arenes Balneari Resort, a large and very beautiful hotel on the beach. I managed to secure the last two suites they had available, both with beach views and a private terrace. The expansive lobby was beautifully decorated with chic contemporary furniture in off-whites and beige giving it a clean, elegant feel. Tourists and locals milled about.

The desk clerk greeted me with a smile and welcomed me by name. Something I wasn't quite used to. Edward was always in charge of hotels and airplanes and hired cars. But I reminded myself I was the one in charge now. As I so aptly told Kincade.

"Your suites are on the top floor, Miss Walker. Enjoy your stay." The woman smiled as she handed over the card keys.

I happily took them and headed for the elevator. The guys followed. Once we were inside the elevator, I handed a key over to Ronan.

"Your room."

"This is the presidential suite," he said, staring down at the plastic card.

"Yeah. One of two," I replied.

"Anna likes amenities," Kincade said.

Well, he wasn't wrong. If he was, I'd argue with him until I was blue in the face. So, I remained silent until the elevator dinged and we disembarked, heading down the hall to the two side-by-side suites.

"What's the plan?" Ronan asked.

"The plan is I take a nice long nap and then I have a date with a cathedral. You boys are free to do whatever you wish," I said.

Ronan gave a nod and stuck the key in the door. "I'll come with you when you're ready."

Kincade practically growled.

I ignored it. "In two hours then."

Ronan shoved open his door and paused, waiting for Kincade. He made no move to enter and suddenly I understood why. Heated tendrils went right up my spine at the thought of sharing a room with him. Not that we would actually be sharing. The suite had two bedrooms. I pinpointed him with a look over my shoulder and a raised eyebrow.

"I guess you're rooming with me?" I asked.

"You guessed right."

I kept the sigh to myself as I shoved open the door to the palatial room. It was as divine as I'd hoped with crisp, clean linens on the bed, personal bathrooms, thick, fluffy towels, and Bulgari amenities. The curtains to the terrace were open showing off the spectacular view of the beach, the crystal blue sky and the cerulean sea. It was breathtaking.

I heard Kincade moving around in the bedroom next to mine.

"You don't have to babysit me, you know."

"I'm not worried about you," he said.

Oh, I got it. He was worried about Ronan. The anger punched through me as I stalked to his room, my hands on my hips.

"He has a girlfriend already, you know."

He sat on the edge of the bed and toed off his boots. He reached into his duffle and pulled out his demon killing gun. I was very familiar with this gun. It made a high-pitched whine before releasing whatever ammo it held and destroyed demons. Usually in close proximity to me and also usually splattering guts all over me.

"Doesn't matter."

He took an interest in said gun. He pulled back the chamber, looked inside it, closed it. I observed his muscled hands, fascinated with the movement and idly wondering what made the high-pitched sound come from the gun. He tucked it under his pillow. I had no idea he slept with his gun.

"Yes, it does," I insisted.

He looked at me as though I should be wearing a dunce cap.

"The marriage contract means nothing. Not to me. Not to him."

"You think I'm worried about a piece of paper?" He shook his head.

I was taken aback. "Then what are you worried about?"

He clenched his jaw tight, the muscles flexing under the skin. Something I'd seen him do when he was frustrated and annoyed with me.

I dropped my hands to my side, my shoulders slumping, defeated. "You're worried about *him*. You don't trust him."

"I don't trust anyone."

I tried not to be insulted by that. "You trust me." I turned on the toe of my boot and left him to consider that.

I went back to my giant room and shut the door. I didn't want to talk to him anymore. He was being unreasonable. Ronan would not tag along just to take me out. I didn't believe that for one second. His father may be a prick, but Ronan wasn't. And everything inside me trusted him. He was a dream walker, a member of the clan that belonged to the Order. I truly believed he wanted to help, not hinder.

But maybe that wasn't Kincade's problem. Maybe Kincade's problem with Ronan was the fact he was tagging along and he was a guy. And Kincade was...jealous.

I'd suspected it before when I interacted with Darius. He didn't like the warrior angel, but he tolerated him since we all lived under the same roof.

He had a serious beef with Ronan because, well, he was like me. A dream walker with some sort of divine ability I had yet to understand. Perhaps Kincade felt threatened by him.

I pressed my cold, shaking fingers to my lips and perched on the edge of the bed. If Kincade was jealous, did that mean he *liked* me?

No, that was silly. I shook it off. I didn't believe Kincade had any sort of feelings for me whatsoever. What sort of future did we have together anyway? What would happen to us once I saved the world and kicked Lucifer's ass?

I'd think about all that later. Not now. I was too tired. A giant yawn nearly split my head into. But first I had to make arrangements for a car to take us from the hotel to the cathedral. One quick phone call and it was done. I kicked off my pink combat boots and crawled onto the bed, staring out at the blue expanse of sea and sky. Moments later, I was fast asleep.

CHAPTER 11

I AWOKE TO A pounding on my bedroom door.

"Two hours are up, Anna. Let's go."

Ugh.

Kincade sounded pissy again. I didn't have the energy to deal with that, but I knew I would have to face him. I sat up, pushing my fingers through my long, tangled hair. A glance out the terrace doors made me long for a real vacation. Out there, people walked the edge of the beach while the surf rolled in. Somewhere on a sunny restaurant terrace, they were drinking cocktails, ordering appetizers, and living their best life.

What was I doing? Chasing after holy relics with a grump and a guy I barely knew.

Another pounding on the door. "Anna, come on."

"I'm coming!" I snapped in my angry voice.

Silence on the other side.

I pulled on my boots and stood. For good measure, I checked to make sure my jade-handled dagger and my uncle's sword were safely hidden in the cloud. I quickly drew them down one at a time, then put them back. Satisfied, I opened the bedroom door.

Kincade stood near the hotel room door with his arms crossed. The gun at his waist didn't escape my notice. At least we were both prepared for the worst.

A certain weariness took up residence deep in my bones. From running all over the world looking for the relics, to the death of my uncle, to everything in between. I was tired of it all. And despite being tired of it all, I muscled through it and kept going. Because that's what I had to do.

"You don't have to look like you're ready to murder someone, you know," I said as I walked by Kincade. I pulled open the hotel room door without waiting for his response.

He was right behind me, letting the door close. I paused at Ronan's door and knocked. I was certain Kincade's glare would bore into the back of my head at some point. Ronan answered a moment later and we were off.

We headed down the thick-carpeted hallway, our boots nothing more than a quiet swish on the plush fibers. I was aware of the uncomfortable silence lingering in the air between us and it was all because of Ronan's presence.

The elevator ride was also silent.

All the silence was about to make me bat shit crazy.

"Where is this cathedral?" Ronan asked.

"In the heart of the city," I said. "Valencia Cathedral. It's too far to walk, so we'll have to drive."

Outside the hotel, the car I'd arranged waited for us. The driver stood outside the black sedan holding a sign reading A. WALKER. He wore a black suit, white shirt with black tie, black chauffeur cap and dark sunglasses. He was tall with broad shoulders that put Kincade's to shame. His perfectly tanned face sported a dark goatee.

"You hired a car?" Kincade asked.

"I did," I replied in my most chipper voice.

"Miss Walker, *sí?*"

I gave him a jaunty wave. "You must be Mateo."

I took in a deep breath to check for demon smell but sensed none. He gave a grin and opened the back-passenger door for me. I slid inside. When Kincade bullied his way between the driver and the door, I frowned but slid across to the other side. He got in next to me and pulled the door closed. Ronan got in the front passenger side.

Kincade, however, gave me his best glare which I ignored.

If I was a girlie girl, I'd have a powder case to pull out and check my face, pretending I didn't give a flip about Kincade or his glare. However, I was not a girlie girl and had no such thing. All I carried was my hotel room key and my cell phone.

I huffed and turned to him. "What?" I said through my clenched teeth.

"Do you know this driver?" He nodded to the man behind the wheel.

I sighed and turned to the window. He was so suspicious these days. "Not personally, no. Why?"

He said nothing as he sat back in the leather seat, the material squeaking with his movement.

"What's your problem?"

"Nothing."

I didn't have an internal lie detector, but I sensed he wasn't giving me the whole truth. "Wrong. What gives?"

He didn't meet my gaze as we headed down the street, his big hands on his knees.

I had a feeling this had something to do with Ronan, but I wasn't sure why or what.

"Fifteen minutes to the Cathedral, *señorita*."

"*Gracias*, Mateo." To Kincade, I said, "Maybe you start trusting me, eh?"

He didn't respond. I didn't expect him to.

We headed down Carrer del Mediterrani, a densely populated street with cars parked on either side. Kincade shifted in his seat as we passed the tennis courts on our right. Another silent ride later. When we arrived, I paid the driver and headed across the plaza to the cathedral. I paused to take in the massive building.

Since my questing began, I'd been to several cathedrals and churches. The architecture never failed to impress me. This particular building was consecrated in 1238 and built over the site of a Visigoth cathedral. Predominantly gothic, it also contained Renaissance, Baroque and Neoclassic elements.

The gothic door, called the Door of the Apostles, was breathtaking with its four-pointed arches. There was so much going on around the door, it was hard to take it all in. Statues carved in the upper frieze were thought to be Kings of Israel from the Old Testament. Above the door, a delicate and beautiful rose stained-glass window housing the Star of David.

I hadn't stepped foot into the building yet and already I had a reverence for it, much like I did in Acre when walking through the Templar fortress. Though the postcard led me here, something told me I would not find the actual Holy Grail.

I took a deep breath and stepped across the threshold into the church.

We made our way to the Holy Grail Chamber, across the black and white checked floor, past the ornate architecture. Walking through the cathedral, hushed voices whispered in this place of reverence. Kincade and Ronan were silent as they followed me through to the Holy Grail Chamber.

We entered at the back of the chamber. A few wooden pews were on either side where tourists perched to listen to the audio portion of their walking tour. I paused inside the doorway, my heart in my throat as I looked toward the altar, a faded red and yellow rug led. The Grail resided in a nook in a backlit glass case. Well, where the Grail should have been. Instead, it was nothing but an empty place behind the altar. Kincade stood to my left. Ronan to my right.

"I don't understand. The postcard led me here."

"The postcard was wrong," Kincade said.

Ronan didn't question what postcard. He moved further into the chamber toward the alter stopping to examine the niche as close as he dared. I remained rooted in place, Kincade at my side.

"The postcard is never wrong," I said.

And it hadn't been. Every time I received a new one, it led me to the location of the next relic. Or, in the case of Antarctica, to my biological mother.

"Perhaps it's not on display at this time," he suggested.

But something was off. The back of my neck tingled.

Ronan returned to us. "It looks like the cup has been removed from display by the cathedral."

I sighed. "If it's not on display, now what?"

"Now, we figure out Plan B," Kincade said.

He made it sound so easy. In my experience, nothing was ever easy.

"What's Plan B?" I asked.

He shrugged.

I huffed. "You're no help."

A buzzing sound came from Ronan. Kincade and I both looked at him as he fumbled to pull his cell phone out of his pocket and quickly silence the vibration.

"My father." He gave me a sheepish look.

I raised an eyebrow. "And you silenced him."

"I can't very well take the call in here." He swept his hand around the Holy Grail Chamber.

"Then by all means return the call outside." Kincade thumbed over his shoulder.

Any chance to get rid of Ronan, I guess. I rolled my eyes. He excused himself and left the room, leaving me and Kincade alone. Well, as alone as possible in a room of tourists. I glanced back toward the empty place where the Grail should have been.

The description of the chalice was burned into my mind. I'd read up on it when I first received the postcard. Carved from agate, it had two large gold handles inlaid with precious gems. Some claimed the cup's origin was somewhere between the 2nd Century BC to the First Century AD, created in the Middle East.

If it was the most legendary artifact of all time, resting quietly in a glass case in a cathedral in Spain...well, this was too easy.

And maybe that was the point. But, again, I wondered why the postcard sent me here.

Unless there was some other reason why I was supposed to be in Spain.

"Come on, Anna. No use standing here all day." Kincade slipped is hand around my upper arm and gently tugged me away.

He was right. Standing around wasn't getting us anywhere.

As we exited the chamber, Ronan approached with his phone in his hand and his cheeks pink as though he'd just had a good lashing.

"Everything okay?" I asked.

Next to me, Kincade bristled. I ignored him.

"My father wanted to know where I was. So, I told him." He paused and we waited.

"You told him you were in Spain?" I asked.

"I told him I was with you."

"And?"

"And he demanded I return to England at once."

"Finally, something that makes sense," Kincade said.

I shot him a heated glare.

"But I'm not going." Ronan's defiant gaze landed on Kincade. "I told him I had a vision and why I must stay close to Anna's side."

"Great," Kincade muttered.

My stomach rumbled. "Now that that's cleared up, who's hungry?"

I didn't wait for an answer as I headed out of the cathedral, not caring one whit if Kincade or Ronan followed.

CHAPTER 12

I EXITED THE CATHEDRAL onto the plaza surrounding the church. It was busy for a brisk January afternoon. I halted, taking it in and trying to decide my next move. Kincade was to my left. Ronan to my right.

"What's our next move?" Ronan asked.

Before I was able to answer, I saw him. Or rather them—three men heading straight for us. The one in the middle had black eyes that appeared to glow gold every so often and were pinpointed right on me. I stiffened as I watched them head across the plaza toward us. They were not human or demon. I wasn't sure what they were.

Kincade rested his hand on the holster on his hip. On my other side, Ronan sucked in a breath.

"Are we going to stand here and let them come for us?" he asked.

"I don't know who or what they are yet," I said.

"It doesn't look good," Kincade added.

I agreed with him. My fingers flexed, ready to draw down one of my weapons. The world turned fuzzy. That usually happened when demon magic was at work. Suddenly, the three of them bolted into a run right for us. Kincade drew his weapon without hesitation. The high pitch whine was unmistakable just before he fired. The one on the left dropped to the ground, dead.

No shouts from humans which told me they couldn't see what was happening behind the veil of magic. I took a deep breath, but they weren't close enough for me to scent them yet.

The death of the one only slowed the other two. The one in the middle bared his teeth. Sharp, pointed teeth that reminded me of a vampire. His eyes glowed gold.

I'd seen a vampire one other time and that was in the underground club in Dallas under Azriel's cemetery.

Ronan gripped my arm and dragged me away at a run. I stumbled before I got my footing and followed him. Kincade was right behind us. We ran across the plaza and back to the street where we hung a right. The other two were right on our heels.

Ronan didn't slow down as he took a left, down a small alleyway and headed toward another street.

A shadow flickered overhead and the two of them were in front of us. We all skidded to a halt. The one with the glowing eyes bared his teeth as he moved closer to us.

"You have something we want, Miss Walker."

Who is this? Kincade's voice floated into my head.

"Oh, yeah? And what is that?" I answered, trying to sound as calm and cool as possible.

Meanwhile, my heart pounded from the sprint. Adrenaline rushed through my veins. I wish I'd drawn down the dagger or the sword. A quick glance around confirmed too many people in the plaza. I didn't want to draw that much attention to us.

He smiled, still showing off those teeth. "You stole it."

Well, then. I'd stolen the Horn of Gabriel and the Staff of Moses. The Spear of Destiny I found fair and square. I wondered which relic these jokers were after.

"Did I?" I lifted an eyebrow and pretended to be unconcerned.

The glowing eyed vampire glanced at Kincade, then Ronan and finally back to me. "In Hong Kong," he added.

Ah, so the horn. "No idea what you're talking about."

He hissed. "We want it back."

"Who's we?" Kincade stepped forward, shielding me from these two.

The vampire met his gaze, utter disdain on his pale face. What kind of vampire could be out in the blinding light of day?

"Consider this a warning, Miss Walker." Though he mentioned me by name, he never took his gaze off Kincade.

They both leapt up the side of the nearest building to the roof and were gone. Kincade turned to me.

"What the fuck, Anna?"

I shrugged. "You got me."

"Those were vampires," Ronan said as though he just realized.

"Yep," I agreed. "How much you want to bet the one you shot in the plaza isn't dead?"

Kincade scowled. "I'll not be taking that bet."

Because I was right. And, as far I knew, his gun killed demons, not vampires.

"What now?" Ronan asked.

"We'll go back to the hotel and regroup. Besides, I need food." As I said it, my stomach rumbled loud enough for them to hear.

We hailed a taxi and headed back to the hotel. The short ride back gave me time to think about this new development of meeting the vamps. They were clearly aware I stole the Horn of Gabriel from Chen back in Hong Kong and they wanted it back. Did Chen have these guys working for him as henchmen or was something else going on?

In Hong Kong, I found the horn in a high-rise office building—Two International Finance Centre. My cousin, Lexi, and I went in under the guise of the cleaning crew and broke into Chen's office. I recalled Lexi telling me Chen funneled money into a religious organization called Partners for the Sanctified. They were fanatics in search of holy relics.

A cold sweat washed over me as the blood drained from my face.

"You all right?" Kincade asked next to me.

I chewed on my lower lip and nodded, though he knew damn well I wasn't. He didn't press further, and I was glad. I wasn't ready to tell him in the back of the taxi what I surmised. Nor did I want Ronan to overhear. Not that I didn't trust him. I did. But the less information he had, the better. And I would have to explain too much about Hong Kong, Chen and the stolen Horn of Gabriel.

The taxi stopped outside the hotel. We got out and headed inside, each to our own rooms.

"See you in the morning." Ronan gave a half-hearted wave over his shoulder as he entered his room.

Kincade and I said nothing as we entered ours. As soon as the door swung shut behind us, he turned to me with that expectant look on his face.

"Tell me."

"I think I know who those vampires work for." I paused, bit the edge of my thumbnail as I mulled over what to say next.

"And?" he prompted.

"You'll recall I stole the Horn of Gabriel from Chen Tso Lang in Hong Kong."

He nodded.

Kincade had followed me trying to track me down after our initial run-in. That was early in our relationship and we didn't know a lot about each other. He was trying to figure out who I was and what I was up to and I was busy trying to avoid everything about him. Hell, I still would if he wasn't living in my house, working out in my gym, and eating my food.

I paced the room. "Well, he was a proud member of Partners for the Sanctified. They're a bunch of zealots searching for holy relics."

"I'm familiar with who they are. And you think these vampires work for them?"

Of course, he was familiar with them. Why was I surprised?

"I do. And they want the Horn of Gabriel back."

"I thought you told me this Chen had it because he was a collector."

"He was." I halted, trying to work out the details. "But...perhaps he was merely holding the relic for them."

"Why would he keep it in a conspicuous place like his office if he was merely holding it for them?"

I shrugged. "I'm not the criminal mastermind here. And since Chen is dead, I can't exactly ask him."

"If what you think is true, how did they find you?" he asked.

"I have no idea." My stomach rumbled again. I walked through the posh living area to the coffee table and picked up the room service menu. "Maybe I'm famous."

He scoffed. "Don't get cocky."

I flipped the page looking for something on the menu that sounded tempting. "Something else is bothering me."

"What is it?" Kincade moved to the sofa and sat, propping his ankle on his knee.

I tossed the menu back on the table. "I'll be right back."

I headed into my side of the suite to my bedroom, rifled through my duffle and grabbed the small envelope I carried with me everywhere. This had been a niggling sensation at the back of my mind for a long while. Unanswered questions were a part of my life now.

I slid out the postcard of Valencia, Spain with the picture of the cathedral. On the back were the words *Holy Grail* in that blocky handwriting. I took it back to the living area where Kincade waited and handed it to him.

He looked it over, then at me. "What about it?"

"The postcard clues haven't been wrong. But this time it was."

His brows drew together in question. "What do you mean?"

"I mean, every time I've gotten a postcard it led me to something or someone. Hong Kong led me to the Horn of Gabriel." I held up the Hong Kong card with the picture of Two International Finance Centre. Then showed him the plain piece of white paper with the words *Station 211 Antarctica*. "This one led me to my biological mother." I held up the one of Istanbul with the words *Spear of Destiny*. "This one the spear." And finally, Jerusalem, Israel. "And this one the Staff of Moses. So, my point is, why did that card lead me here?"

He peered down at the one of Valencia in his hand. He ran his free hand over his scruffy chin, the coarse hairs bristling against the palm of his hand.

"It doesn't make sense," I added.

"Who is sending these to you?"

"I have no idea. They merely...appear."

He tilted his head to the side. "Appear how?"

"The Hong Kong one was in a thick envelope in my old apartment. You were there when I found it."

Nodding, he said, "I remember. The Istanbul one?"

"My apartment in Hong Kong."

"The white paper?"

"My room in Walker Manor. That's also where I found the Valencia, Spain one."

His mind worked as he tried to work out a pattern trying to connect some commonality between the appearance of all the cards. The one thing in common with all of them was me.

"And you've never seen anyone leave them?"

I shook my head. He flipped over the card and examined the written words. "Recognize this handwriting?"

"No."

He held it closer to his face and squinted as he examined the lines of the words. "Someone wrote this in a heavy hand. With a black fine point marker."

"Right. But who?"

"I know as much as you." He handed me back the postcard. "But if you think you were sent here for a reason, we better figure it out."

"What if it's for something else and not the Grail?"

"Like what?" he asked.

I shrugged as my stomach growled again. "No idea."

"I guess it's a mystery." He rose and headed for the hotel room door.

"Where are you going?"

"Downstairs to the restaurant to get you food so you'll stop making so much noise."

He was out the door before I formed a reply.

After he left, I paced the room. The appearance of the postcards did not make sense to me. Nothing much in my life made sense to me.

A knock sounded on the door. I halted mid-step and stared at it, wondering who was on the other side. As I opened the door, I expected Ronan.

Instead, four strangers stood in the hall. I stiffened at the sight of them and took a deep breath. Not demons. Not vampires, either. They all looked rather official.

"Yes?" I asked.

"Miss Walker?" the man who appeared to be in charge asked.

"Yes?" Hesitation and uncertainty laced the one word.

He flashed a badge then produced a set of handcuffs. "You're under arrest for the theft of the Staff of Moses."

Fuck.

CHAPTER 13

I WAS HANDCUFFED AND taken away from the hotel room. My blood pressure rose to an indeterminable rate as I broke into a hot-cold sweat. My mind raced, trying to figure out how this was possible. When I left Israel, Tamar told me she had erased all trace of our stay in her hotel. Apparently, something had gone awry.

When Kincade and I left the country with the staff, we were chased. I assumed by police or some sort of legal authority that didn't take kindly to me removing the staff from their country.

The arresting officer from the local district in Spain was accompanied by someone from Interpol. The charges were for a cultural heritage crime, something to which Israel did not take kindly. I was in deep shit. And I had no idea what to do next.

I kept my mouth shut, did not admit guilt to anything, and followed their lead. It was my best chance at getting out of here without being sent to prison for the rest of my life. My stomach still rumbled, but that was the absolute least of my worries.

How was I going to contact Kincade? I'd left my cell phone behind.

Duh. I remembered I could mindspeak. As I rode in the back of the *policía* car as we headed toward the station, I closed my eyes and tried to connect to him.

Kincade...respond if you can hear me. I'm, um, arrested.

There was no reply. I opened my eyes and watched as the night flashed outside the car window. And then his voice burst into my head.

What the fuck, Anna?

That was Kincade. Never one to mince words. And I kinda liked that about him.

They're taking me somewhere. I'm not sure where, yet.

Silence and then, *I'll find you.*

My stupid heart skipped a stupid beat at hearing his words. If anyone could find me and bust me out of jail, Kincade could. I leaned back into the leather seat confident I would not be spending the entire night in jail.

◆————◆

I SPENT THE ENTIRE night in jail.

No idea why or how or what was going on, but I didn't appreciate being behind bars with the other miscreants of Valencia. I was no common criminal after all.

I got wind this was a temporary situation and they planned to move me. Extraditing me back to Israel where I would face more charges for looting, destroying a historical site, and some other bullshit.

Okay, so, yeah, Tamar set off explosions. There was a fight between Azriel and Kincade and some demons died. But that was totally not my fault. I had been busy in the Holy of Holies retrieving the staff to know exactly what was going out in there.

Where was Tamar? Did she give me up to save her own skin? Or had something happened to her?

Tamar was acquainted with my uncle and helped me find the staff and leave the country. I hadn't given that a second thought as we headed home and celebrated Christmas and New Year's at Walker Manor. Until today. Now I worried about her.

An officer arrived and opened the cell. She waved for me to follow her. Shit. I didn't want to follow her.

They cuffed me, as though I were a flight risk, and led me through the station. I scanned the faces looking for Kincade but didn't find him. Where was he? Why hadn't he come for me yet?

It was mid-morning judging by the level of the sun in the sky. The loaded me into another police car. The female Interpol agent slipped in beside me.

"We're taking you back to Israel," she said. Her words held a hint of a Spanish accent.

She reminded me of Isobel Marquez, my cousin who was murdered by Azriel. Tall, dark haired wearing haute couture with pouty lips painted red. She was someone I didn't want to mess with and yet, my mouth had a mind of its own.

"Why?"

"I think you know why, Miss Walker."

"I don't, really."

"You're wanted in the theft of a valuable artifact from a construction site." She gave me a glance, mystery in her dark brown eyes. "Or did you forget you stole something?"

"I forget nothing." I gave her a thin smile. "You don't know what you're doing."

"I know exactly what I'm doing. I'm taking you back to Jerusalem where you will face charges and you will be convicted." She pushed a lock of dark hair off her face and tucked it behind her ear.

"What happened to innocent until proven guilty?" I asked.

She scoffed. "Americans. So entitled. So arrogant." She gave me a pointed look. I wanted to shrink back into the seat. "You do realize the artifact you stole was of significant historical importance, don't you?"

I said nothing.

"And that you will have to turn it over at some point. In fact, there are agents at your home in England now looking for it."

My heart leapt into my throat, but I said nothing, still. I didn't want to admit to anything, much less the fact the Staff of Moses along with the other three relics were hidden at Walker Manor. I thought of Darius and Ophelia, Natasha, Piers, and Grace in her comatose state. What would happen to them if those agents tore the house apart?

The silver lining in all of this was they would *never* find the relics. No one but me had the combination to the vault. I was the only who *knew* where the vault was. That gave me some comfort. But, still, I was super pissed strangers were in my house looking for the Holy Relics.

"Your silence speaks volumes," the woman said.

I had no reply. Why should I when anything I said would incriminate me? They must have found some evidence on me to be able to track me down. Maybe Tamar had been questioned and cracked under pressure. Maybe she was the one who led them to me. I had to get out of this predicament and fast.

In a moment of desperation, I reached out again with my mind. *Kincade?*

His response came almost immediately. *Working on it. They fucking moved you.*

I'm on the move now. In the back of a car headed to the airport. They are extraditing me to Israel.

And his succinct reply. *Fuck all.*

That was exactly how I felt.

I needed him to get on with it and fast.

Suddenly, the car swerved in a violent jerk to the right. I fell into the Interpol officer with a grunt as she smacked her head into the window.

"What the hell is going on?" she barked to the driver.

Another swerve the other way. And somewhere in the distance up ahead, an explosion.

Shit was about to get real.

I stretched to the side to see out the front windshield. Ahead, there was a plume of smoke and a fiery column of orange and red. The car came to an abrupt halt. Someone landed with a loud *thud* on the hood, denting in the metal as though pliable. The man on the hood leaned down and punched through the windshield. He grabbed the driver by the collar and jerked him out as though he weighed nothing. The poor driver went flying out the windshield with an ear-piercing scream.

The Interpol agent next to me drew her gun and fired off several rounds. But to no avail. It didn't stop the intruder on the hood. All it did was slow him down. And suddenly I understood why. It was one of the vampires.

Fuck and fuck and fuck again. Could this day get any worse?

We're being attacked by vampires, I said to Kincade.

I got no response.

The Interpol agent popped open her door and fired more shots. I sighed. It wasn't going to do any good. All she was doing was wasting ammunition. But it was pointless to try to tell her otherwise. Most humans did not have the ability to see the supernaturals as I did.

Two more vampires approached the car, one on each side. The one on the passenger side grabbed the agent's gun right out of her hands and tossed it away. Then put his hand around her throat and squeezed.

The second one ripped the car door next to me right off the hinges. He reached for me. I shrank into the backseat as far as possible, but his hands found me anyway. He clamped a hand around one of my wrists in the handcuffs and physically dragged me from the back seat of the car. I stumbled out, banging my shins along the way.

Chaos abounded on the street around us. Banged up cars were everywhere. People running to escape the inferno ahead. Shouts and screams of terror.

Just another day in the life of me.

The vampire dragged me away from the car toward the billowing smoke. I took a quick glance over my shoulder to see the other vampire feeding off the Interpol agent. The other humans were dead. That was grand. How was I going to explain that?

I tried to dig in my heels, but the vampire was stronger than me. It occurred to me he was out walking around in daylight like it was no big deal. I thought vampires were nocturnal. Guess these guys, like the ones who attacked us at the Cathedral, weren't.

We turned down a corner into an alleyway. A man stood at the end waiting as we approached. He was tall, of Asian descent, and beautiful with a thick head of dark hair and piercing green eyes.

"Hello, Miss Walker." He gave me a grin, showing off his pointed vampire teeth.

I stood my ground despite being in handcuffs and planted my feet shoulder-width apart. I lifted my chin a little. "I'm afraid you have me at a disadvantage."

He continued to smile. "Indeed. I am Akio."

He paused as if I was supposed to know who he was or applaud or something. "And?"

"You have something of mine."

I had a hunch where this was going, but I played along anyway. "Which is?"

"I heard you were difficult to deal with."

"Great. My reputation precedes me." Sarcasm was my best armor.

"Give me the Horn of Gabriel." The demand in his voice indicated he was sick of my shit.

"I don't have it."

"You stole it from Chen. I want it back," Akio said.

I was trying to make the connection as to how he knew I stole the horn from Chen and why he wanted it back. When I took the horn, some kind of silent alarm tripped in Chen's office sending demons after me and my cousin, Lexi. We narrowly escaped death. That was moments before she betrayed me.

Getting the horn back hadn't been easy. I locked it locked away in the secret vault back home. Which made me think about what was going on there. I wondered if Interpol and the other local authorities were having a great time ransacking the house. They would never find the relics.

"What does a vampire want with a Holy Relic?" I asked.

"That's no concern of yours."

"It is if you want it back." Not that he was going to get it, but I'd let him think so.

His gaze flickered to the vampire still holding my wrist before turning back to me. "Perhaps you've heard of Partners for the Sanctified. They own the relic. They want it back. I've been sent to retrieve it."

"Ah, so you're a hired goon."

His eyes flashed fire. "We *will* find the horn, Miss Walker."

"Good luck with that."

"If you will not hand it over, then…" He paused, looking at his henchman again. "I will force you to tell me where it is."

"I told you. I don't have it." It was a half-truth.

He gave a jerk of his head to his man who then yanked me toward him. He wrapped his free hand around my hair and jerked my head back, exposing my neck.

Shit.

"Zhèng, turn her."

The one holding me bared his teeth and hissed.

"You leave me no choice, Miss Walker, but to turn you. And once turned, I will get answers and be able to control you."

That's what he thought. I wiggled against Zhèng, trying to free myself but it really did no good. Panic welled inside me as his mouth came down to my neck. He took a deep breath as he inhaled my scent. His teeth scraped my neck. I sucked in a sharp breath and struggled against him. I was not going to let him win or turn me into the undead. Determination seared through me and something popped, much like before when I was captured by Lucifer in Hell.

Before I realized what was happening, brilliant white light exploded all around. Zhèng screamed a high-pitched scream and then he was nothing but ashes at my feet.

The Godlight saved me from becoming a vampire.

Emboldened, I turned on Akio and called upon that which was inside me. It burst forth again and fried the poor guy, leaving nothing but ash behind.

That was the end of Akio and Zhèng, but somehow, I knew that was not the end of run-ins with Partners for the Sanctified.

CHAPTER 14

I was still handcuffed in some random alley. I turned from the piles of ash trying to decide my next move. Sirens pierced the air.

I flattened against the brick wall, my heart racing as I watched police officers run by. No doubt I would be framed for killing those officers and the Interpol agent. The last time I was framed for a crime I hadn't committed Kincade took care of it.

But he wasn't around at the moment to help me out of this jam, was he?

I was paralyzed by indecision as I stood with my back against the wall.

Where are you?

Kincade's voice burst into my mind. Relief flooded me as my eyes fluttered closed.

In an alleyway somewhere. I didn't kill those police officers.

A beat of silence, then he asked, *What happened?*

The vampires attacked and killed them. Now what?

I'll find you. Stay where you are.

Kincade would find me, but I did wonder why he was detained. I slid to the ground and drew up my knees, wrapping my arms around them and resting my chin there. I shivered as the wind whipped down the alley tunnel, gooseflesh rising on my arms. I had no coat. My stomach rumbled. I hated everything about this.

Hopefully Kincade would find me soon.

As I sat shivering in the shadows, a man ran by then halted and backed up. He paused. I stiffened.

"Anna?"

It was Ronan. Relief flooded me as I got to my feet. "How did you find me?"

"I followed the path of destruction. I saw the vampire drag you away." He glanced around with question in his eyes. "Where are they?"

"Dead."

He gave a nod and waved me out of the alley. "Come on." As I approached, he noticed the handcuffs. "We need to hide those."

"Yes, but how?"

He took off his jacket and tucked it around my hands and wrists to hide the cuffs. "That should do for now."

He slipped a hand around my upper arm and guided me out of the alley, pausing on the street. He glanced both ways and took off to our right.

"Kincade is looking for me."

"I found you first."

Was that a note of triumph in his voice? We hurried down the street. Ronan wrapped an arm around my shoulders and pulled me close.

"Don't make eye contact with anyone. And pretend you like me a little."

To make a show of it, I buried my face in his warm neck. Damn, he smelled good. We turned another corner, but I hadn't a clue where we were headed.

"It's not far now," he said.

We made our way inside a building. Once we were inside and away from prying eyes, I lifted my head. Up several flights of stairs and down a hallway and to the last door which he opened with a key.

We entered a tiny apartment. He closed and locked the door and moved around checking the windows to make sure they were all secure.

I glanced around. The living, dining and kitchen were basically all one room. There was a bar with several tall stools at it. The kitchen was small and non-functional. A fridge, a stove, a few cabinets, the sink. A hallway led to what I supposed were bedrooms and bathroom.

I glanced around the posh apartment. In the small living room, a brass and glass coffee table sat in the center on top of a white shag rug on top of the white tile floor. A white three-seat sofa was on one side. One navy blue chair on the other next to the one window with a view of the city and, beyond, the sea. At the end of the table, a blue velvet ottoman. Lamps on the side tables were brass. Beyond the furnishings, a large floor-to-ceiling window with gold and silver threaded curtains.

"Kincade is going to be pissed," I said. "You know that right?"

I did not want to imagine the wrath I would face when he discovered Ronan got to me first. He already didn't like the guy. The fact he managed to rescue me out of that alleyway first might send him over the edge.

"I do." He paused at the door, peering through the peephole. "We appear to be safe for the moment."

"Where the hell are we?" I demanded.

"A safe place." He turned to me, his gaze meeting mine. He was a man on a mission.

"And you knew of this place how?"

"Dream walkers have a network around the world. I called in a favor when I discovered you were missing. Meaning, I called my father and asked to use the apartment."

Ah, so his family owned the place. Super.

"You didn't answer my question, so I'll ask again. How did you find me?"

"We are dream walkers, Anna."

I stared at him, dumbfounded. My mind raced, trying to recall if he dream walked me in the night. I didn't remember anything of the sort. Something wasn't right. My senses went on high alert.

"What the hell is going on? And I want answers now."

"Yes, I dream walked you," he said. "You don't remember because..." He paused, a sheepish look on his face. "I have the ability to enter dreams without the dreamer remembering."

My eyes arrowed to slits. "That doesn't explain how you found me."

"I found you because of your dream. You don't remember it."

"I *always* remember my dreams." I clenched my fist, ready to down draw down my dagger.

"Not this time." He moved toward me with his hands stretched out as though he were surrendering. "You have to believe me, Anna."

"Why didn't you tell me this before?"

"It wasn't pertinent."

I folded my arms across my chest. "How did you find me in the alley?"

"When they put you in a car to transfer you, I followed. I didn't make it in time to stop the attack, though."

Where the fuck are you, Anna? I've searched the alleys in the vicinity of the attack.

Kincade's voice burst into my head. I put a hand to the bridge of my nose and pinched.

"Kincade wants to know where I am."

Ronan's brows flew up. "How do you know that?"

"Because I can hear his voice in my head. We're connected somehow."

Silence, then Ronan said, "Because he's your guardian."

My head snapped up, startled. This was the first confirmation of that I'd ever had. "We're connected because he is my guardian?"

"I've misjudged him and you. Tell him we're at 52 Calle Cirilo Amorós." He rattled off what I guessed was an address.

I relayed it to Kincade.

How did you get there? he demanded.

Long story. I'll tell you when you arrive.

Because I didn't want to make him more irate than he already was.

"He's on his way," I said.

Ronan merely nodded.

I held up my wrists still encased in the cuffs. "Think you can get these things off?"

KINCADE ARRIVED WITHIN THE hour. I'd practically worn a hole in the floor with my endless pacing. The knock on the door halted me, my heart in my throat. Ronan went to the door and peered through the peephole. When he was sure it was Kincade, he opened the door.

The man barged in as though he owned the place. Red fury was written all over his face as he glared at Ronan. If looks could set someone on fire, that would be the one. He turned his level gaze on me. I wanted to shrink into oblivion.

"At least you're safe. The National Police are combing the city for you. Now you're an international thief as well as a killer," Kincade said.

"Super. Then I have achieved all my life's goals and dreams." I didn't bother to keep the sour note out of my voice.

He glanced at the discarded cuffs on the dining table. It had taken Ronan a while to pick the lock with a couple of paperclips he'd found in the apartment.

"You two want to explain what the fuck is going on here?" Kincade demanded.

"Ronan found me in the alleyway," I said, before the other man answered.

"I know that." He practically growled the words. Kincade glanced from me to him. "You knew where to find Anna. How?" He crossed his massive forearms over his chest, an accusatory tone to his words.

Ronan shifted from one foot to the other. "I dream walked her as she slept in the jail. I found out where they were keeping her. I went to break her out but discovered from listening to them talk they were planning to extradite her back to Israel for stealing the Staff of Moses."

"And you told me none of this?" The words practically exploded out of Kincade.

"At the time, I had no idea where you were. I tried to get to her before the vampire attack, but I was too late." Ronan kept his voice level, completely unintimidated by Kincade's wrath.

"I was trying to break into the jail, but the local police had her guarded like she was a serial killer."

Well, that answered why he wasn't first. When we first met, Kincade masqueraded as a Dallas police office, but he didn't exactly blend in with the locals here.

I kind of admired that about Ronan and wished I had a similar ability. Kincade's presence was overbearing most of the time.

"You sorry son of a bitch—" Kincade charged him.

I lunged, reaching him before he got to Ronan. "Kincade, stop! We need him."

He shoved me off and turned his fury on me. I took a step back but decided to stand my ground.

"*We* do?"

"He has the gift of foresight. He saw my death," I reminded him.

"He's not the only one who can keep you safe, Anna." Something about the way he said it stabbed me right in the heart.

"And he has divine magic," I added just to needle him some more.

"You are her guardian," Ronan added. "Together, we can keep her safe."

Kincade's head snapped in his direction, his eyes narrowing to slits. "*I* will keep her safe."

I suddenly felt like a bone two dogs were growling over. I moved to stand between them, holding up my hands between them.

"Listen. I don't give a shit if you two hate each other. I don't care who wants to be in charge of my protection. The biggest problem I have right now is the National Police and Interpol are looking for me not to mention the vampires. I managed to obliterate the two in the alley, but I doubt that's the last I've seen of that group."

Ronan and Kincade said nothing. My stomach rumbled again but I was too tired to care. I was tired of everything. Them fighting over me. Me running for my life. Searching for relics. Never getting enough sleep. Being dogged by one supernatural being after another. I rubbed my forehead, the beginnings of a headache.

"I'm going to take a shower and I'm going to bed. And neither of you ass hats better wake me up unless the place is on fire. Got it?"

I stalked away without waiting for a reply.

CHAPTER 15

I STOMPED DOWN THE narrow hallway, hoping I was heading toward a bedroom and a bathroom. I took the first bedroom I found on the left, slamming the door behind me. I clicked on the lamp by the bedside. I'd picked the master suite and was grateful for the attached private bath. The queen size bed dominated the center of the room. But the best part of the room was the sliding glass door with the terrace and a view of the sea. A small club chair sat in the corner by the door.

I toed off my boots, walked to the door and pushed it open. Cool night air with the scent of the sea fluttered my hair. I closed my eyes against the wind, letting it sooth my ragged, tired nerves.

I had a laundry list of problems and no idea where to start.

I still didn't understand why the Grail wasn't where it was supposed to be. For the first time, the postcard I received was wrong.

Which made me wonder if the person who left it for me was wrong.

I felt the presence behind me. My eyes fluttered open. I turned my head to glance over my shoulder. Sariel stood in the pale light of the lamp. Something about seeing his familiar face sent relief flooding through me. I turned toward him as he approached, his emerald green eyes full of concern.

"You are troubled."

"I am." I nodded. I pushed my hands through my tangled hair. "I don't know what to do next."

"Tell me how to help."

I smiled. "I'm not sure you can."

"I am a very good listener, Anna." A faint smile flickered across his ageless, chiseled face.

I plopped down in the club chair as he perched on the edge of the bed. His enormous white wings threaded with gold spread out behind him.

"Where should I begin?" It was mostly a rhetorical question.

"Wherever you wish."

"I was arrested for a cultural heritage crime. Apparently, Israel didn't take kindly to me taking the Staff of Moses."

"They do not understand who or what you are."

"Very few do. And now I'm on the run from the authorities."

There was more, but I didn't want to bore him with details of my mother showing up at the manor. Or that I was betrothed to a man I hardly knew. Or that a group of vampires were after me to take back the Horn of Gabriel.

"Perhaps all will work out."

"I have my doubts."

"Have faith, Anna. The Holy Relics are more important than anything you are facing now."

"I know that, but—"

"Lucifer grows desperate in his attempt to find them as well as find a way to control you. He has failed every step of the way. And he will continue to fail as long as you hold true to your faith."

I sighed. Perhaps he was right. All I needed to worry about right now was the relics. Nothing else. I had enough people on my side to keep the authorities at bay while I continue to search.

"What do you know of the Holy Grail, Sariel?"

He was silent a moment, contemplation on his face. "Is that the relic you seek now?"

I nodded.

"Many have written about the Grail. Many have searched for it. None have found it."

"It was supposed to be in the cathedral, but it was gone."

His dark brows drew together. "What made you think the Grail was in the cathedral?"

I instantly thought of the postcard, but *damn*, I didn't have my bag. I'd left it back in the hotel room. And now I wondered if it was still there. Or had the police ransacked the room and taken what little possessions I had left?

"It doesn't matter now."

"Tell me, Anna," he urged.

I met his gaze. "It's strange, really, but with every quest, I've received a postcard pointing me in the right direction."

He remained perfectly still as he gave an encouraging nod. "Go on."

"And, well, every card led me to something. One of the relics. My mother."

"But something was different with this one?" he asked.

"Yes. It led me to the cathedral here in Valencia, but the Grail wasn't there when we arrived. I'm not sure what to make of that. I don't know if it was moved or stolen or what."

"You believe these...postcards to be a clue to your quests? Why?"

"Because someone wrote a note on each of them. Like the one sending me to Hong Kong for the Horn of Gabriel had the words *begin your search* written in this thick, blocky handwriting." I put my head in my hands, rubbing my forehead trying to stop the throbbing headache. "I can't figure out why I was sent here if the Grail wasn't on display."

He contemplated this for a moment. "Perhaps there is another reason you were led here. Something more important for you to do here. You said one led you to your mother."

I lifted my head as I met his gaze. "Yes, one did. I believe whoever sent them wanted to help me. He or she wanted me to find the relic and my mother."

I pressed cold fingertips against my lips with the dawning. It had never occurred to me that way before but whoever sent me these messages in a cryptic way must know who my real mother was, that she was still alive, who I was—that I was the Keeper of the Holy Relics—and I was on a search for these Holy Relics.

Who? Who would be connected to me, my mother, *and* the Holy Relics?

My gut twisted in a knot. Only one person would want me to find the relics and my mother.

My father.

My *angelic* father.

I peered at Sariel again, looking at him in a different light. Could he be?

No, that was ridiculous. But words haunted me. From my uncle and Kincade, both.

You are divine, Anna.

Born of the light.

The Bringer of Light into Darkness.

Be the light of the world.

I pushed to my feet. I suddenly needed a long, hot shower. "Thanks for your help."

He held his hands out toward me in invitation. "I did nothing."

"You listened."

I took his hands. He pulled me into a quick, tight embrace. Then he held me at arm's length.

"What will you do next?"

I shook my head. "I'm in some trouble. Not sure how I'm going to get out of it so I can get back to searching for the Grail."

"You will find a way, Anna. I have faith in you." He kissed my cheek.

I turned away and headed into the bathroom for that shower. When I glanced over my shoulder, he was gone.

CHAPTER 16

I SLEPT LIKE THE dead. It was the best sleep I'd had in a long while. When I spent the night in jail, I hadn't put up my mental walls. I'd been too stressed to think about it. That was probably why Ronan was able to find me with such ease. But this time, before I fell asleep, I put up my mental walls to keep everyone out.

When I awoke, I was ravenous with a raging headache. I was desperate for coffee.

After showering, I threw on a bathrobe and slept in that under the thick blankets. I rolled out of bed, running my hands through my tangled black hair with a giant yawn. I tightened the belt around my waist, feeling a little awkward about going commando underneath the terrycloth. I didn't have much choice, though, since I left everything behind back in the hotel room.

I shuffled out of the bedroom. As soon as I opened the door, the delectable aroma of freshly brewed coffee tickled my nose. I hurried down the hallway to see Ronan standing in the tiny kitchen cooking. The distinct scent of bacon hit my nose and my stomach growled.

He turned to swipe some eggs onto a plate. When he did, a memory hit me swift and hard and nearly sent me to my knees. I froze where I stood, remembering Ben cooking me breakfast before he left for work in the mornings as I arrived home from my night shift.

I clenched my hand into a fist, my nails biting into my palm as I tried to maintain my cool and not burst into tears.

Ronan noticed me then. "Oh, you're up. I was going to wake you but Kincade said I might lose an eye if I did."

I shook out of my memory and glanced around the small apartment but Kincade was nowhere to be found. "Where is he?"

"He left before dawn." Ronan poured a steaming mug of coffee and pushed it and the plate toward me. "I cooked you breakfast."

I descended on the bar stool and snatched up the coffee cup first, inhaling the rich aroma. I took my first sip, letting the warmth cascade through me willing the caffeine to do its job.

"Oh, you darling man. I could kiss you right now."

He blushed and quickly turned away. Realizing what I said, my cheeks heated as I snatched up the fork and shoveled in a heaping bite of scrambled eggs. They were fluffy and cooked to perfection. Toast popped up in the toaster. He placed a piece on the side of my plate, then placed butter and jam next to that.

"Thanks," I muttered around a mouthful.

And it was all too domestic for my liking reminding me far too much of living with Ben and having a morning routine.

"I retrieved our things from the hotel room. Yours is there." He motioned toward the living area.

I glanced over to see my bag on the sofa. My throat suddenly closed up with the threat of tears. He didn't realize what this meant to me. I had my clothes. More importantly, I had the postcards back.

"Did you sleep ok?"

I dropped my fork. "Stop."

Ronan was taken aback. "Stop what?"

I waved my hands to encompass my surroundings. "Stop *this*. The breakfast. The retrieving my clothes. The small talk. *Stop.* I can't take it, ok?"

He blinked with surprise and confusion. "I was just trying to help."

I snatched a piece of bacon off the plate and stomped to the living room. I grabbed my bag and spun on him.

"I know what you're trying to do. I appreciate it but I'm not..." I paused, trying to decide how to say it without sounding like a total unfeeling bitch. Instead, I blew out a breath. "I'm going to get dressed. Thanks for getting my clothes."

And I ran away to the bedroom to hide.

Like a coward.

I leaned against the closed door listening to the furious pounding of my heart.

I wasn't good with feelings. I never had been. I never would be. I wasn't a mushy girl. I wasn't the flowers and chocolates and sweet nothings girl. I was thick skinned. I didn't talk about my feelings. I hated to cry. I hated for *anyone* to see me cry, though Kincade had managed to be present on at least two occasions for that event. I drank whiskey and cussed a lot. I killed demons and liked it.

I did not know how to process someone like Ronan. Maybe because he reminded me too much of Ben. Sweet Ben who was taken from me too soon because of my arrogance and stubbornness.

Kincade was like me. He didn't talk about his feelings either. He drank whiskey, too. And killed demons. And if he did something nice for me, he didn't broadcast it or make me feel all squishy inside.

No, that wasn't right. I felt squishy inside when he gave me the pendant. I brushed a finger over the kneeling angel.

When he gave it to me, nothing romantic was involved. It was basically, *here I got this for you now shut up and wear it.*

The thing about Kincade was I always knew where I stood with him. There were no games. He gave it to me straight and didn't fuck around. He cussed a lot, too.

And, still, to this day, he never talked to me about how or why he left the Brotherhood. My uncle told me he left to protect me. Kincade said he was here to protect me. Nothing more. Hell, he wouldn't admit he was officially my guardian.

I heard the front door open and close and then their muffled voices. I pressed my ear against the door and listened hard.

"...Anna?" It was Kincade asking about me.

"She's getting dressed. I think I offended her."

More muffled words I was unable to make out. Then Kincade said, loud and clear, "She's not a touchy-feely kind of person."

Bingo. He totally got me. And I crushed on him harder.

I tossed the robe aside and quickly dressed. I wanted to find out what Kincade had been up to today. I had my doubts he would tell me, but I was going to grill him anyway.

I exited the room, trying to maintain my cool and keep my steps light. Like I was unaware he had returned. When I entered the dining area again, he stood there in his big, foreboding presence like he owned the universe.

"Oh, hey." I gave him a nod of hello as casual as possible. I pretended I didn't eavesdrop on their conversation.

He lifted an eyebrow in suspicion.

I grabbed my half-empty cup with the now-cold coffee and stalked into the kitchen to dump it out and start fresh.

"You look well rested," he said.

"I am, thanks." I poured and turned to face him holding the warm mug between my hands. The steam rose over my nose. "Probably the best sleep I've had in ages."

"Good. We have work to do."

I snorted. "Like what? I can't leave this apartment. By the way, where part of town is this apartment located?"

"In the heart of the city," Ronan said. "I figured the best place to hide was right under the National Police's nose."

I frowned. That didn't sound like the best idea to me, but I wasn't in charge. Kincade ignored him as he kept his gaze pinned on me.

"Don't you have a Grail to find?"

"Yes, but—"

"Standing around here isn't finding it."

"And where am I supposed to look?" I demanded. "I got nothing. The Grail was gone when we went to the cathedral—"

"It was removed," he interrupted.

I pondered this, recalling all the information I'd read.

"The Grail has been removed from the cathedral a handful of times. Once when during wartime and again when the pope came..." My words trailed off. "Oh. Is the pope coming?"

No way the pope was—

"Yes."

The words died in my mind as I stared at him. I was baffled. "Why? There aren't any high holy days in January. Right?"

"No, but there is unrest in the world. I do realize you've been distracted and oblivious to the word news, Anna, but there are things you need to know."

He glanced at Ronan who reached for a newspaper and handed it to me. I placed the mug on the counter to take the paper.

Which I found odd. Like they had pre-planned this little conversation. My uncle was the only person who seemed interested in the printed news these days. As I glanced down at the black and white print, I couldn't ignore the large, bold headline.

Pope to visit Valencia Cathedral to quell fears of religious unrest

"Well, shit. Now what?"

"We have an opportunity," Kincade said.

My body broke out into a sudden hot sweat. "What are you saying? We *steal* the Holy Grail out from under the pope? Are you *insane?*"

"Quite possibly."

I glanced at Ronan hoping he was the voice of sanity. "What do you think?"

I didn't miss the annoyance passing over Kincade's face as I asked Ronan's opinion.

"A dangerous plan," he said. "I haven't had any premonitions, good or bad, so perhaps doable."

Kincade smiled, smug.

"Doable?" I threw my hands up. "You are both crazy. I'm not stealing the Grail from the pope!"

"It may be our shot," Kincade said.

I huffed out a shuddering breath. "When is this supposed to happen?"

"Tomorrow."

"Great. Then tomorrow, I will be the most hated person and wanted by every jurisdiction in the world."

CHAPTER 17

WE DISCUSSED AT LENGTH how we were going to pull this off. But with so many variables and unknowns, there was no way to plan. The Swiss Guard wasn't exactly going to share the pope's travel itinerary. All we knew for sure was that the pope would be at the cathedral at around ten the following morning to perform mass.

So, we went our separate ways to rest and prepare for the next day. I decided to do some news digging.

Kincade was right. I hadn't been paying attention to the local or world news in some time. I suppose that's what my uncle did. He kept me shielded from the outside world in many ways, mostly to keep me focused on my task at hand. And so, I never worried myself about it. I read the article and discovered murders and suicides were on the rise. Violence was at an all-time high in the city. There was a little mention about the death of several National Police officers, the Interpol agent, and the armed and dangerous suspect at large. Yay, me.

I pulled out my smartphone and flipped through major headlines around the world. Turns out it wasn't just Valencia experiencing the uptick in violence and hate crimes. Other major cities were having a similar crisis. London. Melbourne. New York. Los Angeles. Hong Kong. Istanbul. Jerusalem. Some of these cities I visited in my questing.

Most of the hate crimes targeted Jews and Christians. Churches bombed. Hostages taken at synagogues. Guns in Catholic schools. I think I understood why. It was a signal to me from Lucifer. He was displeased with the fact I didn't want to help him. And I hadn't seen Azriel about lately, so I figured he was keeping busy with other devil-assigned tasks.

There were also many, many headlines about a pandemic starting to spread worldwide. For now, it was contained to one country—India. But the exact origin was unknown. It was a sickness for which doctors and epidemiologists around the world had no explanation. The illness struck young and old alike. Killing some. Leaving others permanently debilitated with a weakness and loss of appetite which then caused them to die of malnutrition. Like an anorexic.

I thought of those patients who died in the hospital back in Dallas. The ones I tried to save, but whose guardian angels were killed. The ones who, like Ben, were murdered by a high lord like Azriel and their soul taken for Lucifer's dark army. No mention of catatonic patients dying from strange circumstances, but perhaps it wasn't as newsworthy as everything else they liked to sensationalize.

More headlines spoke of a famine spreading across portions of Africa. Once lush green lands that produced plentiful harvests were dried up and turned into a desert. Organizations rushed to help feed the people of these areas, but still numerous people were lost to the hunger. It was horrible.

Pandemic.

Violence.

Famine.

I understood what was happening.

I'd read Revelation.

Next was Death.

The Four Horseman.

Whether I wanted to admit it or not, things were happening in the world I could not control. Things, I suspected, that were controlled by the very factions I tried to fight.

Demons and Satan and vampires.

Oh, my.

It reminded me of something Lucifer said to me the day his vampire wraith attacked Grace.

There will be consequences unlike you have ever seen.

I had to find a way to retrieve those remaining Holy Relics—the Grail and the Ark of the Covenant. And then I had to find out how I was supposed to use them to defeat this evil.

All this weighed heavily on me. This and the very idea I was supposed to steal the Holy Grail from the pope tomorrow.

I laid awake staring at the ceiling trying to calm my raged nerves. Sleep eluded me.

I finally shoved off the blankets and left my room, wondering out to the living area. No lights were on. The only illumination of the tiny room was that of the moonlight and streetlight filtering in through the window. The view was spectacular as I watched the ebb and flow of the surf and, beyond, the sapphire water. Below, the street was quiet. But then movement caught my attention.

A man on a horse. Odd that a man would ride a horse through the town.

He paused under a bright lamplight. He held the reins of the white horse in his left hand and carried a bow in his right. He wore a shining crown of gold. He turned his face up to me, meeting my gaze. For a long, cold moment, I was frozen, staring back at that deathly face. The details were fuzzy as I tried to conjure a memory or some forgotten lore or a scrap of bible verse. And then it hit me. I stood gazing upon the first of the Four Horsemen of the Apocalypse. Conquest.

Come.

A dark oily voice slithered through my mind. I jumped back from the window, my hand at my throat. My fingertips pressed against the wild beat of my pulse, my breathing erratic. I stood in the dark, shivering. I waited several heartbeats before I had the nerve to peer out the window again.

But the rider was gone.

The words of Revelation came flooding into my mind.

I looked, and behold, a white horse, and he who sat on it had a bow; and a crown was given to him, and he went out conquering and to conquer.

We were all fucked.

I ran to my room, panic welling inside me, and shut the door. I crawled into the bed, pulling the blankets to my chin, still shivering. Cowering under the blankets like scared child. Wishing my uncle was still around to give me reassurance and quiet my mind. To tell me what I saw wasn't what I thought it was.

I made a valiant effort to push the vision of the rider on the white horse out of my mind. I would never sleep now. My teeth chattered. My anxiety and stress were at an all-time high. I wasn't going to be able to go through with stealing the Grail out from under the pope in mere hours. I was not ready.

No, I refused to do it.

I would have to tell Ronan and Kincade in the morning it wasn't happening.

I don't know how long I quivered under the blankets wishing I was a child again, that the weight of the world wasn't on my shoulders, that I didn't have any moral obligations whatsoever.

A sharp knock on my door startled me and I nearly jumped out of my skin.

"Anna, it's time. Come on." It was Kincade's stern voice on the other side of the door.

But I remained in the bed, hiding under the covers like a coward, willing him to go away. He knocked again.

"Anna, come on, will you?"

Still, I refused to move.

Finally, he opened the door. "What the fuck, Anna? You're not even up."

"I can't do it, Kincade." My voice was muffled against the thick cotton.

"Yes, you can. Don't make me drag you out of that bed."

Terrified he would make good on that, I shoved back the blankets and sat up. Still shaking. Still terrified. "We shouldn't do this. I have a really bad feeling about it."

And I always listened to my gut. It was rarely wrong.

He stood, larger than life in the doorway, his face shadowed. But I sensed his piecing gaze was on me as he tried to decide if I was full of shit or not. He had that internal lie detector. He would know I wasn't lying.

"Okay," he said slowly. "Then how do we recover the Grail?"

"I don't know but we have to find another way. Any other way." I clutched the blankets to my chest.

His eyes narrowed. "Did you have a dream walk?"

I shook my head. "No."

"Did someone dream walk you?"

Again, I shook my head. "No. I never slept."

"Then what's bothering you?"

Shit. It was annoying how he read my emotions with such ease. I swallowed hard, took a deep breath. "I think I was sent here for another reason. Not to steal the Grail but to do something else."

He tipped his head to the side as he considered this. "Which is?"

"I don't know but my gut is telling me stealing the Grail is wrong. Even though the postcard led me here, I think it was for another purpose."

Sariel's words rang in my ear. *There is something more important for you to do here.*

"All right then we change our game plan. We don't try to steal the Grail. Maybe…" He paused, ran his hand over his chin. "We try to protect it."

I nodded slowly. But something else was bothering me. "There's more. I saw one of the Four Horseman of the Apocalypse, Kincade."

He stared at me a long, quiet moment as though he processed what I said and he didn't have an answer. Which scared me. Kincade always had an answer. His jaw clenched and he stood completely still.

"Describe."

"A rider on a white horse. He carried a bow and wore a crown. I heard his voice in my head when he looked at me. He said one word. *Come.*"

Another long pause. "Where did you see him?"

"Last night on the street below."

He took a deep breath, expelled it. "All right then. We won't steal the Grail from the pope. But we *are* going to that mass."

"We are? Why?"

"Because, Anna, the End of Days is upon us. It has begun."

Judgement Day cometh.

From the tone of his voice, it sounded like Kincade expected something bad to happen.

"Get dressed." He shut the door.

I didn't waste another minute. There was a chance he was right and something was about to go down. Perhaps that was why I had a cloud of impending doom hanging over me. I didn't doubt Kincade just as I never doubted my own gut.

I dressed in my normal attire. This time, I drew down my jade-handled dagger and strapped to my waist. If shit was going down, I wanted to be ready. I emerged from the room. Ronan and Kincade waited. Ronan handed me a black hoodie.

"It's not much of a disguise but you'll need to wear it. And these." He handed me a pair of black sunglasses. "The police are still looking for you."

"Of course, they are." I slipped on the hoodie, zipped it up and then pulled up the hood. It was long enough to hide most of the dagger. Then took the glasses and put them on. "How do I look? Incognito?"

"Not really," Kincade said, deadpan.

"It'll have to do."

Outside, the streets were crowded as people rushed to the plaza of the cathedral. We managed to stick together but it was hard as we jostled through the throng of people. I didn't worry too much about being recognized since all the police would be preoccupied with the security of the pope.

I still had a bad sense about the situation. Though Kincade said we weren't going to try to steal the Grail, something was niggling at the back of my mind that would not go away. I kept telling myself it was due to seeing the rider on the white horse and nothing more. I tried to convince myself it wasn't one of the Four Horseman though I knew the truth of it.

Barricades lined the sidewalks to keep people from getting too close. Police and security were everywhere. I pulled the hood down over my face and shoved my hands deep into the pockets of the hoodie as we pushed our way through the masses. The car with the pope came through heading for the plaza, where they had set up a small altar with microphones.

Kincade pushed his way through to get as close as possible. I followed with Ronan behind me.

The pope took up his position behind the altar. Even from my distance, I spotted the Holy Grail on the altar. I nudged Kincade and nodded toward it. His keen eyes were on the Grail. He nodded understanding.

As the pope began speaking, I sensed the demons coming in from every direction. I sucked in a sharp breath. They reeked like they always did—death and decay and rot. I glanced around but didn't see any. Nor the usual veil that came down to hide them from humans. My hand moved toward the handle of my dagger, but I wasn't ready to pull it out yet.

"Kincade?"

"I sense them, too." His gaze flickered over the crowd, trying to pinpoint them. "I don't see them yet."

"Me, either."

Which worried me. If they were in the crowd, then that meant other beings were in the crowd. Maybe even Azriel. And the vampires. I didn't need the vampires to catch me again.

Something was different this time about the demons. I sniffed them but couldn't find them. Which made me wonder if they had managed to put on some sort of glamour to hide in plain sight from me and the humans.

I grabbed the dagger and slid it out of its sheath. Next to me, I heard the distinct click of Kincade's gun. Glancing down, he gripped it in his hand.

"What is the plan?" Ronan asked.

"To not get killed," I said, "and to kill as many demons as possible."

"Demons?"

"They're here." I nodded toward the throng of people.

"Where?"

"Don't know." Kincade kept his voice low as his gaze flickered over the sea of heads. "We need closer to that altar."

He pushed his way through. I stayed right behind him. Ronan behind me. Though we made our way closer to the front, barricades to keep people as far from the altar as possible were guarded by a line of police.

"How are we going to get closer?" I asked.

As the words escaped, gun shots rang out.

One of the cardinals went down immediately as his chest exploded. He was dead. The pope jerked backward. Blood spread on the shoulder his white cassock. Shouts and cries went up as the crowd panicked. A stampede started. More gun shots from somewhere to our right and a second cardinal went down. Mass hysteria immediately erupted.

Security officers jumped into action as one tried giving the second cardinal CPR. Another shoved the pope to the ground and covered him like a human shield as he shouted into his radio. No doubt calling for backup and an ambulance.

"Get to the altar!" Kincade said.

He plunged into the masses, holding his demon killing gun aloft. He aimed for what appeared to be a regular man, but it was a demon instead. He fired. It emitted that high-pitched whine moments before the flash of light. Black guts exploded all over the ones standing nearest the demon.

Chaos ensued. The police swarmed in. Kincade ignored the onslaught of police as he spotted more demons. He recharged his gun and fired again. More dead demons. More screams and shouts and panic. I lost sight of Ronan.

I wielded my dagger as one charged me. I stabbed him and he immediately turned to ash.

But the thing was he did not look like a demon. At least, not like the demons I had killed in the past. This demon had the appearance of a regular, everyday person. The only difference was he *smelled* like a demon. This was a new development and one for which I was not prepared.

"*Anna*!" Kincade shouted.

I glanced at the altar to see the Grail sitting unattended. Now was my chance. I re-sheathed the dagger and shoved my way through the bodies toward the altar. It was really no use. They were stronger and I was unable to push my way toward the front. Suddenly, Ronan was next to me using his brute force to shove them all out of the way and make a path toward the barricades.

Two demons—at least they stank like demons—barred our way. Ronan halted, put his hands up as though to surrender. His hands glowed bright white. He lunged, putting one on each of the demons. Both of them turned to ash and fluttered to the ground in a heap.

He flashed an uncharacteristic grin as he continued pushing his way through the throngs of people. I followed him blindly toward the altar. I failed trying to protect the pontiff and the others but maybe I had a shot at grabbing the Grail.

Movement on the edge of the raised dais caught my attention. Glancing that way, the vampire paused at the edge and then transformed into a giant bat. I sucked in a gasp as it flapped into the sky and descended toward the altar. I stared at it a long moment as my eyes translated to my brain what the vampire now bat intended to do. I shouted Kincade's name and pointed. He used his demon gun to kill off several more as he pushed and shoved his way toward the front. He recharged his gun, pointed and fired at the winged creature.

And missed.

The bat hissed as it dove toward the altar, heading right for the Grail. It snatched the cup by the handle in his claws, swiping it with ease, then jerked upward again and flapped away into the sky.

CHAPTER 18

Now what? I stood, dumbfounded, as I watched the vampire bat disappear into the late morning bright blue sky with the Grail.

My only consolation was at least it wasn't Azriel, who I hadn't seen in a while. Not that I was complaining.

"Fuck, Anna!" Kincade's voice exploded somewhere to my right.

Then he grabbed me by the wrist and dragged me from the carnage. Ronan followed behind me. The ground was littered with dead demons bleeding the ground black. And every single one of them looked human.

I stole a glance at the altar. A Swiss Guard hovered over the pope who was still on the ground. Sirens pealed through the air heading for the plaza.

"What is *happening*, Kincade?"

"Your gut feeling was right. That's what. We have to get out of here."

He wasn't wrong about that. I let him drag me along the street and turn down another one to put distance between us and the crowds, the police, and the dead.

"That vampire...he stole the Grail," I panted.

"I saw."

"He transformed into a bat!"

"Saw that, too."

"What the *hell* is going on?" I demanded.

We came to a halt outside a small shop that boasted pie and lattes with a CLOSED sign on the door. Kincade shoved me against the storefront window away from the street. Ronan was on the other side of me. We all paused, staring at the traffic rushing by and people running from the hysteria in the plaza. I gulped in air, trying to calm my ragged breathing and erratic heartbeat. Sweat poured down the side of my face. Somehow, through the pandemonium, I managed to keep my hood on.

"We are in some serious shit," Kincade said, his voice low.

"No kidding. Those demons appeared *human*. Why?"

Kincade shook his head. "I don't know."

"What do we do now?"

"We cannot leave the relic in the hands of..." Ronan paused and glanced around but there was no one within earshot.

"Why would they want it?" I realized this was a rhetorical question.

"Because they know you do, and you have something to trade them." Kincade gave me a pointed look.

Crap. The horn. But I didn't have the horn. It was back in England.

My cell phone vibrated in my pocket. I forgot I had it. I pulled it out. Ophelia was calling.

"Ophelia, this isn't a good time—"

"Where the hell have you been? I've been calling since yesterday. I've left messages."

"I've been busy—"

"It doesn't matter. Listen. The police and a couple of Interpol agents showed up here asking a lot of questions. They had a warrant."

I stiffened. This was not news to me. The Interpol agent had said as much but I'd forgotten about it during all the mass hysteria and stress of the last few days. "Did they find the vault?"

"No. But your mother didn't take kindly to them searching the house."

The hairs on the back of my neck stood on end. "What are you saying?"

"Something inside her snapped. She used her super dream walker powers and killed a couple of them."

"Fuck."

"What is it?" Kincade demanded.

I held up a hand to shush him as Ophelia rushed on.

"They tried to arrest her, but she wasn't having it."

"What happened?"

"She...well...she escaped. And I have no idea where she is."

Well, shit. This was not the news I wanted to hear today. "I don't care what you have to do. Find her. Get her back to that manor house."

"See, I'm not sure that's a good idea. She killed two cops and now she's on the run..." Her words drifted away letting the implication hang.

I rubbed the skin on my forehead between my thumb and forefinger. "What about Grace?"

"She's fine. Still comatose. They didn't make it upstairs."

"Find my mother, Ophelia."

I hung up before she could rebut.

Kincade gave me an expectant look. "The cops showed up at the manor with a search warrant."

"Great."

"And my mother used her super dream walker powers to, um, take out a couple of them."

His lips thinned. Disgust and disappointment flickered over his features. "And?"

"And now she's gone. She escaped."

"Super."

Confusion etched Ronan's face. "What do you mean your mother? I thought she was dead?"

"Um, yeah...about that..."

An ambulance sped by with lights and sirens blaring.

"We can discuss this later. Let's go back to the apartment." Kincade gave me a nudge.

Ronan nodded and led the way.

We made it back to the apartment without getting stopped in the street, which was a miracle in itself. Once we were inside, I shrugged out of the hoodie and ditched the sunglasses. If there was a time I needed a drink, now was it.

The pope had been shot by demons or vampires. The Grail was stolen by a vampire transformed into a bat. And my mother was missing in action. What else could go wrong?

I sat on the sofa, crossed my legs in front of me, my beat-up hands on my knees, and closed my eyes hoping neither of them would talk to me.

"I have questions about your mother," Ronan said.

"Forget her mother. We need to figure out a game plan," Kincade said.

"Shh. Both of you."

"What's she doing?" Ronan asked.

"Dream walking."

I huffed out a breath. "For your information, I am *trying* to meditate. I *could* if you both would *shut.up.*"

I didn't bother to open my eyes to see their reaction. I sat there listening to the deep inhale and exhale of my own breathing.

"She's dream walking. Don't let her fool you." Kincade's voice was conspiratorial as he spoke to Ronan.

The apartment door opened and closed. I assumed he left. Then I heard retreating footsteps. Probably Ronan. Which meant I was finally alone with nothing more than my thoughts.

Kincade was right. I was trying to dream walk, but I didn't want to explain why. I was looking for the Grail. In my past experience, I had some luck dream walking while awake. The problem was, I didn't really know who my target was other than the vampire thief.

I did recall his features, though. He was pale faced with a shock of black hair and bright blue eyes. And his fangs were spectacular, at least from the memory of the way he hissed at me.

Why *would* the vampires want the Grail? Unless they were working for someone like, say, Lucifer.

And why were demons masquerading as humans now? What changed? Kincade said Lucifer was building his army but I already knew that. His high lords were killing guardian angels and stealing human souls to turn them into demons. The difference now was the demons were in human form. Which meant something had to change for that to happen.

But I was getting off track. I turned my attention back to the vampire who stole the Grail. After several tries, I found him.

He was still in bat form and in flight but descending toward the top of a building somewhere in a Spanish city with which I was not familiar. He turned back into human form as he landed, holding the Grail between his paper-white hands with long pale blue nails. He walked toward three other vampires waiting on the rooftop. The one in the middle was dressed as though he stepped out of the eighteenth century with long flowing blond hair, pale eyes and deep red lips. His skin was the color of chalk. His hands had a roadmap of blue veins and were clasped in front of him. There was wisp of lace at each wrist peeking out from the crushed velvet jacket he wore. He reminded me of Brad Pitt in *Interview with the Vampire.*

The rider took the Grail to him and extended it as an offering. "The cup, Lord Barnabas."

Then was he a vampire lord?

"Thank you, Silvan." He took the cup and held it up to examine it. "Such a beautiful thing. Alas, none of us need eternal life."

They all laughed.

I clenched my jaw.

"You shall be rewarded," Barnabas said. "Find the relic hunter girl and turn her. She will make a wonderful blood slave for you."

"She was there today, my lord. A beauty, she is."

Yuck. I shuddered.

"Then she shall be yours. As for the Grail, I promised the high lord I would meet him at the gala in Madrid with the cup. My friends, we travel by train in the morn."

I closed the connection as my eyes snapped open.

The vampires were going to Madrid to hand off the Grail to a high lord. Azriel?

And that was our next move.

CHAPTER 19

I THOUGHT ABOUT WHAT the vampires said. That I was a prize for Silvan. That he had permission to turn me. I would rather die than be a prize for anyone or anything.

One already tried and failed. Thanks to the Godlight.

Then there was the other thing about bringing the Grail to a high lord. I suspected Azriel but I had no concrete evidence. I hadn't seen him in the real world since he kidnapped Astrid off the lawn. Not that I was complaining. He was a major thorn in my side.

Footsteps and, a moment later, Ronan entered the small living-dining-kitchen. He paused with questions written all over his face.

"Go ahead. I know you want to ask," I said.

"Ask what?"

"Whatever questions that are boiling in your brain."

"You dream walked while awake."

Not exactly a question, but I answered it like one. "Yes."

"You can do that?"

"I can."

Confusion flickered over his face as he pondered this. "I have never known a dream walker who can do that."

I shrugged. "I guess I'm special."

"How do you do it?"

I thought about that for a long moment before I answered. The only explanation I had was I always had the ability. For the longest time, I needed to be in contact with the subject. That changed when I learned to control it without touching the other person while trying to save my skin in Antarctica.

I shrugged. "Not sure, really. I just do."

"Fascinating. Can you teach me?"

I shook my head. "I'm not sure. We can try some time, though."

"Who did you dream walk?" he asked.

"The vampires. I was trying to find the Grail."

"Did you?"

"Sort of. They're heading to Madrid."

"And so are we then."

I nodded. "That's the plan."

He seemed satisfied with that answer, but something still bothered him. Some burning question he needed to ask. He clasped his hands behind his back and walked to the window. The one I stood at last night when I spotted the white horseman. I bit my tongue, unwilling to share that information with him.

"What is it?" I asked. "There's something more."

"Your mother is alive?"

"Yes."

"How?" He kept his gaze on the outside world. Seeing but not seeing.

"I don't know."

"Was she at the manor house when my father and I visited?"

"Yes."

He turned to face me. "And you said nothing."

I shrugged a shoulder. "What good would it have done? Except infuriate your father even more. And besides, she is not the same person who she once was."

His brows drew together. "What do you mean?"

I wasn't sure how much to share with him, so I summed up. "She was somehow captured by the Knights of the Holy Lance. They wanted to find out how she dream walked so they tinkered with her brain. It gave her these super dream walker powers."

"Which means what?"

"It means she can squeeze your brain with her powers until you're dead."

Or almost dead. She had tried to kill me that way on more than one occasion. Even now I had my doubts she understood who I was to her. Something, though, made her stop trying to kill me.

Ronan turned back to the window. "I see."

"She came to the manor not long before you did. I have no idea how she made her way there. I got the idea she sensed where she was, not that it was her childhood home. Hell, she doesn't know who I am."

He didn't say anything to that. I didn't have any more explanations. Finally, he turned from the window and met my gaze.

"It makes no difference to me if your mother is dead or alive. It will make a difference to my father, though."

I found the very idea that Alexander Harred gave a shit about my mother ridiculous and refused to hold my tongue.

"Because she scorned him? Like who cares. That was thirty years ago. He found someone else." I waved in his general direction.

Ronan clenched his jaw as though he bit off an acid retort.

"And," I added for good measure, "you don't want to marry me anyway. You said so yourself."

I might have pointed out, too, I would not be the person I was had my mother married his prick father, but I kept that to myself.

"No, I don't."

Something about the way he said it made me suspicious. "But?"

"My father can be very...persuasive when he wants to be. He found out about Kiara FitzGerald. I have to give her up."

I stared at him in shock. "This is not the dark ages, Ronan. You can love and marry whomever you wish."

He gave a half-hearted laugh. "You don't understand my father, then."

"No, I don't. And when we get back to England, I intend to give him a piece of my mind."

"The damage has already been done, I'm afraid. He has spoken to Colum. Our romance is no longer secret."

My heart sank for him at how devastated he sounded. If there was a way for me to fix this then I was going to find a way. I had to break the marriage contract. I'd set the damn thing on fire if I had to. I stood and moved to stand next to him at the window.

"I'm so sorry, Ronan."

"It's because I left to follow you on the Grail quest. He was furious when I told him."

"Why did you tell him, anyway?"

"How do you think I got permission to use this apartment?" He motioned toward the ceiling. "I had to tell him the truth. And when he discovered Kiara and me...well, things got worse."

"You don't have to stay here. You can go back to England."

He shook his head. "I can't. I made a promise I'd help you. That I'd keep you safe. And besides." He gave me a sad little smile. "Am I so awful?"

Aw, hell. Why did he have to ask me that? Of course, he wasn't awful. He was handsome and soft spoken. Unlike Kincade who didn't take shit off me. Didn't pressure me to tell him my feelings or what I was thinking. He inherently knew.

The thing about Ronan was he reminded me of Ben. Azriel stole his soul and turned him into a demon. He died because of my stubbornness. I wondered where he was, if he was still alive in demon form.

Ronan awaited my answer. I took a deep breath. "You aren't."

He took my hand in his and held it in a way that sent warm tingles up my spine. His thumb brushed over the top of my hand. "You and I will do great things together."

Before I realized what was happening, he cupped my face and kissed me. His gentle mouth was warm and soft on mine as he tasted me.

I froze, unsure how to react.

My hands clenched at my sides. I'd been kissed before so I realized I should feel something. I felt nothing for Ronan. I didn't want to kiss him back and encourage him. Why wasn't it Kincade, instead? Why wasn't he the one to take my face in his hands and kiss me?

I imagined kissing Kincade would be a very different experience with lightning and power and sparks. My stomach would bottom out. My toes would curl. Not the gentle kiss of a young man, but the fiery kiss of an ancient man who knew what he wanted and how to get it.

That's what Kincade witnessed when he returned to the apartment. The door slammed closed. Ronan and I jumped apart. He released me and stepped back, clearing his throat. My mouth still tingled where his had been.

Fury was written all over Kincade's face, but he quickly regained control. He had an armload of bags which he dropped on the counter with a *thunk*.

"Sorry to interrupt. I brought food."

The amount of controlled calm in his voice was unnerving.

He grabbed one of the bags off the counter and stalked away, disappearing down the hall and closing his bedroom door not so gently.

Sometimes, I really hated my life.

Ronan stiffened next to me. "Are you two—"

"No."

"But it seems like—"

"It's complicated."

No, we were not an item. Yes, I had a major crush on the man. And for sure it was totally complicated.

When Kincade first came into my life, I had no idea who I was or what I was capable of. He followed me from the States to England to Hong Kong. He'd dream walked me. And we'd kissed in that dream walk. But that was so not real life. That was a dream walk. And though it *felt* real, both of us realized it was not.

"Do you want me to talk to him?" Ronan asked.

"No. Leave it. Let's eat."

"Not hungry."

He walked away, disappearing down the hall to his room.

This was the worst day ever.

The delectable aroma coming from the greasy bags smelled suspiciously like a cheeseburger and fries. My stomach rumbled loudly. Unable to resist, I went to the bar in the kitchen and opened one of the paper bags. Melted cheese oozed out of the burger to the wrapper. In the bottom, a pile of fries.

I didn't question where or how Kincade found a place that had American burgers and fries.

As I dove into the burger, not caring the grease smeared my hands and face, I wondered what to do about Kincade. He would never want an explanation as to why Ronan was kissing me. He probably wouldn't buy it.

I polished off the burger and fries in record time and discarded the trash. I stood in the tiny kitchen wishing my uncle was around. I needed to talk to someone with a level head about the vampires, the Grail, Kincade.

I wished Joachim, the messenger angel, would pop in. I hadn't seen him in a while either.

A deep, palpitating loneliness pressed through me. I went into the living area and sat on the small couch as the sun dropped below the horizon. Outside, the streets lights came on, casting long shadows through the tiny apartment.

After a while, Kincade returned carrying a crumpled paper bag in one hand and a bottle in the other. He gave me a sideways glance as he entered the kitchen, opened the cabinet and selected two glasses. He placed the bottle on the counter, pulled out the cork and poured. Two fingers, neat, in each glass.

As he approached, glasses and bottle in hand, my heart did a little thud. He handed me one, then took the chair opposite me and stared out the window. I wasn't sure why he wanted to talk to me. Hell, I wouldn't want to talk to me. I was the type of person to hold grudges over the smallest infractions until the day I died. However, I wasn't going to argue. I'd take the free whiskey any day.

I said nothing as I downed the first one.

In Acre, we made a pact that we drank whiskey when Anna had a crisis. This wasn't a crisis, but we drank whiskey anyway. I'd take it without complaint.

He downed his, refilled, then held the bottle out to me. I took it and refilled, then placed the bottle on the table between us.

"Well?" I finally said. The silence was getting to me.

"Well, what?"

I wanted to ask why he was here. I wanted to explain to him Ronan kissing me was not my idea. That all I thought about was kissing him instead. He cut me a swift glance before looking away and I blushed to the roots of my hair. I'd forgotten that he sometimes was able to read my thoughts. It was hard for me to guard them, especially when I was emotionally fragile.

It seemed I was emotionally fragile all the damn time.

So, I asked, "Are you going to ask me about my dream walk?"

"I thought you were 'meditating.'" He put the word *meditating* in air quotes with one hand.

I kinda wanted to punch him for that. "You and I both know that was a lie."

"I do." He nodded, holding the glass with the amber liquid in his big hand. He didn't drink. Something glittered in those green-gold eyes of his. Something I was unable to read.

"I know where the Grail is."

"Do you?"

He infuriated me. "Do you want me to tell you or not?"

"No doubt with the vampires."

I nodded. "Yes, but they aren't interested in a trade with me. They're taking it to a high lord in Madrid."

That got his attention. "A high lord?"

"That's all he said. This...Lord Barnabas. He told his lackey he awarded me as his prize to turn into his very own blood slave."

His hand tightened on the glass. He didn't like that. Truth be told, I didn't like it either.

"Then I assume we're heading to Madrid."

Again, I nodded. "They're going by train."

"Very well." He took a shot of whiskey but didn't refill. "There is still the issue of these other vamps looking for you. The ones you say belong to Partners for the Sanctified."

"They're the least of my worries. I need to get that Grail back before this Barnabas hands it over to the high lord."

"Azriel?"

"Not sure. He didn't say."

A long pause, then he asked. "And Ronan?"

"Going with us, naturally."

He clenched his jaw. He didn't like that answer. I didn't elaborate, either. I was sure he didn't want to hear about the kiss or why it happened. The worst part of kissing Ronan was wishing it had been Kincade instead.

Ronan said we would do great things together. I hadn't the heart to tell him I didn't intend to marry him. At least, not yet. I would have to break it to him eventually. When we had the Grail and were safely on our way back to England.

Kincade dropped his glass on the table and stood. "Rest up, Miss Walker. We have a long journey ahead."

As he left me sitting there, I was absolutely sure he was right.

I didn't go to bed. I stayed up all night trying to find the bastard vampires and what train they might take. There were several options, but nothing direct from Valencia to Madrid. One was a two-hour trip. Another went through the countryside and took double that.

I tried to dream walk the vamp again. It was no use. I lost the link and was not able to reconnect to the undead.

Frustrated, I pulled up the latest headlines on my smartphone. The first one was about the blood bath in the plaza. The pope was rushed to the hospital. After several hours in surgery, he was stable.

That was good news at least. However, two of his cardinals were dead. They had no information on the shooter.

My guess was one of the vampires working in cahoots with the high lord's demons. They used the shooting as a distraction to snatch the Holy Grail.

Out the window, the sky began to lighten with the coming dawn. I rose and walked to the window, tentatively peeking out in the hopes I wouldn't see the white horseman. Thankfully, he wasn't there. The street was beginning to come alive with activity. It was time to say goodbye to the city and move on to the next.

I turned away and noticed the postcard on the table next to the whiskey bottle Kincade left behind. It hadn't been there before. And I scented nothing that indicated an archangel came for a visit.

Gooseflesh rose on my arms. My hair stood on end. How did it come to be there? I sensed no one enter or leave. I turned my back once to gaze out the window. I bent to pick it up. The picture was of the Royal Palace in Madrid. I flipped it over.

Attend the Royal Gala was written in that familiar blocky handwriting. Another clue? What was the Royal Gala and did I want to go?

All I thought about was Ronan telling me something happens that puts my life in grave danger. That he'd seen my death.

I was fairly certain I did *not* want to go.

CHAPTER 20

KINCADE WAS THE FIRST to make an appearance. He came out his bedroom freshly showered. He still managed to keep that scruffy three-day growth of beard though. I told myself that was not sexy at all. Not one bit. That clean sandalwood scent followed him. I took a moment to inhale and appreciate it.

"There are two trains. One leads through the countryside. The other is a high-speed train," he announced without morning pleasantries. Then he paused as he regarded me with a critical eye. "You look like shit. Did you sleep?"

"Good morning to you, too. Nope, I didn't sleep. Thanks very much for asking. And I know about the trains. The question is which one will the vamps be on?"

"If they're in a hurry, they'll choose the high-speed train."

"And if they're not?"

He gaped at me as if that was the dumbest question. "Then the other one."

I huffed.

"I don't think they'd want to take the scenic route," I said. "They want to deliver their prize as soon as possible. My assumption is there is money involved."

"There's always money involved. So, we take the high-speed train. Fare is about twenty Euros departing from *Joaquín Sorolla* train station. I already bought tickets."

Surprise flickered through me at how Kincade took initiative. I was impressed. "You did?"

"Figured it would be better since your identity is likely being tracked."

"Oh, good thinking. There's something I want to show you."

He gave me a sideways glance as one eyebrow raised. "Oh?"

I pulled the newest postcard from my pocket and handed it to him. He stared at the photo of the Royal Palace, then flipped over the card.

"What's the Royal Gala?"

"I have no idea."

"And we're supposed to attend?"

"That's what the card says. But I hesitate to go. If you recall, Ronan said he saw my death there."

Skepticism flickered over Kincade's face. "You believe that horse shit?"

"Why shouldn't I?"

"Because nothing he's said has come true."

"*Yet.* Nothing he's said has come true *yet*," I pointed out.

His mouth pulled down into a sour grimace. "Because he hasn't predicted anything other than you dying. Do you always do what the card says?"

"Yes," I said with an emphatic nod. "I believe I was sent here for the Grail and to try to protect the pope. I failed. Now, there is another reason I'm to attend this Royal Gala."

"Yeah, so you can die." He was less than amused.

"Well, I plan to not miss it."

"Well, great. Then I guess I better figure out how to keep your ass alive. We need to know what the fuck this royal gala involves and how high and mighty it is." He gave me a pointed look. "For the record, I don't do high and mighty."

That's what I liked best about Kincade. He never minced words.

Ronan made an appearance then, bag in hand. Neither one of us had packed yet. I hadn't showered. Kincade handed me back the postcard as if it was no biggie. I pocketed it. Ronan pretended not to notice the sleight of hand.

"I'll grab my stuff," I announced in a too-happy voice.

I disappeared to my bedroom to collect my bag. The envelope with the postcards rested on the bed. I slipped the one of the Royal Palace inside. I was getting quite the collection. I put the envelope in the bag and zipped it up, ready to go. I took one last glance around the small, tidy room to make sure I had all my belongings.

Sometimes, being in other cities was a very strange thing. Other times, it seemed completely normal.

I headed out of the bedroom, my mind on the Royal Gala and the palace in Madrid. A Royal Gala suggested formal clothes, of which I owned none. Since I was a wanted criminal, I wasn't sure how I was going to pull off attending such a fancy event. But I'd worry about that later.

We left the tiny apartment behind and headed for the train station. Kincade had a taxi waiting, which surprised me. He'd never been the one to take care of arrangements. It had always been my uncle, now me. I said nothing as I slid into the backseat. He followed. Ronan took the front.

Awkward silence prevailed. It seemed to be the way of things between the three of us these days. Which was fine with me. It gave me time to think. How was I going to retrieve the Grail from the vampires? My Godlight killed them, but it wasn't wise to use my power in the general masses. I didn't need to call more attention to myself.

We arrived at the train station and entered the glass and metal building. At this time of day, it was full of early morning risers and mostly commuters. The overhead digital board showed departures and arrivals along with a giant white and green digital clock.

Kincade showed our tickets and then we entered through their version of security. Much like flying commercial these days, the station had a baggage x-ray. Unlike with TSA, we didn't have to remove shoes or everything from our pockets or potentially undergo a strip search. I took a glance around and noticed numerous security guards and police walking through the place. My gut twisted into a knot as one eyed me.

"I don't know about this," I said low so only Kincade heard.

"Just act casual. And stop looking at the cop. If you keep looking at him, he'll think something is up."

We made it through the scanner, but I couldn't help myself. I took another glance the cop's way. As we exited and picked up our bags, he had his radio to his mouth talking and still looking right at me. Kincade gave me a shove to move.

"I said stop looking at the cop."

I complied as he wrapped his free hand around my upper arm. As we walked through the terminal heading for the train, two cops made right for us. I did my best to keep my eyes averted, but they were locked on us. Kincade cursed something under his breath I didn't hear. Ronan took up the position on my other side, both of them flanking me like my protectors.

"What do we do?" I asked.

"Keep walking," Kincade said. "And keep your mouth shut."

One of the officers put up a hand to stop us. We halted. They halted. They both gave me the hairy eyeball.

"Morning." Kincade gave him a head nod.

"Where are you headed?" the one who held up his hand asked.

"Madrid." Kincade flashed a smile. "It's the second leg on our vacation tour of Spain."

He glanced from Kincade to me. I gave him a bright smile. Then he turned to Ronan who stood ramrod still. The tension came off him in waves.

"I'd like to see your passports."

Well, shit. Before either of us spoke, Ronan whipped out his passport and showed it to the officer. He said something in rapid fire Spanish. The officer took it, listening intently to whatever Ronan said, and then peered down at his passport. He replied in Spanish with what sounded like a question.

Ronan laughed a forced laugh, then replied. He made hand gesture to me and Kincade. I had no clue what he was saying and wasn't sure I wanted to find out.

As we stood there wasting time, the scent of death and rot wafted over me. I sucked in a sharp breath. Demons. I peered at the two officers in front of us, but they seemed normal. Human. I sent out a query to Kincade.

Do you smell them?

Yes, he replied in my head. His hand moved to his hip where he kept his demon killing gun.

I wondered then how he managed to sneak that through security. Ronan was still talking to the cops, keeping them occupied for as long as possible. I had no idea what he was saying or trying to do. Not that it mattered. The veil that separated the humans slid into place.

I dropped my bag and immediately drew down my dagger. Kincade had his gun in hand, cocked and ready. Ronan did not bother to hide the surprise on his face when we produced weapons.

The worst thing of all was the two officers stood within the veil. It meant what I suspected—they were demons.

The first cop took out his gun, pointed it right at me. Kincade fired his demon gun. The high pitch whine followed by the flash of light. He killed him at point blank range. Demon guts exploded all over me and Ronan. The second one lunged at Kincade but he turned his gun on him and fired a second time. High pitched whine followed by more exploding demon guts.

"What...?" Ronan began. He didn't bother to hide the disgust on his face at having been splattered with guts and black blood.

"You get used to it. They were demons. We have to go!" I snatched up my bag.

Kincade was already running through the terminal toward the train platform. I followed him, Ronan on my heels. I tried not to gag at the sewage scent clinging to my clothes and skin. I was starting to think Kincade enjoyed killing demons in such close proximity to me so I would stink to high hell.

I was still several paces behind him when suddenly he dropped to the ground as though he'd been hit with something. He groaned and rolled to his back, trying to stand. Blood seeped from his left shoulder around the arrow sticking out of it.

"Kincade!" Fear spilled through me.

He pointed the gun and tried to fire off a round, but his gun was out of juice or something. It didn't work. I skittered to a halt next to him, frantically glancing around for the attacker. I saw nothing and no one. Ronan was on the other side of him and knelt. He helped Kincade to a sitting position.

"What happened?" he asked.

"That bastard fucking shot me!"

"Where? I don't see him." I gripped my dagger in one hand and my bag in the other.

"Who shot him?" Ronan was clearly confused. I hadn't said anything to him about the white horseman.

The unmistakable sound of horse's hooves clopped on the tile floor. He appeared through the veil on horseback, pausing several feet away from Kincade. Overhead light glinted on his golden crown. He held his bow aloft. A quiver of arrows was on his back, the fletchings sticking up over one shoulder. He sat astride the massive white war horse with no saddle. He nocked another arrow in his bow and pointed it directly at Kincade's head.

"NO!" I shouted.

I'd seen enough death of the people I loved. There was no way I'd watch him kill Kincade. I couldn't...wouldn't...allow it to happen. I moved to stand in front of him, blocking the shot.

"Anna, don't be an idiot," Kincade said through gritted teeth.

Next to him, Ronan got to his feet, his hands clenched at his side.

Conquest peered at me out of insanely bright blue eyes. I met his gaze, my stomach twisting in a tight knot, but I refused to show my fear. He was handsome. Blond. Clean shaven. Wearing a pale blue shirt open at the throat and soft white pants. Nondescript shoes. The golden crown shimmered on his head.

"I won't let you kill him." I was proud my voice didn't waver despite the fear pumping through my veins.

He lowered his bow and arrow. "Come, then."

My mouth went dry. "Where?"

"With me." He held out a hand to me in invitation. "Your life for his."

A flashback from when I was possessed by darkness burst through my mind. Abaddon had given me the same invitation. Holding his hand out to me, beckoning me to come to him. To give in to the darkness. But this time I was not poisoned with evil. I was within my right mind.

I lifted my chin, my heart ramming hard in my chest. "If I do, he will live?"

Anna, don't do it. You can't go with him. Kincade's voice seared my mind. It took every strength I had not to flinch.

A faint smile flickered over Conquest's pale lips and then he chuckled. "You cannot escape your fate, savior. And neither can the guardian."

"What fate?" I asked.

"He dies and you join me."

There was no way I was going to join him. Nor would I let him kill Kincade. Conquest was a mere distraction to keep me from getting the Grail. I pushed back the terror gnawing at me, the panic clawing its way through me. I swallowed hard, drawing all the strength and courage I possessed. Deep inside, that glimmer of Godlight flickered on. It was the first time I was able to actually sense it before it exploded out of me. And that gave me hope.

Somewhere in the dark recesses of my mind, my uncle's voice echoed.

Be the light of the world.

I shook my head.

"That isn't my fate. Whatever power I have in me, whatever strength I have, I will fight you. I will fight you to keep him alive. I will fight you to the death to keep from joining you. I am not afraid."

"So be it."

The light left his eyes as he lowered his bow.

What the bloody hell do you think you're doing? Kincade's voice exploded in my head.

My sweaty hand tightened around the dagger. I dropped my bag at my feet. *What I have to do.*

I planted my feet shoulder-width apart and waited for his attack, allowing the training I had with Gilli and Gideon and even Kincade to give me the confidence I needed to beat Conquest.

"You think you'll win, savior?"

I cocked my head to the side and tossed my dagger to the other hand. "Why do you call me that?"

He smirked. "Isn't that what you are? What they all call you? Savior of the world." He scoffed at the title as though it meant nothing.

"I am the Keeper of the Holy Relics." To punctuate my words, I drew down Edward's sword from the cloud, proud it was already flaming when it appeared in my right hand. "The hope for mankind. The one who will defeat evil."

Ronan moved to stand next to me. "I stand with her."

Conquest glared at him. "Be gone, paladin. This is not your fight."

I blinked surprise as I glanced from Conquest to Ronan, but Ronan's face remained impassive as he stared down the horseman. I heard movement behind me and glanced back. Kincade had managed to climb to his feet.

"It's his fight and mine." He cocked his gun and pointed it at Conquest as he moved to stand on my other side.

Conquest chuckled. "A paladin, a guardian and the Flaming Sword. You are well protected, savior. But they cannot protect you forever."

He fired the nocked arrow. Everything seemed to move into slow motion then as the arrow slid through the air heading straight for me. Light puncture the area around me and the arrow dropped to the ground, useless. But the light did not come from me.

Ronan moved to stand in front of me, light crackling around his hands. Defiance was written all over his face.

I froze, holding the flaming sword in one hand and the dagger in the other. Conquest lowered the bow and arrow, triumph on his wicked face.

"As I said they cannot protect you forever. Our fight does not end today." He dug his heels into the side of the horse.

"Until next time, savior," he tossed over his shoulder as the animal turned around.

The horseman's voice sounded distant as the veil dissipated, leaving us standing there exposed to the humans.

Fuck all.

I hid the dagger and sword back in the cloud. In a fit of fury, Kincade broke the arrow off as close to the tip as possible and discarded it. I reached for him, but he batted my hand away.

"I'm fine," he said through gritted teeth. "Let's get on the fucking train."

"We're going to just waltz onto the train with you bleeding like it's no big?" I asked.

"Yes." Kincade hissed through his teeth. He pulled his jacket tighter around his thick frame and zipped it. As if that would hide the blood. I rolled my eyes.

Our next stop was a ticket check before we were able to board the train. I took all our tickets and showed them to the clerk, who eyed Kincade with a curious glance. Her gaze flickered to the hole in his jacket and the suspicious wet spot. The saving grace was his jacket was black and managed to hide the spreading red stain.

She stared me down, too, then Ronan. And I remembered then we both had fresh demon guts splattered all over us. There was no doubt in my mind we looked like death and destruction, not to mention we smelled to high hell. I flashed a bright smile.

"We're heading to Madrid to see the Royal Palace," I chattered nervously. "Never been to Madrid."

Stop talking, Kincade boomed in my head.

Kincade was right. I pressed my lips together to stop talking. Finally, she waved us through. We stumbled onto the train. I still hadn't seen the vampires but that didn't mean much. We'd purchased first class tickets which meant we had more legroom and nicer seats. Kincade took the seat by the window, then pointed to the one next to him indicating that was for me. Ronan took the one across the aisle from me.

I stashed my bag in the luggage rack along with Kincade's. Then sat, my knee bouncing up and down as I bit my thumbnail.

"What about your—" I started.

"I'll be fine," Kincade said, anticipating my question. "When we get there, I'll clean the wound and remove the point." He pinned me with his piercing gaze. "You'll have to help."

"Can't wait for that." My sarcasm was lost on him.

Three vampires stood in the aisle. The very three that had the Holy Grail. Their leader, Barnabas, smiled. He was unaware of who I was, but I recognized his face, his ridiculous outdated outfit and his pale skin. He took his seat several rows ahead of us.

I slowly pushed to my feet, ready to pounce. My hands flexed.

"Not yet, Anna. Sit."

"They have the cup."

"Fighting them for it right now will do no good. Sit."

"And wait until we get to Madrid? No."

"*Anna.*" There was a roughness in his voice.

I glanced down at him, saw the stern look on his face and sank to my seat. "Fine. We'll do it your way then."

"Good. Now be quiet so I can think."

As he said the words, the train lurched and began its journey toward Madrid.

CHAPTER 21

KINCADE PASSED OUT NOT long after the train pulled out of station. I took the opportunity to find my way to the toilet to clean up. When I entered the tiny room, I gasped at my horrid appearance. Black demon guts stained the side of my face and caked in my hair. I frowned, disgusted with my appearance. No wonder the ticket girl stared at us. I looked a fright. We all did.

I used a mountain of paper towels to clean the guts off my face. I tried scrubbing my clothes but that did no good whatsoever. My hair...well...that was going to have to wait until a shower. I swept the long locks into a high ponytail hoping to conceal most of the gunk.

I swear, I think Kincade took perverse pleasure at killing demons and seeing their guts splatter all over me. I often wondered if he did it on purpose.

Back at my seat, Ronan announced he was heading to the cafeteria compartment. When he returned, he looked refreshed and somewhat clean and, the most important part was, he had refreshments. He handed me a bottled water and a sleeve of chocolate cookies. I wanted to hug him. He took his seat across the aisle from me, munching on his own snack cakes.

"His wound needs to be cleaned before infection sets in," he said, not looking at me.

I nodded. "I know." Kincade had plans for me to help him with that. I was not looking forward to it.

"Where are we headed?"

"I haven't thought that far ahead," I admitted.

I'd been so focused on getting out of Valencia and on the train, I had no final destination in mind once we arrived in Madrid. I thought about the Royal Palace postcard in my bag and the directive giving me to attend the gala. The very one in which Ronan had seen my death. I did not have warm fuzzies thinking about it. I also hadn't told Ronan that was our ultimate destination.

"Who was the man on the white horse?" Ronan asked then.

I cut him a sideways glance. "You don't know?"

"I have my suspicions."

Ah, so he wanted confirmation from me. "Conquest."

He leaned back into the leather seat, the material squeaking with the movement. "I thought as much. You realize what this means?"

"Don't you?" I countered.

He glanced around to see if there were any listening ears. "The Four Horseman."

"Ding! You win." I was unable to hide the sarcasm in my voice.

"Why are we headed to Madrid?"

"Because that's where the cup is headed," I said.

"No. There's another reason. Why?" he pressed.

"Why did Conquest call you paladin?" I countered.

He clenched his jaw and looked away. Stalling, he took a sip from his water bottle. "I thought that obvious."

"Enlighten me." I popped a cookie in my mouth and chewed.

"My family line can be traced back to the Early Middle Ages, back to the time of Charlemagne. We were once dream walkers—or paladins—to the medieval king." He gave me a sheepish grin.

I stared at him, dumbfounded, amazed at the brush of history surrounding me. Kincade was once holy guardian to the Knights Templar. Ronan had ancient knights' blood running through his veins. Of course, I'd heard of Charlemagne's legendary paladins, or Twelve Peers. They were akin to Arthur's Knights of the Round Table.

"Are we going to discuss that kiss?" he asked suddenly.

I tried not to flinch at the thought. I'd put it out of my mind after seeing the anger and jealousy on Kincade's face. I tried hard not to give Ronan any encouragement, to keep him at arm's length.

"There's nothing to discuss."

"My father suggests we marry upon our return to England."

"Your father can stuff it," I snapped, then softened when I realized how rude that sounded. "Ronan, you are really a nice guy and I appreciate you trying to do the right thing by your father. But I don't want to marry you."

"I don't want to marry you, but the marriage contract is unbreakable."

"Nothing is unbreakable," I said.

A flicker of hurt passed over his face. "I'm not a bad guy, you know."

I softened. "I never thought you were. You are really a great guy. Any woman would be lucky to have you."

"And that woman is not you."

I have him a weak grin. "We'll discuss it when we return to England. Right now, I have other things on my mind."

He nodded. "Of course, we will. Is this also when you admit you're in love with someone else?"

My head snapped in his direction, my eyes wide. I started to protest, but he waved me off.

"Even a blind man can see it," he added.

I sat back in my seat, avoiding stealing a glance at the sleeping Kincade. I didn't confirm or deny, but Ronan was right. It was becoming more and more difficult to ignore those feelings for Kincade. Especially as we traveled more and more together. Plus, his reaction when he saw Ronan kissing me told me a lot. I thought he would never speak to me again after that.

"I'm in love with someone else, too, but my father managed to ruin that for me."

He sounded so forlorn, a pang or sadness stabbed me right in the heart. I wanted to pummel his father into oblivion. How dare he push together two people who had no interest in being together? I would find a way to fix this if it was the last thing I did.

"Not if I have anything to say about it," I muttered.

He chuckled. "If anyone can twist my father's knickers, Anna, it's you."

I laughed, taking that as a wonderful compliment.

⸎

AFTER A WHILE, RONAN took a nap and I was left to my own devices. I found a hotel near the Royal Palace and made reservations for the three of us. Two suites. Kincade was right to suspect my identity as Anna Walker would be tracked by every agency on the planet. I was a wanted criminal after all.

One of the things my uncle taught me in our travels was the beauty of fake IDs. He'd had one made for me a while back under the name Summer Williams. I had a credit card in that name. I still had it stashed in the back of my wallet from that trip. I used it to book the fancy hotel. Still living the high life for as long as possible.

Frankly, I was shocked I was able to get on the train without at least one person recognizing me in the station. I was certain my face was plastered over every news station and newspaper in the country. I called that shear dumb luck.

I eyed Barnabas and his two cronies ahead and wondered if they had the Grail stashed in their luggage. It would be an easy thing to find out. I slowly pushed up out of my seat so as not to disturb Kincade who snored softly. It was relief he was out cold while Ronan and I had our little marriage discussion.

With my heart in my throat, I stepped into the aisle and paused. I stared down at the luggage rack wondering which ones were their bags. I hadn't a clue and I didn't want to paw through other people's bags and look like a crazy person.

I inched my way down the aisle and reached for my own bag, pretending to open it and get my phone charger. All the while scanning the other luggage.

There was a velvet bag that matched Barnabas' latest outfit. I zipped my ugly canvas duffle that paled in comparison and reached for his. My hand landed on the crushed velvet and pulled the bag toward me when I felt the cold prick of steel at my throat.

"What do you think you're doing?"

The vampire standing behind me reeked of dust. I lifted my hand off the bag and held it up in surrender.

"Nothing."

"Doesn't look like nothing." He quickly frisked me with his other hand. "Gods, you stink."

"It's my natural scent," I quipped.

He removed the knife. I turned to face him. Barnabas eyed me up and down. He didn't miss the guts stuck to my clothes.

"Who are you?"

"Just a girl standing in front of vampire."

He was less than amused. "You know what I am?"

"I know a lot of things about supernaturals. Including vampires. Including you."

"Like what, may I ask?" His eyes narrowed.

"You may ask. But I may not answer."

He pressed the knife against the base of my stomach. "Answer or I gut you like a fish."

"You have the Grail." Narrowed eyes widened slightly. He blanched though it was hard to tell since he was a bloodless, undead creature. "Hand it over and I'll be on my way."

A lazy smile creased his pale lips. "You think to steal it from me?"

"You stole it, didn't you? Right out from under the pope's nose. Very bold of you."

"Who *are* you?"

"Your worst nightmare."

Without thinking, I reached behind me and grabbed his bag off the luggage rack in one swoop, then took off down the aisle. I had no plan, really, other than to run away from him. He was hot on my trail. When I made to the end of the car, I had to wait while the door swished open to allow me to step through to the next car. It gave Barnabas enough time to catch up.

He snatched a handful of hair and jerked me into his arms, the knife point in my kidneys. Pain seared across my scalp. I clutched the velvet bag to my pounding chest.

"Drop the bag, my friend." He pressed the point of the dagger harder.

"Drop the knife, *friend*." Kincade's voice wafted over the vampire.

Barnabas removed the knife and released my hair. I stepped away from him, spinning around to face him, still clutching the bag. By sleight of hand, he sheathed the knife. He held up his hands.

Kincade stood behind the vampire with his gun in hand. I wanted to cheer until I noticed how pale he was. He wavered slightly on his feet. It took shear strength of will for him to stand there and threaten the vampire.

Because of me.

"All I want is my bag."

Kincade's gaze flickered from the vamp to me. *What the fuck are you doing?*

He has the Grail.

You know this for a fact?

Well...no...

"Give him the bag, Anna."

"But—"

"Now."

Barnabas smiled, triumphant.

"On one condition," I said. "I see what's in it."

A dark glower flickered over Kincade's face, but Barnabas smiled.

"As you wish."

He held out his hand for the bag. I handed it over. He opened it and showed me the contents. More fluffy outfits. Miles of velvet and lace.

"Take everything out," I demanded.

He looked horrified. "Surely you jest."

"I never jest. Take everything out."

Barnabas gave Kincade a sidelong plea for help. Kincade pressed the nuzzle of his gun into his side. He would get no help from my guardian.

"Do as she says."

Barnabas removed all the clothing and spilled it onto the floor of the train. I knelt and pawed through it. No cup. Only fancy clothes that stunk like mothballs. Disgruntled, I rose to my full height.

"Satisfied?" Kincade asked.

"For now."

"I've never been so humiliated." The vampire shoved his clothes in a haphazard fashion back into the bag and closed it. He clutched it to his chest as he hurried away.

Kincade holstered his gun and glared. "What the bloody hell were you thinking?"

I shrugged. "It was worth a shot."

"Anna, we have at least another hour on this train. Don't make me tie you to the seat."

"Sounds kinky." I smirked. The words exploded out of my mouth before I was able to stop it. Why did I insist on saying things like that?

He scowled as he stomped back down the aisle to first class. There was little doubt in my mind he would make good on that threat. Sulking, I followed him.

As he headed down the aisle, he lost his balance. He caught himself on the empty seat to his left. I was at his side in an instance, offering an arm. He pushed me away with a glare and a scowl.

"I don't need help."

I lowered my voice so only he could hear. "Clearly, you do. How much blood have you lost?"

"Don't worry about me. I just need to sleep," he groused.

Kincade made it back to his seat without giving me a second glance or a second thought. I tried not to be offended by that. I took my seat and noticed Ronan had slept through the whole vampire affair.

I was still convinced the Grail was somewhere on this train. Why else would they be on it heading to Madrid? Barnabas had it hidden elsewhere. I was determined to find it. But how? It had to be in the bag of one of his cronies.

Kincade reached for me, clamping a hand on my wrist.

"You will stay put."

How did he do that? It was like he sensed what I was thinking. Oh, right. He *did* sense what I was thinking. I had to get better at guarding my thoughts.

"There will be time for that," he said, his voice low.

I met his gaze. "The cup—"

"We will find it."

He sounded so certain it was hard not to believe him.

"Rest. We'll make a plan in Madrid."

"But, what if—"

"No more what if. Rest, Anna. You need it. You're exhausted."

He wasn't wrong. I'd been pushing myself so long with sleepless nights, I was used to the ever-present palpitation of fatigue. I leaned my head back on the seat and closed my eyes. It wasn't long before I was fast asleep.

CHAPTER 22

WE ARRIVED IN MADRID and took a taxi to our hotel. On the way, I thumbed through a search on my phone trying to find information about this gala at the Royal Palace. I mistakenly opened contacts and Tamar's name stared me in the face. An impulse to call her flashed through me. Was she okay? Had she given me up to Interpol? Did she have a choice? I squashed that impulse since now wasn't the time.

I got back to my search. From the news stories I managed to piece together, it was going to be held in four days in honor of the King of Spain's sixtieth birthday. It was supposed to be a glitzy star-studded affair including heads of state and other monarchs from all over the world along with Spain's elite.

How the hell were we going to procure an invitation?

I'd think about that later.

I'd booked an executive terrace suite at The Plaza with a view of the Royal Palace. It was two bedrooms and two full bathrooms with a lounge-dining room and a built-in kitchen. The terrace went the length of the suite and had three doors that opened up to views of the city. My uncle had spoiled me with fancy hotels while traveling. I wasn't ready to give it up.

The apartment was light and airy with a bamboo flooring. The kitchen and dining area had gray slate flooring. We were on a corner of the building and the sunny terrace went the length of the apartment. The furnishings were Neo-classic and mostly in white and beige with a pop of color here and there. Very much like the other fancy hotels we'd stayed in previously.

"I'm taking a shower," I announced.

Without waiting for a reply, I took the master suite with the queen size bed, leaving the other bedroom with the two twin size beds to the guys. They would be roomies and Kincade would have to get over it.

I dropped my bag on the floor of the small room with the one large window. I expelled a breath, still stinking of demon guts and in desperate need of a shower. I stripped off my disgusting clothes and headed to the bathroom. It was equipped with a shower, which was fine by me. Even the bathroom had a door to the terrace. It was hard to resist despite the cold weather.

It felt great to strip out of those stinky clothes and into a hot shower. I scrubbed until my skin was bright pink and my hair squeaky clean. I stepped out, toweled off and dressed. All I needed now was a bottle of whiskey and I would be a boneless chicken for the rest of the day.

But I couldn't stop thinking about Tamar. I called her number and waited while it rang. It went to voicemail. I hung up, not wanting to leave a message, not knowing what to say.

A knock sounded on the bedroom door. I opened it to see a pale faced Kincade on the other side. He sweated. His skin held a sickly palor.

In my hot-shower haze, I'd forgotten he still had an arrow point in his shoulder. Guilt flickered.

He put a hand on the door jamb and leaned heavily on it. He held a bottle of unopened whiskey in one hand.

"We should clean that wound," I said.

"Yes." He gave a jerk of his head inviting me to follow him.

I paused in the kitchen to thoroughly wash and dry my hands. We headed out to the terrace in the waning light of the day where there was a two-seat sofa. A wicker table in front of it held all sorts of first aid items including gauze bandages, rubbing alcohol, antiseptic. A cool breeze shifted across the terrace. I shivered.

"Out here?" I asked.

"Sit." He pointed to the sofa.

"Where did you get this stuff?"

"You ask too many damn questions, Anna. Sit, dammit."

I sat and waited for more instructions, eyeing the bottle of whiskey in his hand and wondering where the glasses were in the midst of the bandages.

There were none. Dread curled up my spine.

However, there were what appeared to be surgical thread and a needle. I made a valiant effort to pretend that wasn't really what I saw.

"You didn't answer my question."

He huffed. "Ronan bought it in the hotel store. He left again for provisions."

Disbelief flickered through me. "He found *all* this in the hotel store?"

Kincade didn't answer as he shoved off his jacket, then stripped away his shirt and tossed it to the ground. The wound on his shoulder looked like rotted meat.

"It's already festered. How?"

"Demon poison," he replied, his voice flat.

I tried to avert my eyes but the more I tried *not* to look, the more I did. It was disgusting. The only other place to fix my gaze was on Kincade's naked torso, and, well...

I swallowed the lump that rose to my throat. My heart immediately went into a hard palpitation.

"Draw down your dagger," he said.

I did, pulling it out of the cloud. He took it from me and then doused it with the rubbing alcohol on both sides. Then he used a soft cloth to wipe it clean. In all the time I'd had the blade, I never recalled cleaning it. It'd killed a hell of a lot of demons. He handed it back to me. I took the jade-handled dagger. He took the bottle of whiskey from my other hand and spun open the cap one handed. He dropped it on the ground next to his shirt, then took a long, healthy swig.

I stared at him, frozen, trying to decide what he wanted me to do.

"Are you going to sit there all day?" he snapped.

My ire rose. "What the hell are you expecting me to do?"

"Cut the damn thing out, Anna."

A beat of silence as I blinked surprise, peeked at the ugly wound, and then back at him. "You want me to cut the arrow point out of your shoulder?"

"I don't think I stuttered." A dark look of pain and anguish mixed with a touch of anger flickered over his face. He took another swig.

It always amazed me the range of emotions his face projected. Especially when he dealt with me.

"Okay," I said slowly.

Hot sweat exploded all over.

I clutched the dagger in my right hand, trying to figure out how to do it without actually touching him. My mouth had gone bone dry.

I reached for the whiskey bottle and snatched it from him before he protested. I took a healthy swig, letting it burn my gut and giving me liquid courage. I handed it back to him. He smirked as he took it.

"Are you sure about this?" I asked. My real question, though, was he sure he wanted me to do this. "Maybe Ronan can—"

"Do it." He clutched the bottle in his hand so tight, his knuckles turned white. "You're the only one I trust."

I flushed. He trusted me?

Had we come to that place in our relationship where we had unconditional trust for one another? Maybe we'd crossed that threshold, though I had no idea when or what event had trigged it.

I did not doubt it was going to hurt like a son of a bitch. I licked my dry lips, trying to decide how to go about cutting the arrow point out of his shoulder.

"Just do it, Anna, for the love of all that's holy."

I took a deep breath.

I placed my left hand to the side of the wound. I tried hard not to think about how warm his skin was under my palm. Heat radiated from the wound.

No, I had to focus.

As gruesome as it was. I clutched the dagger in my sweating right palm and gave the wound a tentative poke.

"For Christ's sake, just dig it out," he said through clenched teeth.

"I've never done this before!" I snapped.

His tense body relaxed under my hand. Like all the fight had gone out of him.

"Hey."

I met his green-gold gaze. A tender look I did not expect.

"You won't hurt me. But you have to remove it before the poisonous infection gets worse."

I nodded.

I bit my lower lip and stuck the tip of the dagger into the wound.

He sucked in a sharp breath.

I ignored him as I dug into the wound, trying to find the point of the arrow. The tip of the blade bumped against it. I dug down deeper.

He grunted and took another swig of whiskey. His free hand landed on my hip, his fingers digging in. I was practically in his lap as I pushed the tip of the dagger deeper, trying to get under the arrow point. I felt something pop and then pushed. The metal tip pushed upward. I saw a hint of the metal peek through the red, pus-filled skin.

Bile rose to my throat. I tried hard not to gag and swallowed hard, pretending this was no big deal. He clenched his teeth. His fingers dug deeper into my side.

"Push it out," he said.

"I'm trying," I replied through gritted teeth. God, this was so not easy!

I shoved the dagger point deeper into the wound. I gave it a little wiggle and a pop upward. The metal arrow point burst through his skin. It was coated in blood as I plucked it up and tossed it to the ground. The open wound streamed blood.

I dropped the bloody dagger in my lap and grabbed the gauze, pressing it hard against the wound.

Warm blood flooded beneath my palm.

My breath came out sharp as I twisted to reach the rubbing alcohol. I lifted the gauze just long enough to douse the wound—no hesitation, no warning.

He growled deep in his throat through is teeth. His hand tightened on both me and the whiskey bottle. I snatched another piece of gauze off the table and pressed it against the open wound, trying to staunch the bleeding. I held it for a long moment, my heart doing a rapid beat and my stomach threatening to heave.

"Clean it again."

"Gosh, you're bossy."

I removed the bandage and doused it again. This time with the antiseptic spray. The dirty wound foamed immediately. He sucked in a sharp breath in his nose, keeping his gaze focused on something across the way. I wiped it with a clean gauze, but it was still bleeding.

He held the bottle between his knees, then pressed my hand holding the gauze against his wound a lot harder than I would have. My gaze flickered up to his, but he was looking at the wound and the red spreading in a little pool on the gauze.

"You need stitches, I think," I said.

"I do," he ground out. "You have to do it."

I stared at him. "Oh, hell, no."

"You have to, Anna."

"Do you want me to puke on you?" I asked.

"I can't do it myself or I would. Don't you sew?"

"Badly, yes!"

"Like stitching a seam. I'll talk you through it." He was not fazed by my retort. He nodded to the suture kit on the table. I was no longer able to pretend that stuff didn't exist.

"Oh, God," I moaned.

"You can do it." Despite his weak tone, he managed to cheer me on.

"I hate you." I whispered.

"I know. Now, use the needle driver to grab the needle."

He held the gauze on his shoulder as I slipped my hand away. My stomach clawed its way to my throat. I reached for the needle driver, which actually looked like a pair of scissors. I pulled the threads out of the suture kit, wondering where in the world Ronan was able to find this stuff. I threaded the curved needle with a shaking hand. It took several tries, but I finally got it.

"Line up the edges as much as you can."

He removed the bloody gauze from the wound. I wasn't exactly weak at the sight of blood but having to stitch up a wound...yeah, so not my forte.

"You owe me for this," I said on a roughened whisper.

He grinned. "I do. Now, push the needle through at a ninety-degree angle. Don't go below the fat. Stay right above it."

I had to tell myself this was not skin I was sewing up, but instead drapes. Cloth drapes that needed a hem. Not flesh and blood.

I stuck the needle in his skin. He didn't flinch. Perhaps the whiskey helped.

"Good. Now twist your hand clockwise and come up the other side. Keep it straight."

"I guess you've done this before."

"Many times."

He talked me through the first stitch and how to make an overhand knot. I kept my mind on the sound of his voice, doing every step as he said while he drank and observed. His free hand was still on my hip as if to steady me and, perhaps, himself.

I closed the gaping wound after an intense process. Once I was finished, all the knots lined up on the left side of the wound in perfect order.

"Not bad for your first time." He gave me a weak smile, then drank again.

I noticed the whiskey bottle was half empty by this point. I covered his wound with fresh gauze and taped it down. Then grabbed the whiskey with a shaking hand.

I gulped in the alcohol until my gut, throat and mouth burned from the taste. When I had my fill, I handed the bottle back to him, wiping my mouth with the back of my hand. My stomach roiled from the emotion and the booze.

"Let's never do that again."

He chuckled. "Thanks."

Blood stained my fingers and crusted under my nails. I looked over my handiwork and was slightly impressed I managed to dress the wound. Conquest's bloody arrowpoint was still on the table. I glared at the offending thing.

"I'm impressed. You weren't queasy at the sight of blood."

"No, just having to do stitches for the first time in my life. And anyway, why should I be? I watched my boyfriend's blood spill all over the floor."

He blanched. I instantly regretted the words. I don't know why I said it. I hadn't thought of Ben's murder in a long while. I wasn't sure why it came to me now. Maybe because I was slightly drunk, hungry, and weak at having to play nurse to a shirtless Kincade.

I snatched the bloody arrow off the table along with the rest of the trash and carried it off to the kitchen to dispose of it. I washed my hands in the hottest water available and scrubbed until there were no more remnants of blood.

He followed me, stumbling slightly. He still held the whiskey bottle. The amber liquid sloshed. He leaned heavily on the door-jamb to the kitchen as I dried my hands on a thick white towel.

"I shouldn't have said that." I refused to meet his gaze. Because I didn't want to see the pity.

Ben's death had been my fault. I refused to listen to Azriel. Ben was collateral damage. He'd been killed because of my own stubbornness.

"Ben's death wasn't your fault."

"Shut. Up." I turned on him. "It was. And you and I both know it."

Kincade shook his head. "No, Anna. Azriel was going to find a way to kill him if you agreed to help him or not."

Hot, blinding tears filled my eyes as I shook my head. "No. It was my fault. I killed him as if I'd been the one to slash his throat."

With a slow, purposeful stride, Kincade entered the kitchen. He placed the whiskey bottle on a nearby counter and then took me by the shoulders. He gave me one little shake.

"Stop it. Stop blaming yourself for his death. There was noth-ing you could have done to save him. You know it. I know it."

"But—"

"No more buts. No more guilt. You have to let him go, Anna."

A sob hitched in my throat and I hated myself for that. Hated I was unable to stop the shed of tears for a man I barely knew but lived with. A man I thought I might marry one day but didn't. A man who didn't deserve to die. But Kincade was right in that I couldn't stop it. Ben was meant to die as I was meant to become Keeper of the Holy Relics.

I shoved Kincade's hands away, trying to ignore the fact he was still shirtless and standing in close proximity to me. I stumbled backward a step, but the kitchen was small. He blocked the only exit.

He took a step back, then grabbed the whiskey bottle off the counter.

"My turn to shower."

And he left me alone and bereft in a sea of my own emotions.

CHAPTER 23

I TOOK A DEEP breath trying to force my erratic heartbeat under control. I didn't want to admit how much Kincade affected me when he stood so close. Or how much I wanted him to keep standing close. I ran a hand through my still damp hair, my fingers tangling in the locks, and blew out a breath.

Ronan entered carrying several shopping bags full. He placed them on the counter and started to unload. I peered at the bags with things like meat and vegetables and wondered how we were supposed to eat all that. I was no cook.

"Do you have a chef in those bags, too?" I asked.

He flashed a grin. "I can cook. And not just breakfast either." He put eggs and bacon in the fridge, then turned to me. His face registered concern. "Are you all right?"

"Fine."

I didn't want to rehash anything with Kincade. I moved out of the kitchen wishing he hadn't taken the whiskey bottle with him. I spied the remnants of the first aid on the table outside, so headed to clean it up. When I came back in, Ronan was done putting the food away. I held up the suture kit and bandages.

"Where did you find this?"

"I have connections."

"In Madrid?" I lifted an eyebrow, skeptical.

He flushed. "Kiara is a nurse. She helped me buy what I needed."

Kiara. His girlfriend back in England. The one he was forced to cut ties with because of me. "That was nice of her."

"Were you able to help him?"

"Yes. You conveniently disappeared."

"I thought it best I not be here."

I snorted. "You didn't want to be a witness to the carnage."

He flashed another grin as he reached back into the fridge for a canned drink. It was a Spanish beer. On the train, he'd asked what the plan was, and I sidestepped, not wanting to tell him the answer. But we were here in Madrid now, a stone's throw from the Royal Palace. And another step closer to my fate. It was probably time to tell him the truth.

"I want to show you something. Stay there."

I went to my room and pawed through my bag until I found the envelope with the postcards. I pulled it out of the bag and headed back to the kitchen.

"On the train, you asked where we were headed next."

I slipped the one of the Royal Palace out and handed it to him. He peered down at the card, then flipped it over to read the words on the back. He slowly lifted his gaze back to mine.

"Where did this come from?"

I shrugged. "I often receive postcards of the places I'm supposed to search for the relics. One led me to Valencia. This one here to Madrid."

His face paled as he handed it back to me. "Who sent it?"

"I have no idea. The postcards appear out of nowhere." I dropped it back into the envelope with the others.

His hand shook slightly. "You suspect the Grail is headed there?"

"Yes."

"And you intend to go despite my warning?" he demanded.

"Yes."

"Even though you know the outcome."

"I have to. I have to try to recover the Grail."

"Then you'll die." He sounded so sure a pang of fear skipped through me.

"You don't know that."

"I do. I saw your death."

"You said you had a vision. You—"

"My visions always come true."

"Our destinies lie within our own hands, Ronan. Not visions or prophesies."

"And yet you are embracing the prophecy of Keeper of the Holy Relics," he said. "You can't go to the Royal Palace."

"I can and I will. I have to follow the cup. If I have a chance I can get it back—"

"And risk your life for it?" He shook his head in disbelief.

I was baffled. "Isn't this the whole reason you came? Because you had a vision of my death? Because you said you had divine power? I witnessed the display of it when your hands crackled with light against Conquest. I understood what that was."

He pressed his lips together in a thin line. "You're right. It is the reason I came."

"Then what's the problem?"

He left the kitchen and entered he lounge area, taking a seat near the terrace door. "There is more to the vision. More I didn't tell you."

I put my hands on my hips. "And what is that?"

"If you die, others will die. Kincade dies. All those people in the Royal Palace. All Hell is unleashed. You have already seen the beginning with Conquest. There will be more. A darkness will reign. Mankind will be destroyed and all hope will be lost."

The situation sounded dire. I didn't like the sound of it one bit. Especially all the dying stuff.

"Your visions are certainly detailed."

I hadn't meant to sound sarcastic, but it came out that way. It wasn't that I didn't believe him. I preferred to believe there were alternatives to this than death and destruction. I wasn't ready to give up. I wasn't ready to see the End of All Days.

"If you're right, it means everything I've done, everything I've worked for has been for nothing. I refuse to believe it's for nothing. I truly believe there is a way to stop it. To alter the future. To save mankind. If I didn't, I may as well pack my bags and go home."

He took a deep breath, expelled it. Then took a swig of beer. "If you're determined to go, then I'm determined to follow you. I cannot allow you to enter that Royal Palace alone."

"She won't be."

Kincade's voice boomed across the hotel room, startling me. His hair was damp from the shower. He had on fresh clothes. A fierce look creased his face. I moved to stand between the two of them, making myself a barricade in case things got ugly.

Ronan downed another healthy draft and slowly came to his feet. My heart quickened as I glanced from him to Kincade and back again.

"Oh, yes, of course. Her valiant guardian. You think you can protect her better than I can?"

"I know I can, *paladin*."

Aw, hell.

Ronan's eyes narrowed as he moved a step closer. Kincade was not one to back down from a fight and inched closer, too. Suddenly, this was a pissing match over who was better at protecting me. A teensy bit of me wanted to love it so hard, but the other part of me wanted nothing to do with it.

"You claim to be her guardian, but so far I haven't seen you do much guarding."

Red fury creased Kincade's face.

Shit. I didn't like where this was going. They both puffed up their chests like they were ready to do battle. Ronan was a head shorter than Kincade. I was pretty sure Kincade would pummel the man.

"She and I have history. You don't."

Heat crawled up my neck and pounded in my cheeks at the way he said that. Like he was boasting about our relationship. Like we even *had* a relationship. We had an uneasy alliance at best, but I was starting to rethink that.

"Her family and my family have been connected for generations. Who are you to her?"

"Kincade was in the Brotherhood of Watchers," I blurted.

Silence descended. I planted my body between the two of them. I put one hand on Kincade's chest and one on Ronan's and gave them both a mighty push.

"Fighting about who gets to protect me isn't going to do me any good," I said. "I'm going to that gala whether either of you like or not." Ronan started to protest but I held up a hand to shush him. "Kincade will be the one to escort me. You, Ronan, will attend to keep an eye on the surroundings. I'll see if I can find you a date."

I almost smirked at the way his face twisted into a scowl at my last words.

"No more fighting, either of you. I do not want to hear another word about who's going to protect me." I pointed to first Ronan and then Kincade. "We're going to go into this thing as a team. Fighting each other isn't going to do us any good and it certainly won't help find the Grail. Got it?"

I pinpointed Ronan with my best stern expression. He nodded slowly, turned on his heel and exited to the terrace with his half-empty beer can. Then I gave Kincade a pointed look. He put his hands up in surrender.

"He started it."

I shook my head. "No more fighting, Kincade."

"Fine."

He stomped off to his room with his bottle of whiskey. The one he shared with Ronan. I almost laughed when I realized this suite was way too small for the three of us.

I hadn't a clue how to dress for a gala. I was going to need assistance and these two manly men were not the ones to offer it. It didn't help I was missing a girl gene.

Only one person I would be able to help.

Ophelia.

I took my cell phone out of my pocket and dialed her number. She answered on the first ring, panting as though she were running a marathon.

"Hey, Anna, I can't talk right now."

"Drop whatever you're doing. I need you in Madrid."

Silence on the other end. "You gave me instructions to find you mother. Now you want me in Madrid?"

"It's a girl emergency and I don't have time to explain. How fast can you get here?"

"I'll be on the next plane if I had the cash for that."

"Ask Piers to buy the plane ticket. He knows how to access the household money. Here's the address of the hotel where we're staying." I rattled it off to her.

A long pause, then she asked, "But what about Natasha?"

What, indeed. Natasha was the least of my worries at the moment. Perhaps she was out terrorizing the world with her super dream walker powers. I didn't have time to worry about at the moment. I would find my biological mother when I could pencil her between finding the Grail and not dying.

"She'll be fine. See you soon. Oh, and bring your sword. You might need it."

"How the bloody hell am I supposed to get that through security?"

"You'll think of something."

I hung up before she gave me a tart reply.

And despite my bravado about the whole Royal Palace gala, I was terrified of what was to come.

CHAPTER 24

AFTER I HUNG UP with Ophelia, I went to work researching invitations to the gala. How did one obtain an invitation anyway? I could do only so much with a smartphone. From what I gleaned from searches the event was invitation only. We weren't exactly royalty, so how we were going to get into this shindig was beyond me.

When I was in Hong Kong, I used the cleaning crew as cover to enter the building. There had to be a servant's entrance in the Royal Palace. And if the event was as big as the news touted, then surely vendors would be assisting with the preparation.

The more I thought about this, the more I doubted we would be able to pull this off. I paced the length of the small living area, biting my thumbnail. As I did so, my phone vibrated, buzzing in my hand. Tamar was on the other end.

"Tamar—"

"Anna, listen. Please understand I had to tell them." Her voice was raspy, low. He words rushed.

I blew out a breath. "Interpol?"

"I cut a deal with them after I was arrested."

"Where are you now?"

"It doesn't matter. I'm sorry, Anna, but I had to."

To save her own skin. I understood despite the bite of betrayal cutting through me.

"Please don't contact me again."

The call ended. Numb, I held the phone in my hand as though it were a foreign object. At least now I had my answer as to what happened to Tamar and how I was tracked down by Interpol.

Ronan wandered back inside from the terrace with an empty beer can. He crushed the aluminum in his hand as he headed to the kitchen and tossed the crumped can in the trash. Our gazes met. We stared at each other a long moment.

"You seem out of sorts," he said.

I shoved the phone deep into my pocket and said nothing. My mind turned back to the current situation. Questions rattled around in my head, but not about him. About the palace, the gala, and how the bloody hell we were going to get an invitation.

"Something is bothering you. I can tell."

I resumed pacing, biting my thumbnail, and nodded.

"The gala?" he asked.

Tamar, the gala, everything. I nodded again, then stopped pacing.

"We need an invitation but we're not royalty or heads of state or Spain's elite."

He took a deep breath, expelled it. "You are still determined to go through with it."

"Yes."

A flicker of disappointment went over his face, as though he hoped I'd come to my senses.

"If you're that determined, then I'll find a way inside."

"How?"

"I'll worry about that. You worry about recovering the Grail so we can all go home."

With that, he shuffled off to the bedroom he shared with Kincade. The door opened, closed, and then silence. I waited, my breath pooling in my throat, as I listened for an explosion of words or fists.

Silence remained.

I wondered if they talked to each other. What they said. If they were talking about me. My imagination ran wild.

When I was certain Ronan and Kincade were not going to kill each other, I took myself to bed. Exhaustion hit me hard and fast. I climbed onto the bed, not bothering to kick off my boots, and was asleep in minutes.

The dream started immediately, and it wasn't my dream. Someone invaded my dream. Instantly, I realized I had forgotten to put up my metal wards in my haze of fatigue.

"Hello, *chérie.*"

Azriel. He looked as he always did—sinful, savage, yet handsome with this black hair, black eyes, black wings glistening. He circled me like a predator, his wide face with that wolfish grin I had come to despise.

"I missed you."

I hadn't seen him in a while and, honestly, I hadn't missed him one iota. "What do *you* want?"

He clutched his chest as though wounded. "Do I have to want something to visit you?"

"Yes." I kept my gaze fixed on him, turning as he turned. Keeping him in front of me at all times.

He smiled that wolf grin. "Aren't you going to ask me about Astrid?"

I stiffened at that. He'd taken Astrid from the front lawn of Walker Manor. He'd hidden her somewhere in the depths of Hell. I promised Killian, her Fae King lover, I would find her and bring her back. And yet, I hadn't. It would mean a trip into Hell and, well, at the moment, I had other priorities. Leaving Astrid wounded me. I hated it as much as I hated the Fallen high lord in front of me.

"She's doing well. Becoming more and more compliant every day."

I clenched my fists. "If you've harmed her in any way, I'll—"

He chuckled. "You'll what? Kill me? You and I both know that's impossible. Just as I know it's impossible to kill you."

Even if he wanted to, he was forbidden by Lucifer. Because the dark lord needed me alive. I was the only one who could touch the Holy Relics before Lucifer or any one of his Fallen high lords. That included Azriel. Which made me wonder...how were the vampires able to touch the Holy Grail?

They were undead creatures, so perhaps being in that state made them immune to whatever the relics did to Fallen.

"Did you come to taunt me?"

"I came to warn you. We have a mutual acquaintance. One who has something he intends to deliver to me."

"Barnabas will never give you the Grail. Not while I live."

That wolf smile again. "My point, *chérie*."

A coldness swept through me. "Is that a threat?"

"No, my dear." He stepped closer, a breath away. "A promise." Then he brushed his cheek against mine, landed a soft kiss on my brow, and was gone.

I cried out and awoke in a cold sweat, still feeling the stroke of his cheek against mine, the touch of his warm lips on my skin. I sat up on the bed, panting and shivering. Darkness pressed all around, the shadows creeping closer and closer. Suddenly, my door burst open. Kincade stood as a silhouette, gun in hand.

He startled me so much, I stifled a yelp. My heart pounded.

"You okay?" His voice was gruff, as though he just woke up.

"I...I'm fine."

He lowered his gun, still standing in the doorway, his other hand on the knob. Something about his hulking shadowed form gave me comfort. My heart finally slowed to a normal beat. He didn't move and though I was unable to see his face in the darkness, I sensed his gaze on me.

At last, he nodded and stepped out of the room, closing the door behind him. But I would never sleep again that night. I flopped back onto the bed, staring at the ceiling, and waited for morning to come.

✦————✦

DAWN CREPT INTO THE room, chasing away the gloom of night. After Kincade left, I curled on my side, the pillow bunched up under my head, and stared at the window, willing daybreak.

Despite the exhaustion pressing through me, I refused sleep. But I was getting used to the bone-tired sensation crushing me. I sometimes longed for my old life back with dreams free of angels and demons and other supernatural things. Without worrying about Holy Relics or saving mankind or wondering if you were strong enough, brave enough, or even enough.

A gentle knock on my door, then Ronan's voice. "Anna, you have a visitor."

I bounced from the bed and shot to my feet. I flung open the door and shoved past Ronan to see Ophelia standing in the hotel room with a bag at her feet. Dark circles rimmed her eyes. The freckles dotting her nose and cheeks seemed darker than normal. Her cheeks were flushed. Her curly blonde hair was pulled back in a ponytail. She looked like she hadn't slept in weeks, something of which I related.

I wrapped her in a tight hug, relieved she was here. She gave me an awkward pat on the back before I released her. Confusion flickered over her face as she gave me an up and down cursory glance. I wasn't the hugging type. Not really, so to her, I must have seemed like I'd lost my mind.

"So, what's the big emergency?" she asked.

"Coffee?" I bounced to the kitchen, busying myself with making a pot. I hadn't a clue what the time was nor did it matter. I wanted coffee.

"No. Anna, I was in London closing in on your mother when you called. I had her in my sights. What is all this about?" She folded her arms across her chest.

"A certain Royal Gala," Ronan said.

She cut him a glance. "And who are you?"

"Oh, that's Ronan," I said flippantly as I scooped coffee into the filter.

"Her betrothed." He said the words as Kincade made an appearance.

I flinched.

Ophelia sucked in a sharp breath, her eyes wide as she glanced at Kincade who stood rooted in place as though he'd been flayed.

"Um…" she began. "I'm going to need more information."

I came out of the kitchen and halted in front of her. "In two days, a gala at the Royal Palace will celebrate the King of Spain's sixtieth birthday. We're going. But it's a formal event and well..." I waved at my attire which wasn't suitable at all for a formal event.

Her pale brows drew together. "And what exactly do you need me for?"

"You're a girl," Kincade said. "She's not."

"Hey!" I barked. But he wasn't wrong.

Ophelia sank to the nearest chair. "I'll take you up on that coffee after all."

⊹———⊹

THIRTY MINUTES LATER, AFTER we'd all decimated a pot of coffee and started another one, we gathered in the small living area. Ophelia and I took the sofa. Ronan the chair across from us. Kincade hovered in the kitchen, leaning on the counter keeping a watchful eye on all of us.

I caught up Ophelia on everything that had happened since we left England. It seemed an eternity ago but in reality, was only a couple of weeks. When I explained to her about the postcard and that we needed to crash the party at the Royal Palace to steal back the Holy Grail, she was all on aboard. In fact, happiness lit her tired face as if I'd given her carte blanche to dress me as needed.

In a ball gown.

I shuddered at the thought.

I was not a ball gown kind of girl. I was a cargo pants and demon killing kind of girl.

"Oh, and by the way, I was able to bring the sword." She held the half-empty cup of coffee in her hands.

I glanced around but didn't see it anywhere. "Where is it?"

"Darius showed me a trick. Watch this." She drew down the sword from the cloud. "No worries about getting this baby through security."

"I'm glad you still have the sword," Kincade said. "It may come in handy."

Once upon a time, Ophelia worked for Kincade as part of a task force hunting down the Fallen who were killing guardian angels and stealing souls. We met in Istanbul kicking demon and high lord butt.

"How's Grace?" I asked, changing the subject.

"The same, really."

At least that was some comfort. I was glad her condition hadn't worsened. "And my mother?"

She put the sword back into the cloud. A grim look slipped over her face before she concealed it. "Agents came to the house with a search warrant looking for you and the relics. They said you were an international thief of artifacts of significant cultural importance. They wanted to recover the property you stole and arrest you."

This wasn't news to me. I nodded to encourage her to keep going.

"Natasha was..." She paused, took a deep breath and shook her head. "She must have heard them downstairs. I didn't know she was there until...well, she was. Something triggered her. She kept telling them to get out of her house. *Her house.*"

Gooseflesh rose on my arms. Perhaps my mother, who now called herself Natasha, had a memory breakthrough.

"Then what happened?" I asked.

"She saw the men going through the house, tearing things apart, searching for the Holy Relics. As if we'd keep them laying around." She snorted and shook her head. "They didn't find them, by the way. Anyway, it upset her. She used those super dream walker skills of hers. I've never seen anything like it."

"What did she do?" This from Ronan.

"She killed them," I answered.

Because I knew how. Somehow, she used those skills to make the person hemorrhage from the inside out. I had first-hand experience.

"Yes," Ophelia replied. "With her mind. One of the officers tried to stop her, but she turned on him. She killed him, too. She managed to escape. After you told me to find her, I tracked her down in the streets of London. She was like some feral animal with a wild-eyed look."

"But she's still alive?" I asked, worry gnawing.

"She is. I wanted to get her off the streets, but I'm not sure she would recognize me at that point. Something inside her snapped."

I sat back in the chair and drew up my knees, my heart hurting. She needed me and I wasn't there for her. She was lost on the streets of London. Alone. Scared. Not knowing who she really was. I failed her.

"It's not your fault, Anna," Kincade said, sensing my thoughts.

"Isn't it? I wasn't there to protect her. Her mind is broken."

"If you had been, you would have been arrested," he pointed out.

He wasn't wrong. Likely, I'd be rotting in some prison cell awaiting extradition back to Israel. Still, it was hard not to blame myself for not being there for her.

"When we're back, we find her," he added.

I nodded. The impatient me didn't want to wait that long. It was hard not to worry about her, though I hardly knew her. I was one person. I understood that. Though I was tasked with saving all of mankind, I had to remind myself I was a human who could not possibly save every one of them.

But I was damn sure going to try.

Ronan rose from his chair. "If we're all going to that gala, I have work to do." He headed for the door.

"Where are you going?" As the words escaped me, I regretted them. Especially when Kincade rolled his eyes.

"We need invitations, don't we? I'll be back later." With that, he left.

I had no idea what he intended to do. Perhaps he would return with fake invitations or a way inside the palace. There was no telling with Ronan.

"And I have my own tasks to handle. What are the sleeping arrangements?" Ophelia asked.

I didn't miss the hopeful glance she cut at Kincade, then back to me. She, like my uncle, liked the thought of Kincade and I as a couple.

"You can room with me." I thumbed to the bedroom behind me.

"Great!" She picked up her bag and headed to the room. A moment later, she returned with her phone in hand. "I have some window shopping to do."

"Not window shopping. Take this." I stood up and pulled the credit card out of my front pocket. I handed it to her.

She peered down at it. "Who's Summer Williams?"

"Undercover me," I said. "Happy shopping. And try not to go overboard."

She flashed a smile as she tucked the card away. "I will do my best."

And she, too, was gone. Leaving me alone with Kincade. I remained where I was, my legs tucked underneath me as I sat holding the mug. He remained where he was. And neither of us acknowledged the other.

Awkward silence ensued.

I shifted, forcing myself to remain and not bolt from the room. It took all my strength to stay seated, to not fidget, sipping the remnants of my now cold coffee.

"Are you ever going to tell me what's going on between you and Ronan?"

Of all the questions Kincade asked me, I didn't expect that one. Or perhaps I should have expected that one. I'd seen the smoldering annoyance he gave Ronan. I didn't want to think he was jealous. Instead, I chalked it up to his overprotectiveness.

"There's nothing between us."

"Bullshit." He moved from the kitchen to stand in front of me to stare me down. "You intend to marry him."

I would have laughed if he didn't look so angry about it. He practically vibrated out of his skin. "I do not."

"I heard him tell Ophelia you were betrothed."

"Because that's what he thinks. I told him I intended to break that marriage contract whether his father likes it or not. His father is pushing him into it. He doesn't want to marry me either, though he's giving it a valiant effort."

The fury seemed to dissipate at bit. He relaxed his stance as he lowered his body to the chair across from me. He leaned back, crossed his massive forearms over his massive chest.

"Explain that kiss, then."

Ah, so that's what was bugging him. I sat gazing at him across the top of my coffee mug, wondering why he cared. And it struck me then. *He cared.* I gazed at him, appreciating everything about him. His thick forearms with the sprinkling of hair. The muscles in his hands. The way he sat all defensive and handsome and ready to kick Ronan's ass. I admired the scruff of beard on his face, the way his short-cropped hair stuck up in spikes all over his head. As though he'd been running his hand through it in agitation. I adored the way fire flashed in those green-gold eyes of his. They mesmerized me.

It was official. I had a major crush on Kincade.

It was hard not to think about trying to save him from Azriel's clutches when the high lord had captured him. When I stepped into his mind and he told me I couldn't save him, to let him go. But in my stubbornness, I refused. He cupped my face, his thumb brushing over my cheekbone.

It means a lot you tried. Let me go.

He'd said that to me. And I refused to let him go. Refused to allow Azriel to have his soul for Lucifer's dark army. Something, some deep desire, drove me to save him. To trade the Spear of Destiny for his life.

And then, before that, in Hong Kong he dream walked me and didn't realize it. It was before we both understood he had the ability. He'd kissed me then, in that dream, his hands cupping my face. His mouth molding to mine in a perfect way, as though they were made to fit.

As I sat peering at him from the safety of my sofa, my heart thudded hard in my chest. My stomach twisted in a tight knot. My skin felt tight, as though stretched thin across my muscles and bones. It was an ache I had not experienced for anyone ever. Not Ben. Certainly not Ronan.

I took a deep breath and finally replied.

"For the record, *he* kissed *me*. I wasn't exactly a willing participant. You happened to walk in at that moment."

I waited for him to call me a liar. Of course, he wouldn't because he had that internal lie detector. He always sensed when I lied to him. Right from day we met in that hospital in Dallas.

He dropped his arms from his chest and relaxed, leaning back in the chair. He stretched his long legs out in front of him, crossing them at the ankles. I pretended I didn't notice the bulge of thigh muscles.

"How are you going to do it?"

"Break the marriage contract?" I shrugged. "I have no idea."

"His father is a dick. I doubt he will let it go."

"I guess I'll worry about that when the time comes. In the meantime, I have bigger things to worry about."

He ran his hand over his scuff of beard, the stubble bristling against his skin. "What if the vamps don't have the real Grail?"

I blinked. It was something I had not considered. "What makes you think that?"

"There are all sorts of Grail stories, Anna. Do you honestly think Valencia Cathedral would keep it in sight for all to see?"

"Why wouldn't they? Christians and pilgrims from all over the world want to see the cup. They want to believe. It's the search for the divine in all of us." My brow furrowed in question. "You have doubts."

"Yes."

"Because? You rarely have doubts without good reason."

He took a deep breath. "The Knights Templar were said to have hidden it."

My eyes widened. He, of course, would have that information since he once had a connection to the Knights Templar as a member of the Brotherhood of Watchers. He'd been at the siege of Acre when they faced their downfall in 1291.

"Was it at Acre?" I asked.

He shook his head. "I'm not sure. I never saw the actual treasure they moved. They moved it before the fortress fell."

The Templars were great at hiding their treasure. No doubt it was hidden all over the world, buried under churches and old fortresses. Now Kincade had planted the seed of doubt in my mind, too.

"The Templars were all over the world. They could have hidden it anywhere," I said.

"Then if this doesn't work out at the gala, we better hope you get another postcard." He unfolded his large frame from the chair.

He left me alone as he headed down the hall to his room.

The thing was, I never knew when I would get another postcard or where it would send me. But he was right. If things went awry at the gala, then we'd need a backup plan. I had no idea what that plan was going to be. Yet.

CHAPTER 25

TIME PASSED SLOWLY IN the small hotel room. I spent a lot of time on the terrace, alone with my thoughts which was not necessarily a good thing. My mind tended to run amok with worst case scenarios and what ifs.

I was so close to finding the Grail. And yet, so far. And maybe Kincade was right in that the vamps didn't have the true Holy Grail. If they didn't, then where was it? I hadn't a clue. I wished my uncle was around to help calm my nerves. Kincade wasn't exactly warm and fuzzy.

Ophelia returned with an armload of boxes and bags. I hopped to my feet and hurried to help her. She dropped the pile on the sofa and stood back, her cheeks flushed and beaming as if she'd had the best day ever.

I was glad. I hated shopping.

"What's all this?" I waved at the mound.

"Oh, wait until you see!"

She clapped her hands together and bounced up and down once. She reached for a large white garment bag and carried it to the nearest doorway, hanging it up. Before she unzipped the bag, she spun to face me. Her face was lit with such joy it practically vibrated out of her.

"I want you to keep an open mind, Anna."

That didn't sound good. "What did you do?"

"I bought you a ball gown. A simply *stunning* ballgown." She spun back around and unzipped it so slowly, I heard every tooth from the zipper one by one.

Footsteps shuffled in behind me. I sensed Kincade halt there. Ophelia shoved the garment bag aside, letting it fall to the floor. I gaped at the gown hanging there. My mouth had gone bone dry.

The strapless emerald-green dress shimmered under the lights, the full skirt dusted with crystals that caught and fractured every movement. Tiny handmade appliqué roses climbed the bodice in an intricate lattice, elegant and unmistakably *not meant for someone like me.*

Behind me, Kincade went very still.

Not breathing still.

"Isn't it magnificent?" Ophelia clapped and bounced again. "I can see you on the dance floor, those crystals catching all the light." In her exuberance, she twirled in a tight circle.

"It's...what did that cost?" I tried to hide the horror in my voice as I eyed the skirt.

"Don't you worry about that. Look at the skirt!" She swished it. The crystals winked in the light. "They're Swarovski crystals. You will be envied!"

Blood whooshed out of my head. Dark pinpricks of light danced in my vision. "I think I need to sit."

Kincade's hand was on my elbow instantly—steady, warm, too aware. He guided me to the nearest chair, his grip lingering a second longer than necessary before he let go.

I sank down, pressing my palms to my temples.

"You don't like it." She sounded devastated.

"I love it, but…" My voice trailed off as I stared at the amazing ball gown.

I didn't belong in that gown any more than a clown belonged at this gala. I was so not a ball gown kind of girl and that was…well, it was way beyond anything I had imagined.

"I got these, too."

Ophelia pulled out full length emerald satin gloves and then boxes of jewelry. I peered at the matching emerald and diamond necklace, earrings, and bracelet and tried not to pass out. The girl was mad. *Mad.* How in the world did she think I was this fancy?

"What do you think?"

She looked so proud of herself it was hard to knock her down a peg. I put on a faint smile.

"It's all amazing."

Her shoulders slumped. She glanced at Kincade, who had been mute the entire time. "She hates it, doesn't she?"

"No." He shook his head and glanced from the gown to me. "I think she has sticker shock."

Ophelia tucked the price tag into the side of the gown. "Don't worry. We'll return it after the gala."

My head snapped up. "Is that…allowed?"

"Just don't bleed on it or anything," Ophelia said. Then she picked up another garment bag and held it out to Kincade. "This is for you."

He stared at it as though it were full of disease. When he refused to move, she rolled her eyes and pulled down the zipper, showing him the black tuxedo inside. He blanched.

A laugh bubbled up my throat.

"Ha! You have to wear a tux!"

His gaze cut to mine—heated, warning, very aware of the irony—before he looked back at Ophelia.

"I'm not wearing that."

"Oh, yes, you are." I jumped to my feet and got right in his space. "You're the one escorting me to this ridiculous, fancy thing." Then I paused and took a step back. "Unless, of course, you prefer it to be Ronan."

He growled, then snatched the garment bag from Ophelia. "Fine."

"You should try that on to make sure it fits. I guessed on your size."

He stalked back to his room and slammed the door.

"Well," I said. "That went well."

Ophelia and I both fell into a fit of laughter.

There was another garment bag lying across the sofa. I nodded to it. "Is that one yours?"

She smiled. "Yes."

She opened it to show me the delicate pink gown inside. Flower-shaped appliqués covered the bodice, cap sleeves, and a tulle skirt. It was the perfect princess gown. Ophelia didn't strike me as a pink princess kind of girl.

"It's lovely," I said. And then I thought about shoes. "I really hope you didn't get heels for me."

She laughed. "No. I found these for you." She pulled a box out of one of the bags and showed me the delicate soft-soled slippers.

I scanned the shoes, the dress, the jewelry. I tried hard not to think about the price tag of all this, but also understood it was necessary.

"Don't worry, Anna. You will look amazing," she said.

"I hope you're right."

And I hoped the vampires and that Grail were going to be there. Like Ronan, I was ready to go home.

⸺⸺⸺

Kincade hadn't emerged from the bedroom since he stomped off with the tux. Ophelia was exhausted after her shopping trip and retired to our shared room to rest. I, meanwhile, sat alone in the small living area watching the sun set outside the terrace trying to ignore the hunger gnawing at my insides.

Ronan returned late into the evening. Fatigue lined his face and deep shadows were under his eyes. He looked like someone had beat him down all day.

But as soon as he walked through the door, he held up his hand with what appeared to be an envelope in his hand. His fatigue turned to triumph. I got to my feet, hope blooming in my breast. He handed me the envelope, which was actually two.

"I called in a lot of favors for those." He headed to the kitchen and grabbed a beer from the fridge.

I examined the shiny gold envelopes. I flipped one over and pulled out the fancy invitation with the script lettering, embossed with the coat of arms of the King of Spain. My heart nearly stopped as I read the invitation. It was our ticket inside.

You and a guest are cordially invited to the King of Spain's 60th birthday gala

"You did it." I glanced up at Ronan who took a swig of his Spanish beer. He moved to sit in the chair across from me. "How?"

"I know people. My father knows people."

Ah, so that was why he looked so beat down. I understood then. His father must have given him hell to pull strings and call in favors for the invitations to the gala.

"It's a shame I have nothing to wear." He leaned back in his chair, running a hand over his face.

"Oh, I wouldn't be too sure about that. I sent Ophelia on a shopping trip today. She returned with formal clothes for all of us."

He shot me an incredulous look. "I have a tuxedo?"

"Yes. She guessed on your size, so you'll want to try it on as soon as possible."

"Shoes, too?"

I nodded. "The whole bit."

Silence stretched between us as he gripped his can in one hand and stared out the terrace at the waning evening light.

"I suppose you'll be going with Kincade," he said, sounding a little despondent.

"I suppose I will."

Because there was nothing on this planet that would keep me from having him escort me to this gala. Not Ronan. Not anyone. I wanted it to be him and no one else.

Ronan gave a slow nod and a small smile. "I understand, of course."

"It's just that—"

"I know." He didn't want or need an explanation. He downed the rest of his beer and rose, trudging to the kitchen. He tossed the can in the trash. "Tomorrow we will need to make a plan for what happens once we go to this gala."

He didn't give me a chance to answer as he walked through to the bedroom he shared with Kincade and disappeared inside.

He was right. We needed a plan for when we arrived at this gala. I had no idea what that was going to be. Yet. I'd think about that tomorrow.

I expelled a breath. Sometimes, it felt like I could not win with either Ronan or Kincade.

I stretched out on the long sofa, crossing my feet at the ankles, and quickly fell to sleep.

CHAPTER 26

I AWOKE TO THE aroma of coffee brewing and bacon frying. It was the single most heavenly scent I'd smelled in days. My stomach approved by the way it growled. Yawing, I sat up on the sofa and eyed the kitchen.

There was Ronan cooking breakfast for the four of us. As if we were in a vacation rental having the time of our lives.

I wished.

I rolled my shoulders, trying to ignore the aches and pains from sleeping on the too-short sofa. I stumbled to my feet and staggered to the kitchen. Ronan poured a cup of coffee and slid it to me along with the creamer.

"You're awesome," I muttered around a yawn.

Moments later, Ophelia made an appearance, yawning and stretching as if she'd had the best night's sleep ever. And she probably had. She had the bed to herself while I snoozed on the sofa.

"Oh, coffee!" Her blue eyes lit up with elation at the sight of the carafe.

Ronan poured her a cup.

"I thought you only drank tea?" I asked, holding the warm mug between my hands. Steam rose over my face, giving me a sense of comfort I hadn't felt in a long while.

"I like tea. But I also enjoy coffee." She sipped the black brew. No sugar. No creamer. Nothing.

"You drink it black?" I asked, shocked.

"Yep." She flashed a smile.

"Psycho."

She giggled.

Ronan then slid a plate piled high with bacon onto the counter between us. "Hands off until the eggs and toast are done."

"But—"

"Hands off, Anna."

"Fine." I pouted, eyeing the crispy pork. My mouth watered.

Kincade made his entrance then looking grumpy as ever. His brow was furrowed. He gave off an unapproachable vibe.

"There's coffee," I said, sounding more chipper than I had intended.

He scowled. Ronan handed him a mug full of the steaming brew. I decided at that moment Ronan was our personal barista and loved it. Kincade took the mug in his hand, dwarfing the porcelain cup in his large hand.

"The gala is tomorrow." Kincade said what was on all our minds.

I tried not to think about the gala as the future place of my death.

"Yes, and I have things to do today to prepare for that," Ronan replied.

I cocked my head to the side. "Like?"

"We need to stay in contact. I will get us all earpieces. Ophelia and I will arrive as a couple," Ronan replied. "You and Kincade will arrive first."

"You already have this planned?" I asked.

"Somewhat. Kincade and I discussed last night."

Surprise swooped through me. I glanced at the brooding Kincade, who stood there stony faced. I reached out with my mind. *You did?*

His gaze met mine, but his face remained impassive. *We did.*

He did not elaborate, which left me frustrated and annoyed.

Ronan scooped scrambled eggs on a serving plate and put it on the kitchen bar right in front of me and Ophelia. Kincade brooded in the terrace doorway.

"We will stagger our arrivals," he continued. "Anna, you and Kincade scope out the room. Ophelia and I will enter the gala after you. We will look for anyone who appears to be out of place."

"Anyone like Barnabas?" I asked, eyeing the bacon. "He'll be the one wearing the crushed velvet with lace at his wrists and throat. That's his signature style."

Ronan gave a go-ahead nod. I snagged a piece.

"Who's Barnabas again?" Ophelia asked, perplexed.

"He's the vampire dude who we think has the Holy Grail." I munched on the perfect piece of bacon, content with the crispiness.

"Right."

"Once we know who all the players are, we'll be able to make our move," Ronan said.

"My assumption is Azriel will be there," I said.

"Which is why your life is in jeopardy," Ronan added.

Ophelia's head snapped around to me. It was a piece of information I had left out when I told her the story.

"Why is your life in jeopardy?"

I started to reply but Ronan beat me to it. "I foresaw her death at the gala."

"And you didn't think to tell me this?" she asked.

"She didn't want to upset you." Kincade moved from his position at the terrace and entered the kitchen area. He reached over me to swipe a piece of bacon.

I got a whiff of his sandalwood scent and felt the warmth of his body near mine. My heart skipped. I managed to keep myself in check and not react to how close he stood.

"It would have been nice to have all the information," Ophelia said.

"I'm sorry I didn't tell you. It didn't cross my mind because it's not going to happen." I gave Ronan a pointed look.

"No, it's not," Kincade agreed.

A warmth bloomed in my chest at the certainty in his voice. I had no doubt in my mind he, Ronan, and Ophelia would do whatever they had to do to keep me safe. Kincade seemed to have conceded to work with Ronan in the endeavor.

"Which is why I have preparations to make. And Ophelia has more shopping to do. My tuxedo didn't fit. I need a different size."

She beamed, excited at the opportunity to shop again. The two of them headed to the bedroom. Ophelia emerged a moment later with the garment bag, gave a jaunty wave, and was out the door. Minutes after that, Ronan made his exit.

Leaving me and Kincade alone. Again.

How did this keep happening?

He walked around to the kitchen and helped himself to a plate of eggs and a heaping portion of bacon. I was content to munch on another single piece. I watched him as he doused his eggs with hot sauce. He paused with the fork halfway to his mouth.

"You have questions," he said.

I pondered. I did, but I wasn't sure how to ask it. Instead, I shrugged and flashed a smile. It was better than saying anything he'd detect as a lie.

"Spill." He spoke around a mouthful.

"You told me you didn't trust Ronan."

"I don't."

"Yet you two had a discussion about the gala."

"Your point?"

"I thought you didn't like him."

"I still don't. And I don't like sharing a room with him. He snores."

I stifled a giggle. "Then I for sure don't want to marry him if he snores." And then I idly wondered if Kincade snored.

He put down the plate that was already half empty. "I don't snore."

Curse him and his mind reading abilities.

"How would you know? You're *sleeping*."

"I just know." He didn't elaborate.

I lifted a brow and decided I didn't want to know how he knew because it was likely going to be an answer I didn't like. I didn't want to think about another woman with him anymore than he wanted to think about me marrying Ronan.

"As much as I dislike the guy, it's best if we work together instead of against each other," he said.

"I bet that pained you to say that," I quipped.

"You have *no* idea."

Oh, I had a pretty good idea. Kincade struck me as the kind of guy who didn't like to share. Somewhere along the way, he'd decided he was my guardian and no one else would do.

He'd decided he was the only one able to protect me from whatever Lucifer threw at me. Maybe even from the coming war between the dark lord and mankind.

And he seemed to have relaxed some after we had our discussion about Ronan, the kiss that wasn't my idea and the fact I was going to find a way to get out of marrying the guy.

I'd also been thinking about the seed Kincade had planted about the Grail. If it wasn't in the vamps' hands, then where was the real one?

"I hope you're ready for this gala, Anna."

I took a deep breath, expelled it. "Me, too."

Because I really didn't know what to expect. That scared me.

The only thing I was looking forward to about this gala was seeing Kincade in a tux. The thought gave me warm fuzzies all over.

After he washed and put away his plate, he headed for the door.

"Where are you going?" I demanded.

I hadn't left the hotel room since we arrived. Mostly because I suspected my face on wanted posters were plastered all over the place. I didn't need that kind of trouble.

"I have recon to do."

And then he was gone.

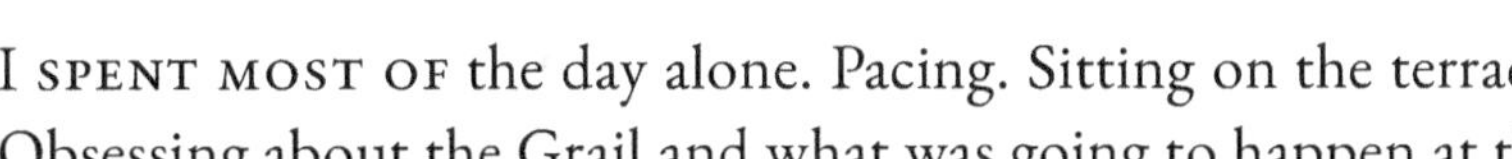

I spent most of the day alone. Pacing. Sitting on the terrace. Obsessing about the Grail and what was going to happen at the gala.

Ophelia returned first with Ronan's exchanged tuxedo. She yawned and headed to the bedroom. Ronan was next armed with wireless earbuds that were so small, they fit inside the ear and were practically invisible. After explaining to me how it worked, he then grabbed a beer and headed to the other bedroom.

Dusk settled and finally Kincade returned. He stepped out onto the terrace and took the seat across from me, stretching out his long legs and crossing them at the ankle. His expression was serious. I instantly sensed something was wrong.

"I have news," he said at last.

"Oh?"

"You aren't going to like it."

I clenched my jaw, preparing for the worst. "What is it?"

"Russia has launched an invasion of Eastern Europe. They think President Ivanov's intent is to recreate the USSR." His mouth flattened into a thin line. There was more he wasn't telling me.

A cold fear trickled through me. "And...?"

"Ivanov has a new military advisor that quickly rose through the ranks, gained his trust, and is now the one calling the shots."

He paused. I waited. Acid churned in my gut.

"This new advisor," Kincade continued, "is Conquest."

I swallowed the fear that clotted my throat. "You know this for a fact?"

"I saw the papers. He's pictured with the president. Bright blue eyes and pale blond hair."

Conquest, it seemed, worked quickly to gain Nikolai Ivanov's trust. The last time we saw the horseman was when he'd shot Kincade with the arrow.

He must have been thinking of it, too, because he reached up and brushed a hand over his shoulder.

"How is it healing?" I asked, trying hard not to think about the fact that one of the Four Horseman of the Apocalypse had started a war.

"The stitches are slowly dissolving. I'll live."

We lapsed into silence, the only sound that of the breeze rusting the trees. I clutched my elbows to ward off a shiver.

"If Conquest helped start that, then…" I let my words trail off.

"I think we both know what happens next."

I met his level gaze, afraid to ask the question though I already had the answer. "And what is that?"

"We should expect to see the second horseman."

War riding the red horse.

"Also," Kincade continued, "the pandemic is no longer contained to India. It's spread through the Middle East. There are talks about travel bans from the bigger countries."

If that happened, then getting home would be damn near impossible. "The US and the UK?"

He nodded.

Which made recovering the Holy Grail even more important. We had to get home before travel was restricted.

"There's more."

"More?" I didn't like the sound of this. My gut churned hot.

"A few African countries' economies have collapsed. They have no way to feed their people."

"So, what you're telling me is," I began, choosing my words slowly. "Not only should we expect to see the second horseman, but the third as well."

"Yes."

Conquest.

War.

Famine.

I understood what this meant. Just as I understood who the fourth horseman was.

Death.

CHAPTER 27

THE BIG DAY ARRIVED. I didn't sleep a wink after Kincade and I had our conversation. I laid awake on the sofa, staring out the terrace doors waiting for sunrise. When I closed my eyes, sleep would not come.

Meanwhile, everyone else seemed to have no problem sleeping.

It was going to take more than a pot of coffee to keep me going.

Ophelia was a driving force, though. I didn't have time to let fatigue hit me. When she got up that morning, she ushered me into the shower. Apparently, she had big plans for my appearance, which terrified me. Even more scary was she didn't want to share what she had in mind.

I exited the bathroom with a towel wrapped around me, my damp hair still dripping on my shoulders. She frowned.

"What?" It was hard not to sound defensive.

"We have some work to do." She motioned to the dining chair she'd pulled into the room. "Sit."

"What are you going to do to me?"

"I'm going to turn you into a princess." She flashed a smile.

I didn't want that. But I sat anyway.

Ophelia went to work. First, she pulled my damp hair back and stuck it on top of my head. Then she began the long and arduous task of applying makeup to my face.

I nearly fled the room.

But I remained where I was for her. She took her time with the makeup sponge, applying first the base and then the translucent powder. She gave me instructions along the way as she did my cheeks, eyes, and brows. As if I'd do my own makeup. I almost snorted. When she handed me a mirror, I didn't recognize myself.

She'd given me a smokey eye in greens and blues which complimented my skin tone. I stared at my face for the longest time, trying to recall the last time I stopped long enough to put on makeup, I couldn't remember.

"Well?" she asked, sounding hopeful.

"I look...different."

"Different? That's all you got?"

"I don't own makeup, Ophelia. This is very different for me."

She nodded then. "I understand. You're amazing. Wait until Kincade sees you."

My heart nearly stopped. "Did you do this for *him*?"

"No, of course not. I did it for *you*. Because you can't go wearing cargo pants and a Henley looking like something dragged out of a sewer."

"Hey!"

"Well? Am I wrong?"

My shoulders slumped. "No."

"That's what I thought. You are going to outshine anyone else." She beamed.

"I think the idea here is that I blend in with everyone else."

"Oh, you will. But that dress is going to a real showstopper."

Something in my gut twisted. The last thing I wanted was to be a showstopper. I didn't need to call more attention to myself than I already did. I was a wanted criminal. I was sure Ophelia missed the point of this whole ordeal.

But looking at her beaming face, there was nothing to say about it. I had to go along with it. I had to keep my mouth shut.

Glancing at my face in the mirror again, I wondered what Kincade would think. Not that I cared what he thought. I didn't.

Who was I kidding? Yes, I did.

"Time to do your hair."

She produced a hair dryer and a whole lot of hair pins. I was terrified just looking at them. She quickly went to work without waiting for me to answer. After putting a mound of mousse in her palm, she spread it through my damp locks. Then she dried it and pulled it back into a low ponytail, then twisted and turned my hair, stabbing my head with all the hairpins. I called her a masochist and she told me to hush. Finally, she achieved the style she wanted—a perfectly coifed chignon. Made more interesting by the two strips of white hair at my temples. The white appeared in my hair after I had a visit with Michael, the archangel.

I was stunned at my reflection. This was certainly not *me*.

"What do you think?" she asked.

"I think you should be a hairstylist."

She beamed.

While I thought her handiwork was pretty spectacular, I had a feeling my hair and makeup would not be long for this world.

Then she said the words that nearly sent me to my grave.

"Now let's get you into this dress. We don't have much time and I still have to dress."

I wanted to faint.

I didn't deserve as dress like the one she'd bought for me. I stood and allowed her to help me into it. She zipped up the back. It fit like it was made just for me. The skirt swished to and fro from what seemed like miles and miles *and miles* of petticoats. The crystals winked in the light of the room. I was afraid to sit in it. I slid my foot into the slippers she'd bought and for a moment, I did feel like a princess. But, like Cinderella, I was afraid the spell would break at midnight.

Then came the jewelry. A diamond and emerald necklace, matching chandelier earrings, the upper length gloves, and the bracelet. It was really all too much.

"Oh, Anna—"

"No gushing," I said, cutting her off. The last thing I needed was her telling me how beautiful I was.

I understood who I was and beautiful was never on that list. Somewhat attractive? Sure.

She pressed her lips together as she bit off whatever compliment she'd readied. "Fine. Then you look adequate. Does that work?"

"Yes, thanks."

She disappeared into the bathroom, leaving me alone and wondering what the hell I was supposed to do in a ten-thousand-dollar dress.

So, I did what I thought I needed to do. I drew down my jade-handled dagger, found my holster and rigged a way to strap it to my left thigh. I was not leaving without it. And it gave me some comfort to know the weapon was on my person instead of hiding in the cloud. If I had a way to conceal my uncle's sword, I'd carry that, too.

Ophelia appeared moments after I'd finished hiding the dagger. Her face was done, her hair in soft waves about her shoulders and she was dressed in the perfect pink gown. If anyone was a princess, it was definitely her not me. I smiled.

"You look wonderful."

"Too bad Darius can't see you now."

She blushed, her cheeks turning bright pink. "Thanks. And it's time for us to leave. I hope you don't mind, but I took the liberty of hiring a limo."

My eyebrows rose. "You hired a limo?"

"You paid for it, of course."

"Of course."

A sharp knock on the door, then Kincade's gruff voice. "How long does it take you two to get ready? We have to go."

I almost laughed. Ophelia and I exchanged a grin. She whisked open the door and exited first. I followed, trying to walk with miles and miles of skirt swishing around my legs. It wasn't easy and I was typically a klutz.

This should go well.

I stepped out of the bedroom, fussing with the oversized skirt as I made my way across the hotel room. I tried really hard not to notice Kincade's stare. But I stole a glance anyway and glimpsed his obvious examination and approval.

"We don't have all night. Let's go," I barked.

I didn't want to notice how handsome Kincade was in his tuxedo. It might turn my knees to water. Besides, I needed to keep calm and act the same as I always did—with my no-care attitude.

I flung open the door and exited without waiting for them to follow. Kincade must have exited next. He was at my side in an instant. My heart—my stupid heart—beat so hard I was sure he heard it. The rustle of Ophelia's skirts swished behind us. Her footsteps and Ronan's were silent on the hallway carpet.

It was the longest, most uncomfortable walk down the hall I'd ever had. Kincade said nothing. I said nothing. We made our way downstairs and to the front of the hotel where the limo waited for us outside.

I managed to stumble my way into the car, holding up my glittering skirts and cursing Ophelia for buying something so extravagant. I feared I was going to lose crystals as I pushed the voluminous skirts underneath me and sat. Kincade, of course, sat next to me. Ronan and Ophelia took the seats opposite us.

She was stunning in her pink gown. He was rather handsome in his black tux with the shiny pinstripes down the sides of the pants. His black shoes were polished to a high shine. Under the suit jacket, he wore a white shirt, black bow tie and cummerbund and silver cufflinks. He was the perfect prince to her princess.

I finally braved a glance at Kincade. My heart nearly stopped. He, too, was dressed in black tux. His pants were pressed with a perfect crease down the front of each leg. Like Ronan's, the sides of his pants boasted a shiny pinstripe in glossy black. I wasn't certain, but I thought his waistcoat had tails. His white shirt was neatly pressed and his bow tie perfectly tied. And, also like Ronan, he wore silver cufflinks.

But the thing that struck me the most was he was clean shaven. I hadn't seen him clean shaven in a while. He seemed to prefer to keep the growth of beard going for that scruffy, rough and ready look. Which I much preferred. Though it was hard not to admire how bloody hot he looked with that smooth face.

Ronan, however, was all business. He handed us both an earpiece.

"Put this in. We will connect via our cell phones."

I flushed hot. "Um, I don't have mine."

A sour expression crossed Ronan's face. "How are we supposed to stay in contact?"

I waved to the bodice of the dress. "Where the hell am I supposed to keep a cell phone in this thing?"

He pinpointed Kincade with his sharp gaze. "Did you bring yours?"

Kincade spread his hands as if in surrender. "Sorry. I don't carry one."

A flicker of annoyance went over Ronan's face. Kincade had let him believe, wrongly, he was a cell phone kind of guy. He was so far from that. I started carrying one when my uncle made me. I was hard not to have sympathy for Ronan. He was, after all, trying to keep me out of harm's way. It occurred to me then the folly in Ronan's plan. I probably should have curtailed it, but I'd been thinking only about how to recover the Grail and not dying.

"Then why did I waste my money and time on these earpieces?" Ronan asked of no one in particular.

"It's fine," I said, trying to diffuse the situation. "We'll figure it out once we arrive."

"The whole point of the earpieces was to be able to stay in contact." Ronan sat back in the seat, the leather squeaking with his movement.

"Change of plan, then. We don't need to stay in contact," Kincade said. "I'll be at Anna's side. You and Ophelia will be right behind us. You said something happens to her here, so make sure nothing happens to her."

"Easier said than done since I have no idea where the threat is coming from. I will do my best."

"See that you do," Kincade said.

I stiffened at Kincade's words. The tension between the two of them was thick. I put a hand on his wrist.

"No need to get testy," I said. "Whatever is going to happen is going to happen. There isn't much we can do to stop it. Let's just hope we find the Grail without an incident."

"I don't think it will be that easy, Anna," Ronan said.

Nor did I but I didn't want to say that out loud. Instead, I remained silent the remainder of the ride. Ronan stashed the earpieces in his pocket, a grim expression on his face.

The limo pulled to a halt outside the Royal Palace. The driver parked and got out to open the door for us. Ronan exited first, then turned to help Ophelia. Then it was Kincade followed by me. He held a hand down to help me step out of the car. I was reluctant to take it but forced myself because I didn't want to trip over the gown and fall flat on my face on the pavement.

I tried not to notice how his fingers tightened over my gloved ones. I gathered the skirt of the gown in my other hand and took a tentative step out of the car. His hand squeezed mine to keep me steady. With two feet flat on the ground, I rose to my full height. But he didn't release me. I lifted my head to gaze up at him as he was a head taller than me. Our eyes met. My heart thudded. Something tender and soft was in his gaze that nearly ripped me in half. I was conflicted. Something I didn't want to acknowledge was there. Something I *wanted* desperately to be there.

Finally, he released my hand and we all walked toward the front of the Royal Palace with the giant double doors. My heart was in my throat as we paused at the door to show our tickets to the guards. They gave us a nod, welcomed us, and waved us through. Probably wondering who we were to garner an invitation to the king's birthday.

We entered the lobby of the palace and were directed to the banquet hall through the main corridor with the most hideous red and gold patterned carpet I'd ever seen. Two sets of stairs on either side of the enormous hall lead up to the landing where most of the guests gathered.

Gripping a handful of skirt, I headed up the grand staircase, grateful the steps were not that steep. Kincade remained at my side, matching me stride for stride and keeping close. I suspected to lend a hand if he thought I was going to trip and fall. It was likely, after all.

At the top of the stairs, we were directed to the ball room where there was dancing until dinner, which would be held in the state dining room across from the ballroom. I took a glance that direction. The long table was set and servants bustled about to prepare for the formal dinner.

We stepped inside the entrance of the ballroom, moving to the side. Ophelia and Ronan remained a few steps behind us. I took a deep breath and gazed out at the ballroom with all the beautiful rich people mingling and dancing and looking glitzy and glamourous and tried not to feel like an utter fraud.

I did not belong here with all the beautiful people of Spain.

Kincade's overbearing presence helped. Knowing he was right next to me gave me a semblance of confidence.

"I feel ridiculous."

I shifted from one foot to the other. The list of times I'd wore a dress this fancy was zero and never. I didn't fit in this world. I would never fit in this world. I pushed a tendril of hair off my forehead. The three-inch wide diamond and emerald bracelet on my right wrist winked in the light of the overhead chandelier.

He leaned close to me, his heated breath whispering over my exposed ear as he spoke. "You look magnificent. Stop fidgeting."

My cheeks heated. The blush crept up from the depths of my soul. Kincade was not one to hand out compliments, so I was flattered.

"Thanks," I muttered.

I wanted to tell him how good he looked but everything sounded so ridiculous and silly. I couldn't bring myself to say the words aloud.

He held out his elbow to me. I glanced up, saw a twinkle in those green-gold eyes that threatened to buckle my knees.

"Are you ready?" He punctuated that with a cocky grin.

It was in that moment my feelings for Kincade went beyond anything I had ever felt for anyone before. My heart fluttered. My stomach bottomed out. Heat flashed through my entire body as I slipped my satin-encased hand on his tuxedoed arm.

"As I'll ever be."

But, deep down, I wasn't.

"Then into the fire we go."

He wasn't wrong about that. It certainly felt like we were headed into the fiery cauldron of Spain's rich and famous. He took the first step into the room, pulling me with him. And for a moment, I thought I might hurl.

Instead, I took the steps with him, my slippered feet silent on the floor. He propelled us into the room, melding with the other guests as though we were meant for that place. But we both knew better.

On one side of the enormous room, a small six-piece orchestra played a familiar classical tune. A few men and women remained on the side of the room, as if it were in style to be a wallflower. Somewhere embroiled in a deep conversation. Others gazed longing out at the dance floor tapping their foot to the tune. Everyone was dressed in their best formal attire.

But Kincade and I weren't there to dance the night away and moon over each other. We were on a mission to recover the Holy Grail.

I spied Ophelia and Ronan following us. He took her in his arms. She appeared to fit nicely against his taller frame as he whisked her into the waltz. Meanwhile, Kincade said nothing as he stepped onto the dance floor. I sucked in a sharp breath through my nose.

"Are you crazy?" I said it through gritted teeth. Panic flooded me. "I don't know how to dance."

"Just follow my lead."

With his catlike movements, he turned onto the floor and took me into his arms. He planted one hand firmly at my waist. I tried hard to ignore his heated palm through the material of the gown.

"Hand on shoulder, Anna." His voice was quiet, intimate between us.

I flushed hot again as I reached up and placed my left hand on his broad shoulder. He pulled me close and I was thankful for the voluminous skirt to give space between us. The pulse in my neck pounded so hard, I was sure he saw it. He held my right hand in his left and then we were on the dance floor, my eyes plastered on his feet.

This was the closest we had ever been. My heart beat hard and fast. It was hard not to inhale his clean scent. He smelled so damn good.

"Chin up," he said.

I tilted my head up and met his gaze and something twisted deep in my gut. I understood then why dancing was so intimate and how a woman could easily get swept off her feet. Kincade moved me at will around the dance floor. I stumbled over every other step stepping on the edge of the gown.

"You really are bad at this, Anna." A hint of a smile flickered over his face.

"And you're perfect," I blurted. Oh, hell. Where did that come from? I hoped he took it as sarcasm.

He lifted an eyebrow. "I do try."

"You're also cocky."

"And you're maddening," he retorted.

But still he had a hint of a smile. His gaze flickered to my lips. Panic welled inside me as my heart fluttered. I knew that look all too well. But he lifted his gaze once again to mine. Even so, heated desire flashed through me.

The way he regarded me, the way he held me as we danced, the way his physique filled out that five-thousand-dollar tuxedo made me wish—*wish hard*—that he would kiss me.

And I hated myself for that.

His hand was warm at my back. Steady. Certain.

This was the man I trusted with my life.

Which made wanting him like this the most dangerous thing of all.

No, I wasn't ready to acknowledge the warmth stirring deep inside me—or the quiet, dangerous intimacy humming between us.

He pulled the hand he held close to him, clutching it against his chest. The wild pounding of his heart did not escape my notice.

Fuck all.

"Anna." He said my name on a breath.

"Yes?" I whispered.

His gaze dropped again to my lips. An almost hopeful glint pierced his eyes. An unexpected anticipation shimmered through me. And I wanted to shout for him to *do it already*. Because all I thought about was that dream walk where we'd kissed. My imagination ran wild with what his mouth would actually feel like on mine.

His head dipped. I was ready. His mouth was close to mine. So close.

And then, all hell broke loose.

CHAPTER 28

THE SOUND OF BREAKING glass interrupted our romantic interlude. That followed by a shriek or two. We broke apart and spun to face the noise. Ophelia was at my side in an instant. I sensed Ronan behind me. Like my posse had gone into super protective mode. My adrenaline kicked into high gear, my mind already trying to figure out a way to reach the dagger strapped to my thigh.

Everyone on our end of the room stopped and gaped toward the sound of breaking glass. But I didn't see anything other than a servant girl blushing furiously as she kneeled to pick up a tray of broken glasses. Another servant shooed her away to clean up the mess she'd left behind. She turned and hurried from the giant ballroom looking as though she was about burst into tears. Poor thing.

"Well, that was exhilarating," I said.

I pressed a hand against my racing heart, realizing how much Ronan's dire warning of imminent death got to me.

"Exhilarating? It nearly gave me heart failure," Ophelia said.

Kincade's hand was on my elbow, ready to lead me into another dance. Ophelia and Ronan melted in with the rest of the crowd. I lost sight of her blonde head as they blended in with the others.

"You're jumpy," Kincade said.

"And you're not?" I pressed my lips together in a frown.

"Just because Ronan said something was going to happen here doesn't mean it will."

He had a point, but I still wasn't convinced all was well. "I don't want to dance anymore."

I slipped away from him. I needed distance and to think about what almost happened. He was going to kiss me. I was going to let him. And then what? Would our relationship change because we actually, finally lip locked in real life? I was terrified of that. I didn't want anything to change between us. I liked our standoffish relationship just fine.

But he fell in step beside me. "Where are you going?"

"I need some air. You don't have to babysit me."

I had no clue where I was headed. I was out of the ballroom and into the hallway. My gaze landed on the grand staircase and I veered toward it.

"I'm coming with you," he said.

It took some serious restraint to not tell him to back off.

I wanted out of this dress. I felt as though I was suffocating. And the fact he was so close to me, sucking all the air around the two of us did not help. I started for the stairs, holding my gown up so I wouldn't trip. As I took the first few steps, the vampires ascended in their perfect, elegant gait.

Barnabas and his two vampire cronies. The head vampire lord was dressed in his signature crushed velvet—a deep navy-blue jacket and pants, white shirt with lace at the wrists and throat. Like he'd stepped out of another century and didn't care if anyone thought he looked ridiculous. I admired his bold fashion choices. The other two were dressed in a more contemporary tuxedo.

I halted. Kincade halted next to me. He put his feet shoulder-width apart, ready for a rumble. We both blocked the staircase and waited. Barnabas paused several steps below me, looking up at me with a coy smile.

"We meet again. Would you care to search me?" He held out his arms from his side. The other two laughed.

"Where is it?" I demanded.

"Where is what?" His innocence made me irate.

"The Grail."

He held up his hand and glanced over his nails. "I'm afraid, miss, I've no idea what you're talking about."

"Yes, you do."

I started down the stairs, but Kincade caught my arm and held me in place. My head whipped around to tell him off when I glimpsed the warning in his eyes. He gave a nod with his chin, a silent signal for me to turn around and look.

Behind Barnabas and company heading up the stairs was Azriel, Astrid and a few other lesser demons. I inhaled. Their unmistakable scent clung to the air. Azriel's was cinnamon. The demons were death and rot. Quite a contrast for the olfactory senses.

Azriel and his sister were dressed in formal attire. The demons not so much, but I suspected normal humans wouldn't be able to see them since they tended to hide behind a glamour. Astrid wore a tight-fitting black gown covered in sequins with a scooped neckline. Azriel wore a tux. His wings weren't visible which meant he had them hidden with his demon magic. He had his hand clamped around Astrid's wrist, dragging her along beside him.

Barnabas moved to the side to allow Azriel to halt next to him. There was no doubting the way his lusty gaze raked over me from head to toe, an appreciative smile on his wide face. I hated him all the more.

"My, my, *chérie*. What a delight you are. You are absolutely stunning."

My hands clenched into tight fists. I itched to snatch my dagger but since it wasn't ladylike to pull up your skirts in the middle of everything, I refrained.

"I don't give a shit what you think," I said. "Where is the Grail?"

He laughed. "You think it's that easy?" He paused, cutting a glance at Kincade. I didn't miss the way he scrutinized him before he returned his attention back to me. "Tsk, tsk, my dear."

The man was infuriating. I realized it wasn't that easy, but I also realized it was worth a shot to ask. I glanced at Barnabas wondering where he'd stashed the Grail. If he and Azriel were converging here together, did that mean someone else had the cup?

Astrid refused to meet my gaze. There was something different about her. She appeared as though Azriel beat her into submission. And I hated that for her. Her stint at his hands in Hell must have changed her, deeply, and not for the better.

I tried not to let the guilt consume me for leaving her there, for breaking my promise to Killian.

"Step aside, *chérie*. We have important work to do here."

"I'm not going to let you harm these people."

Astrid lifted her gaze to mine. A little spark of life flickered in the depths of her gaze.

"Whatever makes you think I would do something like that?" Horror crossed his face at the thought. "Come then, Lord Barnabas. There is another staircase."

The group of them headed back the down the stairs. My heart rammed hard as I turned to Kincade, about to ask him what to do next but he was already moving.

"We'll cut them off."

He took the stairs back up two at a time. I followed, cursing the damn gown the entire time. We waited on the landing. Ophelia and Ronan popped out of the ballroom. Her cheeks were flushed. Panic creased her face. Relief swept over her when she found me.

"There you are! We were worried."

But my focus was on Barnabas, Azriel, and Astrid.

"Ah, so you brought the paladin and the demon killer with you," Azriel said when he spotted them next to us.

Meanwhile in the ballroom, the music never stopped. The dancers continued to twirl. Behind us the clank of dishes indicated servants setting the table for the coming feast.

I kept my gaze on Astrid, who seemed to perk a little more the closer they got. Azriel had not released her wrist as he pulled her along. Her eyes flickered from Ronan, to Ophelia, to Kincade, and finally to me. Almost as if she realized she finally had a way out from her current hell.

I had to help her. I may never have another chance.

"You really are making this more difficult than it has to be," Azriel said to me.

"It doesn't have to be difficult. Hand over the Grail and we'll call it day," I said.

He chuckled. "You speak as though I have it."

"You don't, but your vampire buddy does." I thumbed to Mr. Fancy Pants.

Barnabas shook his head. "I'm afraid you are mistaken. I didn't have it on the train and I don't have it now. Wherever did you get that idea?"

I stood there, frozen, thinking back to my dream walk of the vampire thief. There was no way I got it wrong. I never got it wrong. The vampire handed it over to Barnabas. They talked about going to Madrid to meet the high lord for the exchange.

What the fuck is going on? Kincade asked in my head. *I thought you said he had it.*

I had no clue. *I did say that. Something isn't right here.*

"She's clearly confused, my lord." One of the vampire lackeys spoke up. "She saw Silvan steal it out from under the Pope's nose, but she has no idea what happened to it after that. She merely guesses."

I wasn't guessing. I *knew.* I *saw.*

I clenched my hands so tight, my nails dug into my palms. My patience snapped. My temper flared. I'd had it with these jokers. Since it was too difficult to get to my dagger, I reached for the next best thing. I drew down my uncle's flaming sword. The orange and white light flamed bright as I took a stance, holding it in front of me ready to do battle.

"What do you think you're doing?" Kincade said through gritted teeth.

"Damn. Why didn't you tell me to bring my sword?" Ophelia's fingers twitched, as though she wished she had the forethought to bring it. "Oh, wait! I did." She produced her own shimmering sword from the cloud, a bright grin on her face.

Next to me, Kincade heaved a sigh.

"Fuck all. If the ladies are going rogue, we may as well join the party, Ronan." He palmed his demon killing gun, pulling it from the waistband of his pants.

Impressive. I never realized he brought it.

"We may as well," he agreed. Lightning danced between Ronan's fingers.

Shit was about to get all the way real.

Azriel's grip tightened on Astrid. "Show them what you can do, dearest."

I gripped the sword tighter in my hands. Astrid was a time warper. She had the ability to alter time and space. All she had to do was use a little bit of her magic to wipe out everything that had happened since she arrived.

Before anyone moved, the shadowy veil separating the humans from demons shimmered around us, blocking us off from any prying human eyes. I stiffened, glancing around looking for who might be responsible for the veil.

He ascended the stairs with a smooth, fluid grace. His back was ramrod straight. His face was upturned to the group of us standing on the landing. He wore a tuxedo like the others, his shiny black hair slicked back from his angular face. He had a strong nose, square jaw, high cheekbones, prefect arched brows, and sharp assessing eyes the color of honey.

I took a deep breath. Aside from the cinnamon smell Azriel always exuded, I scented undertones of vanilla. Kincade immediately turned his demon killing gun on the man as he arrived at the top step and paused. A smile stretched his thin lips.

"I'm late to the party, I see." His voice was deep and mellifluous. "Put away your weapons."

"Who the hell are you?" I demanded.

"Oh, Anna. You dazzle me."

He walked toward me with his fluid grace. He paused right in front of me, unconcerned about the flaming sword in front of his face. The firelight flickered over his features. My breath caught in my throat as he placed a hand on my wrist.

Kincade went into protective mode and shoved the muzzle of his gun against the guy's temple. "Touch her again and you die."

He lifted his hand off my wrist and put both up in surrender. "Hello, Kincade. It's good to see you again."

"Kincade, who the fuck is this?" I demanded.

Hadrian. High lord like your buddy here, but far more dangerous.

I wasn't afraid of dangerous. I'd offed Mammon and Abaddon.

Azriel gave the high lord a look of disdain. "Nice of you to join us. Your presence is unexpected."

Everything about this situation was wrong. Fear pumped a wild beat through me, making my senses stand on high alert. I hadn't felt this way in a long while. Kincade said Hadrian was a high lord and more dangerous than Azriel. Had to admit the worry gnawed at me trying to stay one step ahead of him. I wasn't good at mental chess or any other chess for that matter.

"I pop up in the least expected places."

Hadrian flashed a grin, gave a jaunty wave, and headed into the ballroom. The veil followed him. I wasn't about to let him out of my sight. I stumbled over my skirt but managed to keep my footing as I followed him into the room.

Suddenly, the room spun in a whirling flash of color and motion. My stomach bottomed out. The sword disappeared from my hands. My mind turned fuzzy. Everything was a blur. But then I was in Kincade's arms waltzing across the dance floor. He held me tight, his hand on my waist. His other hand clutching mine against his chest over the frantic beating of his heart.

My gaze was pinned on his as our feet moved together in flawless time to the music. While it seemed as though it were a moment of perfection, something was off. Ophelia and Ronan danced away, brushing by us. I caught her pink perfect gown flutter by out of the corner of my eye.

"Anna." Kincade said my name on a breath.

A ferocious case of déjà vu overwhelmed me. My fingers dug into his shoulder as I tried to understand, to make my fuzzy mind remember. Why did it seem as though we'd done this before?

"Yes?"

His gaze dropped to my lips. His head lowered. I tipped my head back. It was the moment I had waited and hoped for with prolonged anticipation. I held my breath. My eyes fluttered closed.

He stiffened and came to a jarring halt in the middle of the ballroom.

"We've done this before."

I blinked my eyes open and focused on his face. His green-gold eyes, sharp and assessing, surveyed the room. Searching for something or someone. I searched, too. Couples whirled around us, seemingly oblivious to our stillness. There was Ophelia and Ronan dancing, looking cozy and happy as they clung to each other. As blissful as they appeared, my brain rejected the sight. It wasn't right. Ophelia liked someone else. But who? And why couldn't I remember?

Frustration edged through me.

I scanned the crowd again. There! I sucked in a sharp breath. The vampire in the blue crushed velvet mingling through the assemblage along the walls. And then Azriel, exhibiting a sort of smugness. The dark-haired man with the cat-like grace named Hadrian. And Astrid.

I gasped. It came back to me in a flood. The dancing, the almost kissing, the trying to push air into my lungs but instead running into vampires and high lords on the grand staircase.

"Astrid! She time warped us!"

Kincade disengaged from me. I tried not to be disappointed about that. "Where is she?"

"With Azriel and the new guy. Over there." I nodded toward the other side of the room.

Kincade said nothing as he charged through the crowd toward them.

I needed to attract Ophelia's attention. I pushed my way past dancers, stepping on my gown and cursing its length. When I got to her, I shoved between her and Ronan and took her by the shoulders.

"Anna, have you lost your mind? Ronan and I were—"

"Darius. You're in love with Darius. I'm pretty sure he's in love with you, too. He's waiting for you back at Walker Manor." I gave her a little shake to jar the memory loose.

She shook her head, her brows drawn together. "Darius? Who is—"

"The warrior angel. Now, snap out of it. I need you and that shimmering sword."

She stared at me for a long moment as though I'd grown a horn out of my forehead. Then, she shook her head. Clarity came back into her bright blue eyes. She sucked in a sharp breath.

"What happened?"

"Astrid happened." I cut Ronan a glance. He had two fingers pressed to his forehead as if he had a splitting headache. I reached for him, put a hand on his shoulder. "You all right?"

"Yes, but I feel something dreadful is about to happen." His head snapped up. "You need to leave this place, Anna."

And that's when all hell *really* broke loose.

CHAPTER 29

KINCADE BRANDISHED HIS GUN and fired toward the two high lords. I thought he aimed for Azriel but no. He aimed for Astrid. Even from this distance, the high-pitched whine of his gun pierced the air. The flash of light followed. Astrid yelped, jerking her left shoulder backward. She stumbled back away from Azriel, who had finally released her wrist from his death grip.

Screams erupted in the ballroom. Chaos ensued as people stampeded for the one and only exit. But only a few were able to escape when the doors abruptly slammed shut. Those at the door tried the handles but it was no use. We were sealed inside.

Lightning flickered between Ronan's fingers. Ophelia drew down her shimmering sword from the cloud. I reached for my uncle's and readied it, flames and all.

That magical veil came down in the ballroom, hiding us from the humans. Hadrian walked toward me with slow, stealthy steps, ignoring Kincade and his gun. I realized, then, Kincade appeared to be frozen in time.

I looked back at Astrid, who had regained her footing. Her left shoulder streamed blood. Azriel had hold of her again, talking to her, his face a mask of fury.

Silence descended as I met the gaze of this high lord making his way toward me.

"You have been nothing but a nuisance, Anna."

I clutched the sword in my sweating palm. "I'm a thorn in everyone's sides."

Next to me, Ophelia and Ronan were not moving at all. My heart clawed its way into my throat as understanding dawned. Azriel was making Astrid use her powers to freeze them, too.

There was no one to save me from Hadrian.

But I didn't need anyone to save me. I was capable of saving myself.

"You've been asking about the Holy Grail far too much. I understand you tried to recover it in Valencia. And now you think to steal it from me. Here."

"From you?"

Oh, damn. Hadrian was the high lord the vampires were meeting, not Azriel.

Then why was Azriel here? As backup? As a delivery boy to Lucifer? I had no clue. A savageness was on Hadrian's face as he approached me, pausing only feet away.

"That flaming sword will not protect you from me."

"Wanna bet?" I clutched the sword tighter.

A cold, joyless smile creased his face. Then he put his lips together and puffed out a breath of air right towards me. The sword flames extinguished as though they'd been covered by a snuffer.

Oh, shit.

"Lucifer wants you alive, but your life is not worth anything. No matter how much jewelry you wear. You are nothing but a lowly human."

He said *lowly human* as though something distasteful coated his mouth. As though a human were the scrapings off the bottom of his shoe. But I wasn't just a human. My uncle told me I was special, that I had powers beyond my comprehension. I didn't believe him then and I should have. Only after his death did I begin to realize the power within me.

"So, you're going to kill me against your master's wishes?"

I still stood there, clutching the sword trying to figure out my next move. Kincade had said he was far more dangerous than Azriel, but I had no evidence of that. Not yet.

"I don't see why you should continue to live, no."

"But I have the other relics. I'm the Keeper."

He scoffed at that. "The Keeper. It doesn't make you invincible. It was merely a title made up by those who would try to defeat us. You do realize we cannot be defeated."

"You can be defeated and you will."

"By you?" He laughed. "You have no one of worth supporting you. No one with the power to stop Lucifer and his army. Already, the world is falling into utter despair. War begins to ravage the place you call Eastern Europe. You cannot stop our forces any more than you can stop a freight train."

This guy was starting to really piss me off. He may have snuffed out the flaming sword with a breath, but I had another weapon at my disposal. I felt the beginnings of the Godlight stirring within me.

"You stand there telling me who I'm not. But let me tell you who I *am*. Better yet, let me show you."

"Let *me* show *you* who I am."

He didn't give me a chance to release the Godlight. He crossed his wrists and pushed his hands out, flat. The raw, white power smacked into my chest so hard, I stumbled backward tripping over the long skirt. It knocked the breath out of me as if someone had punched me right in the gut. I nearly lost my balance. The sword dangled in my left hand at my side. The acrid odor of smoke filled the air around me.

Ophelia, Ronan, and Kincade still hadn't moved. I gasped for breath, trying to push away the pain burning through me. I searched the room for Astrid. Her face was pale with a sadness she didn't bother to hide.

"Astrid!" Her name came out as a roughened whisper. I tried again. "Release them!"

Azriel jerked her closer to him and said something in her ear. She cast her eyes down, hiding her face.

"You say you have the other relics," Hadrian continued as if nothing happened. As if we were sitting down for afternoon tea. "Do you think we cannot find them? Do you think we don't know you have them hidden?"

He used his power again and this time sent me flying. Again, that reek of smoke and I realized that it wasn't *me* that smelled that way—it was his dark demon magic. The sword fell from my hand and clattered to the marble dance floor. I crashed against the hard floor, my right elbow smacking it first. Pain exploded up my arm to my shoulder. I groaned and rolled to my good side. Using my left arm, I pushed to my feet, staggering a bit to get my footing. But then the high lord was on me before I realized what was happening. He sucker-punched me in the gut, knocking the wind out of my lungs. I gasped for breath. Then his fist connected with my face.

"You are worthless." He punched me again. I fell to my knees. "You are weak."

Cradling my injured arm against my mid-section, I reached deep down for the Godlight, trying to coax it to life. It was there, glimmering, but I sensed the fear overtaking me and suppressing it.

"And now you will die."

He placed his palms together then and closed his eyes, his face going into repose as he concentrated. I tried to get up but then something dark and oily slammed into me, shoving me backward. I peered through the shadow to watch Hadrian using his power to control the shadowy monster. The thing latched onto me, twirling around my body, suffocating me, sucking the breath from me.

I tried to gulp in air. I tried to brush it off, but it was no use.

"Behold, the shadow of death. Also called a shade. How do you like it?" Hadrian said. "Oh, that's right. You cannot speak. How utterly unfortunate."

He conjured another shade that converged on me, shoving me back and back and back away from the others. They stole the air from my lungs, the words from my tongue, and the thoughts from my mind. My body weakened. They managed to extinguish the first glimmers of the Godlight, leaving me defenseless.

"They will suck the life out of you. Take all they can take and leave you as nothing but a shell of what you once were."

My fingers twitched, but I was powerless. I collapsed to the floor, my hands flat on the cold marble as I stared down at the intricate pattern of gray and white. My mind faded into nothing.

Hadrian emitted a deep guttural sound of intense pain. A shrill scream sent the shades scattering as I collapsed to the floor. I pressed my cheek against the cold floor as air whooshed back into my lungs, burning as I gulped it in. A weakness pressed through me as I lay there, motionless. They'd manage to suck most of my energy away but left me conscious. Perhaps that was what Hadrian wanted. He wanted me to feel and know what they were doing to me until my last breath.

I wasn't sure what was happening but there was a familiar presence by my side. I pried my eyes open and gazed at a pair of ratty sneakers with holes in the toes.

"Who are you?" Hadrian asked, his voice weak as though something dreadful happened.

The person did not answer. My head was so heavy it felt as though it was packed with lead. It took a massive effort to lift my head to see the person standing there. It was a woman with long dark hair.

"You don't frighten me," he added.

"I should."

I recognized that mellifluous voice. How the bloody hell did Natasha find me here? She lifted a hand toward Hadrian and though her face was out of view, I understood what she was doing. Hadrian gasped, the blood gurgling in the back of his throat. She was killing him. Making him hemorrhage from the inside out.

"Enough of this," Azriel said. He was closer than he had been.

But my mother did not release Hadrian from her super dream walker powers.

I pushed to my knees, cradling my arm against my mid-section and looked up at him. He still had his hand clamped around Astrid's wrist. The others were still frozen in time. She had yet to release them. Pain and anguish lined her face, as though she were conflicted with her powers.

"Astrid, release them. You don't have to do what he says." My voice was weak and raspy, as though I'd spent time in a smoky bar drinking gin.

"I...cannot..." Her voice was weak, strained.

Azriel beamed as though he'd won the lottery. "She is under my complete and utter control. No one can release her. Not even you, *chérie*."

"But I can."

Despite the intense pain, my head snapped up. Killian pushed his way through the mist holding a bow and arrow. He released the nocked arrow in one fluid motion and, with precision and speed, it hit its target—Azriel. The high lord cried out in pain as the arrow embedded into the fleshy party of his shoulder. Blood dampened the cloth of his tux giving it a sheen. With a shriek, he ripped it out of his body and tossed the bloody thing to the ground.

He released Astrid, breaking their connection. As soon as it was broken, it released the spell on Ophelia, Ronan, and Kincade. Astrid's eyes rolled back into her head and she collapsed to the floor. Killian rushed to her side, pulling her into his arms cradling her against him as though she were a precious gift.

Astrid's eyes fluttered open. She reached for him, her fingers grazing his cheek. "You came for me."

"Always." He cradled her against him, protecting her.

Kincade was at my side in an instant, helping me to my feet. I leaned heavily against him, letting him take most of my weight. Even so, I reached for Natasha and put a hand on her shoulder.

"He's not worth it," I rasped.

Natasha dropped her hand and turned to me, blinking her purple eyes that were so much like my own. Hadrian wiped the blood from his nose with the back of his hand. After all his posturing, he'd been weakened by my mother's super mind skills.

"Anna, a dead high lord is the best high lord," Kincade said in my ear. "He nearly killed you."

"You're absolutely right." I glanced at Natasha and gave her the go-ahead nod.

She continued to use her superpowers on the high lord. Blood streamed from his nose, his ears, and the corners of his eyes. He faltered, stagged backward a step. He clutched his heart, fisting his dress shirt as blood dotted the snowy white material. He wobbled and then crashed to his knees, his hands flat on the floor, his head down.

Natasha's hands shook. She gave a weak cry of pain. Her eyes squeezed shut as she dropped her hands and slumped forward. Kincade released me to catch her before she pitched forward to the floor. Her breath see-sawed in and out. Her chest rose and fell as though she'd run a one-hundred-meter sprint. Color leeched from her face in her weakened state.

The high lord was too strong for her and managed to resist. Hadrian lifted his head. He wiped his nose with the back of his hand, leaving a slash of blood behind.

"You bitch. You will pay for this. You both will."

He glanced from me to her. A trickle of cold dread skittered up my spine. I had no doubt he'd make good on that threat. Azriel moved to his side and helped him to his feet.

Kincade wrapped an arm around her shoulders and helped her to stand straight. She waved him off, regaining some of her strength.

"Are you sure about that? We'll see when the reckoning comes, won't we?"

Hadrian smirked. "You still don't have the Holy Grail, though which means your quest failed." He waved Barnabas toward him.

I'd completely forgotten about the vampire. The flashy vamp lord entered our little circle. The bastard had the cup the entire time. He carried it wrapped in a white cloth and smirked at me as I eyed it, trying to formulate a plan to get it from him. He handed it to Hadrian who started to reach for it.

"Wait. You cannot touch the sacred relic, Hadrian," Azriel said.

"Why not?" Hadrian demanded.

"Because I have to touch it first." My heart kicked into high gear. And then I added, "As the Keeper of the Holy Relics. You know, that made up thing."

If the Grail were the true Cup of Christ, then I would know the second my fingers brushed against it. It would reveal its history to me in a flash as though I watched a movie in fast forward.

"Why does she have to touch it first?" Hadrian asked, clearly annoyed he couldn't take off with it.

"Because she is divine, as is the relic," Azriel said. "Once the relic's secrets are revealed to her, we will be able to hold it without consequences."

Hadrian motioned for Barnabas to uncover the cup. "Then allow her to touch it *only*. If she tries to steal it, kill her."

Kincade's hand wrapped around my uninjured upper arm. I wasn't sure if that was for comfort or a warning. Either way, I was glad he stood right next to me. Barnabas pushed the cloth off the Grail. It was the very same one the vampire stole at the mass in Valencia. He stretched the Grail toward me.

I took a deep breath. I glanced up at Kincade for reassurance. He gave me the go-ahead nod.

Do it. If it's the cup, we will find a way to take it, he said in my head.

I swallowed the fear and anticipation climbing its way into my throat and reached out. My fingers brushed along the cold, smooth surface. I sucked in a sharp breath, my spine stiffening as I threw back my head. A moment later, my shoulders slumped, my head falling forward. Kincade was there, though, and caught me in his arms. I slumped against him, making a good show of it.

"It's the true cup, then?" Hadrian asked.

"What did you see?" Azriel interjected.

"I saw…" My voice was weak as I clutched Kincade for strength. "The Last Supper. Joseph of Arimathea collecting Jesus's blood when he was crucified."

Satisfied with my answer, Hadrian snatched the cup from Barnabas and tucked it under his arm. "Then we are done here. Lord Barnabas, collect your reward."

He and the vampires left the ballroom. The doors opened. The veil lifted. And everything returned to as it was before.

Azriel moved toward Killian, his hands clenched. "She is my property."

"Try to take her from me and I will kill you," Killian warned.

"You lost her, Azriel," I said. "Leave before I allow the Fae king to have his vengeance."

The Fallen high lord pierced me with utter hate as he hurried out of the ballroom. Killian scooped Astrid into his arms. She was only somewhat lucid.

"Nice of you to join the party," I said. "But I think we've overstayed our welcome."

Kincade wrapped his arm around my waist and steered me toward the exit. "Thought we'd never get out of here," he muttered.

But as we turned to leave, we faced a new problem.

More vampires. And boy did they look pissed.

CHAPTER 30

I ASSUMED THEY WERE the Partners for the Sanctified. They'd managed to track me down here.

This day kept getting better and better. I sighed. I didn't have any more fight left in me.

"How the hell did they find me?" I didn't bother to hide the incredulous whine in my voice. "What are we going to do?"

Kincade still had a hold of me. Whatever the shades did to me, I was still too weak to move. Around us, the humans were confused as to what was happening and what had happened. There was no way to explain it to them.

Natasha stepped out in front of all of us and began to lift her hands.

"Natasha, no!" I warned.

But it was too late to stop her. She thought using her super dream walker skills on the vamps would diffuse the situation. It did nothing. They were undead. Her powers were worthless on them.

She tried again.

And again, she failed.

She looked at me over her shoulder, clear confusion on her face. "I do not understand."

"You can't kill them. They're vampires."

Her brows drew together as she glanced back at them and dropped her hands. Ophelia brandished her shimming sword. Ronan used his lightning fingers. Both of them moved to stand in front of me and Kincade like a blockade.

The three vampires halted in front of them. Why was it always three? Was that some mystical strength in number for them? They were dressed in formal attire, as though they expected to find me here. The tall one in the center had long dark hair brushing his shoulders. His yellow eyes pierced through me. The other two flanked him but didn't appear to be nearly as menacing as the head vamp.

"You cannot hide from us forever, Anna," the yellow-eyed vamp said. "We want the horn back."

Yep, Partners for the Sanctified. They were new-to-me vamps. I'd fried the others with the Godlight in the alley in Valenica. I reached for that glimmering power within me, trying to invoke it but it wasn't there. I was still too weak to conjure it thanks to the shades trying to suck me dry.

"I don't have it with me," I said. "It's not like I can magically produce it."

"If you don't have it, then we will punish you for your theft. You will become our blood slave."

At that point, Kincade stepped forward, nudging me behind him. "You'll have to go through me and the rest of us to do that."

I rested my hands on his waist to steady myself. However, I stood on tiptoe to peer over his broad shoulder and flash them a wicked smile. "In other words, you're fucked."

They were undeterred by Kincade's threats, Ophelia's sword, and Ronan's lightning fingers.

"She must pay for what she's done. We want retribution," the middle vampire said.

"Too bad." I glanced over at Killian who still held a semi-conscious Astrid in his arms. "Can she help?"

He shook his head. "She's too weak." And then a small smile came across his face. "But I can help. No one move."

He closed his eyes, his face contorted into one of concentration. A flash of light surrounded all of us and we were whisked from the dancefloor to the humid hidden forest of the Fae. They called it sifting and it did nothing for my current weakened state. My knees buckled and I collapsed onto the soft ground, exhausted. Kincade was there, though, kneeling next to me.

"I'm fine." I tried to wave him off, but he was having none of it. "Where's my mother?"

"She's fine. She's here, too." He hoisted me to my feet.

When I swayed against him, he wrapped his arm around my waist. I held my injured arm against my side, trying to keep from moving it.

"Where are we?" Ophelia leaned heavily against Ronan, who also appeared to be weakened by the sifting of time and space around them.

"The sacred Fae Forest," Killian said. "Come. I have accommodations for all of you."

Killian had managed to bring all of us—me, Kincade, Ophelia, Ronan, Natasha—to his hidden forest away from the vampires and the Royal Palace in Madrid. It was a handy trick, the sifting. Kincade helped me walk as we followed the Fae king. The other Fae popped out of their woodland homes to stare at us as though we were part of a parade. Curiosity on all of their faces.

We must have looked strange in our formal attire. And me with my beat-up face.

"You know it's not over with those vampires," I said to Kincade.

"I know."

"They'll find me again."

"They will."

"They won't stop until they have the Horn of Gabriel."

"They won't," he agreed.

"And then what?" I asked.

We climbed a wooden spiral staircase that curved around a massive tree. I held up my skirts with my injured arm, wincing the entire time, to keep from stepping on them. I was amazed I had escaped with the entire gown still intact.

"Then we find a way to kill them off." He gave me a wicked grin.

"Good idea," I said with a nod. "I like the way you think."

"We better find a wooden stake."

"I thought it was a silver bullet?" I asked.

"That's a werewolf."

"Or just behead the bastards," Ophelia interjected. "You should have let me do it with my sword."

I hadn't realized anyone was eavesdropping on our conversation. "If your sword can kill high lords, why not vampires? I should have let you."

"You realize you narrowly escaped certain death, don't you, Anna?" Ronan asked.

I cringed. "Yes, thanks to my mother."

"Your...*mother*?" The disbelief was strong in his voice. He peered at Natasha wearing ratty clothing looking like a street beggar. "That is your *mother*?"

"Yes, and I will explain more later."

And, thankfully, none of them had asked me about the Holy Grail. None of them asked why I let it go so easily. Not even Kincade, though I suspected he already realized the truth. I sensed he had questions about it, but he kept them to himself for whatever reason. Perhaps he wanted to discuss with me in private. That was fine with me. I wanted to discuss with him in private, too.

We arrived high in the trees at a cluster of small houses built in the top. In my mind, I likened it to Sherwood Forest populated by Fae instead of Merry Men.

"Wait here," Killian instructed.

He ducked into one of the houses for a moment and then returned without Astrid. No doubt leaving her to rest in the small house.

"This area of the forest houses my private apartments. Come." He motioned for us to follow him.

"This one has three bedrooms. Perfect for the three of you." He paused at the first little house. He motioned for Ophelia, Ronan, and Natasha to enter.

"My mother—"

"She will be fine." Ophelia patted my arm in reassurance. "We'll watch over her. I promise."

I gave her a skeptical look.

"I *promise*, Anna. I know I failed you before. I won't again."

The way Ophelia said that tugged at my heart. I gave her a small reassuring smile and nodded. "I trust you." I mustered the strength to step toward my mother, putting a hand on her shoulder. "Natasha, you'll be going with them."

She glanced at Ophelia and Ronan, then back at me with question in her purple eyes. "Who are they?"

"You remember Ophelia, don't you?" I motioned to her. "She was at the manor with you. She tried to protect you."

"Those men tried to destroy the house."

"I know." I nodded, give her a reassuring pat. "But they're all gone now. And Ophelia will take good care of you. And this is Ronan." I motioned toward him. "He's a dream walker, like us."

"A dream walker?" She repeated the words as if they were foreign on her tongue.

"Yes. We'll talk more later. You should get some rest. It's been a long journey for you."

She started to go, but then stopped and turned back to me. She reached for me, her gentle hands on my upper arms. Her gaze searched my face and for a moment, there was a flicker of familiarity in that look.

"I wanted to tell you...something. But now...I cannot remember."

"That's okay," I said and smiled. "When you do, find me. We'll talk."

But she paused there for the longest time, still staring at me as though she had questions she didn't know how to ask.

"I found you...because..." She paused, biting her lip. Something I'd done a hundred times myself. "Because...somehow, we are connected, you and I. I do not know how or why. I tracked you there. To that place in Spain. I *sensed* you were in trouble. The shades are deadly and would have killed you."

I gave her a slow nod, goosebumps rising on my flesh. Bless her soul, she didn't understand how or why we were connected because she didn't understand she was my mother and I was her daughter. I would explain it to her someday when she was more coherent. When she could grasp the words and understand. Maybe that day would come.

Something about her had shifted, though. Almost as though she was starting to remember who she was and why she felt at home in Walker Manor.

"You saved my life. Thank you." I kissed her cheek. "Rest, now. You need it."

My mother paused there another long, quiet moment. She placed a hand on my cheek, smiled a little smile, and then turned to Ophelia who held her hand out to her. Natasha took it and the three of them disappeared inside the small wood house.

My heart twisted in my chest. A myriad of uncertain feelings fluttered through me. Kincade took my elbow again, pulling me to him. I let him, drawing on his strength.

"You okay?" he asked.

I nodded.

Killian, who had witnessed the scene, said nothing as he continued down the wooden bridge. He paused at the next house.

"A two bedroom, for the two of you. I am sorry that this is the only other spare apartment I have."

"It's fine," I said, understanding his implication.

He thought we'd want to be in separate places. But after everything that had happened, I wanted Kincade as close to me as possible. Killan motioned toward the door.

"I'll send for my healer for you," he said.

"That's not necessary." I trudged toward it but paused and turned back to the Fae king. "I do have a request, though. Do you think you could find us some other clothes?" I waved at the formal attire. While the gown was starting to grow on me, I needed to feel like myself again.

"I will see that you all have suitable clothes." He gave a brief bow before leaving us to head back to his own little house.

Kincade pushed open the door, then held it open for me. I entered and was not displeased at the sight. The area was a small open concept with a living, dining, kitchenette. Not much different than the one I'd visited when Killian whisked me to the Fae Forest before. The furniture was all made of wood with thick cushions on the sofa and the two seats. A plush garnet rug covered the floor. Beyond the living area to the left was one bedroom. To the right, another.

I headed to the two-seat sofa and went to work removing all the jewels Ophelia insisted I wear. Necklace, earrings, bracelet. Then stripped off the gloves and dropped them on the table next to the diamonds and emeralds. I plopped down. I somehow made it here without my shoes. I drew my knees into a cross-cross position. Some of my hair had come loose from the chignon she had so carefully crafted. Now I ripped out hairpins and tossed them on the table. Then I ran my fingers through my tangled hair, grateful to be more like myself again.

I allowed my tired body to sink into the thick cushion. Kincade, meanwhile, rattled around in the kitchen. He came out with two glasses and a tall thin wine bottle.

"Judging by the sickly-sweet smell, this is mead. It will do in a pinch." He poured two glasses and handed me one.

"Thanks." I sniffed it. Sure enough, it smelled like mead.

"Your face looks pretty bad," he said. "And your lip is split."

I brushed my fingers over my cheekbone where Hadrian had punched me twice. It throbbed. I suspected I would have a black eye soon. I was more worried about my elbow I smacked on the floor. The pain had subsided some but continued to throb. I slowly straightened it out, thankful I was able to still move it without too much agony. I shouldn't have refused the healer, but I didn't want to inconvenience Killian anymore.

"I'll be fine. I've been in worse condition before."

He looked skeptical but didn't press it. "You want to tell me about your act back there?"

"What act?" I blinked innocence, hoping my tarnished halo didn't show.

"Oh, please, Anna. You could have been nominated for an Academy Award for that performance." He took a seat across from me, lowering his large body into the chair. It creaked with his weight.

I giggled. Not only did I appreciate his joke, there was something almost comical about seeing the large man perch in the smallish chair with the red cushions. He was almost too big for it. His muscular hand clasped the delicate highball, the veins along the back of his hand visible under the skin.

It was hard not to admire the way he looked in that tux. He tugged the bowtie loose, untying it, and then tossing the material on the nearby coffee table along with my collection of accessories. Then he toed off his shiny dress shoes.

Why did it seem as though that was the most domestic thing he'd ever done in front of me?

"It wasn't the real Grail, was it?"

I shook my head, sipping the mead. "No. I felt nothing when I touched it."

"You lied." He grinned.

"You know I did. I gave them a vague but realistic answer in the hopes it would make them take the fake cup and go away," I said.

"That's why you didn't fight, and you let them have it."

"Well, that and Hadrian handed me my ass. I didn't have the energy. Besides...imagine Lucifer's ire when he realizes it isn't the real cup."

A rare smile spread across Kincade's lips and then a low chuckle rumbled deep within his chest. It sounded so divine. I closed my eyes and soaked it in along with the sweet mead in my cup. I downed another sip.

"Are we safe here?" he asked.

"For now." I opened my eyes and met his gaze. "As soon as Lucifer realizes that cup is one of many fakes, he will be determined to find the real one. I doubt we have much time."

"Any clues?"

"None." I downed the rest of the mead, allowing the warmth of the alcohol to burn through me. "Not yet, anyway."

He unbuttoned the top button of his dress shirt, then shrugged out of the tux coat. My heart quickened. I had no explanation as to why it did that, unbidden. Perhaps it was because I liked seeing Kincade go all casual and get comfortable around me.

Meanwhile, I was one-hundred-percent sick of this ballgown.

And the dagger digging into my thigh.

I placed the highball glass on the nearby table and, without thinking, hoisted up my skirts and unbuckled the dagger sheath from my thigh.

When I glanced up, Kincade stared long and hard at me. It was in that moment I realized I had exposed the entire length of both legs.

The room suddenly felt too small, too quiet, too everything. I was aware of my ragged breath and his—carefully controlled.

Heat flashed over me. I shoved the skirts down as I tossed the dagger in its sheath on the table. Then I snatched up my half-empty glass.

"You had your dagger the entire time?" he asked, his voice steadier than his expression.

"It gave me peace of mind to have it on me. I wanted to be prepared."

He tipped his head to the side. "How did you expect to retrieve the thing?"

I shrugged. "No idea."

He laughed which surprised the hell out of me.

I laughed in response.

When he regained his composure, he said, "Why do that when you had your uncle's sword?"

I frowned. "A lot of good that did me. I didn't even get to use it." I sat up straight, my heart in my throat. "Oh, shit! I left it behind!"

"No, you didn't." He refilled my glass and his.

"I didn't?"

"Ophelia picked it up and put it in the cloud with hers."

My shoulders slumped as I fell back into the cushions holding the almost full glass. The pale liquid sloshed near the rim. "God bless Ophelia."

"You should get some sleep," he said then.

I gave him a resigned smile. "I should."

"You haven't been sleeping," he pointed out.

"I haven't," I agreed and downed the glass of mead in one gulp. It burned all the way down and back up, giving me the warm fuzzies.

"Go rest, Anna. I'll be here."

The way he said it—quiet, certain—made it sound less like reassurance and more like a vow.

It gave me the heart squeeze. I wondered, distantly, if he realized how easily he did that to me. It was probably the sweetest thing he'd ever said to me.

I was too tired to move from the sofa, though. I tucked my feet up. I used my voluminous skirts as a blanket. I yawned so wide, my jaw nearly cracked as I laid down, my head on one of the sofa pillows.

"Night, night, Kincade."

"Sweet dreams."

And then I was dead to the world.

CHAPTER 31

I AWOKE TO A knock on the door. It jarred me awake and I bolted upright, my heart pounding hard and fast. Kincade crossed the room in his sock feet. His shirt was untucked and wrinkled. He looked good rumpled.

I swung my legs off the sofa and turned toward the door as Killian entered. Kincade closed the door behind him. The Fae king held a stack of clothes and some shoes I assumed were for the two of us. He handed them over to Kincade.

"It's the best I could do," the king said.

Kincade gave him a nod. "Thanks."

But then Killian took a swing at Kincade and landed a punch right on his jaw with an audible crack that made me flinch.

I sharp escaped me.

Kincade was so shocked by it, his head snapped back and his teeth clacked together. Red fury creased his face. He dropped the clothes in a heap on the floor as I leapt to my feet to intervene.

Kincade balled his fists to swing back, but I grabbed his arm and held him. His muscles were rigid under my hand. He did not resist me, though he was strong enough. The king did not back down.

"What was that for?" Kincade demanded.

"That was for shooting Astrid. The only reason you're not dead is because she begged me not to kill you. She said the only reason she was able to break free from Azriel's connection was because you shot her." His body relaxed, his shoulders drooping a little. "For that, you have my thanks."

Kincade's fingers relaxed, the tension easing from his arm. He wasn't going to fight back. "I'm sorry I shot her. It was the only thing I thought might work. Is she all right?"

"She's fine. My healer tended her." He cut me a glance then. "Are you certain you don't want my healer to tend you, Anna?"

"I'm certain," I said with a nod. "I just need rest. That's all."

"If you insist. My servants will bring food for you shortly. You'll find fresh linens in the bathroom."

He started to go, his hand on the door.

"Killian, wait." He paused, turned back to me. An overwhelming sense of guilt swarmed me. "I'm sorry, too, for not being able to rescue her from Azriel. I dream walked her, but she wouldn't tell me where she was. She told me not to come after her."

Killian's face was impassive as he nodded. "She told me. I don't hold that against you, Anna, if that's what you think. You did what you had to do. She did what she had to do. The most important thing is she's out of Azriel's hands and back with me."

"He won't let her go that easily," Kincade warned.

"I don't expect him to. But next time, I will be ready." He cocked a grin as he opened the door and departed.

I ran a hand through my tangled hair as the adrenaline subsided. Fatigue slammed into me again. "I can't believe he hit you."

"I can't believe I didn't see it coming." He bent and picked up the pile from the floor, sorting through the clothes. He picked out what appeared to be his size and handed me the rest. "Go shower and then go to bed. That's an order."

I took the tunic and pants from him. The pants were soft suede. I kind of loved the Fae and their material choices. I started to go but then remembered there was no way I was able to reach the tiny eyehook or the back zipper on my gown.

"I will but I, uh, need a favor first."

He lifted a brow. "And that is?"

"Can you—" I stopped, then forced myself to finish. "Unzip me? I can't reach it. Ophelia got me into this dress, but it's not exactly designed for a quick escape."

As soon as the words left my mouth, the heated blush crawled up my neck and into my cheeks. Because I realized what I was asking and that he'd actually have to *touch* me.

The silence stretched.

When I glanced back up, Kincade hadn't moved—but something in him had. His jaw was locked hard enough to ache, tension carving sharp lines along his cheekbones. His gaze turned molten gold, dropped once, deliberately, then snapped away as if he didn't trust himself to look for long.

He nodded once. "Turn around."

I spun away, my pulse skipping into an impossibly quick rhythm. Maybe I could just cut my way out of this exorbitantly expensive gown instead. I considered telling him *never mind*, but then Ophelia would never forgive me.

I hugged the Fae clothes to my chest, my mouth suddenly dry, acutely aware of how close he stood behind me. Close enough I could feel him, solid and real. Close enough his body heat pulsed against my back.

He hesitated. Maybe he was going to tell *me* never mind. I opened my mouth to tell him I'd go find Ophelia, when—

His fingers brushed aside my hair, slow and careful as he swept it over my shoulder. It sent a shiver down my spine that had nothing to do with the chill in the air. My heart clawed its way to my throat. His knuckles grazed my skin—accidental, I told myself—and his breath changed, the slightest hitch betraying him.

The tiny hook slipped free.

When he reached for the zipper, his touch was firm, controlled—but it burned all the same. The metal slid down an inch. Two. His fingers grazing my skin and I thought my knees would turn to water. He halted for a half a second, then continued until it was all the way unzipped. If I hadn't been clutching the clothes to my chest, the gown would have pooled at my feet in a puddle of crystals and emerald skirts.

My brain fractured.

I couldn't move. Not yet.

Something happened then. His hand slipped beneath the loosened fabric—not a caress, but a steadying touch that still sent heat flaring. The world tilted as dizziness pounded through me.

He was... touching me and I... couldn't stop it.

I also didn't know how to get out of this.

My breath hitched once. And then I felt him lean closer. I tipped my head just enough to glimpse him from the corner of my eye. His head dipped, breath warm against my skin.

Everything I thought I knew about us shattered.

For a split second, the idea of dropping the dress and turning into him flashed through my mind. For the first time, I understood just how thin the line between us really was.

But he was—

And I was—

We were so not right for each other.

He stopped himself.

Then my common sense snapped back into place and I stepped away from him, breaking the contact.

"Thanks," I muttered.

Without waiting for a reply, I hurried off to the bathroom, closing myself in. I dropped the clothes on the bathroom counter and then leaned against it, trying to normalize my breathing. What the hell was I thinking?

I wasn't, that's what. I peered at my beat-up face in the mirror. A frightening sight, to be sure. Beneath the bruising, the heat of the blush remained.

"You are an idiot," I said to my reflection.

I took a deep breath and decided everything would be situation normal. I'd pretend like none of that happened and we would go on with our lives.

I let the gown pool in a sea of green at my feet. Then I turned on the shower, still marveling over the fact the Fae had running water this high up in the trees.

The wonder of Fae magic never ceased.

As I stepped into the hot spray, I wondered how long our respite would last. How long before something happened? Killian assured me the Fae Forest was well hidden from the rest of the human realm, but that didn't mean Lucifer wouldn't be able to find them.

I stood under the hot water until my skin shriveled. Finally, I cut off the water, toweled off and dressed in the clothes Killian brought. We'd left everything behind in the hotel room in Madrid.

Which also meant I'd left behind my bag with all the postcards. A pang of sorrow went through me at the thought of losing them. It hurt to think about that, so I shoved it back into the dark recesses of my mind as I stepped out of the small bathroom and to the first bedroom. I shoved back the covers, climbed into the bed, and burrowed deep into the blankets.

Moments later, exhaustion overtook me and I was fast asleep.

WHEN I AWOKE, MY stomach growled. I rolled to my side, momentarily disoriented until I recalled where I was. Ah, yes. Killian's hidden forest.

Thankfully, I didn't dream. I was glad.

Despite the sleep, I didn't wake rested. My body ached from the beating it took. My face and arm throbbed. I held up my wounded arm and surveyed it. A deep purple bruise spread outward from the elbow. At least it didn't seem to be broken. Just a deep contusion.

I shoved off the blankets and stumbled out of the bedroom in search of sustenance. Kincade was in the living room. He'd changed out of his tux and into black cargo pants and a three-button Henley. My foggy brain did not understand why or how he ended up with cargo pants or a three-button Henley but I didn't much want to quiz him on that at the moment.

"How long was I out?" I asked.

"A while. Hungry?"

"I'm starving. How long is a while?"

He motioned to the small table near the kitchen where a charcuterie board rested in the center. A bowl of black and green olives was in the middle. Surrounding that were several different kinds of cheeses, meats, fruits including grapes, apples, and berries, and bread.

"A little over twelve hours." He shoved the entire board toward me as I sat. "Eat." From a pitcher, he poured a glass of water.

I shoved a piece of rosemary bread in my mouth. "You don't have to take care of me."

He plucked a green grape and popped it into his mouth. "Who says I am? Your stomach is growling so loud, they probably heard it next door."

I gave him a sour look. "Funny." Then I downed the water in nearly one gulp not realizing how thirsty I was.

He left and returned a moment later. "I thought you might want this." He held my duffle from the hotel in his hand.

Hot tears suddenly sprang to my eyes. I blinked them back. "How did you...?"

"I sent Killian and Ophelia to collect our things from the hotel in Madrid."

I stared at the duffle as though it were a foreign object. "I don't understand."

"He sifted, Anna. I knew you'd want the postcards. They're all accounted for in the bag."

I reached for it, took it from him and placed it in my lap. My throat constricted. "Thanks."

"Plus, I can't wear these Fae clothes. They're too..." He paused, his mind working to come up with the right words.

"They're not you," I said. "Not by a long shot."

"Right. Your clothes are in there, too." He nodded to the bag.

To be honest, I was relieved. While the Fae clothes were comfy, I liked my own uniform of black since it hid demon blood much easier.

"Enjoy your lunch."

Then he was out the door before I was able to even form a response. To where, I had no clue. Kincade was often a solitary creature, which suited me just fine. I wasn't the co-dependent type and, clearly, neither was he.

When I finished stuffing myself with as much food as possible, I changed into my favorite clothes, including my pink combat boots that had seen better days, and strapped my dagger at my thigh. It gave me comfort to have it on my person.

I wandered out of the confines of the little house for fresh air. The last time I was in the forest of the Fae, I spent it with Killian and Astrid and never ventured outside his house. Now, I stood on the wooden platform overlooking the ground below. The Fae had built an intricate network of bridges, wooden platforms, rope pulleys and houses high atop the trees in their forest.

Below was much the same. Houses carved into the sides of massive trees and well-worn paths through the forest floor. It was a bustle of activity with Fae going about their daily lives. The air was fresh and clean up here and I inhaled a deep breath, closing my eyes to savor it.

"It's nice here, isn't it?"

Ronan's voice brought me out of my trance. He stood next to me on the bridge, his hand on the railing as he, too, gazed out. He no longer wore the formal clothes. When Killian sifted Ophelia to the hotel, she must have grabbed everything she could, including Ronan's personal items. He wore jeans and a navy-blue polo shirt with a standing collar. Despite the semi-casual dress, he appeared as though he was ready for a business meeting or a pint at the local pub.

"It is," I agreed. "I see Ophelia managed to grab your things, too."

"She did."

We stood in pleasant silence, then he turned to the side and leaned his elbow on the railing as if we were about to engage in casual conversation.

"What happened to her?"

I didn't expect the question he asked about my mother. I didn't particularly want to talk about her to him. He was, after all, the son of the man she was supposed to marry. If I told him the truth, would that then give Alexander Harred more ammunition against me? I didn't trust him. To some degree, where my mother was concerned, I didn't trust Ronan, either.

I grabbed the handrail tight, my hands cramping, as I tried to decide how to answer.

"You don't want to tell me, do you?"

"You sensed that, did you?" I gave him a small smile. "It's difficult to explain."

"You think I'm going to tell my father."

I met his level gaze as he lounged against the railing. "Aren't you?"

"Why?" Ronan stood straight then, his gaze somewhere on the forest in front of him. "And furthermore, why would he care?"

"He has an axe to grind with us Walkers," I reminded him. I thought of the marriage contract between us, the one his father so desperately wanted to enforce. The one I so desperately refused to honor.

"My father is a difficult man. We don't always see eye to eye." He faced me, then, concern flickering over his features. "You have my word what you tell me about her will stay with me. She doesn't know who you are, does she?"

"She doesn't." I continue to grip the handrail. I took a deep breath, trusting Ronan to keep the information to himself. "I found her in Antarctica with a group called Knights of the Holy Lance. Their leader used her DNA to try to create his own legion of dream walkers. He tortured her and tinkered with her brain. It's why she doesn't remember who she truly is. Why she thinks her name is Natasha. He made her what she is."

"And what is that?"

"A super dream walker."

When she used her powers on me, it blinded me for a time until Sariel, the archangel, came to me. He used his healing angelic powers to restore my eyesight.

Ronan was silent a long moment. "That's what she did to that high lord."

"Hadrian. It's what she tried to do," I said with a nod. "I have no idea how she tracked me down in Madrid. Or how she found her way to Walker Manor in the first place."

He said nothing but his mind worked as he tried to decide what to say next.

"Is she all right?" I asked and nodded toward the house he shared with her and Ophelia.

"She is well." He paused, then added, "I do not think you are out of danger yet, Anna."

"You didn't believe what Hadrian said to you, I hope."

"You heard?"

"I heard and saw everything as it happened. We all did. But we couldn't act."

A little Fae girl with her blond curls bouncing up and down her back skipped along the worn path carrying a basket of flowers. Ah, to be so young and carefree. I envied her. I longed for days of no stress. Days I didn't have to think about the end of the world, or the relics, or have the constant worry about my loved ones, or wonder who was going to try to take me out next.

"No, I didn't believe him. All he did was make me mad. Which is likely what he wanted."

I agreed with Ronan, though, that I likely hadn't seen the last of Hadrian. I still wondered why Azriel was at the palace in Madrid. He didn't do anything other than drag Astrid along with him.

Perhaps he expected to use her talents if things went awry for Hadrian upon recovering the Grail from the vampires.

"How long do you expect to be here?" Ronan asked. "Hadrian has the Holy Grail, though I'm sure he's given it to Lucifer by now."

"It's not the real cup," I blurted.

Wide-eyed, his head snapped around to me. "Are you sure? How do you know?"

"I'm sure. I know because when I touch the relics, I see their history. It's a fake."

Relief flickered over his face. "That's why you let them have it."

"Yep."

"Very sneaky."

"I do what I can." I grinned.

His gaze went over my face, no doubt eyeing the deep bruises where Hadrian had punched me. His fingers grazed my cheekbone.

"I came to protect you. I'm sorry I failed you."

"You didn't fail me, Ronan. None of you did. Astrid is powerful and was under Azriel's control. I failed." I turned away from him, unable to hide my disappointment. "And the high lord almost won if not for my mother."

I thought to save myself. I wasn't prepared for the strong demon magic Hadrian possessed or the way he controlled the shades.

"I wouldn't say you failed. What I will say is you are stronger than you think. You are braver than you know. But even with all your bravery and strength, your life is still in danger."

"Did you have another vision of my death?" Even though I said it in jest, I was fearful of the answer and tensed, waiting.

He nodded. "This time of a place much like this." He waved his hand to encompass the forest. "It wasn't clear. All I saw was Hadrian coming after you again."

"He can't touch us here. We're hidden from the normal world."

Worry lines creased his face. "Let's hope it doesn't come to pass. At any rate, your mother has been asking about you. Maybe you should talk to her."

It was something I wanted to do for a while. "Yes, I think I will."

CHAPTER 32

I FOLLOWED RONAN FROM the wooden bridge into the house he shared with my mother and Ophelia. It was much like the one I shared with Kincade, except a little larger. Ophelia and Natasha sat at the small round table with a demolished charcuterie board in the middle. They both had a cup of steaming tea in front of them. And for a moment, it seemed like the most natural, domestic thing to see.

"Hi, Anna," Ophelia said with a grin. "I have something for you."

She pushed back from the table, stood, and pulled Edward's sword out of the cloud. Since she lacked the ability to make it flame, it was merely polished steel. She presented it to me as if it were a prize. I took it from her, grateful to have it back in my possession.

"Thanks for keeping it safe."

Natasha watched with rapt interest. Her eyes lit up as she got up from the table and moved to stand in front of me. Her gaze never left the sword. A glint of familiarity flickered through her eyes. I held it out to her for a better look.

"Where did you get this sword?" she asked.

"It was my uncle's."

"May I?" She reached for it, hesitant.

I nodded. Her fingers brushed down the blade as I held it flat in my hands. She paused at the hilt. Her fingertips brushed over the crisscrossed leather along the handle. There was nothing intricate about the sword handle or the cross-guards. For the first time, though, I noticed the tiny engraving on the rounded pommel—an alpha and an omega. Just like what was engraved on my jade-handled dagger and on Ophelia's own shimmering sword.

Her hand wrapped around the hilt, but she didn't pick it up.

"It is very familiar," she said at last. "I have seen it before."

My throat constricted as I watched her. When she first appeared in Walker Manor, she looked at a picture of Edward. She remembered him, but not from meeting him in Istanbul. She asked his name. I told her was dead.

I never told her he was her brother. Or that she was my missing biological mother.

"Where is your uncle?" she asked.

Before I replied, Ronan ushered Ophelia out of the house and into the late afternoon sunshine to give us some privacy. I appreciated that.

"My uncle died."

Her brows drew together as she thought about my answer. "His name was Edward."

She remembered. I nodded.

"He lived at the manor house," she said.

"He did."

"With you?"

"Yes," I said.

My chest hurt from the pain of remembering, of talking about my uncle, of trying to decide how much I should tell her. She dropped her hand from the sword. Her gaze met mine.

"You have purple eyes. Like mine."

"I do."

"I have never seen anyone else with purple eyes."

She cocked her head to the side, looking me over. We had the same long dark hair, the same nose, the same eyes. I favored her as Kincade pointed out one day after looking at her portrait hanging in the gallery of Walker Manor.

"Who am I to you?" she asked then.

I didn't know how to answer. I deflected instead.

"Do you remember how we met?"

"You were at the lab. He told me to kill you."

The lab in Antarctica. He being Schneider, leader of Knights of the Holy Lance. I narrowly escaped Natasha's super dream walker powers then. Kincade's brother, Decker, managed to extract me from the lab out to the frozen tundra.

"And then again in Rio de Janeiro. On the tarmac," she added.

I remained silent, watching her work it out in her mind. Watching her remember.

"The man with you held this sword." She motioned to it. "It was flaming. He was your uncle?"

"Yes."

"The man in the photo," she said.

I nodded, allowing her to go down the path, to recall all these things hoping it would jar some other memory buried deep in her mind.

"I left you in Istanbul," she said.

"Where did you go?" I asked.

"I hid. The others looked for me even though he was dead."

I assumed she referred to Schneider. I'd killed him under the Hagia Sophia when we were trying to recover the Spear of Destiny.

She released the hilt and moved through the small house. She ran her hands through her long, black hair as she took a deep breath and paced as she told me her story.

"I moved only at night, making my way across Europe. I hitched rides from people who took pity on me. I spent time in farmhouses and barns, crossing country after country. Austria, Belgium, France. It was in Calais I boarded the train to London. I was starving. In ragged clothes I stole from strangers' clotheslines."

She stopped pacing and paused.

"How long did it take you?" I asked.

She shrugged. "Days and days. I lost track of time. I only knew the sunrise and the sunset. I feared I would be found by those I escaped from. I did not want to go back to the lab." She clutched her elbows then and shivered at the dark memory.

I had no grasp of what she went through in that lab in Antarctica. I imagined the worst, though. Especially since Schneider kept vials of her blood in a cooler. I placed the sword across the edge of the table and then perched in the chair next to it.

"In London, I was homeless. I moved from alleyway to alleyway." Still clutching her elbows, she started pacing again. "While the city seemed familiar, I did not belong there. Somehow, I knew that. One night, I had a...dream. Of a place in the country. A large, old house surrounded by a forest and a high wall at the edges of the property line."

The hair on the back of my neck stood on end. She'd dreamed of Walker Manor. I remained silent and allowed her to continue.

"I stole a car." She gave a little laugh, as though she was still impressed with herself. "From London, I drove west. Does it sound odd I had no idea where I was going, only that I had to go west?"

I shook my head. "Not at all."

"I was...drawn to that house. That manor. I abandoned the car in a small village east of the house and walked the rest of the way."

And that's when she arrived at Walker Manor looking as though she'd been through hell. She left out details, either because she didn't want to talk about them or because she didn't remember them clearly.

She stopped pacing and peered at me, concentration lining her face. "I will ask again. Who am I to you?"

I took a deep breath, expelled it. I placed my hand on the hilt of the sword as if it would give me strength.

"Your name is not Natasha. It's the name the neo-Nazis gave you in Antarctica," I said. "My uncle, Edward, is your brother. Your true name is Annabelle Walker and you are my mother."

My mother said nothing for a long quiet moment as she continued to look at me. Then she took slow careful steps toward me. I remained where I was on the edge of the chair as she paused in front of me. Her gaze searched my face, as if seeing me for the first time. As if understanding who I was to her and who she was to me.

She took a tendril of the strip of white hair at my left temple and twined it around her forefinger, then released it. A permanent gift after my visit with Michael, the archangel. Her hand brushed over the crown of my head, then down the length of my hair hanging down my back. Then she took my hands in hers and pulled me to my feet. She held my hands in her cold ones as she shivered.

"Your name is Anna," she said. "Annabelle Marie."

My throat clotted with unexpected emotion. "Yes." The word came out a whisper.

She wrapped her arms around me in a tentative hug. I pulled her to me, hugging her hard. It was a moment ingrained in my mind from the moment I realized she was alive. I wanted to believe she truly remembered me. I hoped a small piece of her did.

When I pulled back, I held her hands, reluctant to release them. Tears burned the backs of my eyes. I blinked them away.

"That's what I named you," she said then.

Gooseflesh rose on my arms. "You remembered that?"

"I remembered the day you were born. In December. A cold, blustery day. In Baltimore."

I blinked surprise. How the bloody hell did I end up in Texas if I was born in Maryland? "Baltimore?"

"There was some danger there." She released my hands and went back to pacing. "I cannot recall what. I only remember we had to leave. We moved south. To a place we thought would be safe. And hidden. But it wasn't." She stopped again, her boots scuffing on the floor.

"When you say 'we' you mean you, me, and my father?"

She shook her head. "You and I." She bit her thumbnail. "Your father. I...cannot recall your father."

"His name?" I asked.

"His face," she replied. Her shoulders slumped. "I have no memory of him."

My heart sank. I was so close to getting answers about my parents. She slumped in the chair across from me, her head in her hands.

"Forgive me, Anna, but I am tired."

"Of course." It was hard not to notice the exhaustion in her voice. I picked up the sword. "We can talk more later."

Maybe she would remember more then. Maybe she would be able to tell me who my father was. I patted her shoulder as I walked by, but she caught my fingers in hers. I glanced down at her. She smiled up at me.

"Thank you."

"For what?"

"For listening. For bringing me here."

"I think it's me who owes you thanks. I'd be dead if you hadn't showed up in Madrid when you did. How did you find me in Spain?"

Thoughtful contemplation came over her face. "I told you before. We have a connection. As though a flutter in my mind. I sense your presence, your fear, your joy. All your emotions." She gripped my hand, squeezing it tight. "I was in London on the streets. I made my way to the train station and stowed away. I arrived in Madrid a few days before I found you at the Royal Palace. I tracked you."

Like a flutter through her mind. Yes, I understood that. She was right—we *were* connected. I was grateful she found me.

I squeezed her hand, then dropped a kiss on top of her head. "Rest now."

As I left the house, closing the door behind me, those hot tears were back. I didn't fight them this time.

I sucked in the afternoon air and got my emotions under control. Thankfully, no one was about. Ophelia and Ronan had disappeared. I still had no clue where Kincade was.

I hid my uncle's sword in the cloud, then returned to the house I shared with Kincade. As I pushed open the door, the postcard laid on the floor on the other side of the threshold. As if someone had slipped it under the door. I bent to pick it up.

The picture was of a red-brick chapel on a base of granite in what appeared to be a secluded spot. No writing was on the card on the front at all. I flipped it over to the familiar blocky handwriting. *Holy Grail* were the only words written there.

Cold tendrils danced up my spine. It was the last and final clue I needed to find the cup. I couldn't wait to tell Kincade.

CHAPTER 33

As soon as I was inside, I dug through my things for my smartphone. My first thought was to search for the chapel, even though I had no information other than it was built with red bricks. When I pulled out the phone, I discovered the battery was dead. Ronan had failed to grab the charger from the hotel room, so it was basically a useless thing. I doubted there were any cell towers in the Fae forest anyway. I tossed it back into the bag, dejected.

I paced the length of the living area holding the picture of the chapel in one hand and biting the thumbnail of the other. My only hope was Kincade would know where this place was. I was certain I'd find the Grail. I was certain this was the final clue I needed.

At last, the door opened and he entered. I spun to face him, my heart pounding wild and fast with excitement and nerves.

I forced myself not to rush him.

"Where have you been?" I hadn't meant to sound so demanding.

He shot me a glance that said I should mind my own business. I fully expected him to blow me off, but he answered instead.

"This place has no way out. Did you know that?"

I huffed out a breath. "Yeah. Fae magic. Duh."

He said nothing as he stood watching me shift from one foot to the other. "What's got you all jittery?"

Hearing him say the word *jittery* was almost comical. But that was exactly what I was. I handed him the card, barely able to contain my excitement. "Look at this."

He took it, studying it intently. "When did you get it?"

I bounced on the balls of my feet, barely containing myself.

I didn't have to explain what it was. He already knew.

"Today. I visited my mother. When I came back, it was on the floor. As if someone slid it under the door."

He flipped it over and read the handwriting on the back. "Like the others. *Holy Grail.*"

"Yes." I nodded emphatically. "It's the clue we needed."

He turned back to the picture to study it some more but said nothing.

"Well?" I prompted.

"Well, what?"

Maddening man. "Do you know this place?"

I watched his mind work as he stared at the picture, not moving. Then he met my gaze. Those eyes glittered with knowledge and a bit of teasing humor. "Yes."

He didn't elaborate. Frustration edged through me. It was like trying to pull information out of an armadillo. I waved my hands for more. "And?"

"It's a chapel in a remote village in western Poland. Built by the Knights Templar."

My heart beat faster. Of course, he would know that. He spent time with the Templars. He was once their guardian in times of need. Until they were all wiped out. Excitement flickered through me. I waited for him to offer more details.

Finally, he said, "Saint Stanislaus."

He let the name sit between us.

"You know where that is in western Poland?"

He nodded. "I do."

"And you can take me?"

He nodded again. "I can."

My elation overcame my good senses. I launched myself at him. I didn't think. I didn't hesitate. I wrapped my arms around his neck and hugged him. I'd lost my head, clearly, as his sandalwood scent permeated my nose and sent a thrill through me. My senses stood up and took notice. My heart kicked hard—not from the excitement of finding the Grail, but from the shock of being this close to him.

Something I had never, ever done.

For a moment, he seemed shocked by my display of affection. His breath stuttered once against my hair.

His arm wrapped around my waist as he gave me a half-hearted return hug. I sensed his discomfort and flushed hot to the roots of my hair.

I pulled away and took a step back.

His hand slid from around my waist and caught my hand, holding me in place. Heat flashed up my arm before I understood what he'd done. Warmth pulsed through me from head to toe as he clutched my fingers in his. Everything seemed to move in slow motion then.

He placed the picture of the chapel on the table. His gaze returned to mine—and something in him had shifted. No longer did he look at me with the mirth of teasing.

The air between us thickened.

He peered at me intently, a vague glimmer of intense danger. His eyes had turned searing gold, edging out the green. A vulnerable longing. As though he had dropped every barrier between us.

My insides jangled with prolonged anticipation.

We had come close to this moment before on the dance floor in the Royal Palace. I remembered that now, but it was nothing compared to this. I stood waiting for him to make the next move.

I realized what he intended to do. He made the decision first.

I was powerless to resist. I froze.

His large hands cupped my face, soft and warm. His thumb swept over my cheekbone. I tilted my head back to study his face, committing to memory every feeling, every movement, every breath, every *everything* as he stepped closer.

Closer.

Closer still.

He hesitated—just long enough for my breath to catch.

His mouth closed over mine. My eyes drifted closed.

The kiss was unhurried at first—exploratory—before deepening with quiet certainty.

My knees threatened to buckle. I swayed.

I reached for him, my hands landing on his waist to steady myself. To give myself something solid for balance. If his waist was this solid, what about the rest of him?

Kissing him was as I imagined—an ancient man who knew what he wanted.

His mouth moved from mine, to cheekbone, to jawline. My fingers clenched in his shirt.

My head fell back as he moved down the column of my neck, pressing a kiss against my rapidly beating pulse. Like he was testing me.

Breathing was now optional. Everything that had happened between us led us to this moment—his mouth on my skin, my body betraying me.

Our relationship was tense and complicated and sometimes strained.

A breath shuddered out of me as he continued down, his mouth against the hollow of my throat. I was not going to last much longer standing upright. His slow drugging kisses returned to my mouth, reclaiming it.

I wasn't ready for the next step. This first step was enough to do me in.

His hands moved from my face to tangle in my hair, fisting the locks and pulling my head back, tucking me into his big body.

Yes, I for sure was not going to last much longer. He must have sensed it—how close I was to unraveling. That's why he clutched me to him, keeping me close, kissing me senseless.

A knock sounded on the door. We both ignored it.

Whoever was on the other side persisted with another, more urgent knock.

"Anna, you're going to want to come out here." It was Killian.

Kincade pulled back, annoyance at the interruption flickering through his eyes.

We stood a moment longer, holding on to each other as if that was the one and only time we would ever engage in the long-burning desire smoldering between us.

"Anna?" he called through the door, then started to turn the knob.

Kincade broke from me, releasing me so suddenly I swayed on my feet. He yanked the door open, positioning himself squarely between me and the hall.

"What?" he barked.

It was fun hearing him bark at someone else.

"I need Anna."

My lips were damp. I pressed my fingers against them, still pulsing in the aftermath of his mouth. I took a deep breath, trying to calm my erratic breathing. When I thought I had it under control, I stepped around him, ducking under his arm holding open the door.

"What is it, Killian?"

He glanced from me to Kincade and back again. Then flushed. No doubt realizing he'd interrupted.

"We have visitors at the edge of the forest. You aren't going to like it."

I shifted from one foot to the other, sensing Kincade's agitation behind me. "Who is it?" When the Fae king hesitated again, I huffed. "Out with it."

"Lucifer," he said at least. "And the high lords."

"Fuck," Kincade breathed.

"Where?" I demanded.

"I'll take you."

I took a mental inventory. Dagger on hip. Sword in cloud. Then nodded. "Let's go."

Kincade followed me out of the house. Ronan and Ophelia fell in step behind us. I didn't see my mother or Astrid and was relieved. I hoped they both stayed safe and out of sight.

We headed down the stairs that lead to the ground, then through the small Fae village. No one was about. As if Killian had ordered everyone inside.

Lucifer stole the four Fae treasures and nearly decimated the entire Fae race by taking out their realm. All that was left were the ones hiding in the sacred forest. How had the dark one managed to find it? It was supposed to be hidden from the human realm.

At the edge of the forest, Killian paused at what appeared to be wall of foliage. He turned to the four of us.

"They are waiting on the other side of this," he said. "I will sift us rather than show them the hidden gate."

"What do they want?" Kincade asked.

"Azriel wants Astrid back, I'm sure. As for the others, I don't know."

"Take us, Killian," I said.

He nodded. A flash of light and a moment later we stood outside the Fae forest facing off with Hadrian, Lucifer, and Azriel. Killian was in the center. Kincade and I were to his left. Ophelia and Ronan to his right. Lucifer's gaze flickered over all of us, a wicked smile on his face.

"Well, this is quite the party, isn't it? Hello, Anna," he said.

"Why are you here?" My fingers twisted, ready to grab the dagger.

"As if you don't know. Where is it?"

"Where is what?" I countered.

He sighed. "Must we play this little game? You lied about the Grail. You said it was the real one when, in fact, it was a fake. That leads me to believe you have the real one."

I shook my head. "I don't have it."

Lucifer cut a glance at Kincade, then Killian, then back to me. "Is the little time warper hiding it? Where is she?"

"Yes," Azriel said. "I'd like my property back."

"How did you even find us?" I changed the subject to deflect the anger I sensed coming from Killian.

"Hadrian has many talents. He's an accomplished tracker," Lucifer said.

"That and I put a tracking device in Astrid's arm." Azriel flashed a wicked grin.

Next to me, Killian stiffened. Anger pulsed off him.

Well, shit. None of us thought to check. And clearly Astrid said nothing of the tracking device. It led me to believe she had no idea it was there. Otherwise, she would not have allowed it to stay.

"Oh, you didn't know about the tracking device, did you?" Azriel added. "Bring her to me now and the rest of you can live."

"You're not getting her back." Killian wielded his sword. The metal made a *shing* sound as it came out of the scabbard.

"I will fight you to the death for her if that's what it takes," Azriel said. "She belongs to me."

"Astrid belongs to no one. And no one is fighting." I stepped forward and placed a hand on Killian's wrist, pushing the sword down. Then I addressed Lucifer. "I don't have the Grail. None of us do."

Lucifer moved closer to me. Behind me, Kincade closed the gap behind me. The warmth from his body radiated over my back.

"It's a pity you won't cooperate with me, Anna. You have so much potential."

He reached for the white tendril of hair at my temple, twirled it around his finger. I remained perfectly still as Kincade growled low and deep in his throat. Lucifer cut him a glance and chuckled.

"Don't like me touching her, do you?"

Kincade said nothing. In my head, he said, *I will kill him.*

Not if I do first, I replied.

"Your power is almost equal to mine. Almost." He stepped backward, taking his place once again between the high lords. "Let us see how you handle my next challenge."

"What challenge?"

He did not reply.

Dark, ominous clouds formed in the sky. The wind turned south, tousling my hair. Lightning flickered between Ronan's fingers. Killian held his sword aloft. Kincade pulled his demon killing gun from his holster and readied it. Ophelia wielded her shimmering sword. I pulled Edward's flaming sword from the cloud.

We all sensed whatever was about to happen. In the distance, I heard a high-pitched sound reminding me of something I'd heard in the depths of Hell the two times I'd been there. Gooseflesh rose on my arms as my eyes remained on the horizon. Lucifer, Hadrian, and Azriel stepped aside to watch the coming horde, unconcerned.

A black cloud smudged the horizon. My heart leapt to my throat. We were about to be overrun.

"What do we do?" I said so only Kincade would hear.

"Stand our ground. Fight or die today, Anna."

"I'm not dying today."

"Good. Let's kill some demons, then."

And then it was on.

CHAPTER 34

THEY CAME FROM EVERYWHERE and nowhere. It seemed as though the demons spilled from the very depths of the earth as they headed right for us. With so many converging on us, we wouldn't be able to defeat them all as they scrabbled over the ground like cockroaches sprinting from the light.

My gut twisted. I stole a glance at my companions. None of them showed fear. They all stood their ground. And it made me proud they were willing to fight for and with me.

Kincade didn't wait until the first group of demons were upon us. He fired round after round, hitting most of them as they ran toward us. The high-pitched whine and flash of his gun was unmistakable as was the exploding black demon guts. The only perk was they didn't explode all over me.

Tired of standing in place, I charged with a deep guttural battle cry. I didn't turn back as I entered the fray, swinging the sword with all my might. I'd never wielded it like this before, so I wasn't prepared for the weight of it in my hand. My muscles quivered from the exertion as I lopped off head after head of demons. Spun one way, killed another. Spun another way, killed more.

A war cry was near me and I glanced up long enough to catch sight of Ophelia using her shimming sword to kill demons. Even Killian was getting in on the action.

A crack of what sounded like thunder split the air. Ronan clapped his hands together. Lightning spun around his hands and then shot outward, taking out large swaths of demons charging us.

I halted, staring at him in awe as he did it again and again. With little or no effort.

"Anna, look out!" Ophelia shouted.

I spun as two demons were on me. I stabbed one with the flaming sword, searing him into a pile of ash immediately. As I turned to take out the other one, the unmistakable whine of Kincade's gun shrieked, then the flash of light, and *BOOM*. The demon exploded all over me. At least I had the sense to anticipate and turned my back before guts splatted all over my face.

"Thanks, Kincade."

"Pay attention, will you?" he shouted back. And then he was out of juice. "Give me your dagger."

Without thinking, I jerked it from the sheath and tossed it to him. He caught it by the handle and went to work killing demons one by one. But we weren't out of this yet. More seemed to be coming.

I lopped off the head of one and turned to take out another and that's when I came face to face with Hadrian. He gave me sadistic grin.

"Shall we finish what we started in Spain? Your face needs more decoration."

I didn't have a chance to respond or react before his power punched through me, sending me backward. The flaming sword dropped from my hand, snuffing out. I landed on the hard, cold ground and skidded several feet before stopping, the wind knocked out of me.

My friends were all busy with their own problems. Even Kincade was happily hacking away demons with the dagger, watching them turn to ash, and then hacking some more. I clutched the ground, fisting damp grass as I tried to shove myself upward to a sitting position. Pain exploded across my chest where he'd hit me with his dark power.

Hadrian used his demon magic to hide us behind his veil. The sounds of the battle faded as we were enveloped. My heart raced as I tried to figure out a way out of this.

I wanted to tell him he wouldn't kill me with his lord master watching. But maybe this is what Lucifer wanted all along. Maybe he wanted me dead after all. I didn't bend to his will, so therefore, I was expendable. With the manor unguarded, attacking it and finding the relics would be relatively easy.

Footsteps and then Hadrian's boots were in my line of vision. He grasped a handful of hair and yanked my head back.

"You are not so invincible, are you? You have no weapon. And no one will witness me kill you. Pity. It will be a spectacular death."

He shoved my face down into the ground, pushing the back of my head. I practically ate dirt and grass but managed to close my eyes. He kicked me hard in the side. I rolled, trying to escape him. I was fairly certain he'd broken a rib or two. So much pain. Breathing was a labor.

"You're nothing but a lying bitch. Do you have any idea how humiliated I was when I returned with the fake cup?"

Ah, so this was vengeance.

In the distance, I heard my name. It sounded like Ronan calling me. But I wasn't sure. It was too hard to make out. My fuzzy brain wasn't able to understand.

Hadrian didn't bother to kick me again or yank my hair or even put another hand on me. He simply used his demon magic to pound me. Blast after blast smacked into me. Somehow, I sensed he held back. Like he was saving the full force of it for the grand finale. I rolled to my stomach, trying to hide from the violent blasts, but it was useless to escape.

A crackling sound exploded around me and then a momentary silence. I realized that was because my ears were ringing from the high-pitched sound. Like I'd been plunged into a tunnel.

A voice in my ear but I wasn't sure who. Hands picked me up off the ground. I sagged against the hard body. My hand landed on the slender chest. It was Ronan. He said something but I shook my head, indicating I couldn't hear him.

He bowed backward then, as if something pierced him. When he turned to face the attacker, Hadrian lowered his hands. He'd used his demon magic on Ronan.

Unable to hold myself up, I slumped back to the ground. In my haze, I glimpsed Ronan turn his lightning hands on Hadrian. I watched, mesmerized, as he formed white streaks of light between his fingers and then flung them out as if he harnessed the power of the sky. He struck Hadrian in the chest. The high lord flew backward and landed hard on the ground.

I spotted the flaming sword nearby and clawed my way to it. Breaking every fingernail and lodging dirt under them as I did. My hand landed on the pommel. Concentrating hard, I slid my hand up the blade, but no flames came.

Dammit, I was too weak.

I pushed to my feet, wobbled, but managed to stay upright as I turned toward the melee. Dead demons littered the ground. Ophelia was covered in black blood. Kincade was somewhere lost in the demon crowd using my dagger to kill one after another. And standing on the sidelines watching it all with a grin, was Lucifer.

Where the hell was Azriel?

My answer came shortly after the thought passed through my mind when his arms encircled me, pulling him against him.

"Give up, *cherie*. You and your pitiful friends have lost."

Hadrian caught sight of us then. I wiggled against Azriel which only made him groan in anticipation as though I was a juicy morsel, he was ready to screw. I gagged on the bile that rose to my throat. Through bleary eyes, I focused and saw the demon army dissipating to almost nothing. We were winning.

"We have not," I managed to croak.

Ronan threw another ball of light at Hadrian, but he deflected it with a black shield of power. His gaze landed on me and Azriel. He turned his attention back to killing me.

"Release her, brother," the high lord called.

Azriel hesitated only a moment before he released me and stepped away. Perhaps Hadrian outranked Azriel. I didn't know. I didn't care. I held the sword in my tired hands, my arms shaking again with the weight. I was determined to defend myself no matter the cost.

Hadrian readied his power between his hands. He released it. Ronan shouted my name, but I stood my ground. And the next thing I knew, Ronan dove in front of me.

He took the blast square in the chest and fell to the ground, his shirt smoking. I shrieked and dropped to my knees next to him.

"Ronan, you stupid fool!"

His face was a map of black and white veins. He gripped my shirt with a bloody, cracked hand. I glanced down to see the light he harnessed between those long slender fingers flickering as though losing an electrical charge. Then he flattened his hand on my chest over my heart.

"It's all you now, Anna."

A pulse of energy pounded through me, shocking me. As though I'd been shocked back to life with a defibrillator. A warm sense of power surged through me outward from where his hand was on my chest. I sucked in a sharp breath as the bright white light converged deep inside me with the Godlight.

Ronan said he had divine power. I understood what that meant now. His divine power merged with mine as he pushed it into me. His hand went limp and dropped back to his body. His sightless eyes peered back up at me, his mouth slack.

Fucking Hadrian had killed him. But that bolt of power was meant for me. And Ronan died protecting me.

I pushed to my feet. The power crackled between my fingers now. A pulsing light beat from my body outward. The Godlight deep inside came to life. I hadn't felt it since the last beating I took from Hadrian. But it was back. Whatever Ronan did to me revitalized it.

And now I was out for blood.

I fixed my eyes on Hadrian, but that sorry bastard turned ran away from the converging demon horde. He and Azriel both.

"Killian! Kincade! Out of the way!" Ophelia shouted.

Because whatever she saw in me, she realized what I was about to do. I focused all my energy, all my wrath, all my *everything* on that bloody demon horde that wouldn't stop. I flung out my hands and shoved the bright white light outward, decimating what was left of them.

They all fell to the ground, dead, leaving behind scorched earth and the acrid stench of death.

As the light dwindled from both my hands and my body, I collapsed in a heap. No energy left. Hot tears sprang to my eyes. My body ached from head to toe but I was alive.

Ronan wasn't.

Guilt swarmed me as I laid in the dirt, gasping for air trying to calm my palpitating heart. Kincade scooped me up off the ground, pulling me into his lap, and holding my boneless body against him. He was my salvation.

"You defeated my demon army. You defeated my powerful high lord. You killed my Prince of Greed and my Destroyer Angel." Lucifer's footsteps crunched on the fried ground as he approached.

"You lose, Lucifer," Kincade said. His deep voice rumbled against my ear.

"Do I? Perhaps not yet." He took a deep breath, lifted his head to the sky and looked up at the foliage behind us. "I should have destroyed all the Fae when I had the chance. When I took their treasures. I was the fool who allowed one king to remain alive. But perhaps he will take this final message to heart."

He gave a fiendish grin and snapped his fingers. Then disappeared.

Silence descended.

Until we all smelled smoke.

Killian's sharp kaleidoscope eyes were on the tops of the trees. Panic etched his face. "The forest is on fire!"

He sifted away, leaving us all. I choked back a sob as fear shuddered through me.

"Kincade, my mother..."

He eased me to the ground and pressed the dagger into my hand. "I'll find her."

"I'm coming with you," Ophelia said.

He pointed at her, his face stern. "Stay with her. Give me your sword."

She obliged. We both gaped in fascinated horror as he hacked his way past the foliage to reveal a wooden gate with iron hinges. He cursed and set about trying to kick it in. Suddenly, the gate flung open. Several women and children ran past him. Kincade jumped out of the way. When it was clear, he ran inside without looking back.

Ophelia and I heard the chaos inside. The screams, the shouts, the cries. She paced, keeping a watchful eye on the foliage. The smoke thickened. The stink of burned trees and grass filled the air. I coughed as the smoke made my eyes water.

"Ophelia, we need to get away from the trees. Help me move him."

Somehow, I found the strength to climb to my feet. I hooked my arms under Ronan's shoulders. She picked up his feet. Together, we stumbled away from the burning forest. Several Fae sifted out to safety while others ran through the open gate. There was no sign of Kincade or my mother, yet.

Killian appeared with Astrid. He left her, then went back inside. Astrid's eyes were bright with shiny unshed tears, her face dirty with soot.

"Astrid, what happened?"

She shook her head. "I can't explain it. One moment, everything was fine. The next, the trees were on fire. As though they suddenly burst into flame. Some didn't make it out."

I was too tired to stand. I collapsed to my knees, watching and waiting. My heart was in my throat as more and more Fae escaped the fire. It seemed an eternity until Kincade appeared with my mother in tow. My shoulders slumped in relief.

She coughed from the smoke. Kincade led her to me as I pushed to my feet. When she reached me, she hugged me tight.

"It's all gone, Anna."

"All?" I asked.

"The houses. Gone," she said.

"I was able to recover this." Kincade handed me an envelope. "They're all there."

I recognized it as the envelope with all the postcards inside. It was hard to choke back the tears. It meant so much to me he thought to grab it. "Thanks."

Killian returned carrying a young girl. He handed her off to her wailing mother. More Fae sifted out, until at last there were no more. The hidden forest burned to the ground until there was nothing left but smoldering cinders and ash.

Killian stood statute still, staring at the destruction with Astrid at his side. Merric, the silver-haired elegant-faced Fae, bustled up to Killian. I hadn't seen him when we arrived. His pale face was red with anger as he glared at Astrid, fire flashing in his pale blue eyes.

"This is the demon girl's fault." He pointed to Astrid.

Killian's head snapped in his direction, ready to fight. But it was me who answered.

"She had nothing to do with it, you old windbag."

He looked positively aghast I dared to speak to him in such a way. Despite the pain riddling my body, I hobbled toward the Fae who had the nerve to accuse Astrid of destroying the forest. Kincade matched me step for step, likely waiting for me to collapse again. At least he'd catch me.

"It was Lucifer," I said. "If it's anyone's fault, it's mine."

"Anna—" Killian began.

"You. I'm not surprised." A sour expression crossed his face as he looked me over in distaste. Then he turned his heated glare on

Killian. "You brought this filth here. Our kinsfolk died because of *her*."

I clenched my fists, wishing I had the energy to punch the guy. Although I was prepared to take full responsibility, I didn't have to be insulted.

"It's not Anna's fault." Killian's voice was surprisingly calm. "Lucifer had a score to settle with me. Or do you not recall him stealing our treasures and destroying our realm? He wanted me to suffer. He wanted us all to suffer."

Merric remained silent as more furious words swirled inside his head. "Then he got what he wanted. Look at them. Look at them all. Displaced. Homeless. Now at the mercy of the human realm."

He waved his hand toward what remained of the Fae huddled together for warmth and comfort. Children clung to their parents, bereft over the loss of their safety and security. I understood that all too well. There weren't many left of the Fae. Less than a thousand, perhaps. Snow started to fall. We had to get out of the elements and soon.

"Go away, Merric, and let me think." Killian rubbed his forehead in frustration.

Merric said nothing more as he charged away, back to the masses. No doubt to spread more lies about who did what.

"Astrid, can't you..." I paused, looking at the destroyed earth.

She shook her head. "No. Even I do not have the power to remake what has been destroyed."

"I don't know what we're going to do now." Killian looked at what was left of his race, his mouth drawn in a frown.

It hurt me to see him like that, to see all the Fae displaced. I had an idea.

"I do. There are woods surrounding Walker Manor. It's safe."

His brows drew together. "What are you suggesting, Anna?"

"Isn't it obvious? I'm suggesting you move your people."

His face remained impassive as he peered at me, contemplating my offer. "You would...have us?"

"Yes. There isn't room in the manor for all of you, of course, but you and Astrid are welcome."

He considered this a long moment. Astrid slipped her hand around his arm and moved closer with a smile. She gave him an encouraging nod.

"We have survived a long time living off the land," he said. "I'm sure they would welcome the new home. For that, I give you thanks."

"It's the least I can do. I wish I could do more."

I watched his people, thinking of all the things that had happened. Things that were yet to come. Of Conquest marching across the land with his armies destroying more lives. Of the famines and the sickness spreading across the world. I understood that with Conquest, the first of the Four Horseman, the others would soon follow.

"What happened here was merely a battle with Lucifer," I said. "He's building his army with stolen souls. A war is coming. One I intend to fight with the Holy Relics."

"My people were not strong enough to defeat him before when he stole the Four Treasures," Killian said. "But, perhaps, we can defeat him together."

"What are you suggesting, Killian?" I asked, mimicking his earlier question. I dared not hope.

"I'm saying I will pledge my sword and those of my people who wish to fight to your cause. The Fae stand behind you. Together, we will defeat this evil."

I was touched. Truly. Emotion clogged in my throat once again. I swallowed it back and blinked away the tears. "Thank you, Killian. We're going to need all the help we can get. Now, can you get us out of here?"

CHAPTER 35

WE DISCOVERED, WITH SOME dismay, some of the Fae were unable to sift like Killian and a few of the others. Merric was an ass. He tried to refuse the offer to move to the grounds at Walker Manor. But eventually he came to his senses when Killian offered to leave him behind in what was left of the sacred forest.

Astrid had regained some of her strength from her imprisonment with Azriel, but Killian wouldn't allow her to expend that energy moving us all. Several Fae leaders, including the Fae king himself, took turns sifting us all back to Walker Manor. The worst part was returning with Ronan's body. Kincade insisted on carrying him.

We arrived as the sun set, drawing long shadows across the vast lawn. Astrid refused to leave the several hundred Fae survivors out in the cold. She set about using what was left of her powers to create a small tent city along the massive grounds giving them shelter and a means to keep warm. Her energy began to drain. I urged her to stop since night was falling and it would soon be dark and cold.

By the time I stepped foot across the threshold, I was exhausted. Still, I was determined to make it to my room on my own two feet. I hobbled toward the door. Kincade followed carrying Ronan's body. Then Natasha and Ophelia followed by Astrid and Killian. Piers greeted us, his face a mask of both surprise and curiosity. When he glanced at me, his expression turned to one of horror. I must have looked a fright.

"My lady, I'm glad you've returned. Not quite unscathed. Are you all right? Should I ring for a doctor?"

"I'm fine." I forced a smile.

Meanwhile, Kincade took Ronan's body into the parlor and placed him on the long sofa. I was dismayed to see many items were out of place, gone or broken. No doubt at the hands of the agents who searched the place when they were looking for me and the relics.

"Master Harred?" Piers asked as Kincade removed one of the fuzzy blankets from the back of the sofa and covered him from head to toe.

"He didn't make it. We'll need to contact his father. I need you to find a room for Astrid and Killian."

Ophelia accompanied my mother through the door then. They both paused in the parlor door. Natasha turned away from the parlor and to me. She gripped my arms.

"I'm so sorry, Anna."

"Me, too," I whispered.

She kissed my cheek, then ascended the stairs as if she knew exactly where she was going. Ophelia didn't bother to hide the tears slipping down her face as she followed my mother. Kincade was still at my side. Ever present. Outside was some commotion. Piers stepped to the door.

"My lady, there appears to be tents erected on the grounds." He turned back to me with question on his aged face.

"Oh, right. We have new residents. I'll explain in the morning. You don't need to worry about them."

I trudged up the stairs clutching the envelope of postcards to my chest and thinking about nothing but a hot shower and my soft bed. I didn't even object when Kincade followed me into my room and shut the door. He took the envelope from me and placed it on the nightstand as I collapsed on the bed. I kicked off my boots.

He went into the bathroom and turned on the shower.

"I don't need help, you know," I said.

"You look like shit."

"Gee, thanks. I feel like shit."

"Let me see your ribs."

"No."

He glared, fire flashing in his eyes. I resisted.

"You're having trouble breathing. Show me. It's not an option."

I sighed, resigned. He was right. I *was* having a hard time breathing because Hadrian kicked the crap out of me. He wasn't going to shut up until I showed him. I lifted the edge of my shirt as high as the pain allowed, wincing the entire time.

"Pretty sure I have a broken rib or two," I said. "Sure feels like it."

I didn't expect him to inspect my ribs. With a gentle touch, he pressed his fingertips against my ribcage. I sucked in a sharp breath.

"Not broken. Just bruised, I think. You need to rest and heal."

"I need to get to Poland," I said.

"The Grail will still be there."

"Yeah? Are you sure about that?"

"They can't find it without you," he said.

I assumed *they* he referred to was Lucifer and company. "How do you know that?"

"Because you're the only one who knows where it is."

I shook my head. "Not true. You know where it is."

"Besides me." He pointed to the bathroom. "Get cleaned up. Then sleep."

I wanted to argue more. That we didn't *actually* know where to find the Grail. Instead, I frowned. "You're not the boss of me."

He reached for my arm and tugged me to my feet. He led me to the bathroom. "For tonight, I am. For once, stop being so stubborn and do as I tell you."

When I was in the bathroom, he closed the door behind me. I leaned against the counter. Every ounce of energy I had was gone. I stared at my face in the mirror, not recognizing the girl looking back. He was right. I looked like shit. Like Hadrian used my face for a punching bag. Dirt smudged my face. Bruises were still evident where he'd punched me. Pieces of dirt and grass were in my hair. Not to mention the demon guts all over my clothes. I smelled awful.

My face hurt. My hair hurt. My body hurt.

Hell, even my teeth hurt.

It took several agonizing minutes to remove my shirt and drop it to the floor. Standing in nothing but my bra, I examined the horrible purple bruises along my ribcage where Hadrian kicked me. A red splotch stained the skin of my chest. I removed my bra and examined it. It faintly resembled a handprint.

Where Ronan had put his hand on my chest.

It's all you now, Anna.

The surge must have been him transferring his power into me. Much like when my uncle died, he had transferred his power to me upon his death. I glanced down at my hand. My nails were ripped and jagged, encrusted with dirt and blood. My hands were red and cracked as though roughened by wind and sun. My joints ached. The hot shower began to steam the mirror, calling to me.

I stripped off the rest of my clothes and stepped under the hot spray. Damn, it was good to be home.

When I finished, I wrapped a towel around me and opened the bathroom door to let the steam escape. Kincade sat in the chair near the balcony reading my tattered copy of *War of the Worlds* by H. G. Wells. When he saw me, he closed the book with a snap.

"I'll give you some privacy."

He stepped out, leaving me alone. I dressed in an oversized long-sleeved shirt and plaid shorts. Every movement sent heated pain throughout my battered body. As I climbed into bed, a knock sounded on the door.

"Come in."

Piers entered with a tray. He brought tea and lemon cakes. He set it down on the nearby dresser and poured a cup. He handed it to me along with a lemon cake. My stomach rumbled.

"Thanks, Piers."

"I contacted Alexander Harred. He and the coroner will be here in the morning to collect his son's body." He stood at the edge of the bed with his hands clasped in front of him. The proper English gentleman.

"How did he take the news?"

"Not well, my lady."

I sipped the tea, letting the steam roll over my chilled skin. I hadn't expected him to take it well. Ronan was, after all, his only son. He likely blamed me for Ronan's death. In my mind, though, he died a hero. He died protecting me. I didn't look forward to seeing Alexander the following morning.

I thought of the girl Ronan loved, the one he was willing to give up to honor the marriage contract. I wondered if she knew he was dead. I wondered if she was as devastated at his loss as I was.

Piers cleared his throat. He had something else on his mind.

"Yes?"

"I took the liberty of cleaning out the master suite. The designer will be here next week to make it more your taste."

"The designer? Piers, I don't—"

"I do realize you wish to keep your uncle's room as is and you prefer to stay in your childhood room. However, it is not fitting for the lady of the manor not to occupy the master suite. I had his things packed up and moved to the attic for storage. You'll want to go through them when you have time."

An emptiness moved through me. I didn't want that enormous room. I wanted to stay put. I did, however, realize Piers was correct. If he hadn't taken the initiative, I never would have. I sighed, resigned, and nodded.

"I trust you, Piers. I leave the design in your hands." Mostly because I didn't want to deal with it.

"If you're certain."

"I am. Thank you."

He started to leave, then turned back. "For all that you've lost, I want to express my deepest condolences."

Then he closed the door and was gone. Tears burned my eyes. Before I gave in to those emotions, though, my door opened again. Kincade entered with a bottle of whiskey and two glasses. He poured one and handed it to me. He took the other glass and the bottle and resumed his position in the chair across the room.

I placed aside the tea and sipped the whiskey. We sat in amicable silence for the longest time, drinking. He was the first one to break the silence.

"I should have been there."

Did I hear a note of regret in his voice? Guilt? His face remained impassive. I started to answer but he continued.

"He stayed by your side. That was my job."

There was no accusation in it. Just fact.

My chest constricted.

"It should have been me."

Horror flickered through me at the thought. I had no words. If I spoke too quickly, my voice would break and the tears would finally fall. The image of Kincade lying under that blanket in the parlor made me feel sick.

"He met his destiny, I think. Besides, I can't lose you."

My breath shuddered out. I said it.

He was my rock. My guardian. The one who stayed, even when I pushed back. What I felt for him went far beyond gratitude or habit. I depended on him in ways I hadn't let myself name before now.

His gaze flickered from the whiskey glass to my face. Something unreadable tightened in his expression.

"You won't."

He said it with conviction. It nearly gutted me.

I finished the whiskey and set the glass aside. We didn't speak again. Not about Poland. Not about the Grail. Not about anything else.

And certainly not about the kiss we'd shared in the sacred forest.

I wondered if it lingered in his thoughts the way it did in mine.

Kincade picked up the book again and began to read, as if there were nowhere else he intended to be.

He wasn't leaving.

I let myself accept that, settled beneath the blankets, and drifted into sleep.

EXHAUSTION HAD TAKEN ITS toll and consumed me. When I awoke, I was alone in my room. No Kincade. The only things left behind were the book in the seat of the chair and an empty whiskey bottle. The tea tray was also gone. No doubt Piers had come to collect it while I slumbered.

Everything was sore as I pushed to a sitting position. I had to admit, though, the rest did me some good. I felt remarkably better. I dressed and then wandered out of my room.

Loud voices wafted up from downstairs. In my bare feet, I hurried down to see what the commotion was about. I was disgruntled to see Alexander Harred and another man I assumed was the coroner in the parlor. Ronan's body was already loaded on a gurney and covered with a white sheet.

Piers stood at the front door and Kincade blocked the threshold of the parlor doing his best impression of a brick wall. As I stepped off the last stair, Alexander's face lit with fury. He charged toward me, trying to shove past Kincade. He blocked him.

"You! You did this. You killed my son," he wailed.

"Anna did no such thing," Kincade said.

But Alexander wasn't having it. "After everything I did to help you. Everything my son did to help you."

"Everything *you* did?" I shook my head. "I don't recall you being with us when we were attacked by a demon horde, Lucifer, and his two high lords."

"I allowed the use of my apartment in Spain. I allowed my son to accompany you against my wishes." He was so angry, he practically spit. "There will be an autopsy. I hope you realize that."

I clenched my sore hands into fists as I approached the man who wanted to blame me for everything that had happened to him and his family.

"Ronan died saving my life. With his last breath, he gave me his divine power."

Alexander scoffed as if he didn't believe it. "That power was a gift to him from the archangels. If he gave it to you, prove it."

I did so love a challenge.

I lifted my hands, unsure how to make the lightning crackle between my fingers as Ronan had. I suspected it was like the Godlight inside me. I had to find a way to tap into it and bring it to life. And since it was all new to me, I hadn't a clue how to do that.

"Anna is telling you the truth," Kincade said. "We all saw it. The high lord intended to kill Anna with his demon magic. Ronan used his body as a shield to protect her."

The man's eyes were bright with tears as he stood looking from me to Kincade and back again. I would forever carry the guilt with me of Ronan's death and so many others. I concentrated hard on how the power pulsed through me when he pressed his hand against my chest.

It crackled to life almost instantly. Tiny flickers of light danced between my fingers. I held up my hands, gazing at it in wonder.

Alexander stumbled backward as if he'd been punched in the gut. He turned to the coroner and said something low under his breath. The man took the end of the gurney and wheeled it toward the door. Kincade stepped aside to let him pass. And out the front he went to a waiting van. He loaded the body into the back, my heart in my throat.

The light dancing around my fingers dissipated to nothing.

Alexander pushed past Kincade and paused in front of me. "You will pay for his death. This I promise you."

"I've already paid enough," I said.

Kincade had enough. He grabbed the man by the back of his coat collar and hauled him to the door.

"And you aren't welcome here anymore."

He shoved Alexander outside, then slammed the door without waiting for a reply. Piers and I stood in stunned silence at Kincade's boldness. I kinda loved him for that.

"So, is there breakfast? I'm starving."

CHAPTER 36

I FINISHED GORGING MYSELF on bacon, eggs, toast, pancakes, and coffee and sat back in the dining chair, my gut full. I sipped one last cup of coffee trying to ignore a hovering Kincade. He hadn't left my side since I landed in the dining room. I had a feeling he was going to be my constant companion from now on.

One brush with death was all it took for him to stick to me like Velcro. Figures.

Piers entered the dining room and paused at my chair. He cleared his throat.

"There is a gentleman here to see you, my lady."

"Oh? Who is it?"

"He said he was an agent with Interpol."

My gaze went to Kincade whose eyebrow rose in question.

"Then I suppose I should speak to him."

"Very good. He's in the parlor, my lady. Shall I bring tea?"

"Sure."

Because every crisis was solved by tea.

I took one last gulp of coffee and pushed back from the table. As I started for the door, I sensed Kincade hot on my heels. Yep, he wasn't going to let me out of his sight.

I wasn't exactly excited about going into the parlor since that was the last place I saw Ronan and had the confrontation with his father. Today was turning out to be a special day. The man stood at the fireplace looking at the few family photos on the mantle. When we entered, he turned to greet me.

I expected him to be accompanied by other agents and other law enforcement, but no. He was alone.

He was tall, with a full head of dark curly hair, a high forehead, high cheekbones, a thin straight nose, and bright green eyes. He sported a goatee on his chin that was neatly trimmed. He wore a black coat over dark trousers. His black shoes were scuffed and probably had seen better days.

"You must be Anna Walker. I'm Agent Bishop." He extended a hand in greeting.

I peered at it suspiciously. "I'm Anna Walker. This is Kincade."

He glanced at the hulking man behind me, pasting on a bright smile. When I refused to grasp his hand, he dropped it.

"Please, have a seat." I motioned to the sofa.

"May I inquire about the numerous tents erected on your lawn?"

"You may not." And that was as much as I intended to answer. I didn't want to have to explain the existence of the Fae or why they camped out on the lawn. "Where are your other agents?"

"Other agents?"

"Aren't you here to search for missing relics? Arrest me for murder? Some other law enforcement type action?" I asked.

Kincade shot me a glare. *Too much information, Anna,* he said in my head.

May as well cut to the chase.

Agent Bishop moved to the sofa, but he didn't sit. Neither Kincade nor I took a seat. So, there we all were, standing around in the middle of the parlor as though we were prepared to face off with one another.

"Can I take your coat?" I asked.

"Oh, no. I won't be here long. I'm not here to search the house."

"Then why are you here?"

He tugged at the collar of his coat, then unbuttoned it. "Perhaps I will take a seat." He shrugged out of the coat and then perched on the edge of the sofa.

I took the chair to his left. Kincade to his right. About that time, Piers entered with the tea tray. He poured three cups from the silver teapot. He handed one to the agent.

"Cream or sugar, sir?" he asked.

The agent waved him away. When Piers glanced at me, I shooed him toward the door. He gave a brief bow and disappeared.

The agent took a sip of tea. "The relics you're accused of stealing...are they here?"

"I don't think that's any of your business," Kincade said.

Bishop grinned over the rim of his cup. "Forgive me, I should explain." He placed the cup on the coffee table in front of him, then angled his body toward me, ignoring Kincade. "Anna, I'm not sure how to explain this."

I was running out of patience. "Why don't you cut to the point, agent? I'm a very busy girl."

He eyed my bruised face. "I see that." Then cleared his throat. "You and I are a more alike than you know, Miss Walker."

"And how is that?"

"You were entrusted with these relics, weren't you?" he asked then.

I tipped my head to the side. "How do you know that?"

"I know many things about you and the Walker family. I was very sorry to hear about the death of your uncle," he said.

Suspicion tingled the back of my neck. I cut a glance to Kincade who's brow was furrowed in question.

"How do you know my uncle, then?"

"He's a bit of a legend. Forgive me. I'm having a difficult time explaining myself."

"No doubt," I said.

"It's not often one meets someone like you," the agent said.

"Like me?"

"You're the Keeper of the Holy Relics."

I shot to my feet. Kincade did, too, ready to do battle.

"Okay, maybe you tell me who the bloody hell you are. No more beating around the bush," I demanded. "Are you really an Interpol agent?"

"I am. And I'm recommending we drop all the charges against you. I have a clear understanding of who and what you are because, well, you see, I'm a dream walker, too."

Shocked, I sat down so hard in the chair it nearly rocked backward. Kincade lowered himself to his chair with much more grace than I.

"You're a dream walker," I repeated.

"Yes, and I'm very good at my job." He flashed a grin. "All of us are connected in some form or fashion across the world. And all of us have an understanding of the prophecy of the Keeper of the Holy Relics."

I had no words. I stared at him, numb, trying to understand. My head began to throb.

"You know about me?"

"Yes, of course. A few of us have been following along as you collect these relics. We also know what's coming. Ther there are others like Agent Harris. Or were, I should say."

"Who's Agent Harris?"

"The one who arrested you in Spain."

Oh. The one who died at the hands of the vampires.

"She did not understand who or what you are," he continued. "I tried to be the one on your case and to meet you in Spain that day as the arresting officer. Things would have turned out much different for you and Agent Harris. I'm sorry it didn't work out. However, after the attack in the street, I used my influence and managed to have myself assigned to your case. And, so, here I am. With a full pardon."

I stared at him in shocked silence, trying to form words. I wasn't exactly sure how a full pardon worked with Interpol but, hey, I wasn't one to look a gift horse in the mouth.

At last, I said, "I see."

He reached for his coat and pulled out a card from the inside pocket. "And when that time comes, please call on me. Us."

I took the card from him. It was plain with nothing but his name, Archibald Bishop, and a phone number.

"I don't understand."

"I think he wants to fight for you, Anna," Kincade said.

"Yes, exactly. As far as Interpol and other law enforcement is concerned, you are cleared of all charges. By way of a matter of misunderstanding." Bishop gave me a sideways grin that indicated he was pleased with that outcome.

"I...don't know what to say."

"You don't have to say anything, Miss Walker. And now I simply must be going. I don't want to overstay my welcome and, as you said, you are busy. Thank you for the tea." He scooped up his coat and headed for the door.

Somewhat in a fog, I got to my feet. "I'll walk you out."

"No need. I can show myself out. It was a pleasure to meet you, Miss Walker."

Then he gave a jaunty wave and left.

It was, by far, the strangest conversation I ever had.

"Well, I guess that means you're cleared to go to Poland," Kincade said.

I stared down at the card. "I don't get it."

"Don't get what?"

"First the Fae, now there's apparently a whole network of dream walkers who want to help me." Confused, I met his gaze. "Where were they when I needed them?"

"You didn't need them yet," he said. "But you will. And soon."

"With one horseman released, I expect the others are not far behind."

"Which means we need to find the Grail and the Ark."

I nodded agreement. The last two relics. But first the Grail.

"Then I guess we better pack our bags."

"Our?" He quirked an eyebrow.

"Oh, please. Like you're ever going to let me out of your sight again." Though I rolled my eyes, I was secretly glad. He tried hard to hide the smile, but I caught a glimpse of the hint of it.

"Probably not," he said. "Are you sure you're up for it?"

"I have to be up for it. Let's do this."

✦———✦

DESPITE MY CONTINUED FATIGUE and beat up body, I was ready to go to Poland and recover the Holy Grail. I made arrangements with the private jet. We planned to fly into Poznań Airport, rent a car, and drive the rest of the way. In the past, I may have been apprehensive about traveling alone with Kincade. Now, it seemed normal.

Neither of us had acknowledged that kiss. I found it difficult to stop thinking about it, though.

Everything I traveled with burned up in the sacred Fae forest. I traveled light anyway. I found a small carryon suitcase to pack my black clothes and underwear. When Kincade gave me the dagger back, I put it and Edward's sword back in the cloud for safekeeping. They would be there again should I need them.

The driver would arrive within the hour to take us to the airport. I used the time to say my farewells to my mother, Astrid and Killian, Ophelia and Darius. Darius remained ever vigilant at Grace's side. I paused by her bedside, taking her hand in mine. Her skin was cold, clammy. Her face was pale. Deep bruises had appeared under her eyes. Her cheeks looked as though they were sinking. My heart hurt. It had taken far too long to recover the Grail. Far too many distractions and interruptions.

I kissed her forehead.

"I will be back with the Grail. I promise," I whispered.

She made no movement or indication she heard me. I placed her hand by her side. I didn't want to think about Grace dying if I didn't make it back without the relic. Kincade waited for me at the bottom of the stairs.

Together, we got in the chauffeur driven car and left Walker Manor behind once again.

CHAPTER 37

IT WAS A TWO-HOUR flight from London to Poznań, then a two-and-a-half-hour drive from the airport. I let Kincade do the driving while I dozed in the passenger seat. I found an inn near the chapel. He parked, we checked in, and headed up to the room. It was very small. One thing stood out to me—there was only one bed.

"I asked for two beds," I said.

"Don't worry. I don't snore." He dropped his bag in one of the gray chairs.

I stood in the middle of the tiny room with the wood flooring and stared at that one bed with my heart in my throat. It was, at least, a queen size bed. But Kincade was a tall guy and I had serious doubts about his large frame fitting the bed without his feet hanging off the end.

The bed faced the brick wall and the two gray chairs with the small round table between them. A full-length mirror sat in the one and only corner of the room. At least we had a private bath which was only big enough for one person. A toilet, a sink, a shower with glass doors. Fresh linens were on the bed and two stacks of plush white towels on the shelf over the toilet.

Despite the small inn and the tiny room, there was, at least, a bar and a restaurant. We wouldn't starve.

He stood at the one window keeping a watchful eye on the outside.

"Tell me about the chapel."

"What about it?" He never looked from the window.

I plopped down in the chair and stretched out my legs. "Why would the Grail be there?"

"Probably because there are secret tunnels and chambers under it."

Excitement tingled through me. "Secret tunnels? How do we get inside?"

"There's a well not far from the chapel. That's the entrance."

"How do you know this?"

Finally, he turned from the window and met my gaze. "Because I helped them build it in the thirteenth century."

The guy sure got around. "Was that before the massacre at Acre?"

"Several years before, yes. In 1232."

"Why didn't you tell me about your connection to the Templars before Acre?"

"It wasn't pertinent." He perched at the foot of the bed.

Meaning, it wasn't pertinent until we were in Acre searching for the Staff of Moses. We never found the staff there. Instead, I found the truth about Kincade's past and his connection to both the Knights Templar and my ancestor, Ezra, who used the Holy Relics to conquer lands.

"You still have dark circles under your eyes, you know."

"That's just the bruises," I said. "They'll fade."

Disdain crossed his face. "You're running on fumes."

"I'm fine," I said automatically.

"You slept," he countered. "That doesn't mean you're rested."

I opened my mouth to argue, but a yawn betrayed me. I didn't want to admit I was still tired. I toed off my boots.

"I think we should expect some type of resistance at the chapel. You need to be ready to face whatever that is."

I cocked my head to the side. "Do you know something I don't?"

"No. But if history has taught us anything, there's always some prick Fallen high lord trying to cash in on your finds."

He wasn't wrong. I stifled another yawn and then finally decided to give in. I was still sore and tired from the ordeal in the sacred forest.

"When do we go in?" I asked.

"Under the cover of darkness. Midnight. I'll wake you."

I crawled up the bed and curled around the pillow with another yawn. I was out in seconds.

⊷⊶

IT SEEMED AS THOUGH I only closed my eyes when Kincade shook me awake. "It's time."

Bleary eyed, I slid off the end of the bed, found my boots and stuck my feet in. Leaving them untied, I trudged to the bathroom with the bleak black wall tiles making it appear even smaller than it actually was. I splashed cold water on my face, pulled my hair up in a high ponytail, and took a deep breath. I was ready.

The drive to the chapel was literally one minute. My teeth chattered the entire time from the bitter cold. All I had was a hoodie. I wished I'd thought to bring a thicker coat, but I was in too much of a hurry to leave England for Poland. Kincade wore nothing but his usual long-sleeved Henley, cargo pants, and boots. He seemed unaffected by the cold. The compact rental car didn't even have a chance to warm before we arrived at our destination.

He parked on the side of the road. As we exited the car, my hard breathing came out in plumes of smoke. He said nothing as he led me across the lawn behind the chapel, which stood tall and dark against the shadows of a moonlit sky. One lone tree, naked from the winter, stood as though a sentry over the well, which was nothing more than a small round stack of stones that had seen better days. The mortar had long since crumbled away.

At the well, he paused, looking down into the darkness as his smokey breath see-sawed in and out.

"This is it," he said.

"This?" I pointed to the black opening.

"Yes."

"How do we get down there?"

"We jump."

I didn't like that answer and frowned.

"Don't worry. It's a short drop." He flashed a grin as he swung a long, thick leg over the short wall. "Follow me down."

Then he disappeared into the shadows like a thief in the night. Seconds later, a thud echoed back to me as he landed. I glanced around, checking for any sign of life or sanity. Taking a deep breath, I sat on the edge of the well, swung my legs over, and pushed off.

I fell for only a few seconds and landed with a grunt next to Kincade in the pitch black. Satisfied with my entrance, he turned toward the wall, his hands roaming the stone. It reminded me much of searching for a way into the underground chamber in Jerusalem where we found the Staff of Moses.

There was an audible click and then the scraping noise of stone against stone. An opening into more darkness.

"Stick close," he said.

He didn't have to tell me twice. A sense of dread and foreboding swept over me as I followed him into the gloom. We walked down a long musty tunnel that seemed as though it had been sealed for eons. I dragged my fingertips along the stone wall. Keeping close, only the back of Kincade's head bobbing up and down in front of me was visible.

"Don't you have a flashlight or a torch or something?"

"Are you afraid of the dark?" Humor tinged his voice.

"No." My voice was small and quiet in the dark.

He chuckled. "Patience."

I made out a yawning black opening ahead at the end of the tunnel. At the entrance, he paused. I heard his movement around the opening, then a scraping noise. He turned to face me and shoved an unlit torch in my hand.

"Hold this."

Like I had a choice. He pulled something from his pants pocket. A striking sound produced small flickers of light. Another strike and a flame came to life. He lit the torch, then using the same match, lit a second torch.

The yellow and orange light flickered over the stone walls. We were in a larger empty chamber with three tunnels to choose from. He held his torch aloft, not moving. I moved to stand next to him and glanced at him. His mind worked as he tried to remember which tunnel to take. Finally, he nodded toward the left one.

"That one."

"You've been down here before." It was more of a statement than question.

"Once many years ago. They built the chapel first, then the tunnels and underground chambers."

Down the tunnel we went. It seemed like an eternity as we walked. At least we had light, though. I wasn't scared of the dark, as he suggested, but I sure wasn't fond of it. Up ahead, there was another yawning opening cloaked in shadows. My heart started to pound at a rapid pace, and I sensed something about the place that was similar to the chamber in which I found the Staff of Moses. Goosebumps rose on my arms even under the hoodie.

"We're close," I said.

"How do you know?"

"I feel it."

He glanced at me over his shoulder. "The Grail?"

I nodded.

We arrived at the opening. Kincade put his torch in bracket just inside the chamber opening. He took mine and did the same on the other side of the opening. We stood inside the musty chamber, my heart in my throat, as I stared down at what was once two Templar knights. Two other bodies littered the floor, long since decomposed. There appeared to have been a struggle. They were nothing but bones, now, but the Templar knights still wore the white mantle with the red cross emblazoned on the chest.

Two on the left looked as though they'd died from a mortal wound, their swords still in their hands. One on the right also appeared to have died defending the man in the middle slumped against the far wall. He held a wooden box, his skeletal fingers still gripping it tight.

I stood, frozen, staring at the scene. My imagination played out the last moments of these four men. The horror of dying in an underground chamber. Or was it horror for the knights? They died with the honor of defending the Grail.

If it was, in fact, in the box clutched by the dead knight.

"Well?" Kincade asked, his voice quiet as though not to wake the dead.

The thought of touching the dead guy made my stomach turn. "I can't do it. You do it."

"Wimp."

"Yes," I agreed.

He said nothing else as he kneeled by the knight. He hesitated, closing his eyes as though saying a quick payer. Then he slid the box out from under the bones. The hand fell into pieces once it was gone from his grip. Kincade stood and turned, extending the box to me.

It looked ancient. Thick dust covered the top which had a latch long since broken. It dangled askew as though someone had broken into it. My heart pounded hard and fast as I opened the lid while he held it. Inside, a nondescript rather ordinary cup. Not made of iron or pewter or any type of metal as the false cup in Spain.

The cup appeared to be made of clay and nothing more than a handle-less bowl with an elongated base. It did not have the handles on either side as the other cup, nor was it decorated with jewels.

I glanced up at Kincade. He wasn't looking at the cup in the box. He was looking at me. Gooseflesh erupted along my arms.

He gave me a nod to encourage me.

"This cup is the new testament in my blood, which is shed for you," I whispered reaching for the cup.

I took a deep breath, expelled it.

As my hand landed on it, the vision exploded through me. The first thing was the forging of the cup by someone collecting clay along a stream. Then he used the clay to shape and form it into the cup. It passed from hand to hand until it was brought to a house. A house that hosted the Last Supper.

Images of the Last Supper flickered through my mind, the apostles and Jesus sitting together as they all shared the cup of wine.

Then the crucifixion and Joseph of Arimathea catching Jesus's blood with the cup. From there, things turned fuzzy as it made its way from hand to hand.

It was on display for a while in a church, then moved again and handed to a man dressed as the pope. It moved again to someone else's hands and a voice saying to take it to safety. But then it moved again, taken by a man wearing a Templar mantle and then, finally, landing in box.

The vision abruptly ended. I stumbled backward, sucking in a sharp breath as my heart raced and my hands shook.

"That's it," I whispered.

"You saw its history, didn't you?"

"Yes."

Silence pounded through us as we stared at each other.

"Your eyes...they...glowed." He sounded awestruck.

I lifted my gaze to his. He had a sort of reverent expression. I flushed.

"Don't look at me like that," I snapped.

"Like what?"

"Like I'm some sort of...saint."

"You possess a power like no other, Anna." He closed the box with a snap. "I've never seen anything like it."

"That's nice. Can we get out of here?" I dismissed his veneration and waved toward the opening.

He said nothing more. Merely gave me a nod. As he walked by the opening, he snatched a torch out of its bracket. I followed the flickering light as he headed back through the tunnel. Instead of going back the way we came, he took a different route. This tunnel was somewhat winding as we made our way through to a set of stone steps. At the bottom of the stairs, he extinguished the torch and placed it in an empty bracket.

Up the stairs we went. At the top, there was a set of wooden doors. He gave the door a tentative push, but it didn't budge.

"Take it." He handed me the box and then turned back to the doors.

Using his shoulder as a battering ram, he pounded against the door several times until at last it burst open. Metal clanged against the wall with a loud bang. He ascended first. I followed.

We were in more darkness, but instead of being in another tunnel or chamber, we appeared to be in some type of basement.

"This way." He motioned through the shadowy confines.

I hadn't a clue where he was going but he seemed to have the route committed to memory. Though he didn't admit it, he must have been at the chapel quite a bit to know the underground tunnels as well as he did. We exited the hallway into the chapel to one side of the altar. He led me through the chapel. I was only able to make out shapes of the line of pews down both sides. An aisle split the center. Inky blackness pressed against the tall narrow windows on either side. Ahead, the door. Finally, we were outside in the crisp night air.

I breathed in a deep breath, happy to be out of the musty underground tunnels and the chapel, clutching the box to my chest. We'd done it. We had the Grail. Now, we could return to England, I could save Grace, and then I'd put the relic in the vault with the others until the time came when I needed it.

"I think we have company," Kincade said.

I followed his gaze to the tree line short distance from the chapel. Moonlight from the full moon illuminate the three figures standing like specters from the depths of Hell. Two high lords, Azriel and Hadrian, with an expanse of black wings behind them, the glow of the blue-white moonbeams making their feathers shimmer. Lucifer stood in the middle with his hands clasped in front of him as though he waited for an invitation, a smirk on his face.

Fear crawled up my spine, a shudder trembling through me. Kincade was right. There was always some prick Fallen high lord trying to cash in on my finds.

"You called it. How the bloody hell did they find us?" I asked, my breath pluming in the air.

"No idea. Let's not hang around to find out."

CHAPTER 38

He took my hand, pulled me into a run, and started for the hidden car. But I had my doubts Lucifer and the two high lords weren't going to let us go so easy.

A punch of demon magic hit me in the back, knocking the wind out of me. Pain exploded thought my already battered body. I pitched forward, unable to control my fall. I landed in the dirt, the box tumbling from my hands. It splintered, shattering into pieces.

Kincade drew his gun, turned, and fired all in one fluid motion. The high-pitched whine followed by the flash of his gun gave me the seconds I needed to grab the Grail. I wrapped my hand around the cup as he fired another round. I tried to catch my breath as I crawled to my knees.

Behind us, the night sky lit up in a brilliant display of white light. "Get up."

Kincade wrapped a hand around my upper arm and hauled me to my feet. Instead of heading for the hidden car, he turned and started back toward the well. I clutched the cup to my chest as I stumbled, trying to keep my footing. I breathed hard, trying to keep up with him but his legs were longer as he pulled me along behind him.

"Faster, Anna."

"I'm...trying..."

Another hit of demon magic smashed into me. This time more vicious than the last. It was that familiar stench of the dark musky scent of smoke and ashes. I stumbled again and headed for the ground. My arm jerked out of Kincade's vice grip. I landed hard, bashing my already injured elbow which hadn't recovered from the previous damage. The cup tumbled from my hands and rolled across the damp grass. I was slow to move. Somehow, I found the energy to push to my hands and knees. Despite the cold, my brow and the back of my neck broke into a hot sweat.

Kincade had his hand on my arm again, trying to pull me to my feet.

"I...can't..."

Everything hurt. Dizziness swept through me, turning my stomach. Pain exploded everywhere.

"Anna..."

My name was an urgent plea on his lips. I pushed him away, holding myself up on all fours watching the ground spin beneath me. Like I'd had too much to drink and was about to hurl.

What the hell had Hadrian done to me?

"We know you have the cup, *chérie*. Give it to us and we will let you live." Azriel's hateful voice carried across the field. "Both of you."

The sulfuric zing of demon magic bit through the air and smashed into Kincade. He grunted, his back bowing, as he fought the urge to fall. He was bigger and stronger than me and managed to stay upright.

"Grab the cup." My voice was weak. "Take it to Grace."

"I'm not leaving you here, dammit," he said through gritted teeth. "Get. Up."

"I can't. It hurts too much." My stomach heaved as I rolled face down.

I stole a glance over my shoulder and saw the three of them—Hadrian, Lucifer, Azriel—standing only a few feet away.

"I have to admit, you two are very good at what you do." Lucifer's silky voice crawled like ants over my skin. "Watching you work together is a delight."

I said nothing. Kincade said nothing. Neither of us moved. The Holy Grail was some three feet behind us in the grass. It would be rather easy for them to overpower us, take it, and be on their way.

Do not move, Kincade said.

He must have sensed me thinking about the relic. He realized, like I did, that if I reached for it, it would signal to the dark lord where it was and that we didn't have it in our possession.

"Nothing to say? Pity." Lucifer tsked. "Do you want to know how we found you?"

I pushed upward, my roiling stomach finally under some control. I sat back on my heels and looked at the three of them, the nausea still pounding me. "I'm sure you're dying to tell us."

In the pale moonlight, Lucifer's face cracked with a smile. "We followed you from England. Oh, it was a feat, to be sure." He took a step, two, closer. He was within reach now. "And, of course, Hadrian has special talents."

"Like what?"

"In Spain, I was going to let him kill you," Lucifer said. "Until I realized that dark magic of his clings to your skin like an invisible parasite. It's quite brilliant, actually. It allowed me to sniff you out." He inhaled a deep breath. "I scent you even now. His dark magic with a hint of honey. Did you know you smelled of honey?"

A bitter taste entered my mouth. At that moment, I had the deep understanding Kincade and I were not getting out of this alive.

Kincade, tired of listening to the filthy devil speak, raised his gun and fired off a round. It was as if Hadrian had sensed his actions before he even did it. The high lord put up a shimmering black shield between them and Kincade's weapon. The flash of light did nothing but illuminate it in a wild arc that went nowhere and then quickly dissipated.

"Ah, the cup. Azriel, retrieve it."

Azriel practically skipped past me to the cup. Kincade turned, tried to fire at the high lord, but Hadrian hit him with another intense punch of dark magic. Kincade went down this time, collapsing to his knees and pitching forward into the grass. The gun fell from his hand.

Well, fuck.

Azriel snatched up the Holy Grail, flashed me his wicked wolf grin and then returned to his little band of darkness. I glanced at Kincade to see if he was all right. His face was beaded in sweat. He clutched his gut as he rolled to his side. His gaze met mine and I recognized that look. It was the same one he gave me when he was Azriel's prisoner and he told me, in the dream walk, to let him go.

I refused then. I refused now.

It's not over, I said, hoping he heard me.

My hand fell on his gun. I had no idea how it worked, if it still had juice. I was willing to try. I pushed to my feet, swaying a little as I tried to stand straight, holding the gun in my hand behind my thigh so the others wouldn't see it. My stomach wanted to revolt, but somehow, I managed to keep from heaving.

"We thank you for finding the relic for us," Lucifer said.

"Do you?" My voice wobbled.

"Yes. Now we will return to England, to Walker Manor, and retrieve the others."

"Over my dead body," I said.

He smiled that oily smile. "That is the plan, my dear."

Hadrian lifted his hand toward me. I didn't wait for the punch of magic from him. I raised the gun, squeezed the trigger. The familiar high-pitched whine followed by the explosion of light burst forth.

I did not expect the gun to kick back the way it did. It jarred my hand, vibrating all the way up my arm, rattling my teeth. I was so stunned by that, it took a moment for me to see Hadrian on the ground, his chest smoking with the hole the gun left there. Black blood trickled from the hole in chest. His black wings spread out beneath him. His lifeless eyes were still open staring up at the night sky.

Ah, so Kincade's gun *could* kill the Fallen high lords. Excellent.

Also, of note was he did not explode into bits and pieces like the other demons.

"You bitch!" Lucifer's face was red mask of fury.

"Anna, three. Lucifer, zero." I smiled, tallying up my list of kills which included Mammon, Abaddon, and now Hadrian. I turned the gun on Azriel. "Give me the relic."

He held it as though it was his prized possession. "You will have to pry it from my cold, dead fingers."

I shrugged. "Suit yourself." And pulled the trigger.

Nothing happened.

Shit.

Kincade's gun was out of juice. I reached for the Godlight, but it wasn't there. My fingers twitched, trying to conjure Ronan's lightning. Nothing. I sensed not even a flicker of either of them. I was out of options.

Lucifer laughed. "If you're trying to conjure your magic, you won't find it. Hadrian's magic suppressed it."

Azriel handed the relic to his boss, turn turned on me.

I was fucked.

But I was forgetting a crucial element. I had a weapon. I dropped Kincade's useless gun in the grass and quickly drew down my uncle's sword, setting it on fire at the same time. Azriel halted, eyeing the weapon.

"You can't kill me," I said. "You need me for the last relic. You need me to find the Ark of the Covenant and touch it, remember? Without me, you will never have all five."

Hesitation flickered through Azriel's eyes. Since he stopped trying to seduce me, our interactions had gone from sultry to toxic. It wasn't lost on me that eventually we would fight each other and one of us would lose.

Finally, Lucifer said, "It is true you are the only one who can touch the relics and release the angelic protection. So perhaps we allow you to live. However, we don't need your overgrown bodyguard. Bring me his soul, Azriel."

Angelic protection. All this time, I had no idea the relics had that. It made sense, though, to keep the relics safe from the Fallen and Lucifer.

I stepped between Azriel and Kincade like a human shield. I two-handed the sword. My arms shuddered with the weight of it, my breathing shallow from the bruised ribs, my body throbbing with pain from head to toe, my breath puffing in clouds.

I swung the sword in a warning arc, but Azriel didn't even flinched. He swooped around me with a speed I didn't expect. He knelt by Kincade's motionless side and reached for him. His hand landed on his shoulder. And then he began to pull Kincade's soul from his body, just as he did when he'd captured my guardian months ago.

Suddenly, Kincade gripped Azriel's wrist and bent it backward at an awkward angle. Azriel cried out in pain as Kincade shoved him backward with a wicked force. I gasped.

All this time, he was playing possum. The Fallen high lord flew backward, landing in the grass with an audible thud. Kincade winced and struggled to his feet despite the pain lancing through him. I charged Azriel, swinging the sword aiming for his head.

Azriel had better reflexes than I anticipated and jumped back, the flaming blade narrowly missing him. In a fit of rage, I swung again, but my arms were quaking from the weight of the blade and my erratic attacks. Azriel stumbled to his feet and produced a knife in one hand. The other hand dangled at a sickly angle from the broken wrist. The only other time I'd seen him carry a weapon was when he slit Ben's throat, killing him before me.

I almost laughed. A small knife was no match for my sword.

But then he lobbed it at me with a precision I hadn't expected. It flew end over end at a rapid speed giving me no time to react. The point made contact with my shoulder, hitting nerves and bone. I cried out, dropping the sword, my arm numb and useless. The flame snuffed out. I staggered backward, my hand on the hilt of the knife. Gritting my teeth, I jerked it out with a yelp, trying hard to ignore the blood staining the steel.

Azriel charged after Kincade again. But Kincade wasn't having it. He ducked his head down and took on the high lord's charge like a linebacker. Azriel pounded into him. They both landed on the ground with a muffled grunt. Azriel punched Kincade in the face. Kincade punched Azriel in the side. Azriel flattened his hand, making a go for the middle of his chest.

The sound of something whistling through the air zinged overhead in a streak of light. Then fire illuminated the grass next to their struggle. I spun around, holding my hand against my wound, trying to staunch the bleeding. Blood trickled through my fingers anyway.

Hooded figures with bows and arrows emerged from the darkness. Azriel ceased his fight with Kincade, rolled away and got to his feet, clutching his broken wrist against his chest. He bolted toward Lucifer, who still had the Grail, and both were heading away from the newcomers.

I swore under my breath and forced my feet after them. I had to recover that Grail before they disappeared into the night for good. I stumbled over a rock, tripped and fell, face-planting. Kincade was at my side then, wrapping his arms around my shoulders and lifting me up.

"He has the Grail," I panted. God, everything hurt.

"Stay here."

Even as he said it, more whistling arrows pummeled the ground around us. These were, at least, unlit, as they embedded in the soft earth. I ducked curling into a tight ball as Kincade sprinted away. He closed the gap between Azriel and Lucifer, but he still wasn't fast enough.

An arrow slammed into Azriel's back and he went down. Lucifer didn't bother to stop and check on his favorite high lord. By then, Kincade was almost to the dark lord. One more push of energy and he launched himself at him. He tackled Lucifer from behind. Back on the ground he went, this time taking Lucifer with him.

From this distance, in the shadows, I was unable to make out what was happening. I sensed someone standing next to me.

"Hands up. Do not move," the man said.

I turned my head to see an arrow nocked in a bow and pointed right at me. I lifted my hands in surrender, my heart ramming hard in my chest.

"Who are you? What are you doing here?" His hood concealed all but his chin which was covered in a goatee.

Gee, those were loaded questions. I had no idea how to answer him. A commotion near Lucifer and Kincade caught my attention. They were surrounded by more hooded, armed figures.

"You and your friends are trespassing on holy land."

"Yeah, no kidding," I muttered.

"We have them, sir. We've recovered the Grail." Another man joined the first, clearly proud they had managed to capture Kincade, a wounded Azriel, and Lucifer.

Great. How was I going to get the Grail back now?

The others brought them forward. I made eye contact with Kincade. He had a cut on his cheekbone and a bloody lip. Other than that, he seemed okay. But as they arrived at our little circle, Lucifer cast a glance at me, then Kincade, and then he and Azriel were gone in a puff of black smoke. Meanwhile, one of the other hooded men used something to extinguish the flaming arrow that had stuck in the ground.

No one else moved.

"Where did they go?" the hooded man asked.

"Back to Hell, most likely," I said. "Where they belong."

"Demons?" he asked.

"Lucifer and his favorite fallen angel," I replied.

He tossed his head back, letting the hood fall away. He had dark, glittering eyes set in a wide face with high cheekbones and a narrow nose. He had an ageless, imperial look about him. He seemed unflustered with my response. With the arrow still pointed at me, he narrowed his gaze.

"I'll ask again. Who are you?"

"Who are *you*?" I countered.

"If I give you my name, will you then give me yours?" he asked. I nodded. "We are the protectors of Saint Stanislaus. I am Hugh de Mornay."

"Descended from the Knights Templar," Kincade added.

Hugh's head snapped in his direction. "How do you know this?"

"I'm Kincade from the Brotherhood of Watchers. I fought for the Templars long ago when they were still known as the Poor Fellow-Soldiers of Christ and of the Temple of Solomon."

Slowly, Hugh lowered his bow and arrow. "Did you know Hugues de Payens?"

What an odd question.

Kincade nodded. Surprise flickered through me. He had never shared this information with me, that he had been there since the inception of the Templars. And I wondered again how old he truly was if he had been walking the earth since the Templars were founded in 1119.

"If you are with the Brotherhood, then who is she?"

"She is Keeper of the Holy Relics," Kincade said. "And the one who was prophesied."

I rolled my eyes. It always sounded weird to be called *the one who was prophesied* like I was some sort of saint or savior or something.

"My name is Anna Walker. Can we move along before I bleed to death?"

"Anna."

Hugh let my name roll of his tongue, as though he tested it out. Then he turned and shouted something in Polish to someone behind him. A woman ran up carrying what appeared to be a first aid kit.

"This is Marta. She will attend you."

"I don't need—"

"Anna." Kincade's tone was warning.

"Fine." I said it through gritted teeth as I pushed off the hoodie, my fingers stained with blood.

Marta went to work on my shoulder. She pulled aside my shirt and doused the wound in alcohol. I clenched my jaw tight so as not to cry out and sound like a wimp. Hugh continued.

"We do know of the prophecy of the one who would collect the relics we protected these many long years. The one who would save all of mankind."

"Yeah, that's me."

I tried to sound convincing but wasn't sure I succeeded. Most days I didn't believe in the prophecy. Marta paused cleaning my wound and gazed up at me with eyes the size of saucers. There was a sort of reverence etching her face. I flashed a half-hearted smile.

"The wound is not deep," she said. "You don't need stitches."

"Funny, it felt like the blade hit bone."

"Then you've come for the Grail," Hugh said, ignoring both of us.

"Yes."

I eyed it in the hands of the second man standing next to Hugh. Marta finished torturing me with her alcohol doused gauze pad. Despite her claim I didn't need stitches, she used butterfly bandages to keep the gash closed while she covered it up with a clean gauze pad and tape.

"Give her the Grail, Antoni," Hugh said.

Antoni glared at me with a suspicious eye. "How do we know she is who she says she is? They were trying to steal the Grail."

"She walks with the Brotherhood," Hugh replied, sounding impatient. "Or do you not remember your history, my friend? Give her the Grail."

Antoni hesitated a long moment. "But…"

"Yes, they were trying to steal it. They didn't understand that those of us who live in this village take our vow to protect the chapel seriously. That we will give up our lives to keep its secrets safe." Hugh granted me a small smile. "Did you?"

I cut Kincade a glance and didn't miss the guilty look on his face. *He knew* but he failed to tell me. Perhaps he thought we would be able to get in and out without being detected. We didn't account for Lucifer and company to show up.

"We did not," I said finally.

"We would have given it to you," Hugh said.

"You knew it was there?" I asked.

"We all did. Two knights died defending it while the rest of us protected the chapel and the village from invaders."

The rest of us he said. As though he'd been here, in this village, since the knights died with the Grail, the underground chamber becoming their tomb. Perhaps they had. Since I began looking for the relics, my expectations and understanding of the real world had changed drastically. Marta finished her bandaging, snapped her first aid kit closed and walked away. I slipped my hoodie back on.

"And now it's yours," he added.

When Antoni still failed to give me the Grail, Hugh took it from him. He stretched it out to me. I slipped it from his hands and held it, realizing just how delicate the cup was. There was a hairline fracture from the rim down the bowl.

"Thank you," I said.

"Go with God, Keeper. May you be the light of the world."

Goosebumps burst along my arms and up my spine. Those were the exact words my uncle had said to me. *Be the light of the world.*

Hugh gave me a farewell nod. He started to turn away but stopped to say one last thing. "You do realize, of course, we could have killed you at any time. We never miss." He held up his bow and arrow.

I swallowed hard. "I realize that, yes. Thank you for not killing us."

Kincade hobbled to stand next to me. Together, we watched them walk away. Hugh stepped over the dead fallen angel as though he were merely an inconvenience. Then they all disappeared along the tree line and back to whenever they came.

"You knew about the villagers, didn't you?" I asked.

He nodded.

"And they're, what, hundreds of years old?"

He nodded again. I sighed.

"One more question. Why didn't you tell me you knew Hugues de Payens?"

He gave a shrug of one shoulder, then winced with the movement. "It wasn't pertinent at the time."

"Huh. You're starting to sound like my uncle." I shivered as snow started to fall. "Can we please go back to the hotel now? I'm freezing."

"Sure."

He retrieved his discarded gun from the ground and holstered it. Then grabbed my uncle's sword and handed it to me. I cradled the Grail in my good arm like a newborn babe, doing my best not to smear it with blood. I took the sword from him and returned it to its hiding place in the cloud. We both limped our way from the chapel to where we'd parked the car.

"By the way," I began, "just how old *are* you?"

"Old enough," he said, his voice gruff.

Which meant he wasn't going to tell me. I was determined to find out sooner or later.

CHAPTER 39

RETURNING TO THE CAR seemed to take a lot longer than when we left it. That was because both of us had gotten the shit kicked out of us. We hobbled our way back. Kincade limping. Me with the bandage on my shoulder and my limp arm.

"Were you aware the relics had angelic protection?" I clenched my jaw to keep my teeth from chattering.

"I did."

"Why do people never tell me things?" I didn't bother to hide my frustration. "My uncle, you, who knows who else."

"Your uncle didn't tell you things because he wanted to protect you." He turned me, his green-gold gaze meeting mine. "And so do I."

My heart squeezed. I looked away quickly, not wanting to acknowledge the flicker of desire coming to life deep inside me.

"Why didn't you use the Godlight or your divine power?" he asked. "You could have taken them all out at once."

"I tried but Hadrian's dark magic did something to me. I was unable to conjure it."

We finally arrived at the car. He opened the passenger door for me. But he held it cracked to keep me from getting inside. I glanced at up at him, about to question what he was doing when there was that look on his face. The one he gave me before he kissed me back in the Fae's sacred forest.

"Then we'll have to find a way to keep you from being hit with dark magic. Won't we?"

My throat went dry. "I suppose we will."

I pushed open the door, slipping into the seat before he made another move on me. Not that I didn't *want* that, but I was still trying to process my feelings about that first real life kiss.

He got in the driver's seat and away we went, back to the hotel. We said nothing more even though I couldn't stop thinking about the way he kissed or that he appeared to want to kiss me again. I tried hard to keep my thoughts guarded because he was so good at reading them. If he heard me thinking about him, he didn't acknowledge it. But Kincade had the best poker face I'd ever seen.

When we returned to the hotel, we climbed the stairs to the room. I immediately kicked off my boots which, I noticed, were dotted with blood. My blood. At least Kincade hadn't blown a demon to bits next to me. Still, though, I had a hard time getting that acrid smoke stench out of my nose. I sniffed the sleeve of my hoodie and frowned.

"What is it?"

"That smell." I held my jacket out to him. He sniffed. "I don't smell anything."

"It's musky like smoke. Not like cigarette smoke. Like maybe a grass fire. Have you ever smelled a grass fire?"

"No."

"Well, that's what it smells like." I pulled my hair down from the ponytail, grabbed a strand and sniffed, then coughed. "My hair stinks, too. Is this what Lucifer meant about the dark magic clinging to me?"

"Possibly."

He took a step closer to me, scrutinizing me in a way he never had before with a critical eye. He lifted my arm, pushed up my sleeve and examined my skin. He turned my arm to and fro, into and out of the light. Then paused. He pulled me closer to him, closer to the light of the one lamp and examined me closer. Holding my arm against his side with one hand, he trailed his fingers down my forearm with the other, leaving gooseflesh in his wake.

A heated blush rose to my cheeks and all the way to the roots of my hair. He, however, seemed unconcerned with the way he affected me.

"I see something. Look at this."

He ran a finger over my forearm again. Aside from the bumps, a shimmer clung to my skin. A shimmer I had never seen before.

"What the hell is that?"

He lifted his gaze to mine. "Dark magic."

I pulled out of his grasp and stumbled away, still holding the Grail. Panic lanced through me. This wasn't my first brush with dark magic.

"How do I get it off?"

"I don't know yet."

I frowned, then handed him the Grail. "I'm going to shower."

"Your bandage will get wet."

"Then I'll redress it."

I stomped away and closed myself in the dark and depressing bathroom. I leaned on the edge of the sink, staring at the stranger staring back. I looked a fright. My hair hung in loose strands about my face, the white streaks on either side brilliant in the bright light. The bruises on my face were fading. Dark circles were under my eyes giving me the appearance of not having slept in weeks. Not far off. I had the stab wound on my shoulder now, thanks to Azriel. I lifted the edge of my shirt. A bloom of black, blue, and purple bruises were along my ribcage. Pretty much everything else hurt.

I started the shower and stripped off my clothes. It was a feat, but I managed to keep the bandage from getting doused with soap and water. When I finished, I wrapped in the plush white towel and stepped out. I checked my skin again, but the shimmer of dark magic remained.

I frowned.

Would this nightmare ever end?

Funny how he and the other demon lords waffled between wanting to kill me and wanting to keep me alive. I did, however, understand Lucifer allowed me to live until I found the Ark of the Covenant, then all bets were off. I didn't want to think about that now, though.

I cracked the bathroom door open and peeked out. Dead silence. No movement. I pushed open the door wider to an empty room. Kincade was nowhere to be found. He'd left the Grail on the nightstand by the bed. I used that moment of solitude to quickly dress into fresh clothes. By the time I was finished and the towel returned to the bathroom, he'd returned with a large paper bag that smelled like heaven.

"Where did you find food this time of night?" Truthfully, I had no idea what time it was. My stomach growled loud enough for the neighbors to hear.

"I didn't. Our new friend, Hugh, brought it to me." He pushed the one lamp back on the table between the two chairs, then placed the bag on it.

I cocked my head to the side. "How did Hugh know where we were staying?"

Kincade gaped at me as though I'd lost my mind. "There's only one inn in the village, Anna."

"Oh." I flushed.

He pulled out makeshift to-go containers. The decadent aroma of food made my mouth water. He pulled the lid off a container and handed it to me with a fork. Inside, pierogis. I dug into them with an overzealous relish I usually only reserved for apple pie. They were potato and sauerkraut and it was likely the best thing I'd ever eaten in my life.

We feasted on cabbage rolls, kielbasas, bread, some type of stew with pork, cabbage, and mushrooms, and ended it with a poppy covered pastry.

I laid back on the bed, my stomach full and all my aches and pains forgotten. My eyes were heavy as I laid there, fighting sleep.

"I hope you paid him for that." My voice was thick with a drowsy happiness.

"He wouldn't let me."

A rustle of containers and paper indicated he cleaned up the aftermath. Then he snapped off the light.

"Sleep now."

"What about you?" I said around a yawn.

"I'm fine. Good night."

And that was the last thing I remembered.

⋯

I slept for what felt like forever. When I awoke, bright sun streamed through the one window, filtered only by the gauzy white curtains shoved to each side. I rolled over, watching the lazy swirl of a few snowflakes. Snow and sun.

The shower started running. I sat up, glancing around the tidy room. Kincade's bag was open on one of the chairs. A book rested on top of the clothes. I shoved off the bed covers and padded over, feeling nosy. The book was my old copy of *War of the Worlds*.

Why did it settle something deep in my chest to see he had brought the book along with him?

I pictured him sitting in the chair, his long legs stretched out before him while he read by the one lamp as I snored. Ever since Ronan's death, Kincade hadn't left my side.

I understood why, of course. He wasn't going to let me out of his sight—not with the guilt pounding into him for not being there when Hadrian tried to kill me. I didn't blame him for that. At the time, he was doing what he had to do—killing demons.

Looking back over what happened, I started to think it was something that *had* to happen. Like it was part of my destiny. Ronan had to die to give me his divine power. Just as my uncle had to die to give me his power.

The water cut off. I perched on the edge of the bed, realizing I'd slept in my clothes. They were wrinkled. I didn't much care.

The bathroom door opened. Kincade came out on a cloud of hot steam, smelling like fresh sandalwood which was quickly becoming one of my favorite scents. I assumed it was his natural scent. He wore nothing but a thick towel around his waist. His torso was still damp. It was hard not to eye the silvery scar snaking down the left side of his chest. The arrow wound on his shoulder had healed, which also left behind a scar.

He halted when he saw me, his face passive as he concealed his reaction and his emotions. Poker face extraordinaire.

"You're awake."

"Just woke up."

He grabbed his bag and headed back to the bathroom.

"I don't blame you," I called.

He stopped, his back still to me. His muscles rippled under the damp skin which, like mine, was bruised from the dark magic he was hit with from Hadrian.

"I blame myself." It was all he said as he started walking toward the bathroom again. He understood exactly what I meant.

"You don't have to."

He paused again, this time looking over his shoulder at me. "The next person to die protecting you will be me."

My heart thudded against my chest as I stared at him, my mind trying to comprehend what he'd said to me. Did he know something I didn't? Did he have a premotion and refused to tell me? Or was he merely stating what he *thought* would happen in the future? My gut churned acid as I tried to form the next question.

He didn't wait for a reply as he entered the bathroom and closed the door.

CHAPTER 40

WHILE HE DRESSED, I made arrangements to check out, hired a car, and called the pilot. I was ready to be home, back in England. I was ready to help Grace. Hopefully, the Grail worked. I packed it carefully in my bag, making sure it was padded between all my clothes. I was relieved we didn't have to go through customs or a commercial airport. Definite perks to flying private.

We spoke no more about premonitions or death or protection or much of anything else. In fact, I kept my mouth firmly shut. I sensed something had shifted between us. Something I didn't understand. I had questions but I wasn't about to ask him anything else. Was it the kiss? The threat of imminent danger I was always in? The fact I was constantly stalked by Fallen and Lucifer? And what about this shimmery stuff on me from the dark magic? No matter how much I scrubbed, it didn't come off in the shower. Not that I expected it to.

Two-hour-plus drive to the airport followed by two hours on the plane and then more driving to get home. We didn't speak much.

We pulled up to the house. The driver got out first and opened my door. Kincade was already out on the other side. I grabbed my bag from the trunk, bid the driver farewell, and headed for the door, relieved to be home.

As I passed by Kincade, he reached for me, pulled me to a stop.

"Anna, what I said before…I meant…" He paused, searching for the words. It was a rare thing to see him at a loss.

I thought about what he said—that the next person to die protecting me would be him. I decided what he said and what he meant were two different things. What he said sounded like he intended to die protecting me, that it was an inevitable event. What he meant was he intended to be the one protecting me should that event come to fruition. At least, that's what I hoped.

"I understood what you meant. You intend to be the one by my side if there's a next time." I thought it best to let him off the hook.

He dropped his hand, gave me a nod, and that was the last we spoke of it. He followed me into the house. Now all I needed was that holy water and the Grail and Grace would be saved. I bolted up the stairs to my room. The holy water was still in its little vial sitting on my nightstand. I picked it up and then carefully took the Grail out of my bag.

I hurried down the hall to Grace's room, where Darius and Ophelia kept their constant vigil. Ophelia jumped to her feet when she saw me, a bright smile on her face when she realized I carried the cup. Darius moved away from the side of the bed to give me room.

Grace looked the same as the last time I saw her. Pale, with sunken cheeks and dark circles under her eyes.

I paused, taking a deep breath. Holding the Grail cup in one hand and the vial in the others, I struggled how to open the vial. Ophelia came to my rescue, slipping the vial from my hand.

"Let me."

I gave her a grateful smile as she pulled out the cork. I held the cup out to her. She poured the holy water into it. She discarded the empty vial, then went to Grace's other side and pushed her to a sitting position. I didn't even have to ask for her help.

I threw a little prayer to Heaven as a just-in-case.

It was messy, but I was able to pour most of the holy water between Grace's lips. The rest of in ran down her chin, dampening her nightgown.

A long, quiet moment passed with nothing but silence pressing between us all.

Then Grace gasped, coughed and her eyes fluttered open. Relief sputtered through me. Hot tears of joy sprang to my eyes.

It worked.

She was alive.

Her gaze landed on me then. She peered long and hard at me, blinked once and then spotted the Holy Grail in my hands. She reached for it, took it, held it her hands as though it were a delicate babe, and gazed at it with reverence.

"You found it." Her voice was quiet and weak.

"I did."

"I'm so proud of you."

I kissed her forehead. "I'm so glad you're all right."

"I'm feeling better." She gave me a half smile. "But tired still. As though all the strength has left my body. As though..."

"Shh. Don't talk. Ophelia, will you ask Piers to bring some tea and lemon cakes?"

She nodded and headed off to do my bidding. Darius with his enormous snowy white wings made his way to the door but I stopped him.

"Darius, wait. Thank you."

He gave me a nod, a small smile on his face. "You are welcome, Keeper."

I perched on the edge of the bed next to Grace, holding her hand. Her skin was cold and clammy and thin, but she was starting to regain some color. The dark circles under her eyes remained but would fade in time as she healed and grained more strength.

"It was very strange," she said.

"What was?"

"The dream. At times it seemed as though someone was with me. Sometimes, more than one person." She shook her head, which was more of a short movement from left to right. She took a deep breath, exhaled it. "There was that man."

"What man?" I tipped my head to the side, concern and a trickle of fear going through me.

"The dark-haired one with the blue eyes."

I stiffened. Lucifer. "He was in your dreams?"

"Sometimes. And when he tried to hurt me, someone was there to protect me."

"Darius?"

"No." Her tongue darted out, trying to wet her dry, cracked lips. "The one who protects you. Your guardian."

Kincade. Gooseflesh erupted along my arms as I sat ramrod straight, stunned to my shoes. All this time, Kincade had been in her dreams protecting her from evil. Keeping her safe. While Darius stood over her, watching her sleep, keeping her safe.

And yet, he had never mentioned it to me. I reached for the pendant he'd given me, ran a thumb over the guardian angel.

I didn't know what to think about that. Aside from being completely and utterly grateful he protected her when I couldn't. All sorts of mushy feelings erupted for the man, reinforcing my damn crush on him.

"Tell me how you found it." Her voice was still weak, breaking through my thoughts. She held the cup in her hands as though it were a delicate baby bird.

"Well, that is a very long story."

"I want to hear it." She leaned her head back against the headboard and waited.

Piers entering carrying the tea tray. He paused in the doorway, gazing at Grace with a mixture of relief and adoration. Grace, in turn, granted him a weak smile. She held a hand out to him.

I stood and took the tray from him, my heart fluttering. He stepped to her, took her hand in his. He closed his other hand over their joined ones. They said nothing with words. Everything was conveyed by the emotions on their faces, the gazes they exchanged, the smile she gave him.

"I'm glad to see you, my dear," he said softly.

"I'm glad to see you, dearest."

"I shall return after you and Miss Walker catch up."

She nodded. He released her and headed for the door. He granted me a rare smile as he passed.

I placed the tea tray on the nearby dresser, pouring first one mug and then a second. He'd also brought finger sandwiches and lemon cakes. I placed one of the sandwiches on the side of the saucer and handed it along with the tea to Grace. She pushed upward in the bed until she had elevated herself enough to take the cup and sip. I shoved a lemon cake in my mouth before perching on the side of the bed once again.

"Where were we?" I said around a mouthful of sticky cake.

"You were about to tell me a story." The steam from the cup wafted upward and over her face. She closed her eyes, relishing it.

"Ah, yes."

And so, I began the long tale from the moment she was unconscious until waking her up.

⟵———⟶

Hours later, I stumbled out of her room, exhausted. I had talked while Grace nibbled, sipped tea and listened. And when I was finished the story—leaving out a few of the more violent bits and the fact that Kincade and I had smooched—she seemed happy and content.

She was glad I was home. So was I.

I left her resting in her bed. She promised she would call on me if she needed me. In the hall, I leaned against her door as I tried to regain some of my energy to walk down the hall to my own room.

Kincade stood on the other end of the hall leaning against the wall with his bulky forearms crossed over his chest. He wanted to give me space but still keep a watchful eye on my whereabouts. I trudged down the hall, my shoulders slumped.

"Did it work?" he asked.

"It did. She was awake and talking, but it made her tired. She still has some recovery. She's resting now."

"Good. Now you rest."

"I—"

"You're barely standing. Go. Everything else can wait."

He was right. I wanted to be stubborn, but the fatigue won. I started for my room, then halted, turned back to him.

"In the sacred forest..."

My chest tightened. I bit off my words, shook my head, pressed my lips together. No sense asking the question. I was too afraid of the answer. "Forget it."

"What about it?" he asked, one brow lifted. A curious glint was in his eyes.

"Nothing."

"You want to ask me a question, so ask." He, of course, would know since he sensed my every thought.

I hesitated a moment, watching the way he stood. No hint of amusement or maliciousness was on his face. Merely curiosity. Kincade had never lied to me or told me something he thought I wanted to hear. Fine. I'd ask. I steeled my nerves, ready to be rejected. I turned back to face him.

"Why did you kiss me?"

He pushed off the wall in a long, slow methodical way that left me breathless. My knees threatened to buckle. He moved toward me with a sort of fluid catlike grace that reminded me much of the first time we met. How dawn stained the clear summer sky that morning and how his face was bathed in the garish yellow lights from the portico. One thing was clear when he looked at me then as he looked at me now—his green-gold eyes pierced me.

As he neared, he paused. I lifted my eyes to meet his gaze, sure he saw the rapid-fire beat of the pulse in my neck.

"Because I wanted to."

And then he moved on to his room, closing the door behind him.

I stood in the hall a long time, clutching my elbows and trying to decide what to make of that. His answer was direct. Not cryptic. So why did I want to try to read between the lines? There were no lines to read between. I asked. He told me.

He *wanted* to.

Finally, I sighed and started for my own room when I noticed Natasha hanging around the gallery of portraits. Her gaze was firmly fixed on the one of her. In the portrait, the younger version of herself sat on the edge of an oversized garnet wing-backed chair wearing a champagne-colored gown. Her black hair, just like mine, hung long and straight over one shoulder. We both had the same purple eyes. She had a small smile on her lips, as though she gazed at someone she was madly in love with.

"I was sixteen."

I froze. My mouth had gone bone dry. She didn't sound like the woman who called herself Natasha. She was someone else.

"I sat in that horrid dress for hours while they painted this portrait. And do you know why?" She glanced at me. I shook my head. "Because my father insisted."

I stared at her, shocked to the marrow of my bones at how lucid she sounded. She remembered who she was. Maybe because I'd been the one to tell her not long ago. I told her who Edward was, who I was. Something had clearly clicked with her and she was...different.

"You...remembered that?"

"I remember many things." She gave a little laugh. "But not everything."

I had no words. Instead, I remained mute.

"I remember Christmas. It was my favorite. I decorated every year."

I thought of the decorations Ophelia had dragged down from the attic. She told me she found them in tubs and that someone took great care organizing and labeling them.

Someone who loved Christmas.

"We had a piano forte. I played carols and made Edward sing." She giggled at that. "He hated it so, but he did it because he loved me."

Piano forte. A somewhat archaic phrase. There wasn't one in the manor these days which made me wonder what happened to it. Perhaps Edward had it removed so as not to conjure more memories of his long-lost sister.

For the life of me, I had the hardest time imagining Edward singing Christmas carols, much less singing period. The image made me snicker.

She turned to me and took my hands in hers. "Anna, I'm sorry."

"For what?"

Confusion followed by indecision flickered through her eyes. "For not having the answers you want. About you, me, your father. I simply cannot remember what happened or even who he was."

I squeezed her hands to reassure her. "I'm not angry. I understand why. And, maybe, in time you *will* remember."

It seemed to be enough for her. She nodded, then hugged me. She left me standing in the hall, emotionally drained, as she went back to her own room.

Kincade was right. I was exhausted.

I stumbled to my door, shoving it open. And halted when at the sight of the winged man standing on the balcony. His huge snowy white wings threaded with gold spread behind him. He turned when I entered. I recognized that ageless chiseled face with high cheekbones, a thin straight nose, and eyes so green they rivaled an emerald.

"Sariel?"

"Hello, Anna. Welcome home."

I stifled a yawn. "What are you doing here?"

"I came to see how you are." He stepped from the balcony and looked me over.

"I'm great," I lied.

He didn't buy it. "I see the shimmer of dark magic on your skin. I smell it, too."

"Yeah, well, not much I can do about that."

"Allow me?" He reached a hand to me.

I shrugged and placed my hand in his. He pushed my sleeve up my arm to my elbow. In the light of the room, the shimmer of dark magic was evident. He ran a hand over my arm in one swift stroke. The shimmer was gone.

"You removed it?" I asked.

"I did." He released my hand and stepped back. "Do not move."

He closed his eyes. He used his hands to outline my body without touching me. When he opened his eyes, I shoved the sleeve up my other arm. No shimmer.

"I have removed all the dark magic," he said.

"How did you do that?" I didn't hide the wander in my voice.

A spark glinted in his eyes as he gave me a half smile. "You have to ask after? I returned your eyesight, after all."

I thought for a moment. "Angelic power?"

He nodded, still smiling.

"Thank you. I'm glad it's gone." My shoulders slumped as exhausted once again creeped in. "Now if you don't mind..." I sat on the edge of the bed and toed off my boots.

"Yes, of course. But one more thing, Anna." He cut a glace to my bedroom door. Odd.

I sensed his hesitation. I glanced up at him, bleary-eyed. My pillow was calling but I managed to hold my eyes open. "Yes?"

"I—" He cut off his words, then asked, "Your mother. Is she well?"

What a strange question. "She seems to get better every day."

"Good. I want to give this to you." He pulled a white envelope from the pocket of his pants.

I took it, opened the flap and pulled out a postcard. It was a picture of the city of Cairo with the Great Pyramids in the background. I peered at it, confused.

"What is this?"

"A postcard."

I flipped over the card. My breath caught. Written in those familiar blocky letters were the words *Ark of the Covenant.*

My head snapped up to him. "I-I don't understand."

"It's your next relic, Anna. And then you will have come to the end of your quest."

"Who wrote this?" I held it up.

"I did."

Again, I stared at him. "You?" The word came out a rough whisper. "All this time...it was...you?"

"It was."

I stared at him, slack jawed. "Why?"

"Is it not clear?"

I shook my head. "No."

"The task put before you was too much for you to handle alone. You needed help. It may not be there in Cairo, but it is a place to start."

"But-but..."

"I left the cards for you as a guide. A clue."

Realization crept through me. "Including Antarctica. You sent me to find my mother. And Acre to find out about Kincade's past."

Strange, cold tendrils skittered up my spine to the base of my skull sending goosebumps across my scalp. My tired brain, though, did not understand why that was significant.

He said nothing.

"Find the Ark, Anna. Save mankind."

And then he was gone.

I sat holding the postcard. The Ark of the Covenant was, indeed, the final relic. And then, the real war begins.

Sneak Peek of *Light of the World*

Blood from the cut over my left eye dripped onto the gray workout mat as I stood on all fours, trying to regain my breath. My chest seesawed in and out. My heart drummed in my chest from exertion.

"Did that hurt?" Kincade asked with a hint of humor in his voice.

I took a deep breath and exhaled. "I wanted to work out, not get my ass kicked."

I lifted my head, closing my left eye and squinted, trying to give him my best angry glare. His eyes widened when he saw the blood oozing from my forehead.

"I didn't mean to do that."

"Sure."

"Come on." He stepped next to me and wrapped his hand around my upper arm. I shoved him off.

"I don't need your help." There was more anger in my voice than I intended.

"You say that a lot, and yet, here I am."

I frowned. "Because you won't ever fucking leave."

The ugly truth was I hated how much my chest loosened every time he proved it.

Kincade became my constant companion since that one incident with the high lord that nearly killed me. The high lord killed my betrothed, Ronan, instead.

"That's right. I won't."

There it was again—comfort disguised as a threat. The kind I couldn't afford to want.

I hobbled toward the door as he fell in step behind me. I swiped the back of my hand over the cut, smearing blood over my skin. A lot of good it did. I still bled and the throbbing wasn't going away. I should have known not to engage Kincade in a workout session.

Kincade wasn't like my uncle. He wasn't going to push me into going after the relic. He wasn't going to prod me into making travel plans. Instead, he was biding his time, living in the manor house, and eating my food while he waited for me to announce my next move.

"You should let me clean that," he said.

"I think you've done enough damage for one day."

I practically growled the words, not understanding why I was so annoyed and angry. I'd been annoyed and angry with everything lately, though. Everything and everyone. Perhaps because I finally decided, deep down, to embrace my true calling as Keeper of the Holy Relics. Perhaps because my life was never the same as it was before when I lived in Dallas. Before I was contacted by both a messenger angel and a fallen angel.

I hurried across the damp lawn, trying to lose him, but it was no use. His legs were longer than mine, and he kept up with ease. At the back kitchen door, I banged through it, startling Piers and Grace, who were cooking something for dinner later that evening. The kitchen smelled of a decadent pastry in the oven. A huge stockpot simmered on the stove. A stack of cookies was heaped on a platter at the end of the kitchen counter. I swiped one on my way past.

Grace gaped at me wide-eyed as I stomped through the kitchen, biting my lip to keep from saying something to Kincade I'd regret later.

"Lord have mercy, what happened?" She wiped her hands on a blue and white kitchen towel as she came around the island.

"I'm fine," I grumbled, then halted and turned toward Kincade. I punched him in the chest with all the force I was able to muster. He didn't even falter. "You stay here."

He looked so surprised, I almost laughed. I managed to contain it as I spun on the toe of my pink boot and left the kitchen, stuffing the cookie in my mouth. I hurried through the house and up the stairs to my room where I paused in the hallway. I stole a glance down to the other end where Edward's bedroom—now mine—was undergoing a transformation. Contractors had been in the house for weeks.

Piers insisted I move out of my childhood bedroom and into the master suite since I was now the lady of the house. I was reluctant. He offered to have it renovated into something more my taste. I refused to pick a wall color or anything else and left it up to the old butler. He seemed content enough to handle the project himself.

Mild curiosity coursed through me. What did it look like behind that closed door?

I heard footsteps that sounded like Kincade and hurried toward my room where I slammed the door, leaning against it. My breath came in gasps, my hands shook. Cookie crumbs were stuck in the back of my throat and I wished I had something to wash it down.

For the last few weeks, I vibrated with unspent energy. I knew what my next destination was, but I was stalling to avoid the inevitable. There was something unsettling about facing what was to come and I wasn't ready to face it. Not yet. So, I asked Kincade to work out with me.

Sometimes Kincade didn't know his own strength. And he forgot I was a girl. Granted, I'm not a delicate flower, but I wasn't prepared for the punch I took to the head.

Honestly, I think he missed and hadn't intended to hit me. Which wasn't at all like Kincade. He was a man with purpose, who always knew what his next move was going to be. He always planned one step ahead.

I padded to the bathroom, trying to forget Kincade and everything else.

War of the Brotherhood (Dark Paranormal Romance)
Set in the Dream Walker Universe
Dark Night of the Soul (Coming 2026)
Fall of the Forsaken (Coming 2026)
Immortal Everlasting (Coming 2026)

Enchanted Realms (YA Fantasy Romance)
Once Upon a Midnight Clear (Cinderella)
Once Upon True Love's Kiss (Snow White)
Once Upon an Enchanted Kiss (Sleeping Beauty)
Once Upon an Enchanted Castle (Beauty and the Beast)
Once Upon a Midnight Dreary (Poe's The Raven)

Enchanted Realms Related Novellas
Once Upon an Ancient Curse (Red Riding Hood)
Once Upon a Silver Strand (Rapunzel)
Once Upon a Woven Wish (Rumpelstiltskin)

Enchanted Realms: Crossroads (Cozy Fantasy)
A Spin-off Series of the Enchanted Realms
Petals and Portals (Coming 2026)

Five Towers (YA Fantasy Romance)
The Sorcerer's Daughter

Highland Destiny (Paranormal Romance)
Desiring the Highland Laird
Loving the Highland Warrior
Captivating the Highland Rogue

Legends of the Five Crowns (Romantasy)
with Misty Evans
The Lost Kingdom
The Flame and the Dragon
Tide of Stolen Thrones

Realm of Honor (Fantasy Romance)
One Knight Only
Only for a Knight
A Knight to Remember
A Knight Like No Other
Shadows of the Knight

Shorts and Anthologies (Fantasy/Paranormal)
Newsletter Subscribers Only
A Dance Among the Faeries, A Short Story
Eorwulf, A Short Story
Dragons of Emhain Short Story Collection

Watch for more at MichelleMiles.net

ABOUT THE AUTHOR

Michelle Miles is an empress with a war map in one hand and a romance vow in the other—writing fantasy, paranormal, and young adult adventures where magic crackles, danger prowls, and love refuses to back down. From fairy-tale retellings to angels and demons to Fae, elves, and time travelers, she builds big-hearted worlds full of quests, curses, kisses, and chaos—often in that order. When she's not plotting her next emotional ambush, Michelle narrates audiobooks and hosts Miles Beyond the Page, a podcast spotlighting writers' real journeys. A proud Texan, she's usually reading, hiking, rewatching favorite movies, or savoring a glass of wine while sharpening the blade for the next adventure.

Quests, Curses, Kisses, and Chaos!

Read more at MichelleMiles.net